Altogether nineteen people sat down to the evening birthday tea, and when the hullabaloo had subsided, Chinese Lady made herself heard. What all the commotion was about she didn't know, she said, it was implorable to turn a tea party into Bedlam. She meant deplorable. She also said she had to apologize to everyone for her youngest son Sammy coming to the party looking like a common costermonger who'd been in a fight with hooligans.

The birthday tea began. It was riotous. So were the birthday games afterwards. Rosie had begged for lots of games, including Forfeits. Lizzy said she wasn't going to play Forfeits, not if Boots organized them. It would mean what it had always meant, that all the girls would get fiendish forfeits and all the blokes would fall about.

'We don't want any hooliganism,' said Chinese Lady.

But they all played Forfeits after all, and just as Lizzy had said, it was a fiendish ordeal for the female members of the party. Somehow or other they all had terrible trouble with their dresses, and all their menfolk fell about pop-eyed and laughing. Chinese Lady said she'd never seen anything more disreputable, and that Boots ought to be arrested.

The Adams family were enjoying themselves together as only they knew how.

A FAMILY AFFAIR

Mary Jane Staples

CORGI BOOKS

A FAMILY AFFAIR
A CORGI BOOK : 0 552 14154 2

First publication in Great Britain

PRINTING HISTORY
Corgi edition published 1993

Copyright © Mary Jane Staples 1993

The right of Mary Jane Staples to be identified as author of this
work has been asserted in accordance with sections 77 and 78

1. This book is sold subject to the condition that it shall not, by way of
trade or otherwise, be lent, resold, hired out or otherwise circulated in
any form of binding or cover other than that in which it is published
and without a similar condition including this condition being imposed
on the subsequent purchaser.

2. This book is sold subject to the Standard Conditions of Sale of Net
Books and may not be re-sold in the UK below the net price fixed by
the publishers for the book.

Set in 11/12pt Linotype Times by
County Typesetters, Margate, Kent

Corgi Books are published by Transworld Publishers Ltd,
61–63 Uxbridge Road, Ealing, London W5 5SA,

The Random House Group Limited supports The Forest Stewardship
Council (FSC®), the leading international forest certification organisation.
Our books carrying the FSC label are printed on FSC® certified paper.
FSC is the only forest certification scheme endorsed by the leading
environmental organisations, including Greenpeace. Our
paper procurement policy can be found at
www.randomhouse.co.uk/environment

MIX
Paper from
responsible sources
FSC® C018072

Printed and bound in Great Britain by Clays Ltd, St Ives PLC

Addresses for companies within The Random House Group Limited
can be found at: www.randomhouse.co.uk/offices.htm

To Janet, Chris, and the boys,
Justin, Giles and Ben

Ronald J. Ponsonby   Pentonville Prison
Rue Thiers 14   London
Dieppe
France   20th April 1926

Dear Ronald,

I hope this letter will reach you. I am having it smuggled out for posting. I am, as you see, in Pentonville Prison, awaiting trial for murder at the Old Bailey in June. You know my predilections, they're identical with yours, and you know too how you and I have always suffered hostility and interference due to that for which we have a common liking. You were wise to leave Nottingham and exile yourself in France when the Nottingham police began an investigation into the disappearance of some silly girl. In not going with you, I now find myself the victim of an infernally hostile and interfering busybody, a man named Robert Adams, who struck me senseless and delivered me to the police. If I'm found guilty of shortening the useless lives of a few girls whom I saved from growing up fat and commonplace, I shall be hanged.

Accordingly, I ask you, my dear brother, to return to England and do what I am sure you will wish to do in the event of my enforced demise. That is, to avenge us, for whatever is done to one of us is

7

done to both, as we have always agreed. It will be too dangerous for you to visit me in prison, even if you were allowed to, as I've been asked questions about the missing Nottingham girl on the grounds that I answer the description of the man the police wish to interview. Wait for the trial and the verdict, and in the meantime find out all you need to about Robert Adams and his family. I do know he has two brothers, with whom he runs a business somewhere in Camberwell, but I believe they are all better known in Walworth. He may have other brothers, and he may have sisters. I suggest you find lodgings in Walworth and begin your enquiries there. Robert Adams has a daughter, by the way, a young girl who would photograph very prettily. In the event of a guilty verdict, I shall go to the scaffold consoled by my conviction that you will attend to Robert Adams and other members of the brood.

I don't think I need tell you that as we're identical twins you must change your appearance, since there are people in Walworth who would see me in you. This letter may be my goodbye. If so, I wish you freedom from the interference that will have brought me to fatal misfortune. But we will remain one, you and I.   Gerald.

Chapter One

May, 1926.

The country was falling apart.

The General Strike was on.

The trade unions had said they'd no wish to call it, and the Government had said it would be calamitous if they did. The coal-miners' union said make some concessions, then. The Government said we'll set up a commission. We've had some of that, said the miners, and out they came at midnight on the first of May. All other trade unions followed.

They've all gone barmy, said the cockney women of London, fearful that they wouldn't even be able to buy bread for their families.

Everything seemed to come to a stop, except public utilities such as water and gas. Factories were suddenly silent, trains ceased to run, and so did trams and buses. Newspaper presses closed down and delivery vans disappeared from the streets of towns and villages. Belligerent strikers roamed around London, some with the Red Flag hoisted high. Unfortunately for their cause, that got up the noses of the general public.

'Bugger the Red Flag,' said cockney housewives when they found that even milk deliveries had disappeared from their doorsteps.

The Government, controlling huge resources, went into action. So did the people. Volunteers poured forward to drive trams, buses, trains and vans, and to get essential services going. Fights broke out. The public joined in, siding for the most part with the volunteers. From Government printing presses issued a one-sheet informative newspaper called *The British Gazette*. It was the brainchild of Winston Churchill, Chancellor of the Exchequer.

Non-union workers did what they could to keep some factories going, but were hampered by a lack of raw materials. People got up earlier than usual to walk to their places of work. Business, however, was still badly affected, and country people didn't think much of a strike at this time of the year. Well, country people saw the first week of May as a time for celebrating the arrival of summer, even if summer had a fit of the sulks and refused to turn up. Come to that, there were some street kids in Walworth mostly of the little girl kind, who liked to do a bit of dancing round a maypole erected on waste ground near Rodney Place. This year, a daft trade unionist, having looked up the rules of a building workers' union, declared that the erection of a maypole could only be carried out by a union member. Which couldn't be done, on account of the strike. Little girls cried and blew their wet noses on their frocks, and six hefty housewives sat on the bloke and stuffed his book of rules down inside his trousers where it would do the most damage. It hurt him as well. But the maypole went up and the little girls danced around it.

There was one boss who'd seen the strike coming and had taken precautions. That was Sammy Adams, the driving force behind Adams Enterprises, Adams Fashions and Adams Scrap Metal.

He'd never favoured strikes. He believed in hard work, initiative, competitiveness and making good use of one's brainbox. Everyone had a brainbox, but not everyone made proper use of what nature had gifted. Sammy believed in using his to the full. He also believed in paying a fair wage, but expected every employee to earn it. Twenty-four, he had striven since his formative years to make a name for himself, and had acquired a talent for looking ahead.

At the moment, Adams Fashions had a highly important contract to fulfil, a contract for supplying ladies' wear to Coates of Kensington. Coates had branch stores all over the South of England. There were mouth-watering profits to be made, providing nothing happened to muck the whole thing up. Late delivery would cost the firm a packet, and Sammy was dead against that kind of thing, which was ruinous and also painful to a businessman of his standing.

However, he had looked ahead, seen the trouble signs and accordingly taken precautions. Adams Fashions were stuffed to the roof of a rented warehouse with materials and fabrics all relevant to the manufacture of ladies' wear and all purchased well in advance of the General Strike. Sammy, in fact, had practically cornered the market in fabrics as far as the London rag trade was concerned. And as his factory in Islington employed seventy non-union seamstresses, production was up to schedule, if not in advance. His East End workers were unshakeably loyal to him and his brother Tommy, their manager. They received bonuses for extra effort, something unheard-of in East End factories, especially in the sweatshops. Sammy's seamstresses kept very quiet about it. He didn't want irate competitors making arrangements to blow the factory up.

As it was, a number of his competitors, those who also employed non-union labour, were already discovering they'd only be able to keep their factories going by purchasing materials from Adams Fashions. The Lancashire supply mills had been shut down by the strike, and London wholesalers were depleted. Tommy had begun to accept enquiries and orders for stocks over the phone. The price per bale, he said to one more enquiring competitor, was five quid.

'It's what?'

Tommy repeated the price.

'Listen, Tommy Adams, if that's the thieving price Sammy's put on the goods, tell him to measure his bleedin' self for a coffin.'

'What's ten per cent extra except to cover 'andling charges?' said Tommy. 'And a bit of allowable profit?'

'Ten per cent my backside, it's nearer twenty.'

'Sammy's got to live,' said Tommy.

'So have I. I don't go for havin' my throat cut by Sammy.'

'It's a hard life,' said Tommy.

'It's harder when someone's crucifying you. But I've got to have that stuff.'

'Pleasure,' said Tommy. 'COD, of course.'

There was a strangled cry of pain at the other end of the line.

Sammy's personal assistant, the former Miss Susie Brown, now Mrs Sammy Adams, informed him she was shocked at what he was doing to his competitors.

'Sammy, it's just not decent.'

'Still, it's good business, Susie.'

'It's profiteering.'

'Same thing, Susie.'

'It's not Christian,' said Susie, a lovely blue-eyed young wife of twenty-one.

'Well, as you know,' said Sammy, 'business ain't quite the same as goin' to church, Susie. I'm as religious as the next man—'

'No, you're not,' said Susie. 'Sammy Adams, you know I didn't hold with you buying up everything you could lay your hands on. I've just been speakin' to that nice Mr Ross of Shoreditch. He says by this time next week he won't have a single yard of material left in his factory.'

'Poor old Georgie Ross, what a cryin' shame, Susie. I'll have to buy him out.'

'No, you won't,' said Susie, 'I've arranged to let him have all he wants from the warehouse.'

'Well, good for you, Susie. What price did you ask?'

'The price we paid.'

'Now, Susie, don't say things like that. Things like that give me a headache.'

'I repeat, the price we paid,' said Susie. 'Of course, there was ten per cent for storage costs and five per cent for handling charges.'

'Susie, you caution, consider yourself me favourite personal assistant,' said Sammy. Susie *was* a caution. They'd been married a month, and he'd said a few private words to her during their honeymoon in Devon.

He began by saying, 'Susie?'

'Yes, Sammy?'

'I want to tell you something.'

13

'Yes, Sammy.'

'You're beautiful, did you know that?'

'Oh, yes, I do know, but it's nice you know too.'

'I've got a certain feelin', Susie, that you're beautiful all over.'

'Well, yes, I am, Sammy.'

'Mind, I haven't seen you all over.'

'Oh, dear, I am sorry, but never mind, you can take my word for it.'

'Seeing we're married, Susie, don't I have the privilege of—'

'Some hopes you've got, you shocker, if you think I'm goin' to do a Lady Godiva act for you.'

'Have I asked you to, Susie, have I asked you to sit on a horse in your birthday suit?'

'Not yet you haven't,' said Susie, who had discovered that Sammy, an electrifying businessman, was also an electrifying lover. She laughed.

'What's funny, might I ask?' enquired Sammy.

'You are, Sammy love. All right, I'll let you see me in my birthday suit, when we turn out the lights in our bedroom tonight.'

'You might not believe it, Susie, but I can't see in the dark.'

'Oh, dear, can't you really, Sammy, what a blow. Still, here we are, sitting on the cliffs, and you can see the beautiful view, can't you?'

'Susie, you saucebox.'

'Same to you, Sammy love,' said Susie.

Sammy never got any change out of speaking to her, privately or otherwise.

Today, the third day of the strike, Susie was at the Camberwell offices and he was at the rented factory in Islington. His faithful seamstresses were being intimidated by strikers. He'd received a

14

phone call from Tommy and had travelled immediately from Camberwell to Islington.

Gertie Roper, his loyal charge-hand, was very upset. A thin woman, Shoreditch-born, she was the kind of gutsy person Sammy liked. She was a worker, an honest and efficient one, and she earned every penny of the extra he paid her for being in charge of the machinists. There was very little Gertie wouldn't do for Sammy and Tommy to ensure productivity was of a kind that meant the firm would make money. She didn't at all mind that Sammy made money. That was what bosses ran a business for, to make money, otherwise there wouldn't be any businesses. But she had her reservations about some bosses, particularly those who ran the East End sweatshops and paid their seamstresses a pittance. She was a Bolshie as far as they were concerned. Sammy Adams was a different proposition. He was a corblimey lovely boss, and Gertie had a cockney woman's frank affection for him. To her two growing sons she had lately been handing out advice and warnings.

'Listen, you grubby 'orrors, either you grow up like yer dad or like Mister Sammy Adams, or I'll put both of yer through me mangle. Either you're goin' to be real men or 'orrible 'ooligans, and you ain't goin' to be any kind of 'ooligans, you 'ear me? Mister Sammy and yer dad was both as poor as church mice once, but they still grew up to be real men, and so will you, the pair of you, or through me mangle you'll go and come out flat all over. You got that?'

'Yes, Ma.'

'All right, then, now go and wash yer faces and stop tryin' to pull the cat's tail orf.'

Gertie was also fond of handsome Tommy, the factory manager. He always lent an ear to the girls and their problems, and their problems were usually to do with family poverty. It was no wonder she was in an upset state today, for the strikers had not only made it difficult for the seamstresses to get into the factory, but were now threatening to smash all its windows unless the women joined the strike. Bert, her husband, was out there, trying to calm the strikers down. Bert was Sammy's maintenance man and also the factory's Jack-of-all-trades. Sometimes he could hardly believe he was actually taking home a regular wage of two pounds five shillings a week. That on top of Gertie's charge-hand wage of twenty-one shillings a week meant they were beginning to feel rich. It also meant they felt they could afford something better than their shabby little flat-fronted dwelling in Shoreditch. Sammy advised them to buy a decent little house in a decent street. Get a mortgage, he said, don't pay rent, not if you can afford a mortgage. Rent's money down a drain, he said. The thought of herself and Bert, and their four children, having a house of their own turned Gertie giddy.

She was beginning now to get steamed up about the strikers. Everyone in Islington and Shoreditch, the strikers included, knew that Sammy and Tommy Adams were good bosses. What sense was there in breaking up the factory of good bosses? What good would it do the workers? Gertie might have sent for the police had she not believed in the East End principle of encouraging coppers to mind their own business.

There was a large blackboard outside the factory.

On the blackboard was a boldly chalked announcement.

'ADAMS FASHIONS SUPPORT THE STARVING FAMILIES OF THE MINERS WITH DONATIONS FROM STAFF AND EMPLOYERS — DROP YOUR OWN DONATIONS IN THE BUCKET.'

Bert was in charge of the bucket. A well-known figure, he was giving the impression that he himself was out on strike. As an ex-docker, he had felt he had to make some gesture, and Sammy had said right, look after the bucket and make known the seamstresses are working to help support the miners' families, which is a sight better than coming out.

The strikers kept listening to Bert. They also kept interrupting him. Now, finally, they'd told him to get the factory shut down or else. Non-union workers were all scabs. They wanted quick action before any rozzers turned up.

'It ain't my job to get it shut down,' said Bert, 'and it wouldn't make sense, anyway. The miners are goin' to get 'alf everyone's wages, plus the same amount from the guv'nor, so stop shovin'.'

The strikers became stroppy. One of them aimed a kick at the bucket. It turned over and clanged about. Coppers spilled from it.

'In ten seconds, mate, we start smashin' the winders,' shouted a striker.

'Don't talk daft,' said Bert.

'Watch yerself, Bert,' said another man, 'yer beginnin' to sound like a bleedin' blackleg.'

'You ever call me a blackleg,' said Bert, 'and I'll break your back.'

Inside the factory, Gertie was talking to Sammy and Tommy.

'I'm goin' out there meself,' she said, 'I ain't 'aving them set about Bert. 'E's me old man, the only one I've got, and I want 'im all in one piece when 'e gets 'ome this evenin'.'

'You stay here,' said Sammy. He had addressed the strikers once, half an hour ago. He'd said nothing about the fact that his factory was a non-union shop, he simply pointed out that the business gave regular work to over sixty seamstresses, none of whom had any complaints, and that it wouldn't help the miners or anyone else if they all walked out. It would damage the business and probably result in cancelled contracts. That would mean laying off more than half the women. If that was what you blokes were after, he said, you'd better send a spokesman into the factory and tell them so. But watch out your spokesman doesn't get his legs broken. The girls ain't partial to bad news. The strikers said that what they were after was workers' solidarity. Well, have a meeting about it, said Sammy, and try to come up with something that won't cut Gertie Roper's throat. Gertie's the girls' spokesman. The strikers muttered and growled, and Sammy left them to deliberate. Now, however, it was all too obvious the strikers weren't going to be satisfied until the factory was shut down. 'Tommy, we'll have to go out and read 'em the riot act. Bert needs help.'

'Time we gave him some, then,' said Tommy, a tall and stalwart young man of twenty-six. 'Time too we thought about callin' in the coppers.'

'Not on your life,' said Sammy. 'People round here have got a kind eye for Adams Fashions. Kind eyes round here, Tommy, turn sour if the law's called in. Come on.'

He and Tommy went outside to stand shoulder to shoulder with Bert, who was facing up to prospective violence. A large man, newly arrived, received a whispered word or two from a striker. He gave Sammy the once-over.

''Ello, you're Sammy Adams, are yer?' he said. 'You're the bleedin' boss, are yer?'

'Dead right, I'm the bleedin' boss,' said Sammy, 'and I've got one man on strike, Bert Roper here.'

''E looks like a bleedin' bosses' man to me.'

'Bert Roper's his own man,' said Sammy, 'don't make any mistake about that. He's come out. I asked him not to. It made no difference. He's out, and it's causin' me considerable inconvenience. I've been a worker, man and boy, all me life, and I can recognize when workers are committin' fatal suicide. I hope you're followin' me.'

'You're a ponce,' said the large man, 'and it's suicide for yer fact'ry if you don't shut it down.'

Sammy eyed him sorrowfully. The bloke was a pain in the neck. Sammy knew the type. They thrived on trouble, not being able to relate to uncomplaining workers. The large size of this one didn't intimidate Sammy, whose dealings with all kinds of people had given him a maturity that belied his twenty-four years. Further, he had a good pair of shoulders and a hard fist.

'I hear you've got some idea about smashin' all our windows,' he said.

'Yer bloody right we 'ave,' said the large cove, 'and that's just for starters. Take a butcher's at me brothers' ammo.'

Several hands were raised to show bricks and half-bricks.

'That's not very friendly, mate, nor reasonable,'

said Tommy.

'See here, cully,' growled the large man, 'me and me brother unionists ain't been brought up to be reasonable on account of bein' victimized from the age of one.'

'Yer bleedin' right,' said a striker. The mood was ugly now. People were looking on from a distance, waiting for the fireworks to begin. 'We gave 'em ten seconds to shut the fact'ry down ten minutes ago, and they ain't taken a blind bit of notice. Time we let fly.'

'Lay off, mates, you still ain't makin' sense,' said Bert. Lean and sinewy, he could take care of himself and hand out a few wallops while doing so.

'Sod makin' your kind of sense!' bawled another striker, and he chucked a brick. It smashed the office window. Flying glass showered around Gertie, watching from the window. A sliver cut her face and drew blood. That did it, as far as Gertie was concerned. She rushed into the workshop as more bricks were thrown. Strikers charged, and Sammy, Tommy and Bert were suddenly in a fight with several of them. Out came Gertie, seamstresses pouring after her, yelling and shouting, slats of wood in their hands.

'I'll give yer try to knock me 'ead orf!' yelled Gertie, and led the charge of her petticoat brigade into the fight. She smote the capped head of a man.

'Oh, yer bitch!'

'You bleedin' 'ooligan, who's a bitch?' Gertie bashed his cap. Then the seamstresses, at least thirty of them, were all at work. The large man couldn't believe his eyes. His brothers couldn't believe what was happening to their heads. Down came the slats of wood, whacking and thumping.

What the hell was going on? Workers against workers, one lot in skirts? It shouldn't be allowed. Who'd got a rule book?

'Give over, yer crazy female, or I'll pull yer drawers off!' bawled a conked striker to a young, smiting machinist.

'Oh, yer common sod, I 'eard that,' cried the girl. 'Did you 'ear it, Mrs Biddy? 'E said 'e'll pull me drawers off. 'Ere, take that!' She conked him again, and so did the woman backing her up, a Mrs Biddy. The striker fell over. Mrs Biddy, a buxom woman, trod on him.

The seamstresses and Gertie were fighting for the factory, for their jobs and for their bosses, and the bulk of the strikers couldn't make head or tail of this development. The rest of them, a small mob led by the large man, were at Sammy, Tommy and Bert, who were doing what they could to hold them off. But Gertie and a dozen seamstresses were at the backs of this mob, clouting them.

'I ain't believin' this,' panted one man, as his cap was knocked off and his head whacked.

Onlookers across the street gawped and gaped. Crikey, what a punch-up, what a corblimey free-for-all. A woman shouted.

'Go it, gels! Up the workers!'

A policeman's whistle sounded from way down the street. The onlookers melted away by instinct. The large man disentangled himself from the mêlée, roared at Sammy that he'd get him, and then made himself scarce. The strikers followed on his heels. Coppers' whistles were always bad news.

'Disappear, girls,' said Sammy, and Gertie and her machinists poured back into the factory.

When two bobbies arrived on the scene, all was

quiet. Outside the factory, only Bert was visible, standing beside the bucket, the righted blackboard behind him. He attended to the coppers' questions. No, no real trouble, he said, just one window that got broken accidental. Sure? What happened to your face, then? Walked into that ruddy blackboard, said Bert. One bobby recommended that the factory should be enclosed within a strong wire fence, with entrance gates that could be locked. It might help to stop your face walking into blackboards, Mr Roper. Bert said a wire fence would make the factory look an unfriendly place, and the boss, Mister Sammy Adams, was against that kind of thing. The other bobby wanted to know what sort of an accident it was that had broken the window. Funny you should ask that, said Bert, I was just about to mention I broke it meself. I was shifting the blackboard and it fell against the glass. Dear oh lor', said the bobby, how unfortunate. You sure there's been no trouble, Mr Roper? Nothing to complain about, said Bert. Well, call the station next time you've got nothing to complain about, said the bobby, keeping his face straight, and he and his colleague left.

Sammy would have dealt with the coppers himself, but he had a black eye and some sore ribs. Tommy had a painful knee and a bruised jaw. Bert came in to report his conversation with the coppers, and suggested he'd better do a night watch in case the large bloke and some of his brothers turned up when it was dark. Sammy, nursing his eye with a cold wet flannel, said, 'No, you might get done over, Bert. We'll ask the station for a couple of bobbies and pay for the service.' Then he and Tommy went from the office into the workshop to see how the girls were. The girls were at their machines and going it.

'Bless me soul, Mister Adams,' said Gladys, an established hand, 'where'd yer cop that fancy mince pie? You ain't been in a fight, 'ave yer? Mister Adams, I'm surprised at yer. And what's happened to Mister Tommy? 'E's lookin' all bruised. You ain't walked into a wall, 'ave yer, Mister Tommy?'

'Something like that,' said Tommy.

'You ought to look where yer goin',' said Gertie, a piece of lint and sticking plaster covering the cut on her cheek. 'Walls is dangerous. Look what one's done to Mister Sammy.'

Mrs Lilian Hyams, designer exclusive to Adams Fashions, came out of her drawing office. A war widow, her exceptional talents as a designer had brought her offers from famous fashion houses. She had turned them all down. Sammy and his electrifying approach to challenges had fascinated her when she first met him. But it was more than that. Sammy alone had had faith in her designs at a time when she was flat broke and desperate. He had offered her a contract on the spot. It pulled her up from the gutter of poverty to become an overnight rival of established designers. She used the professional name of Mimi Dupont. That was Sammy's idea. She knew all three Adams brothers. They were Gentiles who had broken into the rag trade and broken it wide open, with Sammy leading the way. Lilian, extrovert and talented, put her grateful heart and soul into all her work. As far as she was concerned, only an elephant could drag her away from Adams Fashions, and even then she'd only go kicking and screaming.

Now she regarded Sammy with a whimsical smile.

23

'Sammy, is that you hiding behind a shiner? My life, is it?'

'I admit to being injured,' said Sammy, dabbing his shiner again, 'but it ain't fatal, and Bert and Tommy are still alive.'

'I saw it all from the office,' said Lilian.

'Best place,' said Tommy, 'it was dangerous outside.'

'Mister Tommy, we feel for yer,' said the young seamstress who'd given a good account of herself. 'I wouldn't go near 'ooligans like that meself.'

'I heard that, Maggie,' said Sammy. 'I seem to have a picture in me mind of certain machinists interferin' in the argument that was takin' place outside. I'm against you ladies carryin' on like that. It's highly risky and liable not to do you much good, either. I ought to be layin' down the law and remindin' you I don't hold with ladies participatin' in argumentative punch-ups. But I won't, seein' it was a rescue act. Only don't do it again, in case some of you charge me for wear and tear. Do I remark you're sufferin' wounded wear and tear, Gertie?'

'Slightly, yer might say, Mister Sammy,' said Gertie. 'We don't recall no punch-up, not us, yer know. It was just that we wasn't goin' to stand for the fact'ry bein' smashed up.'

'I see your point, Gertie, even if one of me optics is a trifle bunged up,' said Sammy, and seamstresses giggled.

'I'll bring a shotgun tomorrow,' said Lilian, looking eye-catching in one of her own creations, a beaded peach-coloured straight dress with a scalloped hem. Her silk-stockinged legs showed to her knees. Just thirty, she was unable to take on the popular flat-chested look of the flappers, for she had an old-fashioned figure. That worried her not at all, since most men were against straight lines, and none of the Adams brothers had ever suggested that as a designer of flapper fashions she ought to do something about flattening herself.

'No shotguns,' said Tommy.

'I should worry about blowing a few heads off?' said Lilian.

'It's against the law,' said Tommy, and Lilian laughed. She was a happy woman, and she had a good relationship with the seamstresses. Their rushing charge from the factory had exhilarated her. They were all characteristic of East End women, hard-working, resilient and fiercely loyal to their kind. They were afraid only of themselves and their husbands being out of work. That fear was a stalking spectre in the minds of most people in the East End. Working for Sammy Adams kept that spectre at bay for these women, and their action in beating off the militant strikers had been a demonstration of a different kind of loyalty, an unusual one among East End workers. It was a loyalty to their bosses.

Lilian knew that Sammy and Tommy were aware of it.

Sammy arrived back in his Camberwell office just after three o'clock, in time to receive a cup of tea and some biscuits from Doreen Paterson of the general office.

Doreen, taking a look at him, said, 'Crikey.'

'Something bothering you?' said Sammy.

'Mister Sammy, did you know you've got a black eye?'

'Have I? Unfortunate if it notices.'

'Did it 'appen at the factory?' asked Doreen.

'We had a bit of an argument with some of the strikers who've decided to picket non-union workshops,' said Sammy. 'It's a diabolical liberty and saucy as well, but the factory's still workin'.' His left eye was swollen, his ribs tender.

'It's awful, the fights that are goin' on,' said Doreen. 'The strikers are so bad-tempered about the way people are standin' up to them. I just 'ope you won your fight, Mister Sammy, and that the other bloke's got two black eyes.'

'It hurts me to say so, Doreen, but I think the other bloke just had a grin on his face.' Sammy took a welcome mouthful of the hot tea. 'You havin' trouble gettin' to work and goin' home?'

'Well, it's bothersome gettin' on a tram or bus,' said Doreen, 'but I'm managing. Shall I send Ronnie out to buy you a piece of raw steak?' Ronnie was the office boy.

'Too late,' said Sammy, wishing his bunged-up mince pie hadn't happened.

'Well, you've got me deepest sympathy, Mister Sammy,' said Doreen, and departed to inform the general office girls that he'd returned from Islington with a shiner.

Mrs Susie Adams entered her husband's office. As his wife, with a house on Denmark Hill to look after, her hours now were from ten until four instead of from nine until five-thirty. That allowed her enough time for her domestic chores, which so far she counted as a labour of love. Love at the moment was at its most exciting. Boots, her brother-in-law, teased her, of course, with questions like what happened last night, Susie? Last night? Yes, you're wearing a blush this morning.

There her husband was, back from Islington, his head bent as he scanned letters on his desk.

'Sammy?'

'What is it, Miss Brown?'

'Not that old chestnut, if you don't mind.'

'Ah, yes,' said Sammy, 'what is it, Mrs Adams?'

'Was there much trouble at the factory?'

'A slight argument, but the factory's still goin' full pelt,' said Sammy, keeping his head down.

'Sammy, there's a button missin' from your jacket,' said Susie.

'Fell off,' said Sammy.

'Fell off, my foot,' said Susie.

'No, off me jacket,' said Sammy.

'Sammy, look at me.'

'I'm up to me ears, Susie, and all behind as well.'

'Look at me when I'm talkin' to you,' said Susie.

'Oh, well, it's now or never, I suppose,' said Sammy, and lifted his head to show her his damaged eye. Susie blinked.

'Who did that?' she asked.

'Walked into a sandwich-board,' said Sammy.

'No, you didn't. Who hit you?'

'I didn't catch his name,' said Sammy, 'just his wallop.'

Boots, his eldest brother, came in then. Two months short of thirty, he had an air of maturity, gained in advance by his time in France and Flanders. He was, however, a good-humoured man and a tolerant one.

'Sammy,' he said, 'I understand you've been slightly damaged. Yes, I see you have. You've collected a beauty. What happened?'

'All right,' said Sammy, 'I'll use up some of me

valuable time to tell you how our factory light brigade charged the Bolsheviks.' He recounted events.

'Help,' said Susie, 'the machinists set about the strikers?'

'And then went back to work as if they'd only had a tea break,' said Sammy, 'which I suggest is what we do to earn our crusts. Any messages, Susie?'

'Yes,' said Susie, 'Miss de Vere wants a report on progress, she's worried in case the factory gets shut down.' Miss de Vere was the chief buyer for Coates. 'She respects how busy you are, Sammy, and said if you don't have time to phone her, she'd like Boots to.'

Sammy managed a grin.

'Passed to you, Boots,' he said.

'Yes, she's gettin' faint about you, Boots,' said Susie, 'but I won't tell Emily.'

'Nor me,' said Sammy, 'or Em'ly might injure me other optic.'

'I'll try to work my way out of danger,' said Boots. 'Production's up to schedule, Sammy?'

'Production is steamin',' said Sammy, 'all on account of Tommy and the girls keepin' the pot boilin'.'

'I'll pass the good news on to Miss de Vere,' said Boots, and went back to his office.

'Sammy,' said Susie, 'I'll do something about your eye as soon as you get home.'

'I'll appreciate that,' said Sammy, 'I'm sufferin' a bit of vision trouble.'

'What sort of trouble?' asked Susie in concern.

'I can only see half of you,' said Sammy.

Chapter Two

At three-thirty, Mrs Emily Adams, Boots's wife, covered her typewriter and put her hat and gloves on. While she had never been known as a beauty, her nose being peaky and her chin too pointed, she did have a crown of dark auburn hair and striking eyes of a swimming green. When animated or excited, she could sparkle, and people forgot that she was plain. She had an inner energy that could make her eyes look bright and lively. At the moment, she was painfully thin. She'd begun to lose weight months ago, and her Denmark Hill doctor had diagnosed anaemia. Boots eventually came to question that, and so did she herself. She thought it might be something worse. So she asked her doctor if she could consult her previous practitioner for a second opinion. He readily gave her a letter to carry to Dr McManus of Walworth, who came up with his own diagnosis after a careful examination and several questions about her diet.

'Emily, Emily,' he said, shaking his head, 'you're a sad case of starvation.'

'Starvation?' said Emily. 'You're jokin', doctor.'

'From your condition and from what you've told me,' said Dr McManus, 'I'd say you're simply not putting enough food into your system, young lady.'

'Well, bless you, doctor, for callin' me a young

lady when I'm twenty-seven,' said Emily, 'but I still can't think I've got a starved condition.'

Dr McManus, a fatherly practitioner who had earned the gratitude and affection of countless people in Walworth, said, 'Since I last saw you, Emily, there's half of you gone missing.'

Emily said she knew she'd lost a bit of weight. Half of you is more than a bit, said Dr McManus. You're starving yourself, aren't you? Well, I admit I don't have a big appetite these days, said Emily. Dr McManus suggested she probably had no appetite at all, and asked if anything had worried her during the last year. Emily's own real worry had related to the possibility of a woman called Polly Simms usurping her in the affections of Boots, but not even to Dr McManus would she mention that. So she said she hadn't had any worries she could think of, not serious worries. Well, said Dr McManus, something has caused your loss of appetite. I thought that was just my anaemic condition, said Emily. You haven't got anaemia, Emily, you've got an odd complaint called anorexia.

'Oh, my soul,' breathed Emily, 'is that fatal, doctor?'

'Plainly put, it's a dislike of eating.'

Emily admitted she did toy a bit with her food. Dr McManus advised her that that had got to stop, and that if it didn't she'd find herself seriously ill.

'I can't afford to be ill, doctor, I've got my fam'ly and my home life. I don't have time to be ill, and I'm sure Boots wouldn't be in favour.'

'If I know Boots,' said Dr McManus, 'he'll help to see it doesn't happen. It may take time for you to adjust to eating three reasonable meals a day, in

30

which case you could try eating little and often. Or you could start by tackling six bowls of nourishing soup a day, soup made from good stock, like meaty bones from your butcher, with a little solid food in between.'

'Six bowls of soup a day? Six?'

'Six at least, with a slice of bread and butter each time. It's going to be a question of fighting your dislike of food in the easiest possible way.'

'Oh, I'll fight a good fight, if it'll stop me gettin' ill,' said Emily. 'Me ill and in bed and my fam'ly all up and about? I'd go barmy. Can I keep comin' to see you all the time I've got this anex – what was it, doctor?'

'Anorexia, Emily, and yes, you can continue to consult me. I'll write to Dr Thompson.'

'Well, bless you, doctor, you've always been kind and 'elpful to me ever since I was a little girl. Boots asked me to give you his regards.'

'How is he?' smiled Dr McManus.

'He's fine,' said Emily, 'he's so healthy it's almost aggravatin'. I just hope all that soup won't make gurgling noises, or he'll be sure to say something like eat a sheet of blottin' paper first. Do I get any prescription?'

'Yes,' said Dr McManus, and wrote out a prescription for a medicine with a restorative factor. He gave it to her and again emphasized the necessity of putting food regularly into herself.

'I will,' said Emily, 'even if it kills me – Lord above, what a daft thing to say.'

That had been nearly four weeks ago, since when she really had been fighting her odd aversion to meals. Boots's mother, known to the family as Chinese Lady, and her second husband, Mr Edwin

Finch, shared a large house with Boots and his family, and Chinese Lady had been preparing soups so appetizing that everyone was enjoying them. Anyone would think you've all got anexia, said Chinese Lady. Yes, I expect it's anexia that makes us like your soups so much, said Rosie, adopted daughter of Emily and Boots. And their young son Tim said he didn't mind having anexia a bit. Boots said it was generous of Emily to share her complaint with everyone, it helped them to qualify for a measure of soup. Chinese Lady remarked to her husband that her only oldest son still said things no-one understood except himself. Give him some more soup, Maisie, said Mr Finch. That won't cure his tongue, said Chinese Lady. Perhaps not, said Mr Finch, but it might cure his share of the complaint. It's not a complaint Emily's got, said Chinese Lady, it's just a temporary condition.

Emily smiled at her recollections.

And there was something else to smile about. She'd put on seven ounces. Entering her husband's office, she said, 'I'm off now, lovey.' She always finished at three-thirty so that she could go home and spend some time with young Tim, not yet of school age.

'Treat yourself to a large slice of fruit cake when you get home,' said Boots.

'Fusspot,' she said, but gave him a warm kiss just to let him know she still liked being his wife. She also liked the fact that she didn't have to worry now about that Polly Simms, a certain woman who'd been an ambulance driver during the Great War, had met Boots a few years ago and taken a fancy to him. Now she was in darkest Africa, or somewhere like that. 'See you later.'

She collected her bicycle from the ground floor. She'd been using it since the General Strike began. She wheeled it over the pavement to the road, and began to cycle home. Her short skirt, not much longer than a flapper's, showed her knees. As she reached Ruskin Park, a young bloke came out through the gate and whistled at her.

Crikey, she thought, he's whistling at my legs. Wait till I tell Boots a saucy young whistler made my day.

Doreen put her head into Boots's office at five-thirty.

'Good night, Mister Adams,' she said, 'I've just got to go now.' She was one of the staff of fourteen employees working on this floor or the top floor. The strike was causing problems that meant some employees weren't getting away precisely on time.

'Hop off, Doreen,' said Boots, whose looks and whimsical good humour made him a thrill in the eyes of impressionable girls. 'Thanks for slaving away.'

'Been a pleasure,' said Doreen, whose firm but susceptible bosom had sometimes known sighs and flutters in his presence. Most of the office girls had a crush on him. She smiled as she descended the stairs to the street, where she turned left towards the junction of Camberwell Green. She was nineteen. Her fashionably brief skirt of dark green whisked around her knees, her flesh-coloured rayon stockings gleaming in the early evening sunshine, her lemon-coloured jumper cosily cuddling her figure, her little straw hat sitting on the back of her shingled brown hair. Cloche hats were favourites with most young ladies these days, but

Doreen thought their pudding basin effect didn't suit her face. Actually, she had a very nice face, made the nicer by hazel eyes bright and friendly, and she had the quick ready smile of most cockney girls.

There were crowds at the tram and bus stops. Public transport was running on a limited basis, and trams and buses driven by volunteers bulged with passengers during the rush hours. Each driver usually had a protective policeman up with him, since some strikers had virtually declared war on all volunteers. Doreen, seeing the waiting crowds, decided she'd probably get home quicker if she walked, as many workers were doing every day. Her mother would be watching the clock, waiting for her to get home and to start the evening meal. Doreen's dad had died two years ago, her twin brother and sister were both married, and she was now all her mum had.

Mrs Paterson relied on her younger daughter for company and affection, and was affectionate herself, but in a possessive way. She professed fragile health from the shock of losing her husband. Doreen, a good-natured girl, had not yet come to realize she was expected to be her widowed mum's lifelong help and companion, although she knew she was very necessary to her at the moment. It meant friendships with young men were out of the question for the time being. Talk of young men upset her mum. Not that it was a serious matter. She hadn't yet met Mr Right, nor anyone she was really keen on. Perhaps by the time she did, her mum would have got over her loss and become her old busy self.

Doreen crossed the junction into Camberwell

Road, and hurried homewards on quick feet. A couple of horse-drawn carts passed her, full up with people who'd been given a lift. That's what I could do with, a lift, she thought. She lived with her mum in Morecambe Street, off the East Street market. She earned twenty-one bob a week with Adams Enterprises, a nice wage for a switchboard operator. That, with her mum's little pension, generously paid by her late dad's old firm, just about kept them going after the weekly rent was settled.

A crowded tram passed her, and so did a young man riding a bicycle. He noted her hurried walk and her shining legs. He pulled up a little way ahead of her and waited.

'Need some transport?' he smiled.

''Ave you got some, then?' said Doreen. 'Like a bus tucked up your shirt?' She hastened on. The young man followed, wheeling his bike. 'D'you mind goin' away?' she said. She knew all the tricks that the lively fellers of Walworth and Camberwell could get up to when trying to pick up a girl. 'Look, stop following me.'

'If you're in a hurry—'

'Yes, I am.'

'I thought you were,' said Luke Edwards. 'Like a lift on me carrier?'

Doreen cast him a suspicious look, and had to admit he wasn't exactly repulsive. His peaked blue cap and dungarees were those of a workman, his features healthy, his smile friendly. He looked about twenty-four. I think I ought to tell him to push off, I think I should. He might be anybody, he might be what Mister Sammy Adams would call a highly dubious geezer.

'Well, I don't mind a lift,' she said, 'as long as you're not tryin' to pick me up.'

'Perish the thought,' said Luke, 'I'll just be pleased to give you a lift. Where'd you live?'

'Morecambe Street, Walworth,' said Doreen.

'Know it like the back of me hand,' said Luke. 'I'll take you there if you'd care to park your lower 'alf on me carrier.'

'I said I'd like a lift, I didn't say I wanted any sauce.'

'What's your name?' asked Luke, taken with her.

'I don't tell me name to people I don't know,' said Doreen.

'All right, I'll call you Lady Vi,' said Luke. 'Jump aboard.'

'Lady Vi my eye,' said Doreen, but placed herself sideways on the carrier. 'Oh, watch it,' she gasped, for he was away at once, cycling strongly and whistling as he went. She tugged at her skirt, her stockinged knees bright round cups of reflected sunlight.

'Comfy?' he asked, overtaking horse-drawn vehicles on his way to the Walworth Road.

'Well, I 'aven't fallen off yet,' she said.

'Good,' said Luke. 'Um – legs all right?'

'Yes, they're running behind,' she said.

He laughed, the peak of his cap shading his eyes against the slanting sunlight. He sighted something questionable in the distance.

'Hold on to your titfer, Lady Vi,' he said, 'I think there's trouble ahead.'

'Oh, don't get held up,' begged Doreen, 'I don't want to be late 'ome.'

'I'll do me best,' said Luke, and pedalled on.

He approached the corner of Fielding Street,

where Walworth Road·began. A tram was at a stop. A surging mob surrounded it, a mob of belligerent strikers and resisting men. The strikers were trying to board the tram to get at the volunteer driver, and the protective policeman up with the driver had his truncheon out and at the ready. Luke had to stop. The mêlée was blocking the road. He pulled up. The pole of a striker's banner was swinging. Luke knocked it aside. Doreen, on her feet, held the bike steady, troubled little breaths escaping her. The striker, his back to Luke, turned on him, his face red and angry. Few strikers liked the fact that the public had turned against them. While most people had a deep sympathy for the coal-miners, they had no sympathy at all for a strike that could shut off food from shops and medical supplies from hospitals.

The angry bloke went for Luke. Doreen quivered. Round came the banner in an attempt to knock Luke's head off. He caught hold of the banner itself, and applied a violent jerk. The striker lost his hold, and Luke chucked the pole and banner at the man.

'Sod yer!' bawled the striker.

'Watch your mouth,' said Luke, 'I've got a lady with me.'

'Sod 'er too!'

'Oh, yer ruddy 'ooligan!' yelled a woman from among people on the pavement.

'Starvin' our kids, that's what you're doin'!' shouted another woman.

'Bleedin' fried eggs,' bawled the striker, 'I got kids of me own, ain't I?'

'Well, they ain't got much of a dad!'

The mêlée around the tram increased in violence.

The copper aboard was blowing his whistle.

'Come on, mate,' said an old bloke on the pavement, beckoning to Luke. A gap appeared, Luke wheeled his bike on to the pavement and through the crowd of bystanders, Doreen following. Luke took his bike back on the road, Doreen perched herself on the carrier again, and away they went, along the Walworth Road.

'All right, Lady Vi?'

'I'm not Lady Vi, you daft ha'porth,' said Doreen, legs hanging clear of the back wheel. 'Crikey, I thought that striker was goin' to knock you under a bus.'

'I think he thought I was his dog's dinner,' said Luke. 'Legs still all right?'

'D'you always talk to girls about their legs when you give them a ride on your bike?' said Doreen.

'Only when there's a strike on,' said Luke, 'and only when it's you.'

'Stop showin' off,' said Doreen.

Luke slowed down for the turn into East Street. The bike trembled over tramlines. A passing bloke had a word with Doreen.

'What yer doin' tonight, darling?'

'Nothing with you, saucy,' said Doreen, and Luke smiled, liking her lively backchat. He pedalled into East Street, which was clear of stalls. The market had packed up for the day. Approaching King and Queen Street, Luke pulled up again, this time to avoid colliding with a boy cyclist who came riding out with a young girl seated astride his carrier.

'Oops, look where you're goin', Freddy,' said the young girl.

Freddy Brown stopped and let his bike rest. He saw Doreen.

'Watcher, Doreen,' he said.

Doreen smiled at the likeable, fresh-faced boy. He was the young brother-in-law of Mister Sammy. She had met him at the wedding of his sister to Sammy.

'Out with your girl, Freddy?' she asked.

'Not me,' said Freddy, 'I ain't come of age yet.'

'Got a few years yet, 'ave you?' smiled Luke.

'Me dad says a bloke's got to come of age and 'ave a few bob in 'is pocket before takin' girls out,' said Freddy. 'This is Cassie Ford that's on me bike. She's just me mate, and she ain't 'alf a trial.'

'No, I ain't,' said Cassie.

'I'll be old before me time, yer know,' said Freddy.

'Hard luck,' said Luke.

'Me cat's gettin' old before 'is time,' said Cassie, ''e's wearin' 'imself out running after a lady cat.'

'See what I mean?' said Freddy.

Doreen smiled.

'Can't stop, Freddy,' she said, 'I must get home.'

She and Luke went on.

'Let's see,' he said, 'shall I call for you later?'

'What?' she asked, startled.

'Yes, what time?' asked Luke, turning into Morecambe Street.

'Excuse me,' said Doreen, 'but I don't go out with fellers I've never met before. Besides, I've got me widowed mother to look after.'

'I don't mind comin' round to sit with you,' said Luke. 'We could look after her together for the evenin'.'

'Crikey, you're not backward comin' forward, are you?' said Doreen. 'If you think that just because – oh, stop, you've gone past me house, it's the one where the gate's open.'

Luke wheeled round and stopped outside the house, and Doreen put her feet to the ground.

'There we are, Lady Vi,' he smiled. 'All right now?'

Doreen straightened her skirt. Farther up the street, kids were running about.

'Look, thanks ever so much really,' she said, 'but I've got to get in now. Goodbye.'

Luke looked wry.

'I'd like to see you again,' he said.

'No, you can't,' she said.

'I'm capable.'

'Yes, you can stand up for yourself all right,' said Doreen, 'but I've got to say goodbye.'

'You sure I can't come knockin'?'

Doreen was suddenly tempted to give in to what was natural. It hadn't bothered her, the fact that she didn't have a young man. Because of her affection for her mum, she really was quite happy in her role as devoted daughter. She still didn't realize such a role could take possession of her. When speaking of her mum to Mrs Emily Adams, wife of the general manager, Mrs Adams had said well, just don't grow into an old maid, Doreen. Oh, I won't do that, she said. It was simply that her grievously widowed mum came first for the time being. A young man was something to think about later on. Yes, she thought, later on.

'No, I'm sorry,' she said to Luke, 'I'm too busy at 'ome to give time to anyone but my mum. But thanks again for the lift. Goodbye.' She hastened to the front door, pulled on the latchcord and went in. The door closed behind her. Luke was left looking rueful. I hope a girl like her doesn't make a life's work of a mother like that, he thought. I think I'm against taking no for an answer.

A boy came riding down the street, the boy he'd nearly collided with. The young girl was still seated astride his carrier. He saw Luke.

'Oh, 'ello again,' he called, and Luke moved from the kerbside and stopped him. Freddy pulled up, his girl mate Cassie swinging her legs. She was ten years old and a proper caution in the way she used her dreamy imagination. Freddy was on his way to twelve, a rumbustious and energetic boy who quite liked girls as his mates, but was finding Cassie, his current one, a bit of a handful. She didn't always do what he told her to, and on top of that she was as potty as a parrot. 'Doreen Paterson lives down 'ere,' he said to Luke.

'Yes, I've just seen her home,' said Luke, accepting that that was her name.

'I'm Freddy Brown, yer know, and Doreen works in me sister Susie's office.'

'Which office is that?' asked Luke.

'Oh, it's above the firm's shop called The Bazaar that's a little way along Denmark Hill, past Camberwell Green,' said Freddy, and Luke made a mental note of that.

'Mister,' said Cassie, 'd'you ride elephants?'

'Well, no, I don't,' smiled Luke, 'I'm an engineer and ride to work on me bike.'

'Cassie, what're you talkin' about, does 'e ride elephants?' said Freddy. 'Of all the barmy questions.'

'Well, 'ow did I know if 'e did or not?' said Cassie. 'I only asked, didn't I? Me dad used to ride elephants,' she said to Luke.

'No, 'e didn't,' said Freddy.

'Well, 'e was in darkest Africa once,' said Cassie, ''e could've rode elephants then.'

'You'll 'ave to excuse Cassie, mister,' said Freddy, 'she can't 'elp bein' scatty. She was born like it, yer know. Poor woman,' he added, with a bit of a grin. 'Mister, I've never seen Doreen ridin' on a feller's bike before. Are you 'er bloke?'

'Not yet,' said Luke.

'Well, I wish yer luck,' said Freddy.

'I need some, do I?' said Luke.

Freddy, always ready for a chat, let on that his sister Susie had told the family that Doreen's mum as good as kept her under lock and key.

'Oh, that's what 'appened to Princess Sylvia,' said Cassie, 'she was kept under lock an' key by 'er wicked uncle, but a handsome lord sent a magician to the castle, and 'e cast a spell that turned 'er into a bee so she was able to buzz out through the key'ole and fly all the way to the handsome lord. 'E gave 'er some honey that turned her back into a princess an' they lived 'appy ever after. 'Er wicked uncle 'ad a fit that turned 'im into a meat pie and 'e was ate up by 'is servants.'

'Can't believe 'er, can yer?' said Freddy to Luke.

'Why can't 'e?' protested Cassie. 'The wicked uncle's servants liked meat pie.'

'I think I'd better ride 'er home,' said Freddy.

'I ain't goin' 'ome yet,' said Cassie, 'me supper won't be ready.'

'All right, I'll take yer to the Zoo,' said Freddy, 'and leave yer in the Monkey 'ouse. So long, mister, I wish yer honest luck with Doreen.' Off he rode with Cassie. Luke spotted some street kids and had a chat with them too. Street kids were always full of information.

Doreen, having taken her hat off, entered the kitchen. Her mother was seated in a fireside chair. She looked up and smiled at her daughter, and Doreen thought she was still a handsome woman. She was forty-four, and her figure itself was still handsome. And she had a wealth of chestnut hair. She didn't look as if the grievous loss of her husband had left her in fragile health. She looked as if she could turn the rollers of her scullery mangle all day, if necessary, but Doreen accepted that the shock of becoming a widow had dealt her mum a hard blow.

'Oh, there you are, Doreen,' said Mrs Paterson, 'I was just beginnin' to worry about where you'd got to.'

'It's the strike, Mum,' said Doreen, 'I just couldn't get on a tram or bus, they were all full up.'

'Well, never mind, you're 'ome now,' said Mrs Paterson, 'and we can 'ave a nice quiet evening together. But just now, I'd love a pot of tea before you start the supper.'

A pot of tea was always the first thing she asked of Doreen as soon as her daughter arrived home from her work, and it had never occurred to Doreen to point out she could easily make the pot herself. She surprised herself on this occasion by thinking just that. Hastily, she brushed the thought aside. She was simply too fond of her mum to upset her in any way.

'I'll make it now, Mum, I could do with a cup meself,' she said.

'That's my girl,' said Mrs Paterson. She'd managed to get out for a walk during the day, she said, but had felt a bit tired when she got back. Still, she didn't think the walk had done her any harm.

And so on.

Doreen, putting the kettle on, thought about a vigorous young man wresting a banner from a striker and chucking it at him.

Chapter Three

Luke Edwards entered a house in Mason Street off
the New Kent Road, where he and his dad shared a
three-roomed flat on the second floor. The untidy-
looking passage shuddered to the onset of noise
from the downstairs kitchen. Crash, bang, wallop,
the Parslake family were at it again. Father, mother,
sons and daughter could all dish it out. Much of
their spare time activities were devoted to yelling,
roaring and bashing. It was the furniture that took
the bashing. Old man Parslake, beefy and beery,
had been known to give the table a demented bashing with a chair, and to have the chair finish up as
matchwood. They used the matchwood to help fuel
their kitchen fire. Mrs Parslake had been known to
chuck a pint beer bottle at her husband once she'd
drunk its contents. Her sons had been known to
drag the rent collector in off the doorstep and make
an attempt to stuff him up the parlour chimney.
The daughter had been known to knock her
brothers out with a wooden rolling-pin. They all
enjoyed their bruising and uproarious way of life.

Luke and his dad didn't enjoy it quite so much,
and were ready to move to quieter pastures. Not
that the Parslakes were unfriendly. Far from it.
Their attachment to their lodgers was a rousing and
warm-hearted one, and Luke and his dad had an
open invitation to come down and participate in the

family's free-for-alls any time they liked. Bertha, the buxom daughter, all of five feet ten, was willing to take Luke or his dad on in a wrestling bout. In fact, if they liked, she said, she'd take both of them on together, with the kitchen table pushed back.

Luke's dad informed his son he didn't fancy getting his bones broken now he was coming up to fifty. He'd like to preserve them intact for posterity, he said. Let's get out of here while we're still in one piece, he said. Good idea, said Luke. If I fall over and Big Bertha falls on top of me, I've a feeling I'll never get up again. That's my feeling too, said his dad, and it'll be an 'orrible way to go, me lad.

Luke, having carried his bike up with him, left it on the landing and entered the little living-room. His dad was frying sausages on the gas ring in a corner. Mr Edwards was forty-eight and a widower. He had another son, twenty-two-year-old Paul, who'd emigrated to Canada. Mr Edwards, however, preferred Luke not only as a son but as a friend and companion, though he'd not stand in his way once he got married, which was something he ought to be thinking about now he was twenty-four.

Luke was personable and outgoing, his dad lean, leathery and chatty, with muscles of whipcord. He was known as Old Iron. As a young man he had bent iron bars, eaten broken glass and executed escape jobs from a network of shackling chains. He'd performed at fairgrounds, particularly at places like Hampstead Heath or Peckham Rye on a Bank Holiday, or with buskers entertaining theatre queues, or before lunchtime crowds on Tower Hill. However, he met a lively cockney girl when he was twenty-three. She said she'd only marry him if he gave up playing silly devils with iron bars and broken glass, and got himself a steady job. He did just that, but the nickname of Old Iron, attached to him by some wag when he was only nineteen, stuck. He quite liked it. He worked at a metal factory off the Old Kent Road for thirty-two shillings and six-pence a week. Luke's job was with an engineering firm in Camberwell New Road, and his wage was thirty-five bob. He and Old Iron both had a bit of money in the Post Office Savings Bank. They were a sociable pair, with a variety of cockney friends. Old Iron, a widower for five years, was fond of the occasional pint of old and mild at the nearby pub, and he was also partial to the ladies. Having enjoyed a good marriage, he wasn't loath to marry again. At forty-eight he felt he'd still be able to appreciate a warm armful. In his opinion, cockney women were born to be warm armfuls, and you'd have to go a long way to find women who could beat them as wives. Of course, they got into a paddy every so often, and were quick to lay a hand on a rolling-pin, but any bloke who couldn't take a thump or two from an aggravated wife wasn't much of a man. Best to take it like a man, not like they did downstairs, with all that crashing, banging and yelling. Time he and Luke moved elsewhere for a bit of peace and quiet.

'Well, me lad,' he said, as Luke came in, 'how'd you get on, what were the rooms like, and 'as our prospective new landlady got a warm 'eart?'

'We're movin', Dad, I can tell you that,' said Luke. He took a bottle of beer from the larder and lifted two glasses from the dresser. He twisted the stopper free of the bottle, and filled the glasses with foaming light ale. 'Let's have a drink to celebrate.'

'It'll be me pleasure,' said Old Iron, the glass in

his left hand, the frying-fork in his right. He took an appreciative swallow. 'I don't reckon all that bawlin' and screamin' down below will reach our earholes all the way from 'ere to Balfour Street.'

'It's not Balfour Street,' said Luke.

'Eh?' said Old Iron, turning the sausages and the frying potatoes. 'Did our prospective new landlady turn yer down, then?'

'I didn't go to Balfour Street,' said Luke. 'I happened to be in Morecambe Street, and some kids there told me a Mrs Martin at number twelve had the whole of 'er upstairs to offer.'

'But didn't the card in the newsagent's winder say the 'ouse in Balfour Street was offerin' the same and likewise?' asked Old Iron.

Luke said the kids in Morecambe Street had been very informative about Mrs Martin having rooms to let, and on top of that he'd met a girl on his way home from work. A young lady, actually.

'A nice young lady,' he said.

'Ah,' said Old Iron, and a little grin appeared. The sausages sizzled cheerfully. 'Not a girl, a nice young lady. See what you mean, Luke. Fell overboard, did yer?'

'Good as,' said Luke, and filled his father in. She was in a hurry to get home, so he'd given her a lift on his carrier from Camberwell Road to her house in Morecambe Street. He asked her if he could see her again, if he could call on her this evening, in fact. She turned him down, she said all her time was taken up looking after her widowed mother.

'Ah,' said Old Iron again, but without a grin this time.

'Listen, Old Iron, what I'm thinking is 'ave we got another case of the Aunt Rosa abdabs here?'

said Luke. Aunt Rosa was his dad's eldest sister, a woman of fifty-four who had tied her only son to her apron-strings from the time he left school. He was now thirty-one and was still tied. He was Aunt Rosa's insurance for her old age, he'd never had a young lady in his life. Aunt Rosa had taken on the condition of an ailing mother years ago, and her mouse of a husband always said it was only their son Alf who could give her the kind of attention that kept her from being bedridden.

'Bad luck on poor old Alf,' said Old Iron, 'but yer Aunt Rosa wouldn't enjoy life like she does if she didn't 'ave the constant abdabs. It's turned son Alf into a fussy old woman 'imself. All right, sit down, Luke, and I'll dish up the supper.'

They sat down to their usual simple kind of evening meal. This evening it was pork sausages, sliced potatoes and tomatoes, all fried, and eaten with a dash of OK sauce. Old Iron asked to hear more. Luke said he frankly fancied the young lady. Old Iron asked if he meant that honourably.

'Don't come it, Dad,' said Luke, 'I told you, she's nice. Nice doesn't mean tarty.'

'It's still me duty, as yer respected father, to make sure you don't 'ave the wrong ideas about nice young females.'

'Turn it up,' grinned Luke. 'What about your ideas concernin' nice mature females?'

'Well, me lad,' said Old Iron, 'nice mature females 'ave usually got a few ideas of their own, which I'm cautionin' you to watch out for when you're mature yerself. Me own approach is always cautious, as well as honourable.'

'I know what that adds up to – hopeful,' said Luke, and his dad grinned again.

The kids in Morecambe Street having pointed him at Mrs Martin, said Luke, he'd called on her. She was a lively old girl of about fifty, and she and her old man had just seen the last of their offspring get married. That meant they could do with the rent they could get from letting their upstairs rooms. Mind, she hadn't put a card up in the newsagent's window yet, so how did Luke know she was going to let? Luke said a couple of nice kids had informed him. Mrs Martin said that was the first time she'd heard there were any nice kids in her street. They were all 'orrible little hooligans as far as she was concerned. Still, she said, now you're here, you can look at the rooms, if you like. They're all fully furnished.

'And you liked 'em, did you?' said Old Iron, polishing off the last of his sausages.

'The back room has a range nearly as good as a kitchen range,' said Luke. 'We'll have a self-contained flat.'

'Any crashin', banging or broken bones?' asked Old Iron.

'Shouldn't think so,' said Luke. 'In fact, Mrs Martin likes a quiet life. In fact, she made it clear that if we turned out to be a couple of drunks we'd get quick marchin' orders, and 'er old man's boot as well. I said I'd been brought up to behave meself, and that you went to church sometimes.'

''Ere, 'old on, me lad—'

'You needn't go every week,' said Luke, 'say about once a month to give a good impression.'

'I trust, me lad, that you ain't let me in for church-goin' at my time of life,' said Old Iron.

'Only once a month,' said Luke, 'and it means Mrs Martin is allowin' us to move in on Saturday afternoon at ten bob a week rent.'

Old Iron swallowed his residue of beer.

'It's a shock, bein' let in for church by me own flesh and blood,' he said. 'I take it you picked Morecambe Street on account of it'll make you a near neighbour of this nice young lady you fell overboard for. Well, 'er poor old widowed mother's goin' to be a near neighbour as well. What're you goin' to do about 'er?'

'Get you to be neighbourly and find out how she can be cured of tyin' Doreen to her apron-strings,' said Luke.

'I might like that kind of work,' said Old Iron genially. 'Doreen's the lady's name, is it? Who's 'er Ma, then, and what's she look like? I 'ope she ain't skinny. I ain't too partial to flat chests, not on females, I ain't. Not natural, me son.'

'The name's Paterson,' said Luke, 'but I didn't meet the mother. I did meet a chatty lad called Freddy Brown, who told me Mrs Paterson more or less keeps Doreen under lock and key.'

'Don't like the sound of that,' said Old Iron, shaking his head. 'That ain't natural, either. Yer right, Luke, we've got another Aunt Rosa 'ere. Now you sure you've got a young bloke's torments about the daughter? After all, you've only rode 'er home on yer bike. That ain't enough to give you the torments, is it?'

'Not the torments, you old goat, just a certain feelin',' said Luke.

'I'll overlook old goat, seein' you ain't quite yerself. You can't be, not when you've gone out of yer way to get us lodgings in the same street as the young lady. You're overboard all right, me lad, but I'm with yer. We don't want 'er life ruined by 'er over-fond mum, do we? On the other 'and, suppose the young lady don't want to be saved? 'Ave yer thought of that? Take yer cousin Alf, poor sod. 'E does 'ousework and likes it. 'E cooks the Sunday dinner and likes it. 'E wears an apron and likes it. I did me best when 'e was young to save 'im from the 'orrible fate of bein' yer Aunt Rosa's 'ousemaid and nursemaid, and what did I get for me pains? A request not to 'urt his feelings. Now then, me lad, suppose this young lady likes bein' a doormat to 'er mum? Women are funny, yer know, when it comes to sacrificin' themselves. Some get to like it. Most of 'em do a bit of sacrificin' when they get married. Take yer late mum, bless 'er resting bones. She 'ated makin' a Spotted Dick, and nor was she partial to eatin' it. But because it was a fav'rite of mine, she made one regular and ate 'er share. Mind, she always put sugar on 'ers.'

'That's chapter and verse, that lot,' said Luke. 'We'll look into things. You go to work on Mrs Paterson.'

'I'll find a way of invitin' 'er down to the pub,' said Old Iron.

'I don't think that'll work,' said Luke. 'You can be a bit smarter than that, can't you?'

'I do 'ave a certain reputation for bein' agreeable to the ladies, me lad, which is a sight more 'elpful than bein' smart.'

'Well, good on yer, Old Iron,' smiled Luke, 'but I still don't think Mrs Paterson is goin' to let you pour pints of Guinness into her. It's just a feelin' I've got.'

'Good for invalid widows, yer know, Guinness is,' said Old Iron.

'Who said she's an invalid?'

'I'll bet yer she lets 'er daughter think she is. Anyway, me lad, once we've settled down in Morecambe Street, I might just present meself to the ailin' lady as a new neighbour that used to do a bit of doctorin'.'

'What doctorin'?' asked Luke.

'I'll think of something,' said Old Iron. 'Something that'll take 'er mind off 'er daughter and point it at me. It's me fond 'ope that she ain't too old or wrinkled. What age d'you reckon the nice young lady is?'

'Eighteen or nineteen,' said Luke.

'Just right, you bein' twenty-four,' said Old Iron encouragingly, 'and it ought to mean 'er dear old Ma can't be too old. More like in 'er forties, I'd say. Luke, I'm tickled for yer, and I like it that you fancy the young lady in an honourable way, it bein' time you thought about gettin' churched. No good stayin' a bachelor, me lad. If you'd been born a Suffolk cucumber or a Spanish onion, it wouldn't matter, but you was born a human bein' of the male gender, much to yer late mum's pleasure at the time. You're in a good trade and you got money in the bank, so it's up to me, yer respected dad, to do me bit with the widow while you do a Douglas Fairbanks act with the young lady. Yes, I'll knock on Mrs Paterson's door one day and see if I can give 'er some medical advice about 'er invalid condition. Or something. I'm doin' the Tower of London this evenin', by the way.'

'Well, you did a good job with the Bank of England last week,' said Luke.

'That was a real teaser and no error,' said Old Iron.

'The Tower might be really sticky,' said Luke.

'So it might, me lad, with them Beefeaters standin' guard over the Crown Jewels,' said Old Iron. 'It'll be a test of me craft and patience.'

Rosie, the adopted daughter of Boots and Emily, was just eleven, and her birthday party took place that evening. Much to her pleasure, everyone in the family came, and even more to her pleasure they all insisted on being there, at the large house in Red Post Hill, off the south end of Denmark Hill. Rosie was fair-haired, blue-eyed, engagingly pretty and infectiously articulate. If she had forgotten her natural mother, who had left her when she was only five, she hadn't forgotten how her forlorn life had changed from the moment when Boots and Emily took her into their home and their lives, and eventually adopted her. Security, warmth and love had made her a girl who poured out affection. She loved Emily, her adoptive mother. Boots, her adoptive father, she adored.

The whole family sat down to the evening birthday tea. Boots's mother, Mrs Maisie Finch, presided. She was known to the family as Chinese Lady on account of the fact that she had almond eyes and had once taken in washing. In her fiftieth year, she was a slim woman with a well-preserved bosom and an upright walk, and was married to Mr Edwin Finch, her second husband. Her first husband, Daniel Adams, had lost his life fighting as a soldier on the North-West Frontier. Mr Finch accepted that she had fond memories of her Daniel, even if she did think he'd been careless in getting in the way of a bursting shell.

Tommy and his wife Vi were there, together with their one-year-old daughter Alice, and Vi's mum and dad, known as Aunt Victoria and Uncle Tom. Aunt Victoria had a slightly critical tongue but a mellowing outlook, and Uncle Tom was a bluff old bloke who let complaints bounce off him. Also present were Susie and Sammy, together with Sammy's shiner and Chinese Lady's only daughter, Mrs Lizzy Somers and husband Ned, plus their children Annabelle, Bobby, Emma and Edward. Annabelle, in her tenth year, had her mum's chestnut hair and brown eyes, and was Rosie's best friend. Then, of course, there was Mr Finch himself, a distinguished-looking man of fifty-three who worked for a Government department, Boots and Emily, and Rosie's four-year-old brother Tim.

Altogether, nineteen people sat down to the evening birthday tea, and when the hullabaloo had subsided, Chinese Lady made herself heard. What all the commotion was about she didn't know, she said, it was implorable to turn a tea party into Bedlam. She meant deplorable. She also said she had to apologize to everyone for her youngest son Sammy coming to the party looking like a common costermonger who'd been in a fight with hooligans.

'The point is, did he win?' said Mr Finch.

'I don't want to hear no details,' said Chinese Lady. 'You can say grace, Edwin, then we can all start.'

'Good-oh,' said Tommy.

'Crikey, yes, I'm famished, aren't you, Uncle Tommy?' said Rosie.

'I'm hungry as well,' said Tommy.

'Let's have grace,' said Boots, 'then we'll all do a wrecking job on the shrimps and winkles.'

'I can only see half of everything,' said Sammy, 'I've been tryin' to work out why me newly-wed wife Susie has only got one eye, one arm and one leg.'

Annabelle spluttered giggles.

'If you don't mind, Sammy?' said Chinese Lady, giving her youngest a matriarchal look.

'Carry on, Grandpa,' said Rosie, and Mr Finch said grace.

'For what has been provided on the auspicious occasion of Rosie's birthday,' he said, 'let's all be truly thankful to the Lord and to Rosie's mother and grandmother, who have worked overtime in the kitchen.'

'Amen and good on Rosie's mum and grand-mum,' said Ned.

'And bless me too,' said Rosie.

The birthday tea began. It was riotous. So were the birthday games afterwards. Rosie had begged for lots of games, including Forfeits. Lizzy said she wasn't going to play Forfeits, not if Boots organized them. It would mean what it had always meant, that all the girls would get fiendish forfeits and all the blokes would fall about.

'Well, all the other girls will play, won't you, girls?' said Boots.

'No!' shrieked all the other girls except Annabelle and Rosie.

'All right, Sardines, then,' said Boots.

'Oh, me gawd, not Sardines,' gasped Emily, 'that's like assault an' battery.'

'We don't want any hooliganism,' said Chinese Lady.

'Oh, can't we have just a bit, Nana?' begged Rosie.

'A bit's sort of healthy,' said Sammy.

'Not your sort of bit, Sammy Adams,' said Susie.

'I'll play Sardines with Bobby and Tim and Emma and Uncle Tom, but not with you or Boots or Tommy or Ned or Mr Finch. I played it with you lot last Christmas and went home a different shape.'

'All right, what's it to be, Sardines or Forfeits?' asked Boots, the devil lurking in his eye.

'Forfeits, Daddy, Forfeits!' cried Rosie.

'I'm goin' 'ome,' said Vi.

'I'm goin' to call an ambulance,' said Lizzy.

'I'm goin' to lock meself in the kitchen,' said Emily.

'I'm goin' to scream for a policeman,' said Susie.

'Well, I must say it all sounds dangerous,' said Aunt Victoria.

'It's not dangerous, Aunt Victoria,' said Lizzy, 'it's blush-makin'.'

So they all played Forfeits, and just as Lizzy had said, it was a fiendish ordeal for the female members of the party. Every forfeit Boots devised for them may have sounded harmless, but it didn't work out like that. Somehow or other, Emily, Rosie, Vi, Lizzy and Susie had terrible trouble with their dresses, and all their menfolk fell about pop-eyed and laughing. Chinese Lady said she'd never seen anything more disreputable, and that Boots ought to be arrested. Mr Finch said Boots had the makings of an impresario. Chinese Lady said kindly don't use unlawful French words, Edwin, they don't become you and they make you sound like that implorable oldest son of mine.

When the last blush had faded, Emily led the charge of the put-upon females. Boots disappeared under a flurry of vengeful ladies.

'Pull his trousers off!' yelled Lizzy.

'Not here, Lizzy, if you don't mind,' said Chinese Lady.

Rosie rescued Boots.

'Oh, help, there's a fire in the kitchen, Nana!' she cried from the open door of the living-room.

When that false alarm was over, more games were played. They arrived at Postman's Knock, a favourite with the family. That went down well. Lizzy got off to a lovely start by being kissed by Mr Finch, and Mr Finch in turn experienced soft sweetness from the lips of Vi, healthily expectant with her second child. Chinese Lady got kissed by Sammy, who asked tuppence for it. He'd always charged for kisses as a boy. Chinese Lady said how would he like his ears boxed? Not much, said Sammy, I've already got a black eye. Uncle Tom received a kiss from Rosie, then left her to collect a kiss from the next one out.

It was Boots who came out into the hall. Rosie's eyes sparkled.

'Kiss, Daddy?'

Boots smiled and kissed her lightly on her dewy young mouth. Something happened then to eleven-year-old Rosie. Her lips tingled and she pressed them tightly to his. She kissed him adoringly, her eyes closed, her arms around his neck, bliss permeating her young body.

'Steady, poppet,' said Boots gently.

Rosie, flushed and quivering, whispered with a catch in her voice, 'I do love you, Daddy, ever so much.'

Boots knew then that he had to be very careful in his relationship with his engaging Rosie, his adopted daughter, not his natural one.

Chapter Four

'Goin', are we, brother?' enquired Fred Marsh,
shop steward. It wasn't yet half-past five.

'Don't mind, do you?' said Luke. The workers of
Langdon's Engineering Company were on strike
and had been picketing the factory in Camberwell
New Road every day. It was a question of making
sure the bosses didn't break the strike by sneaking
in some volunteer labour. Ruddy disgraceful,
Marsh had said, all these volunteer blacklegs trying
to do the workers' cause a crippling injury. Luke
was in two minds about the strike. In the first place,
he thought a fair deal for the coal-miners was well
overdue. Most of the top-hatted owners were
grubby skinflints under their fat polished look. The
miners began to cough up their lungs before they
were forty. Silicosis it was called, and it killed them.
In the second place, however, Luke had never
thought the General Strike a good idea. Nor had his
dad. They both agreed the public wouldn't stand
for it, not when it meant it could shut families off
from the necessities of life. And so it was proving.
You can make war on us, mums and dads said to
the strikers, but not on our kids. Which was why, in
Old Iron's opinion, the public and the volunteers
were going to break the strike, as sure as chickens
laid eggs and not oranges.

'All right, shove off, Luke,' said the shop

steward, and Luke set off for Camberwell Green on his bike. At the Green, he turned right and entered Denmark Hill. He stopped when he reached a pub that was opposite the shop that was called The Bazaar. It sold Army surplus, and quite decent togs for men, women and children at prices kind to the thin pockets of the working people of Camberwell and Walworth. Above the shop were offices. Gold paint on the windows spelled out *Adams Enterprises Ltd*. There, according to the lad Freddy Brown, Doreen Paterson worked. Her finishing time had to be five-thirty, and Luke intended to offer her another lift home on his bike. Keep at it, Old Iron had said, nice young ladies never think much of blokes that give up too easy.

There was a motor van outside the shop. In blue rimmed with gold, bold lettering advertised that name again. *Adams Enterprises Ltd*. Luke saw her then. She came out through the door at the side of the shop, in company with another girl. They made straight for the van and climbed in beside the driver. That's done me in the eye, thought Luke. He watched the van move off, shrugged his shoulders ruefully, turned his bike and joined the traffic himself. The van, going at a fair lick, soon left him behind.

Well, there's always tomorrow, he thought.

There's a lot of girls about, but this one's a treat. This one's for me, if I don't trip up.

'Done yer down, did it?' said Old Iron, when Luke was home and had recounted his lack of luck.

'It looked like the firm's van was givin' her and her friend a lift,' said Luke.

'I feel for yer, me lad,' said Old Iron. 'But that's

the way it goes. You make yer plans and then the cussed 'and of fate dots yer one in the eye. Did yer nice young lady spot yer?'

'No.'

'Disappointed, are yer?' said Old Iron.

'A mite,' said Luke.

''Ow did she look?'

'The way I like a girl to look.'

'What way's that, might I ask?'

'Nice,' said Luke.

'Goin' broody, are yer, Luke?'

'Not yet,' said Luke.

'Preventive medicine, that's what you need,' grinned Old Iron. 'Say a Guinness.'

'Is there a bottle?' asked Luke.

'Stacks of 'em down at the pub,' said Old Iron, and roared with laughter.

'It ain't all that funny,' said Luke.

'I like it, me lad, I like it that you've got yer first pangs, it shows you've got 'ealthy longings to cuddle up to yer nice young lady. Keep at it, Luke.'

Luke grinned.

That evening, Boots took a cup of coffee into the room his step-father used as a study. Rosie was allowed to use it most evenings for her school homework. She was being set special homework, since she was swotting for a scholarship examination.

'Coffee, Rosie.'

Her fair hair danced as she lifted her head.

'Oh, good old sport,' she said, 'coffee might perk up my French verbs. Daddy, could I speak to you for a minute?'

'Go ahead,' said Boots.

'You're not to laugh,' said Rosie.

'Right, no laughing.'

'Well, then, could I start wearing stockings?'

Boots coughed.

'I've just remembered, I've got some gardening to do,' he said.

'No, you haven't, you're just trying to dodge the question,' said Rosie. 'If you've got to remember anything, Daddy, it's that I'm eleven now, and easily old enough for stockings. Imagine a girl as old as I am having to wear socks all the time.'

'It's a bit like purgatory, is it?' said Boots with a straight face.

'Well, Daddy, if you don't mind me being frank, it's a lot like purgatory,' said Rosie.

'I think you'd better speak to your mother,' said Boots.

'But you're head of the family,' said Rosie.

'Well, you know that, Rosie, and so do I, but I'm not sure if Emily does. And then there's your grandmother, Chinese Lady. She's head of all of us.'

'Daddy, you're dodging again,' said Rosie. 'Bless me, I think I'm having trouble with you. If I ask Mummy and she says no, I'll still be suffering purgatory.'

'Tricky,' said Boots. Rosie eyed him hopefully. His smile that always seemed to be lurking surfaced. Eleven-year-old Rosie. Stockings for her legs. 'Tell you what, poppet, I'll ask her for you.'

'Oh, would you beg her on my behalf?' said Rosie. 'You could do a bit of happy ever after with her first, and then tell her that in socks my legs don't feel as if they're properly dressed, not at my age they don't. Daddy, are you laughing? You promised you wouldn't.'

'Perish the thought, poppet,' said Boots. 'I can see it's dead serious, a girl as old as you going about with undressed legs.'

'People don't half look,' said Rosie. 'I bet they're saying fancy that poor girl having to wear socks at her age. It's nearly calamitous.'

'Well, I'll speak to your mother about keeping calamity at bay,' said Boots.

'Bless you, Daddy.'

'What?' said Emily, who had just put four-year-old Tim to bed.

'Rosie said what?' asked Chinese Lady.

'Say it again, Boots,' smiled Mr Finch, a man of sophisticated maturity, and a specialist in the kind of service he gave to the British Government. He was in Intelligence.

'Rosie feels her legs are undressed in socks,' said Boots. 'She'd like to wear stockings.'

'At her age?' said Chinese Lady in some kind of shock.

'That's the point,' said Boots, 'she's feeling her age.'

'She's doin' what?' said Emily, wanting to laugh.

'Feeling her age,' said Boots solemnly.

'But she's only just eleven,' said Chinese Lady.

'True,' said Mr Finch, evening paper on his lap, 'but to a girl who was only ten a few days ago, eleven might seem old.'

'Old? Old? Can someone make sense?' said Chinese Lady.

'Two of a kind, that's what Boots and Dad are,' said Emily. 'Boots, you sure Rosie wasn't pullin' your leg?'

'Fairly sure,' said Boots.

'I never wore stockings when I was eleven,' said Chinese Lady.

'Rosie mentioned that wearing socks all the time was like purgatory,' said Boots.

Mr Finch coughed and took up his paper.

'I suppose she didn't ask for silk stockings, by any chance?' said Emily.

'Silk?' said Chinese Lady. 'Silk stockings? At eleven? I hope I'm not hearin' you serious, Em'ly.'

'I wasn't bein' serious,' said Emily, 'I was just tryin' to keep up with old funny-cuts here.'

'Silk stockings would be all right for Sundays, I suppose,' said Boots. 'Have you got any thoughts on that, Edwin?'

From behind his paper, Mr Finch said, 'Well, if she's feeling her age, some concessions ought to be made.'

'I'll have 'ysterics in a minute,' said Emily.

'Mind, I won't say our Rosie won't look nice in stockings the way she's springing up,' said Chinese Lady, 'but at only eleven, well, I just don't know.'

'I'd best tell her to wait a bit,' said Emily.

'Say a few weeks,' murmured Mr Finch who, since his days as a lodger with the Adams family, had always found them entertaining.

'A few weeks?' said Chinese Lady.

'Well, perhaps a month,' said Mr Finch.

'That's when it'll be serious,' said Boots.

'Why?' asked Emily.

'She'll be feeling her age a lot more by then,' said Boots.

Emily laughed.

'Boots, you're potty,' she said. She went to the study a few minutes later, just as Rosie was coming to the end of her homework. 'Rosie?'

'Yes, Mummy?'

'Rosie, are you feelin' old?' smiled Emily.

'Well, no, not frantically old,' said Rosie, 'just getting on a bit.'

'Lord above, you poor old thing,' said Emily. 'Never mind, perhaps some nice stockings will take a few years off you.'

'Crikey, who's a lovely mum, then?' breathed rapturous Rosie.

'We don't like to think you're goin' about with your legs feelin' undressed,' said Emily. 'Daddy's goin' to treat you.'

'Bliss,' said Rosie. 'Did you have happy ever after with him?'

'No, I had hysterics,' said Emily, 'he's gettin' pottier every day.'

'Oh, I like potty men, don't you, Mummy? Shall I make you a sandwich before you go to bed?'

'Do I look as if I need one?' asked Emily, who'd spent the day eating little and often.

'No, you look nice,' said Rosie. 'I was only thinking you deserved one.'

Emily smiled.

'We're goin' to let you start wearin' stockings next month, lovey,' she said, and was reminded then that next month Boots was due to appear as a witness at a murder trial. A man called Gerald Ponsonby would be up before judge and jury at the Old Bailey, charged with the murder of three young girls. Boots had been responsible for trapping him and handing him over to the police. Life was very strange.

Emily hated the thought of what Gerald Ponsonby's trial would be like. He'd strangled those three young girls. The man was a monster. Boots was saying very little about the trial, but Emily knew he regarded Ponsonby as unfit to live.

There was another Ponsonby, a Mr Ronald James Ponsonby. He was living in Dieppe at the moment, having absented himself from England several years ago as a precautionary measure. His departure had coincided with the discovery in Nottingham of the body of a young girl.

He was a lean, dapper-looking man, usually seen in a natty suit and a straw boater. Since arriving in France, he'd acquired a beard and moustache, both neatly trimmed, and a passport in the name of Joseph Victor Wright, a British subject.

At the moment, he was set on a return to England. The General Strike over there, however, had closed the ports to shipping. Cross-Channel ferries from France were prevented from docking. There were rumours, however, that the strike would not last long, and Mr Ronald Ponsonby was exercising patience.

Sitting one morning at a pavement café table, enjoying coffee with a small measure of cognac, he extracted a letter from his wallet. He read it, not for the first time. It was from his twin brother Gerald, and had been written over two weeks ago. It referred to his arrest on a charge of murdering three girls, to the man responsible for his arrest, one Robert Adams, and to his wish for his twin brother to avenge him in the event that he was condemned to be hanged.

Mr Ronald James Ponsonby refolded the letter and put it away. He stroked the moustache and beard that made him look much more like King George than his clean-shaven twin. He seemed a man at peace with the passing scene in Boulevard de Verdun. And why not? He had no quarrel with Dieppe, nor Dieppe with him. With Lyons, yes, but that was a year ago. His only quarrel now lay in London, with a family called Adams, Robert Adams in particular. Well, down the man would go, with others of his brood.

Passage on a ferry would be booked as soon as Britain's General Strike was over. He would travel under the name of Joseph Victor Wright, his passport identifying him as such. The passport photograph depicted him with spectacles, as well as a beard and moustache.

Gerald, his twin brother, would almost certainly be hanged, of course. Before he went to the scaffold, however, word might reach him that the Adams family had been destroyed. That, perhaps, would put a smile on his face when the noose was placed around his neck.

Mr Ronald Ponsonby finished his coffee and cognac, placed coins on the table beside the little chit, then got up and went on his way, sniffing fussily at the sea air.

Chapter Five

At twelve noon the very same day, Old Iron left his bench to begin his dinner hour. The firm was a small one, employing just five metal workers, all non-union. I think I'll take a walk, Old Iron said to himself, and he left the little factory in his boiler suit, carrying his packet of corned beef sandwiches. He unwrapped them as he made his way along the Old Kent Road to East Street. He ate while walking. When he turned into East Street, a street urchin came up beside him.

'Cor, give us a bite, mister,' he said.

''Ungry, are yer?' said Old Iron.

'Not 'alf I ain't.'

'That's funny, so am I,' said Old Iron. 'Like ham sandwiches, do yer?'

'Mister, they're me fav'rite,' said the urchin.

''Ard luck, sonny, these are corned beef.'

'They're me fav'rite as well.'

'All right, treat yerself to this,' said Old Iron, and gave the kid half of one of his two sandwiches.

'Ta, mister. I suppose you ain't got a slice of apple pie as well, 'ave yer?'

'No, and I ain't got any rice puddin', either,' said Old Iron, grinning. 'Kindly 'oppit.'

The kid hopped it, the while making inroads into the sandwich. Old Iron ambled on. By the time he reached Morecambe Street, he'd finished his food.

Now, he thought, do I knock on the widow's door and tell her I've come to look at her gas meter, or do I just size things up by taking a look at her front room curtains? You can tell what some women are like by the state of their curtains. If they take a pride in their curtains, they take a pride in themselves. I favour proud and handsome women, even if they do have funny ideas about making skivvies of their daughters when they're widowed. That's it, I'll just take a look at the curtains. Wait a minute, half a mo, if the daughter looks after the curtains, that won't tell me a lot about her mum.

There were few women about. Most were probably at home, serving food. Well, most kids went home for something to eat during school dinner hours.

Old Iron lingered a bit. He saw a woman entering Morecambe Street from Browning Street. Fine figure she had, and a proud-looking hat with feathers in it. Old Iron thought now, could she be a widow? She's wearing a black costume. But I can't say she's my idea of an ailing widow who's thinking of tying her daughter to her apron-strings.

Another woman appeared, moving from her open front door to her gate. She was tidying up her loose hair. She pushed a hairpin in. She had three more between her teeth. She took them all out as the woman in a black costume approached. Old Iron heard her speak.

'Oh, 'ello, Mrs Paterson,' she said, 'how's yerself today? You've managed to get out, I see. Well, it's nice weather, just right for a bit of shoppin' or a bit of a walk.'

'Yes, I thought I'd try and get out for a bit,' said Mrs Paterson, and Old Iron, an interested spectator, noted that she seemed to let her shoulders sag as she stopped. 'Mind, I don't know it's done me much good. I don't 'ave the same health and strength as I used to. But I do me best, not wantin' to be a burden to Doreen.'

Old Iron, still lingering, decided to tighten his bootlaces, and went down on one knee to do so, a little grin on his face.

'Well, I'm sure you always do yer best, Mrs Paterson,' said the woman with the hairpins. 'I was only sayin' to your Doreen the other day that you wouldn't want to be a burden. Yes, yer mum does 'er best, I said, she manages to do a bit of shoppin' now and again. I don't know how I'd manage meself if my 'Arold passed away. 'E ain't much of a talker, 'e's more of a doer, 'e can mend anything. 'E mended me best-lookin' stays once, and made 'em as good as new. I always say that stays that feel new do wonders for a woman.'

Granted, missus, granted, grinned Old Iron to himself as he took his time fiddling with his bootlaces. Here we are, Luke me lad, with our peepers clapped direct on your young lady's widowed mum herself. She's trying to look wore out, but she's a handsome body all right, with a proud pair of stays, I'd say. She just needs a bit of doctoring.

'I'm appreciative you're understandin', Mrs Johnson,' said Doreen's mother. 'I'm lucky I've got an understandin' daughter too. I don't know what I'd do without 'er.'

Well, I could take you out to a pub, buy you a few drinks and do a knees-up with you, thought Old Iron, who didn't know what to do about the grin on his face, exept stay down on one knee and keep it to himself.

'It's a blessin' that when we're a bit down we've got fam'ly consolations,' said Mrs Johnson. 'And I must say Doreen keeps you lookin' a picture of 'ealth, even if you don't 'ave much strength.' Thrusting in a final hairpin, the knowing neighbour added, 'She'll make some nice young feller a lovely useful wife when 'er turn comes.'

'Oh, she don't think about young men,' said Mrs Paterson, 'she likes her own 'ome and knows she's always got me for company.'

Now now, Mrs Widow, said Old Iron to himself, it's the other way about and I'll eat these here boots of mine if you don't know it. I think I've got some patient doctoring to do on you, but you're handsome all right and me doctoring might be a pleasure to me.

'Well, Doreen's grown up very attractive,' said Mrs Johnson, 'and it's surprisin' young men don't come knockin' on yer door.'

'Doreen's more interested in 'elping me to recover from me grievous loss than in young men,' said Mrs Paterson, and sighed. 'I don't know I'll ever properly recover. I'd better go in now, I'm a bit done up from me walk.' She crossed the street in a tired way and entered her house. Old Iron stopped lingering and strolled back to his place of work. His grin was all over his face.

Susie was lunching with Emily in Emily's office. They'd made a tinned salmon salad. They lunched together in this way most days. They liked a little hen party. It gave them a chance to exchange feminine confidences, and to talk about members of the family in a fashion that induced giggles and laughter.

Sammy was at Islington.

Boots was thinking about going across the road to the pub for a beef and mustard sandwich and half a pint of old ale. Doreen put her head in.

'Someone wants to see you, if you've got time, Mister Adams.'

'If it's Gladys Cooper, I'll make time,' said Boots.

'Lor', I'm sorry to disappoint you, but it's not Gladys Cooper, it's a gentleman who says 'is name is Simms.'

'Simms?' Boots thought of Polly Simms, now in Kenya. 'The name's familiar, Doreen. I'll see him.'

The caller was more than mere Mr Simms. He was General Sir Henry Simms, father of Polly and one of the governors of the primary school attended by Rosie and her cousins Annabelle and Bobby Somers, children of Boots's sister, Lizzy. A tall spruce man with iron-grey hair and moustache, he had made a name for himself during the Great War by disagreeing violently with Haig over the Commander-in-Chief's persistent use of the British Army as a human battering-ram. He had met Boots on a number of occasions, usually at the school when teachers and governors were meeting parents.

He knew of his daughter Polly's weakness for Boots. Polly had been an ambulance driver all through the war, and had an unshakeable conviction that if she and Boots had met in France or Flanders, he would have been hers, not Emily's. She always declared that Emily pinched him from her while she wasn't looking. She was in Kenya now, trying to cure herself of her feelings for him.

'Hello, Boots, sorry to barge in. Know you must

be busy, but I was passing and thought I'd drop in.'

Boots came to his feet and shook hands.

'Take a seat, General,' he said. He had a very friendly relationship with Polly's distinguished father.

'Rather you joined me for a modest drink and a sandwich across the road, Boots.' It wouldn't be the first time Sir Henry had been in a pub with Boots. 'If you'd care to.'

'Yes, I'd care to.'

'Good. Shall we go, then?'

In the well-appointed saloon, they ordered beef sandwiches and old ale, and were perfectly at ease with each other, a general and an ex-sergeant of the Great War. Sir Henry had a liking for Boots, and had always understood why he appealed to Polly. He had no side, and none of the weediness and affectation of the young men belonging to the Bright Young Things with whom Polly had chased about during the post-war years. Sir Henry asked him what the General Strike was doing to the family business.

'It might have wrecked the fashion side if Sammy hadn't had the foresight to buy up all the materials he could lay his hands on,' said Boots. 'On the other hand, it did almost wreck his left eye a couple of days ago. He collected a shiner from a striker's fist. A small price to pay for keeping the factory going, but slightly painful. What's the news on the Army front?'

'Glad you mentioned that, Boots. Wanted to have a word with you, as well as a drink. How would you like to go on Officers' Reserve?'

'Pardon?' said Boots.

'An emergency body of the right kind of men the

73

Army can call on in the event of another war,' said Sir Henry.

'Another war? There won't be one, not after the last. That one ended all others.'

'We'd all like to think so,' said Sir Henry. 'Boots, your step-father's in Intelligence.'

'How'd you know that?' asked Boots.

'I do know, and I also know his general background in espionage. I'm fifty-two, Boots, and haven't yet been retired to grow roses. Edwin Finch wasn't always your step-father's name.'

'No comment,' said Boots, and Sir Henry smiled.

'Typical,' he said.

'Of what, General?'

'Of you,' said Sir Henry. 'You are, I believe, the only one in your family who knows your step-father was once a German agent. He's been in Germany recently, as I think you also know. Has he told you anything about the small army the Allies have allowed Germany to form for the purpose of self-defence and the maintenance of law and order?'

'He's told me it's a small army of picked men commanded by a senior officer who intends to turn it into Europe's most efficient fighting force.'

'Some of our Intelligence officers believe it's also intended to make it the model for the German army of the future,' said Sir Henry, and went on to say there were political and military elements in Germany who declared it was not the army that had surrendered to the Allies in 1918, but the politicians of the time. This conviction and a desire for revenge were the principal factors behind the rise of dangerous agitators, in particular a certain man called Adolf Hitler, a fanatic steeped in the legends of German racial superiority. Such men, with the backing of industrialists and an élite German army, would almost certainly set Germany on the road to a war of revenge.

'After the carnage and disasters of the Great War?' said Boots.

'Perhaps, Boots, it will be a different kind of war,' said Sir Henry. He and Boots were occupying a corner table. He had chosen it himself. 'It won't happen next year, or even in three or four years, but your step-father and other Intelligence officers think it will come, say in not more than ten years. The British Army will need a nucleus of tried and trusted men who served in the Great War, some to be officers in the field, others to command the training establishments for recruits. I'm speaking, Boots, of men like you.'

'Count me out,' said Boots. 'In the first place, I was only a sergeant. In the second place, my left eye is nearly blind. In the third place, I'll be too old, and last of all I left all my liking for war behind on the Somme. It's buried out there, General, along with hundreds of West Kents.'

'We all left something behind, Boots. I know your war record. Despite your eye, I could quite easily arrange to get you placed on Officers' Reserve. But I won't press you, not now, only ask you to think about it.'

'Have another glass of old ale, General.'

'I was about to suggest we both had another, Boots.'

'It's my round,' smiled Boots.

'Good man,' said Sir Henry.

'How's Polly?' asked Boots, getting up.

'Trying, I believe, to make something of her life in Kenya.'

'Well, if I'm any judge of Polly, Kenya will know she's around,' said Boots, and went to buy the second round of old ale.

Emily, placing typed letters on her husband's desk at half-past two, said, 'Boots, have you been drinkin'?'

'Not much,' said Boots. 'Why'd you ask?'

'You've got a silly smile on your face.'

'Have a banana,' said Boots, and opened a drawer in his desk. A spotless yellow banana came to light. He did occasionally keep one there for Emily. A banana here and there helped him to help her in the matter of eating little and often. The system was working. The sharper lines of her abject thinness were filling out. Good, thought Boots. A wife should be cuddlesome to bed with.

His smile broadened. Emily regarded him suspiciously.

'Look, you're not one over the eight, are you, at this time of the day?' she said.

'No, not much,' said Boots.

'Don't keep saying not much, it doesn't make sense.'

'I'll sign these letters, Em, and keep us both sane. By the way, what would you say if there was another war with Germany in about ten years' time?'

'I'd give up,' said Emily, 'and so would everyone else if the world went as barmy as that. You must be a bit drunk to even think about it.'

'Oh, I only had a couple of glasses with a friend I met,' said Boots.

'Some friend, I don't think, if he said there'd be another war.' Emily laughed it away. 'You shouldn't 'ave pub friends who are off their rockers, specially as you've got me.'

'Have a banana,' said Boots again, and gave it to her. Then he began to scan the letters for signing. Emily hit him over the head with the banana. Boots swivelled in his chair, took hold of her and sat her on his lap, positively. Being the man he was, one who thought it normal to enjoy his wife, he said, 'It's my distinct pleasure, Em, to inform you your bottom's putting on weight.'

'Oh, me gawd,' gasped Emily, smothering a giggle, 'not in the office, you lemon.'

Doreen knocked on his door a minute later and put her head in, meaning to tell him she'd found an old file he wanted. Instead, she could only say, 'Oh, sorry.' Back she went to the general office. Lottie, a blonde typist whose frizzy hair always looked as if every night was *Amami* night, asked her what she was giggling about. 'It's Mrs Em'ly Adams,' said Doreen, 'she's sittin' on her husband's lap eatin' a banana.'

Luke again got away from his picket duties early enough to begin another wait for Miss Doreen Paterson, a girl he hardly knew but whom he still considered a very nice young lady. Leaning on his bike on the other side of the road, he watched the shop. There was no van present this time.

A few minutes after five-thirty, Doreen emerged from the side door with three other girls. They were all engaged in animated chatter. He heard a series of little laughs. Girls were a lively lot, he thought. Their tongues kind of danced the days away, never mind that most of them in this area of South London often went home from their jobs to

77

hard-up households. But very few cockney girls allowed family poverty to turn them into squashed cabbages. A hint of sunshine around the corner was always enough to make life a lark to them. Doreen and her office friends were bubbling, and Luke could hear little bursts of laughter. Doreen's saucily short skirt caught his eye, making him frankly appreciative of her pretty legs. There's a nice girl, he thought, a really nice girl. Something's got to be done about seeing she doesn't get tied to her mum's apron-strings for good if I'm going to have the pleasure of taking her to Hampstead Heath on Bank Holidays. Let's be honest, I'm already gone on that young lady. The thing is, is there any competition? There might be, even if she has to keep the bloke out of sight of her mum. The world was full of mums, and most of them were good old mums. It was a bit unfortunate that Doreen had clicked for a possessive type. That could point her towards becoming an old maid. What a waste. Can't have that.

He wheeled his bike across the road and followed the girls. Workers going home milled around the junction at the Green. Two stationary trams, one on each side of the road, were filling up. So was an open-topped LGOC omnibus.

Doreen parted from the other girls and ran for the bus. She was the last one to board.

'Room up top only,' said the volunteer conductor.

'I'm not goin' up with you standing there,' said Doreen.

'Hard luck, miss, but it's me duty to stand here while passengers are boarding. Go on, get yourself up the apples and pears, I won't look.'

'I bet,' said Doreen. Out of the corner of her eye she glimpsed someone waving a hand. She turned her head. Luke, assuming the conductor was telling her his bus was full up, beckoned her. 'Well, I'm blessed,' she said.

'So you might be,' grinned the conductor, 'but I've still got to get this public bus moving. You on or off, miss?'

A young man boarded then, and Doreen stepped off. The conductor rang his bell and the bus began to move. Luke wheeled his bike up.

'Evenin', Lady Vi,' he said, 'like another lift?'

'Wait a minute,' said Doreen accusingly, 'what're you doing here? Have you been followin' me?'

'If I said no, I'd be tellin' a lie.'

'How would you like it if I had you arrested?' said Doreen.

'Could you wait till I've seen you home on me carrier?' said Luke.

'I don't like bein' followed,' said Doreen.

'Well, you looked nice from where I was,' said Luke.

'Cheek won't do you any good,' said Doreen, 'but all right, you can give me a lift. Only don't get into any fights this time, I've got to get home to me mum.'

'Right, all aboard,' said Luke.

Doreen perched herself sideways on the carrier, and off Luke went. He swerved to avoid a boy running across the road.

'Here, you nearly knocked him down,' said Doreen.

'I'll try again tomorrow,' said Luke, which made her smile. 'What's your name?' he asked, even though he knew it.

'You don't 'ave to know my name,' said Doreen.

'I'm Luke Edwards.'

'I'm Marie Lloyd,' said Doreen, holding on to her handbag and her skirt.

'Give us a song, then,' said Luke, overtaking plodding vehicles and watching out for trouble in the shape of strikers at odds with volunteers.

'You'll be lucky,' said Doreen.

'Comfy?' said Luke, as they reached Walworth Road.

'You asked me that the other day,' said Doreen, 'but I'm fairly comfy, thanks.'

'Legs all right?'

'You asked me that too. They should be all right, I've had them all me life, and they 'aven't been a nuisance to me yet.'

'Well, I'm pleased for you,' said Luke, cycling on. The road was full of traffic, but there was no sign of any strikers, aggressive or otherwise. It did not take him long to reach her house in Morecambe Street. 'Here we are, Lady Vi.'

'Thanks ever so much,' said Doreen, 'me mum worries a bit if I'm late.'

'Don't mention it,' said Luke. 'Good luck.' And he rode off. That left Doreen a little flummoxed. She'd been sure he was going to ask to see her again. She'd have had to say no. She told herself again that there just wasn't any point in taking up with him or anyone else until her mum had stopped grieving over her loss.

She went in and found her waiting for the usual pot of tea to be made.

'Mum, you don't always have to wait for me to come in if you fancy a cup of tea,' she said on impulse.

'Oh, I know, love,' said Mrs Paterson, a picture of handsome health, 'but about this time of the day me strength starts to run out.'

'All right, mum, I'll put the kettle on.'

'Bless you, pet, I just don't know 'ow I'd manage without you.'

'Well, me lad?' said Old Iron, ignoring a bust-up that was crashing about downstairs.

'Nice girl,' said Luke.

'Got lucky and saw 'er tonight, did you?' said Old Iron, who had pork chops on the go.

'And gave her a lift,' said Luke,

'And what come of that, might I ask?'

'Nothing,' said Luke.

'You didn't press yer suit?' said Old Iron.

'I didn't want to make a nuisance of meself,' said Luke. 'Best thing, Old Iron, not to be a headache to her.'

'You may be right, Luke. 'Ow did yer picketin' go today?'

'No trouble. The strike's already totterin' a bit, anyway.'

'Well, me own news is that I laid me peepers on yer nice young lady's Ma,' said Old Iron, and gave his son the details.

'So that's how it is,' said Luke, smiling. 'She pops out to look at the shops like a normal woman, but likes to let her neighbours know it tires her down to her feet. What's she like?'

''Andsome,' grinned Old Iron. 'I like 'em 'andsome. So I'm pleased to inform yer I ain't reluctant about doin' what I can to take 'er mind off 'er daughter and 'elp 'er point 'erself at me. She's cuddlesome, me lad, cuddlesome.'

'Well, don't rush her,' said Luke, 'or she might cut your legs off.'

Old Iron roared with laughter.

'You're a joker, me lad,' he said.

'What's all the crashin' and banging about this time?' asked Luke.

'Downstairs, yer mean?' said Old Iron. 'Well, I told 'em we're movin' on Saturday. So they're celebratin'.'

'They like it that we're movin'?' said Luke.

'No, they don't like it a bit,' said Old Iron, 'so they're fightin' each other about it. That's as good as a celebration to the Parslakes. I think I'll buff me old bowler hat when we move. Give it a bit of an 'andsome look. I don't want to present meself to the widow lookin' like last week's left-overs. And I'd better 'ave another go at the Tower of London tonight. I'd like to get it over with before we move. But I don't want any 'elp or interference.'

'You can rely on that,' said Luke.

'I'd appreciate that,' said Old Iron, 'seein' I'll be a bag of nerves by the time I get to the Crown Jewels.'

Gertie and her girls willingly put in an hour's overtime that day. Sammy had been at the factory since eight-thirty, feeling it was the least he could do under the circumstances. His presence was a reassurance to the seamstresses and a back-up for Tommy. Bands of strikers had been roaming around Islington and Shoreditch, their mood fretful and resentful. They knew the General Strike was coming apart at the seams, due to the critical attitude of the public and the increasing effectiveness of volunteer labour.

Although the factory wasn't put under threat, Sammy nevertheless stayed all day, and Gertie and her girls knew he was there in a protective capacity. They knew too he was set on maintaining productivity. They were ahead of schedule and earning welcome bonuses, and it was Gertie who suggested an hour's overtime would put them even farther ahead. A welcome safety margin, said Sammy, so good on yer, Gertie. Pleasure, Mister Sammy, said Gertie. Her husband Bert was still operative outside the factory, collecting donations for the miners, which dropped into the bucket at a penny or ha'penny a time.

The girls finished at six and left. The street was clear of strikers, much to their relief. Sammy left at six-fifteen, taking Tommy and Lilian in his car to drive them home. He was satisfied with the day, and he knew Boots, Emily and Susie would have looked after things at Camberwell. The only real trouble all day had been with the firm's van driven by an old soldier called Mitch. Part of Mitch's work was to collect finished garments from the Islington factory for delivery to the firm's ladies' wear shops in Brixton, Peckham and Kennington. Twice today strikers had attempted to stop the van, but each time Mitch had cut up a turning and used the back doubles. Sammy felt, therefore, that it hadn't been a bad day at all. Further, his shiner was less puffy, and on top of that was the fact that when he arrived home, Susie would have a nourishing supper ready. Susie. A saucebox she might be, but what a wife. Come to think of it, every deserving bloke ought to have a wife like Susie.

As he drove away from the factory with Tommy

and Lilian, the large man watched him from a little way down the street.

'I'll get yer, Sammy Adams, I'll get yer,' he said. Two coppers appeared. They were on a beat that would take in the security of the factory. 'I'll still get yer, Mister Sammy Adams.'

Chapter Six

The following day wasn't one of the best for young Freddy Brown. Teachers weren't on strike and schools were open. During the afternoon break at St John's Church School, Larcom Street, he was collared by Mr Hill.

'Ah, young Brown,' said the teacher.

'Yes, Mr Hill?'

'Hail, Caesar,' said Mr Hill.

'Do what, sir?'

'O Mighty Caesar, perhaps I should have said. Duckworth has to have his tonsils out. That puts the kybosh on his role as Caesar on Empire Day. Our new pupil, the irrepressible Miss Cassie Ford, has made a demand for a new Caesar.'

'Oh, blimey,' said Freddy in sudden dread suspicion. Cassie had transferred to St John's after Easter. She told her dad she'd go off and be a lady explorer if he didn't arrange it. Well, her dad said, I don't want you eaten up by crocodiles, Cassie, but why'd you want to go to St John's? To keep an eye on Freddy, she said, I'm his best mate. Well, since Cassie had suffered the trauma of narrowly escaping a strangler, one Gerald Ponsonby, both her dad and the headmistress of St John's gave in to her wish. She made her mark on the staff within her first week, and had been chosen for one of the roles in the Empire Day pageant that took place annually at the school. 'What's the bad news, sir?' asked Freddy.

'It's good news,' said Mr Hill, 'you're to be the new Caesar. Boadicea insists.'

Cassie was taking the role of Boadicea. She'd wanted to be Good Queen Bess, but that role had been given to an older girl who had red hair.

'Me to be Caesar? Me in a nightshirt and leaves on me 'ead?' said Freddy, appalled.

'A toga and a laurel wreath,' said Mr Hill, 'and you're required in the finale to lie beneath Boadicea's chariot, O Mighty Caesar.'

'Me?' said Freddy, in his twelfth year and accordingly not disposed to lie beneath any chariot in a nightshirt, never mind if it was called a toga. A bloke of his age had some rights. 'Am I allowed to say I ain't goin' to do it?'

'Afraid not,' said Mr Hill, a stalwart teacher who had a philosophical approach to what the terrors, the minxes and the big-eyed innocents could get up to at school. 'It's true that history records Boadicea was finally downed by Caesar, but as Empire Day is of a triumphant kind, we're going to ignore that. Boadicea will celebrate her victories in a tableau that puts her in the chariot, with Caesar having a hard time under her wheels. That'll be you, my lad. Oh, and young Miss Ford – Boadicea – would like you to make the chariot. We all would. Just an orange box, a couple of wheels and a shaft. Of course, if you'd prefer to be one of her steeds – no, perhaps not, she insists you're to be Caesar. Good hammering, Freddy, and bring the chariot to the school as soon as you've finished it.'

'Me?' said Freddy again. 'I've got to make the chariot that's goin' to run over me?'

'All in the cause of a good old Empire Day on the twenty-fourth,' said Mr Hill breezily.

'I don't mind Empire Day, sir,' said Freddy, 'but I ain't happy about bein' run over by Cassie Ford.'

'Be brave, O Mighty Caesar,' said Mr Hill, and went away with a smile on his face.

Freddy had several words with Cassie on their way home from school.

'Some mate you are,' he said, 'lettin' me in for doin' Caesar on Empire Day. And I've got to make the chariot as well. Cassie, I'm 'aving to think serious about findin' another mate.'

'You'd better not.' Cassie, ten years old, had raven hair, round brown eyes, and a dreamy imagination. She also had her share of feminine precociousness. 'Me dad'll punch your face in if you do. Oh, did yer know he once used to be champion boxer of the world?'

'No, I didn't,' said Freddy, 'and what d'yer mean by tellin' the teachers I'd got to take Duckworth's place as Caesar?'

'I didn't actually tell them,' said Cassie, 'I just mentioned you'd be best at it because your dad was once an actor on the stage.'

'No, he wasn't,' said Freddy.

'Well, he sometimes looks like 'e was,' said Cassie. 'Anyway, I'll 'elp you make the chariot.'

'Gawd 'elp the chariot, then,' said Freddy. 'And me as well,' he added, 'seeing I'll 'ave to wear a nightshirt like the Romans did.'

'I'm goin' to wear me Sunday frock,' said Cassie, 'with a gold crown, like Queen Boardser. And a spear.'

'Well, don't point it at me,' said Freddy, 'I ain't lived me life to the full yet.'

'Freddy, ain't you proud about bein' Caesar?' asked Cassie.

'No, I'm ill,' said Freddy, thinking he ought to give her what for on account of landing him in it. But he couldn't, not when she had to go to the Old Bailey in June and be a witness. He had to be there himself, and so did Susie's brother-in-law, Boots. They'd all got to be witnesses at the trial of a nasty old geezer, a Mr Ponsonby, who'd abducted Cassie and locked her up in what was left of a factory that had been partly destroyed by fire. Cassie hadn't seemed too worried about going to the Old Bailey. She'd asked if the King and Queen would be there in their royal robes. Freddy said no, but the judge would and so would Mr Ponsonby.

'Ugh, I don't like that man,' Cassie had said, 'he put something over me face and made me faint. I'm goin' to tell on 'im. Freddy, did yer know me dad used to be a judge once?'

Freddy wondered what a bloke could do with a mate as scatty as Cassie. He couldn't drop her down a coal-hole, even if she did let him in for playing Caesar in a nightshirt. He let her walk home with him, as usual, and his mum gave them both a cup of tea and a slice of cake, as usual. Then, also as usual, he took her to her own home on his bike. After what had happened that time, Freddy wasn't keen on letting her be on her own. Her mum had died some years ago, but her eldest sister Annie was just home from work. Annie Ford was a real lively young lady, who acted as mum to her brother and sisters, and was walking out with Freddy's brother Will.

'Here's Cassie, Annie,' he said, taking his mate in.

'Well, thanks, Freddy, you're sweet the way you look after 'er,' smiled Annie, and gave the boy a warm kiss on his cheek.

'I think I like that,' said Freddy.

''Ere,' said Cassie in protest to her sister, 'what're you kissin' Freddy for?'

'For lookin' after you,' said Annie.

'He don't let me kiss 'im,' said Cassie.

'Well, mates don't kiss,' said Freddy.

'When the Prince kissed Sleepin' Beauty, it woke 'er up,' said Cassie.

'He probably gave her a pinch as well,' said Freddy.

'Oh, on 'er botty, d'you think?' said Cassie, imagination springing ahead. 'I read a story once about a fat lady that got pinched on 'er botty on the way to Strawberry Fair. It was in rhyme, yer know, Annie. It said, "*In a dress of very tight cotton, she got pinched by a dwarf on 'er bottom.*" And then it said—'

'She's off,' said Freddy, 'so I'm off meself.'

'But what about me ride on your bike?' demanded Cassie.

'Oh, all right,' said Freddy, and took her, as usual, for a ride on his bike until their suppertimes. Freddy regarded Cassie as his mate. She regarded him as one of her belongings.

Freddy sat down to supper with his family in their kitchen. That is, with his mum and dad, his fourteen-year-old sister Sally and his twenty-year-old brother Will. Sally, who had left school at Easter, had a job as an apprentice assistant in one of Sammy Adams's ladies' wear shops at Kennington. Will, who'd been in the Army, had been discharged on account of contracting asthma. Sammy had found a job for him too, as clerk and handyman in one of his scrapyards, also at Kennington. The work put no strain on his condition and gave him a fair amount of fresh air. The light of his life was Annie Ford, Cassie's sister, who refused to allow his asthma to come between them, as it were. Annie was fond of being kissed. Will was becoming fond of more than a kiss. Annie said she supposed it was natural, her young man letting his hands cuddle up to her blouse or jumper, but not on top of a tram or when anyone was looking. Will said it was a help to his asthma. Annie said you sure? Will said you can feel my chest, if you like. Oh, what a nice change from you feeling mine, said Annie, and sure enough his chest did feel fine and manly, so she said all right, if it does help your asthma, you can have cuddles, but only when we're alone in the parlour. Well, that kind of thing was very recreational, and good for their relationship. Annie was no prude, and Will was hardly a wet weekend.

Freddy put a question over supper.

'Can I say something?' he asked.

'What d'you want to say, Freddy?' asked Mrs Brown, the epitome of a motherly body.

'I'm doin' Caesar,' said Freddy.

'Who?' asked Will.

'What?' asked Sally.

'Eh?' asked Mr Brown, a good-natured dad.

'I'm doin' Caesar,' repeated Freddy.

''Ow much you doin' 'im for?' asked Mr Brown with a grin.

'It's for the Empire Day pageant at school,' said Freddy, making healthy inroads into sausage-toad-in-the-hole. 'That Cassie did it on me. Billy

Duckworth was supposed to be Caesar, but 'e's havin' 'is tonsils out. On purpose, I shouldn't wonder. Cassie got the teachers to agree to me takin' 'is place.'

'Well, that's nice, Freddy,' said Mr Brown.

'Not much it ain't,' said Freddy, 'I've got to wear a nightshirt, like the Romans used to.'

Apart from Mrs Brown, the family fell about.

Freddy said it wasn't funny, especially as he had to lie under the wheels of Boadicea's chariot, with Cassie playing Boadicea. Mrs Brown said she hoped it wouldn't ruin his nightshirt. The others fell about again. Freddy said go on, help yourselves, but it's not making me laugh.

'Nor me,' said Sally, 'I'm cryin' me eyes out.'

Luke had missed out on seeing Doreen again. He wasn't able to leave the picket line until too late. In any case, Doreen managed to board a bus and to arrive home in very good time. Her mother said what a reliable girl she was most days, even when there was a strike on. She'd got through a bit of ironing, she said, and a bit of dusting too, although it had left her a little short of breath. Perhaps Doreen would put the kettle on?

'Yes, all right, Mum,' said Doreen.

'Doreen love, you sure that skirt isn't a bit too short? It might make some young men think you're fast, and you might get one followin' you 'ome.'

'Oh, it's the fashion, Mum,' said Doreen, putting the kettle on.

'What, bein' followed 'ome?' said Mrs Paterson in shock.

'No, short skirts, silly,' said Doreen, keeping

quiet about the young man who'd given her a lift home on his bike a couple of times.

'So you didn't see 'er this evenin', eh, me lad?' said Old Iron, who had a lamb stew going. Potatoes were in the pot as well, but not dumplings. Somehow, he couldn't put a decent dumpling together. His late wife had always come up with lovely ones whenever she made a stew.

'I told you, Old Iron, I was too late leavin' the picket line,' said Luke.

'Well, duty's duty, if you're union,' said Old Iron.

'I think the strike's fallin' apart,' said Luke.

'Nor ain't you far wrong,' said Old Iron. 'When you want to beat the bosses and the government, you need to be able to dig yer heels in by standin' on firm ground, not on top of a bog. The unions are sinkin', Luke, and takin' the miners with 'em. That's one more load of bad luck for the miners. Now then, me lad, we're movin' tomorrow afternoon. You on the picket line in the mornin'?'

'No,' said Luke, 'it's only a few men tomorrow, and I asked to be excused, anyway, on account of our movin' lodgings.'

'Well, good on yer, me lad,' said Old Iron, 'that'll leave you free to do yer stuff. I'll be obliged if yer'll pack our things up and hire a wheelbarrer for takin' them round to our new lodgings sometime in the afternoon. I'm workin' meself in the mornin', but I'll be 'ome in time to give you a hand come midday. Don't take any of the stuff down to the passage, not till we're ready to load it, or the Parslakes will jump up and down on it.'

'Their way of saying goodbye, I suppose,' said Luke.

'And bein' friendly,' said Old Iron. 'Where yer goin' with that towel?'

'To have a wash,' said Luke.

'What, another one? You washed as soon as you came in.'

'Blimey O'Reilly,' said Luke, 'what's up with me?'

'Nothing that's too serious,' said Old Iron, poking the stew. 'You've just got a young man's natural complaint. I 'ad it several times meself, specially when I met yer mum. It looks like yer nice young lady Doreen is special to yer. Well, we'll 'ave to get 'er handsome mum interested in something like the Salvation Army.'

'That's it, give her one of those tambourines,' said Luke, grinning.

'On the other 'and,' said Old Iron, 'there's me and me well-preserved manliness, which could be 'ighly interestin' to a woman like our widow.'

'Well, now you've seen her,' said Luke, 'are you thinkin' of makin' an honest widow of her?'

'Steady, me lad,' said Old Iron, 'she'll make *me* 'er nursemaid then. Mind you, she looks like a good cuddle for a bloke.'

'Best of luck, Dad,' said Luke, ''elp yourself to a bundle of cuddles once you've got those apron-strings untied.'

'Well, I made a good job of the Tower of London,' said Old Iron, 'which 'as got me in a confident mood about yer nice young lady's funny mum.'

'What's next, then?' smiled Luke.

'Lamb stew,' said Old Iron, a versatile charac-ter.

*　　*　　*

Mrs Martin, a typically friendly and chatty neighbour, popped in on Mrs Paterson that evening, as she often did, to help cheer her up. She considered neighbours and neighbourliness were part of the Lord's wondrous works. Neighbours who became suffering widows had a Christian right to be cheered up.

'Would you like a cup of tea, Mrs Martin?' asked Mrs Paterson. 'Me and Doreen always 'ave one about an hour after supper.'

'I won't say no,' said Mrs Martin, due to be a landlady to Luke and Old Iron.

'Doreen'll make it, won't you, love?' said Mrs Paterson.

Doreen, about to do some intricate sewing work on the torn lace hem of a slip, said, 'All right, Mum, I'll put the kettle on.'

'There's a good girl,' said Mrs Paterson. To Mrs Martin, she said, 'I just couldn't do without my Doreen, especially when I've got one of me 'eads.'

'Oh, you poor dear,' said Mrs Martin, 'have you thought about seein' Dr Johnson down by the Elephant and Castle? I've 'eard 'e's a wonder at findin' out what gives a woman 'eadaches, specially if they're chronic.'

'Oh, it's the shock that gives me mine,' said Mrs Paterson, passing a hand over her brow.

'I must say you put up very brave with them,' said Mrs Martin, motherly and slightly plump. 'No-one would know you was sufferin', you always manage to look a well woman. Still, Dr Johnson might give you something to stop your 'eadaches comin' on. He 'as a late surgery on Fridays, up to nine o'clock.'

Mrs Paterson, after briefly registering alarm at

this suggestion, said, 'Oh, you can't cure shock, Mrs Martin, not my kind of shock. It hit me 'ard, bein' so unexpected, and didn't do me 'eart any good, either. It's been weak ever since.'

'I'm admirin' of 'ow you keep goin,' said Mrs Martin. ''Ave you thought about Dr Johnson givin' you some medicine for yer weak 'eart?'

'Oh, medicine can't cure weak 'earts,' said Mrs Paterson.

'Still, it might not be a bad idea to see Dr Johnson, Mum,' said Doreen. 'We can go on a tram before his surgery closes tonight.'

'Oh, I've 'ad a long day, love,' said Mrs Paterson, 'and don't feel I could make the effort. Perhaps some other time, when I'm less poorly.'

'Yes, I remember Mrs Ridley goin' shoppin' once when she was feelin' poorly,' said Mrs Martin.

'Oh, what 'appened to her?' asked Doreen, waiting for the kettle to boil.

'She fell over down the market,' said Mrs Martin, 'and finished up in King's College 'Ospital. She 'ad a lovely time there, and all kinds of doctors came and looked at 'er. She said she'd never been more looked at in all 'er life. Well, she's a pretty woman, and didn't 'ave anything to be ashamed of, and all the doctors were 'andsome. She was like a two-year-old when they discharged 'er sayin' she could be proud of 'erself for not 'aving anything wrong with 'er. Oh, did I tell yer I'm goin' to 'ave two lodgers, a father and son? 'E's a nice young man, the son, and me and 'Arold's goin' to let them rent our upstairs from tomorrow. We can do with the rent. The son said 'e and 'is dad are both respectable and don't drink much, nor keep fast company. I said I 'oped they'd live peaceable in me house, and 'e said it 'ad been the life's work of 'is dad to live peaceable.'

'How old is the son?' asked Mrs Paterson.

'Oh, early twenties, I'd say.'

'Well, I just 'ope he's as peaceable as 'is father,' said Mrs Paterson, 'and keeps 'imself to 'imself.'

'Well, he's 'ighly pleasant, Mrs Paterson, and might just take to a girl like Doreen,' said Mrs Martin cheerfully.

Mrs Paterson looked faint with new shock.

'I'm sure my Doreen won't want anyone's lodger takin' to 'er,' she said, 'she's a nice quiet girl.'

'Me?' said Doreen, a typically lively Walworth girl. If she was living a quiet social life at the moment, it was only because she was devoting herself to her mum.

'Well, you're a good girl, Doreen, that you are,' said Mrs Martin, 'and nice company.'

Crikey, thought Doreen, does she mean I'm nice company for her and me mum? I hope I've got a bit more than that to look forward to.

'I'm grateful I've got my Doreen,' said Mrs Paterson predictably.

Mrs Martin, a woman given to helpful suggestions, said, 'Why don't you 'ave a lodger yerself, Mrs Paterson? Not one you 'ave to run about for, of course. That kind takes advantage. A nice retired gent, say, so that you wouldn't always be alone in the 'ouse while Doreen's at work.'

'A lodger?' said Mrs Paterson, who might have suffered more shock if she hadn't suddenly thought it would mean she couldn't be expected to face up to the responsibilities of a lodger all by herself, that it would keep Doreen at home indefinitely, sharing the responsibilities. 'Oh, I don't know I'd be up to that, Mrs Martin, lookin' after a lodger.'

Doreen thought what a good idea. A nice retired gent might turn out to be good company for her mum, and it might mean that she herself could enjoy a bit of social life. Not only that, a lodger's rent of five bob, say, would be a great help, because there was never any money to spare.

'Oh, I'd help, Mum,' she said, 'and we could really do with a lodger's rent.'

'I wouldn't want to put you out, Doreen,' said her mum. 'There'd be 'is bed linen to wash for a start, and – well, I just don't know.'

'I could manage any extras in the wash,' said Doreen, who usually did the weekly laundry on Saturday afternoons.

'I'm sure a nice retired gent as a lodger would buck you up, Mrs Paterson,' said Mrs Martin. 'Old Mrs Winters 'as got one who's a great 'elp to her. Mind, it's not that you're old, but you're a sufferin' woman that shouldn't be alone all day. You ought to 'ave someone in the 'ouse that you could call on if you 'ad a nasty turn.'

'Well, perhaps – well, Doreen and me'll think about it,' said Mrs Paterson.

'Let's do it, Mum,' said Doreen. 'I'll put a card in the newsagent's window advertisin' for a retired gent as a lodger at five bob a week. We've got two spare rooms upstairs.' There had been two spare rooms since her brother and sister had moved out. She had the upstairs front herself, and her mum had the downstairs bedroom. 'Yes, let's go for a lodger, a nice bloke.'

'Well, all right, love,' said Mrs Paterson, 'if you don't mind sharin' the responsibilities.'

'Of course I won't mind,' said Doreen.

'You might 'ave to wait a bit for the right kind of gent to come along,' said Mrs Martin, 'but bless yer, I'm sure it'll be worth it.'

'I'll put the card in the newsagent's window tomorrow,' said Doreen, which she did, on her way to work. A window card cost threepence a week.

Mrs Martin's right, she thought. A nice retired gent as a lodger might just take mum out of herself.

Tommy and Vi, living upstairs in the house of Vi's parents, were entertaining two visitors, Annabelle and Rosie.

'Uncle Boots sent us,' said Annabelle.

'Uncle Boots?' said Vi.

'Yes, you know, Auntie Vi,' said Rosie, 'Nana's only oldest son.'

'Yes,' said Annabelle. 'Go and wake up your Uncle Tommy, he said, and tell him he's to start making up a four at tennis again.'

'And to start tomorrow afternoon in Ruskin Park,' said Rosie. 'Three o'clock.'

Easy-going Tommy grinned. He'd never touched a tennis racquet in his life until last summer, when Boots had persuaded him to have a go. Tommy took to it like a duck to water, and after only a few games with Boots, Rosie and Annabelle, became a very creditable performer.

'I'll have to improve me backhand this year,' he said.

'Well, your forehand's a walloper, Uncle Tommy,' said Rosie. 'Shall we tell Daddy you'll be there?'

'Uncle Boots said we weren't to take no for an answer,' pointed out Annabelle. In her tenth year she was coming on gamely at tennis, mainly because she didn't want to be left behind by Rosie.

'Yes, go on, join them, Tommy,' said Vi.

'All right, you're on, girls,' said Tommy.

'Crikey, you're a sport, Uncle Tommy,' said Annabelle. 'Would you like a kiss?'

'We'll give him one each,' said Rosie, 'he doesn't charge tuppence like Uncle Sammy does.'

Tommy received a smacker on each cheek.

Chapter Seven

Luke and his dad departed from their lodgings to the sound of the Parslakes going hammer and tongs in the kitchen, Mother Parslake and her daughter setting about their menfolk to celebrate the disaster of losing their lodgers.

'We're well out of that lot,' said Old Iron, walking beside Luke, who was pushing the wheelbarrow that they'd loaded with their personal goods and chattels. Old Iron was pushing Luke's bike. 'Well out, take my word.'

'You're ruddy right,' said Luke, 'we're lucky we're not walkin' wounded as it is.'

'I tell yer, me lad,' said sprightly Old Iron, 'we're lucky not to 'ave been found dead and stuffed 'alfway up our chimney. Well, on we go, sunshine, round to our new landlady, Mrs Martin.'

Mrs Martin, after Luke had introduced her to his dad, said, 'Well, come in and welcome, Mr Edwards, yer son told me you're respectable and church-goin'.'

'Now and again, Mrs Martin, now and again,' said Old Iron amiably. 'The Lord bein' my shepherd, I attend occasional.' He stepped into the passage. 'Well, what a well-kept 'ome, Mrs Martin. Polished lino and all, or me eyes deceive me. You can take pride in that, as a woman of – of forty, might I suggest?'

Mrs Martin, nearly fifty, quivered happily.

'Kind of yer, Mr Edwards, I do take pride in me 'ouse and 'ome, like me 'usband 'Arold takes pride in shining 'is boots,' she said. 'You'll find everything in order upstairs, the beds nicely aired.'

'Well, thank you, Mrs Martin,' said Old Iron, 'I'll 'elp me son Luke bring our goods in.'

They were comfortably settled within an hour, and Mrs Martin made her first friendly gesture by taking them up a pot of tea in return for receiving ten bob rent in advance.

Enjoying the tea in what would be their kitchen and living-room, Luke said, 'What's that?'

'What's what?'

'All that silence downstairs,' said Luke, and Old Iron grinned.

'Yer know what that is, don't yer, me lad?'

'Yes, peace, perfect peace,' said Luke.

'Ruddy 'ooray,' said Old Iron, then got up, took a garment from their open trunk and shook the creases from it.

'What the hell's that?' asked Luke.

'Me new frock coat,' said Old Iron. 'Well, maybe not exactly new, but as good as newish. Bought it from Solly's yesterday.' Solly's was the nearest local pawnbroker. 'Well, when I knock on the widow's door to offer her some doctorin', me frock coat will meet 'er female mince pies authentic, like.'

'Now look 'ere, Dad, I'm serious about gettin' Doreen unfastened from her old lady,' said Luke, 'and I'm not in favour of you dressin' up like a variety turn. All you need to do is find a way of introducin' yourself as a new neighbour and then lettin' your well-preserved manliness do the rest. You don't need to wear any frock coat.'

'Frock coats, me lad, are still a sign of bein' a professional gent, like a doctor,' said Old Iron. 'If you're serious about your fancy, I'm serious about 'elping you to be the love-light in 'er mince pies. I'd like to see you goin' steady, and 'eading for the altar. Bein' married to a good woman is a treat for a bloke, never mind the ups and downs. I'll admit some good women get a bit off balance at times, which can make some blokes take fatal to drink, but there's always one sour apple in a barrel of pippins. 'Owsoever, that don't mean wedlock ain't favourable to a man gen'rally speakin'. I 'ad a good marriage, and I want you to 'ave one. Come to that, seein' I ain't quite past me prime, I might even click for a second good marriage.'

'Come to that, so you might,' said Luke.

'I'm goin' shoppin' now, Mum,' said Doreen.

'Oh, I'll come with you, love,' said Mrs Paterson, 'I like the shops on a Saturday afternoon, and I feel I've got some strength in me legs today.'

'No, you stay home and rest,' said Doreen.

'No, I'll come with you, it's a nice day,' said Mrs Paterson.

'Well, all right,' said Doreen, and thought that just for once she'd have liked to shop by herself. Her mum always insisted on going with her.

On their return two hours later, the first adult she saw in Morecambe Street was the young man who'd given her lifts home on his bike. He was chatting to street kids, and the kids were grinning. As soon as she and her mum had gone indoors, Doreen came out again. Luke saw her.

'Excuse me,' she called, and he went across to her.

'Hello, Lady Vi,' he said.

'What're you doin' in our street?' she asked.

'Well, I live 'ere now,' smiled Luke.

'What?' said Doreen.

'I like your dress,' said Luke.

'Kindly don't mention it,' said Doreen. 'What d'you mean, you live 'ere now?'

'Yes, number twelve,' said Luke. 'My dad and me. We're lodgin' with Mr and Mrs Martin. We're your new neighbours.'

'I don't believe you,' said Doreen, then remembered Mrs Martin had mentioned last night that she was taking a father and son as lodgers. 'Look, why 'ave you come to this street?'

'There was a war goin' on in our other landlady's fam'ly,' said Luke, 'and we decided to move while we were still alive.'

'It sounds suspicious to me,' said Doreen, hazel eyes searching him.

'Tell you what,' said Luke breezily, 'pop round to Mason Street and ask about the Parslakes. You'll find out they're a blood-and-thunder lot. Mrs Parslake broke a window once with Mr Parslake. She bashed his 'ead against it, from the inside. Dad went down to their parlour and asked her what all the noise was about. She said her clumsy old man had just broken the window. Dad asked her where Mr Parslake was now. Gone off to the hospital, she said, to get his 'ead seen to, but look at me broken window, she said.'

'Are you tryin' to be funny?' asked Doreen.

'Me? I'm a serious bloke,' said Luke.

'No, you're not,' said Doreen, 'you're a joker, you are, and I think you're followin' me about.'

'Well, I can't blame meself,' said Luke, 'I like the way you look.'

'Here, d'you mind?' said Doreen. 'I told you, I'm too busy takin' care of my mum to 'ave anyone likin' the way I look and followin' me about. Look, you're not really livin' in this street now, are you?'

'Yes,' said Luke.

'Well, don't you come knockin' for me,' said Doreen.

'I won't, not until you want me to,' said Luke.

'Some 'opes,' said Doreen, and went in. Her mum wanted to know who she'd been talking to. Just a neighbour, said Doreen.

'You've been ages out there,' said Mrs Paterson. 'Still, never mind, neighbours do keep a body talkin' sometimes. I'd love a nice cup of tea now, it might revive me a bit. Would you put the kettle on, love?'

'Yes, all right,' said Doreen. Her mum had done quite well, she'd been out for two hours, and hadn't complained once. She deserved a nice cup of tea now.

Crikey, was that young man really living with the Martins? If he came calling for her, her mum wouldn't half get upset.

Young Cassie Ford pulled on the latchcord of the Brown family's front door in Caulfield Place, and went in. She found plump and placid Mrs Brown in the kitchen with lean and wiry Mr Brown.

'Oh, hello, Cassie,' said Mrs Brown.

'Yes, how yer doin', girlie?' said Mr Brown. Cassie, being Freddy's mate, had the run of the house. She came and went like one of the family.

'Oh, I'm goin' to be Queen Boardser with a chariot in our Empire Day pageant,' said Cassie, school gymslip looking any old how and boater sitting on the back of her head.

'You mean Queen Boadicea, don't you, love?' queried Mrs Brown.

'Yes, that's what I said. I'm goin' to be next to King Arthur and 'is Knights of the Round Table, and Freddy's goin' to be Hail Caesar, did yer know?'

'We know all right,' said Mr Brown, 'but I'd tell a lie if I told yer Freddy can't wait. He's 'aving to wear a nightshirt, he says.'

'Where is 'e?' asked Cassie.

'He's out in the yard, Cassie,' said Mrs Brown.

'Makin' a box-cart,' said Mr Brown.

'Yes, that's me Queen Boardser chariot,' said Cassie, who was carrying a brown paper parcel. 'I'll go and 'elp 'im.' Out she went through the scullery back door into the yard. There was Freddy, fixing an axle with wheels to the bottom of an upside-down wooden crate. He was hammering in large metal staples. ''Ello, Freddy, 'ere I am,' said Cassie. 'Crikey, is that me chariot? What's it upside-down for?'

'So's I can fix this axle,' said Freddy, 'which Mr Greenberg sold to me for thruppence, which you owe me.'

'Oh, I'll pay yer next year, Freddy,' said Cassie. 'I'm expectin' an uncle of mine to leave me a fortune next year, and 'is castle as well. Look, I brought you a flannel nightshirt that me sister Nellie don't want any more.' She unwrapped the parcel and showed Freddy what was in it.

'Here, excuse me,' said Freddy, 'I ain't wearin' that, it's not a nightshirt, it's a nightgown. I ain't wearin' any girl's left-over nightgown.'

'But you've got to wear it or you won't look like Caesar,' said Cassie.

'Caesar didn't wear a girl's nightgown, yer scatty 'a'porth,' said Freddy.

'Nellie said she don't want it back, Freddy.'

'I ain't wearin' it,' said Freddy.

'You'll look nice in it, just like Caesar,' said Cassie. 'Freddy, what's that?'

'The shaft,' said Freddy, 'with a straight 'andle for pullin'.'

'It's not long enough for me 'orses,' said Cassie.

Freddy hammered in another staple.

'There's not goin' to be any 'orses,' he said, 'just two boys.'

'Yes, but they'll be actin' as me 'orses,' said Cassie.

'If you keep on like this, Cassie, I'm goin' to pass away,' said Freddy.

'King Arthur 'ad six black 'orses at his funeral, did yer know that, Freddy? It was when he passed away 'imself.'

'Would yer like a cup of tea and a slice of cake?' asked Freddy.

'Yes, I would,' said Cassie.

'All right, go and get me mum to treat yer,' said Freddy, 'and leave me to pass away peaceful.'

'Yes, all right, Freddy. Oh, 'ave yer made a will?'

'No, not yet,' said Freddy, 'I wasn't thinkin' of passin' away till you arrived.'

'Never mind,' said Cassie. She thought. 'I expect you'll live,' she said, and went to see if there was a cup of tea and a slice of cake going. After all, this was her second home, good as, and Mrs Brown was like a fond mum to her.

*　　*　　*

It was Saturday afternoon, and in Dieppe the news was that across the Channel the strike at some ports was breaking up and that ferries were able to dock at Newhaven.

Mr Ronald Ponsonby received this news in interested fashion. He took himself down to the dockside offices of the ferry company and booked a passage on the Monday morning crossing. The trial of his twin brother opened in June. He'd have to find out the date. But he had the rest of May, at least, in which to make his enquiries and formulate his method of elimination.

'What's cookin', Old Iron?' asked Luke at twelve-thirty on Sunday.

'New potatoes,' said Old Iron, who had a saucepan going on a gas ring. 'Then garden peas. Two pork chops are comin' on, I 'ope. I ain't quite familiar yet with this range. Well, not enough to try a joint.'

'Want any help?' asked Luke.

'Listen, the time for you to 'elp is when you're married,' said Old Iron. 'Meself, when I need 'elp doin' pork chops and a couple of veg, you can start writin' out me 'eadstone.'

'I'll go for a little walk, then,' said Luke.

'Turn left for the pub,' grinned Old Iron, 'or right if yer after a chat with Doreen, which young lady I ain't 'ad the pleasure of meetin' yet.'

'Keep hopin',' said Luke, and went out.

Doreen, who had Sunday dinner going for herself and her mum, was cleaning the outside of the parlour windows. In an old apron and with an ancient straw hat on to keep the dust out of her hair, she jumped as she heard Luke's voice.

'Top of the mornin' to you, Lady Vi.'

She turned, feeling wild that he'd caught her looking like a skivvy.

'Don't do that,' she said.

'Don't do what?' asked Luke.

'Don't creep up on me and make me jump, that's what,' said Doreen.

'I like your apron,' said Luke, pleased that he'd chanced upon her.

'I bet,' said Doreen.

'Like your hat as well,' said Luke.

'Go away!'

'Look, I'll clean those windows for you, if you like,' said Luke. 'I don't favour a pretty girl 'aving to do a job like that on a nice Sunday mornin'. Hand over the dusters, and I'll finish the job for you while you go and 'elp your mum with the Sunday dinner.'

'I've never 'eard such cheek,' said Doreen. 'Standin' there and givin' me orders, as good as. And I'm doin' our Sunday dinner meself. Everything's on, if you must know.'

That wasn't the way it should be, thought Luke. Most Walworth mums, widows or otherwise, seemed to happily sacrifice their Sunday mornings to cooking the dinner. Sunday dinners were always special, even if a family couldn't afford a roast, and Walworth mums knew it.

'Doesn't your mum do cookin'?' he asked.

'Mum suffered grievous shock when Dad died,' said Doreen, 'and it's given her a weak heart. I'm all she's got now. I don't know why you're standin' there lookin' at my hat. It's only an old thing.' She took it off and the sun, braving the smoke of Walworth, danced on the shingled chestnut waves.

What a very nice-looking girl she was, thought Luke.

'Sorry about your mum's weak 'eart,' he said.

'Yes, it's only lately that she's mentioned it,' said Doreen, 'she's been suffering it without telling anyone. You can see she needs lookin' after.'

I can't see that yet, thought Luke, I haven't met the good lady.

'Sure I can't finish the windows for you?' he said.

'No, thanks, I—'

'Doreen, who's that?' Mrs Paterson was at the open front door, staring suspiciously at Luke, and Luke saw a woman handsome of looks and figure. So that's the grieving widow, he thought. Well, she looks ruddy ungrieving to me, and healthy as well. All in the mind, that's what it is. Wait till Old Iron starts working on her. It'll be a fight to the finish. Old Iron liked a challenge.

'It's a new neighbour, Mum,' said Doreen, 'one of Mrs Martin's lodgers. I don't know his name.'

'I'm Luke Edwards, Mrs Paterson—'

'Who told you I was Mrs Paterson?'

'Mrs Martin.'

'Pleased to meet you, I'm sure,' said Mrs Paterson, who looked far from pleased. 'Doreen, could you come in and mix the batter for the Yorkshire puddin'?'

'I'll finish the windows first, Mum,' said Doreen. 'The batter doesn't need mixin' just yet.'

'Well, all right,' said Mrs Paterson, but remained at the door, visibly taking on a watchful role. She managed to make herself look as if her only concern was to ensure her precious daughter didn't lose her virginity while cleaning the parlour windows, and on a Sunday too.

'Nice to have met you and your daughter, Mrs Paterson,' said Luke, and made a tactful departure.

'That young man's got a forward look,' said Mrs Paterson.

'Has he? I didn't notice,' said Doreen, and stretched on tiptoe to reach the top of a window. Two street kids came running, one after the other.

'Oi, D'reen, you got snow in the south!' called one kid.

'Seen yer legs, D'reen, seen yer legs!' called the other.

Doreen hastily stopped stretching.

'Them demons, there ought to be a law against them,' said Mrs Paterson, 'but I did mention about your short skirts, love.'

'I like the fashion,' said Doreen, 'and at least I don't 'ave fat legs.'

'Doreen, you shouldn't talk about your legs out 'ere in the street,' said Mrs Paterson.

'Don't fuss, Mum,' said Doreen, still polishing.

'Well, that's not a very nice thing to say to your own mother. I 'ope that forward young man didn't stop to talk to you on account of your short skirt.'

'He just stopped to say 'ello.'

'You never know with some young men, love.'

'Well, p'raps he'll fall off his bike one day,' murmured Doreen to a window.

'What was that?' asked Mrs Paterson.

'Nothing,' said Doreen. I think I'll go to the park this afternoon, yes, and by myself.

Luke, watching the street from the upstairs front bedroom at fifteen minutes to three, saw her come out of her house, which was a little way down and on the other side of the street. She looked a treat in a light loose-waisted summer dress with a fringed hem that danced around her knees, and a little blue and white hat. A street kid hailed her.

'Where yer goin', Doreen?'

'Ruskin Park, if it's all right with you, Georgie.'

'Come wiv yer, if yer like.'

'D'you mind if I don't like?'

'That's it, break me 'eart,' called the kid.

Doreen quite enjoyed sauntering in Ruskin Park, even if she was on her own. Her mum had wanted her to stay in, but a girl had to have a break sometimes. Fellers gave her the eye, but she hadn't come to the park to be picked up. After a while, she sat down on a bench to watch the tennis that was being played on the four public courts. It looked fun, and she thought she'd rather like to be able to play the game herself.

'Can I join you?'

Doreen jumped for the second time that day. Looking up, she saw Luke, bare-headed and wearing an open-necked shirt and Sunday flannels.

'Oh, you've done it again,' she said.

'Done what again?' asked Luke, who'd managed to catch a tram to the park. There wasn't much public transport about, as it was Sunday.

'Made me jump,' said Doreen, 'and now you're standin' in my way.'

'I'll sit down,' said Luke, and did so. Doreen gave him a look. 'I like your frock,' said Luke, who had hoped to find her in the park, but without wanting her to feel he was making a nuisance of himself.

'Never mind my frock,' said Doreen, ''ave you followed me all the way here?'

'No, I came on a tram,' said Luke. 'Nice to have bumped into you.'

'I'm thrilled,' she said.

'Yes, I like it meself,' said Luke.

'Look,' said Doreen, 'you 'ardly know me, but you follow me about, creep up on me when I'm cleaning windows, sit down next to me when you 'aven't been asked, and then talk about likings you're not supposed to have, not when you don't 'ardly know me. If my mother thought you were tryin' to get off with me, she'd come round to your lodgings with a policeman.'

'Does she go out with a policeman, then?' asked Luke.

'Funny ha-ha, I don't think,' said Doreen, feeling she had to do her best to discourage him.

'Speakin' of your Ma—'

'D'you mean my mother?'

'Yes, and she looks a picture of health. Attractive too. I suppose she wouldn't like me to take her out, would she? To a music hall, say, like the South London Palace of Varieties?'

'What?' gasped Doreen.

'Well, it might cheer her up—'

'What a sauce,' said Doreen, 'I can't believe me own ears. Take my mum out, you said?'

'Well, she's nice-lookin' and a widow, and I'm fancy-free,' said Luke. 'And I know it's no good askin' you, Lady Vi.'

'And it's no good askin' my mother, either,' said Doreen. 'Of all the nerve. She's still in mourning, I'll 'ave you know, and even if she wasn't, she wouldn't go gallivantin' about with someone your age.'

'I'm twenty-four,' said Luke, 'that's not too old for her, is it?'

Doreen wanted to laugh, but thought she'd better not.

'Someone's goin' daft round here,' she said, 'and it's not me. D'you think my mother would go out with anyone who's only twenty-four?'

'I could ask her,' said Luke. 'I mean, she might—'

'Never mind what you mean,' said Doreen. 'Mum's a mature woman.'

'Still, in a woman, looks count for more than age.'

'Crikey,' said Doreen, 'are you tryin' to say you fancy my mum?'

'No, I thought askin' her out might cheer her up a bit.'

'I'll fall off this bench in a minute,' said Doreen.

'Like a cup of tea at the tea rooms?' said Luke.

'No, I'd best get 'ome now,' she said.

'Well, all right.'

'Look, if I do 'ave a cup of tea with you, don't think that'll mean I like you followin' me about.'

'Cross me heart,' said Luke.

'I'll chance it, then,' said Doreen.

'Is it family cricket this afternoon?' asked Boots of Tim and Rosie. They were in the garden of their house in Red Post Hill. The long lawn was perfect for cricket.

'Is it today, Rosie?' asked Tim.

'No,' said Rosie, 'Daddy's gone skew-whiff. Family cricket's the fourth Sunday in the month.'

Family cricket brought all the Adams to the house every month in the summer. Everyone had to play, Lizzy and Ned and their children, Tommy and Vi, Sammy and Susie, Boots and Emily, Rosie, Tim and Mr Finch. Chinese Lady was excused on account of her priorities. Getting a nice Sunday tea for everyone was far more important to her than cricket. About cricket, she said she could understand why men went daft over it. None of it made sense, she said, which was why it sent men daft.

'So we're by ourselves this afternoon, are we?' said Boots.

'Us could play,' said Tim.

'Good idea, young 'un,' said Boots. He patted his son's head. 'You've got something there besides a mop. Right, go and get your mum, Tim, and your grandpa. Tell 'em the sun's out and it's cricket on the lawn. And you can bat first.'

'Crikey,' said young Tim in bliss, and dashed off.

'Rosie, you can get the stumps and bats,' said Boots.

'Yes, Daddy, at once if not sooner,' said Rosie. She laughed. She adored garden cricket because Boots was so fond of it. His loves were her loves, and she would have walked to the ends of the earth with him.

'Hop off, then,' said Boots.

'Daddy, you're fun,' she said, and off she went.

Boots looked up at the blue sky of May, and thought of the hot sky of Africa, from under which the England cricket team had recently returned.

It was evening in Kenya, and the sun had made its usual early descent. Polly Simms, escorted by a handsome white farmer, plunged into the gaiety, the brittle gaiety, of one more cocktail party.

After thirty minutes, her bright smile had become a mask.

My God, what boring, boring people.

Chapter Eight

Mrs Paterson couldn't think why Doreen had gone off to the park. She hoped it wasn't to meet somebody. To Mrs Paterson, 'somebody' always represented a threat to her cosy relationship with her daughter. A woman whose husband had passed unexpectedly on, and whose son and elder daughter had left her to get married, needed one of her children to be a comfort to her. She and Doreen usually spent a nice quiet Sunday afternoon together, but this time Doreen had simply said she needed to get out, and she'd gone out. Was there somebody? Mrs Paterson thought she'd have a turn if there was.

Half an hour after Doreen had left for the park, Mrs Paterson heard a knock on her front door. Opening it, she found herself looking at a man with a weathered face and a friendly smile. In a black frock coat, he looked like one of those old-fashioned preachers who always carried a Bible about with them and read out the fiery bits if anyone gave them half a chance.

'Mrs Paterson, I presume?' said Old Iron, doffing his bowler hat.

'I'm Mrs Paterson.'

'Thunder and lightnin',' said Old Iron, 'I'm overcome. Good afternoon to you, Mrs Paterson—'

'What d'you mean, thunder and lightnin'?'

demanded Mrs Paterson. 'What's your game?'

'I'm overcome by 'ow well you look,' said Old Iron admiringly. 'I'm a new neighbour, lodging with me son Luke at Mrs Martin's. Name of Edwards, 'Enry Edwards. I 'appened to hear you unfortunately lost yer 'usband two years ago, and 'ave been poorly ever since. I also 'eard yer kind 'eart's ailin' a bit. Might I step in and 'ave a consoling chat with yer?'

'No, you might not,' said Mrs Paterson, 'I don't know you from Adam, nor don't I want to. I don't 'old with strangers knockin' at me door on a peaceful Sunday afternoon, and you can oblige me by takin' yourself off.'

'You've got a point, Mrs Paterson, I won't say you ain't,' said Old Iron, 'but me call is a neighbourly one, take my word for it. I've always 'ad a reputation for bein' a good neighbour. On top of that, I used to do a bit of healin'.'

'If you're one of them faith 'ealers, you can get off my doorstep,' said Mrs Paterson. 'I've 'eard about faith 'ealers, and how they tell cripples to stand up and throw their crutches away, and that when they do they just fall over.'

'No, that sort of thing ain't in my vernacular, Mrs Paterson,' said Old Iron. 'Might I mention me son Luke told me he 'ad the pleasure of meetin' you this mornin'? He was that sorry to 'ear you'd been widowed at an early age, said what a cryin' shame it was. You can't be much more than thirty-six at this exact minute. I don't wonder you suffered repercussion'ry shock that I 'ear has made you poorly. I'll admit you look well, but it's underneath, ain't it? I know just 'ow you feel. I lost me own better 'alf a few years back, which makes me genuine understandin' of yer condition. Might I step in and—'

'Stay where you are,' said Mrs Paterson, handsome figure bridling. 'Me lovin' daughter's out and I'm all alone in this 'ouse, and if you try to put just one foot over me doorstep, I'll go and get me parlour poker.'

'I'm understandin' of yer womanly fears, Mrs Paterson,' said Old Iron, nodding sagely, 'but I'm more well-known for bein' a protector of ladies than a Burglar Bill. In fact, I ain't known as a Burglar Bill at all, 'aving lived an honest life from the time I was born, when the Lord gifted me with a bit of a talent for healin'. Concernin' you bein' poorly and 'aving a weak 'eart as well, might I enquire as to what medicine yer doctor prescribes for you?'

'I don't take any medicine, if you must know,' said Mrs Paterson, her fulsomeness a barrier at the open door. 'Medicine's all right for coughs and flu, but it don't do anything for a widow still weak from shock. As long as I've got me daughter lookin' after me, I can manage to put up with me condition, though it's an effort some days.'

'I couldn't agree with yer more about medicine,' said Old Iron, looking professionally dignified in his frock coat. 'Could I take up more of yer time by askin' about the food you eat?'

'Wait a minute,' said Mrs Paterson, 'I never 'eard the like of this, a stranger knockin' at me door on a Sunday afternoon and askin' me questions as if 'e was me own doctor. What I eat is me own affair.'

'Did I tell yer me name's 'Enry Edwards and that I'm a new neighbour?' said Old Iron confidingly.

'I don't care if your name's Stanley Baldwin,

you've got no right to be standin' on me doorstep askin' me personal questions,' said Mrs Paterson. 'What d'you want to know about me food for?'

'It's diet, yer know,' said Old Iron, 'it's the proper diet that's a lot more healin' than medicine. D'you eat well and 'earty, Mrs Paterson?'

'I eat when me daughter Doreen cooks for me. Well, I peck at it, not bein' the woman I was.'

'Mrs Paterson, I can tell yer that the woman you are is a credit to the country. I'm meanin' the look of you. I 'ope I ain't steppin' out of line by advisin' you you're as 'andsome as Queen Mary. Mind, you're a lot younger. Of course, a weak 'eart and an ailin' condition don't always show on women. They've got a brave way of keepin' it from being noticeable. Could I ask if yer daughter serves fish and chips sometimes?'

'Fish and chips?' Mrs Paterson gaped.

'With the occasional Guinness?' suggested Old Iron, looking medically wise.

'I'm 'earing things,' said Mrs Paterson, and would have shut the door on him if she hadn't had a slight feeling of being mesmerized.

'I can't say I'm qualified in me doctorin',' said Old Iron, 'and I don't use me talent professional, like, nor for money. I'm a metal worker, yer know, and I only offer me healin' advice out of me sympathy for sufferin' humanity, more especially sufferin' women. Might I step in for a minute?'

'No,' said Mrs Paterson. 'Well, all right, just for a minute.'

She took him into the kitchen, and there Old Iron gravely informed her that fried fish and chips with a Guinness could do wonders for her weak heart. She told him she wasn't going to be led up the garden by that sort of advice, which sounded like being told to take to drink.

'Don't you believe it,' said Old Iron reassuringly. 'The occasional Guinness ain't takin' to drink, not by a long shot, it's food for the ailing and it gives yer a lift as well.'

Mrs Paterson wasn't ailing, of course, nor did she have a weak heart. What she did have was a widow's wish to keep her daughter as a permanent companion. So she couldn't make out why this new neighbour was getting her into a state of confusion, when she could have avoided it by simply telling him to shift himself off her doorstep when he first began to talk about his healing gifts.

'You don't think I'm goin' to rush off and buy meself fish and chips and a bottle of Guinness come tomorrow evenin', do you?' she said.

'Now I don't want you to do that at all,' said Old Iron. 'Rushin' off anywhere might seriously damage yer weak 'eart, Mrs Paterson. No, a gentle stroll to the friendly fish and chip shop in the Walworth Road is more like it. I'd offer to accompany yer, but I'm usually busy of an evenin'. Still, sometime maybe, as a kind duty to me patient.'

'Patient? I'm not your patient,' said Mrs Paterson. 'The very idea.'

'Well, I'll look in on you occasional out of neighbourliness,' said Old Iron pacifically. 'You'll excuse me if I don't stay for a cup of tea.'

'Kind of you, I'm sure,' said Mrs Paterson.

'I've got things to do just now. It's been a pleasure 'aving this 'eart to 'eart with yer, Mrs Paterson. Good afternoon for the present, like.'

'Good afternoon, Mr Edwards,' she said, and

when he'd gone she sat down and told herself that if he called again she'd get rid of him double quick. She'd been talked to until she didn't know where she was. Now she badly needed a cup of tea. She made herself a pot and drank two cups, which helped her to recover from feeling mesmerized. Afterwards, she emptied the teapot and washed up the cup and saucer. She needn't tell Doreen.

Old Iron and Luke compared notes over Sunday tea. Luke thought his old man had taken things a bit far with Mrs Paterson.

'No, just so-so,' said Old Iron, peeling shrimps. 'You've got to lay it on a bit for a woman like 'er. But 'aving found Doreen in the park, you didn't get very far with 'er, eh, me lad? Treatin' 'er to a cup of tea was all right, but she still didn't let you walk her home.'

'I think I've made the mistake of pushin' her a bit today,' said Luke, 'but a girl like that, well, who wants to keep passin' her by?'

'And you teased 'er, did you?' grinned Old Iron. 'You let 'er think that as she won't go out with you, you'd ask 'er mum instead.'

'She didn't think that made much sense,' said Luke, 'I think she thought I was pushy just bein' there.'

'Well, young ladies don't fancy backward blokes, I can tell yer that for nothing,' said Old Iron. 'What they like is a bit of the old dash and go, and a feelin' they might get kissed as soon as it's dark. Not right off, of course. Give 'em a week, say. Mind you, Luke, your late mum clouted me when I first kissed 'er, and I'd known 'er a fortnight by then.'

'Wasn't it dark enough?' asked Luke, tackling peeled shrimps with bread and butter.

'Wasn't dark at all,' said Old Iron, 'it was in broad daylight, in the middle of a Bank Holiday funfair at 'Ampstead 'Eath. Well, you should've seen 'er in a white hat with flowers all round it, and a white dress with a pink sash. Turned me reckless. So Maggie clouted me, and told me to wait till it was dark. What you've got to do, say, is wait till Doreen starts callin' you Luke. That's the first sign of a girl lookin' for a bit of dash and go. Now, as for 'er unfortunate mum, there's a widow that needs a fairish bit of workin' on.'

'And that's part of it, is it, tellin' her that fish and chips'll solve all her problems?'

'She'll be obstinate,' said Old Iron, 'seein' she don't want 'em solved. Well, she don't 'ave any, except wantin' to turn Doreen into 'er nursemaid, but that's a problem and a 'alf. I think I'll pop round tomorrow evenin'. Might give me a chance to 'ave a look at Doreen, the nice young lady that's makin' the mistake of thinkin' 'er mum can't do without 'er.'

Over tea, prepared by Doreen, Mrs Paterson asked her daughter if she'd met somebody in the park.

'Somebody?' said Doreen.

'Well, I did wonder what you went to the park by yourself for.'

'It wasn't to meet anyone,' said Doreen.

'You've always got me if you ever want someone to walk with,' said Mrs Paterson with a loving smile. 'I could always manage a little walk in Ruskin Park. Here, what d'you think, I 'ad Mrs Martin's lodger call this afternoon, the father of that young man who made a nuisance of 'imself outside our door this mornin'. He 'ad the cheek to tell me he'd done some healin' of people in 'is time, and that he could 'elp me with me weak 'eart. Eat fish and chips sometimes, 'e said, and with a glass of Guinness. Me, that's never been a drinkin' woman.'

Doreen laughed.

'He sounds like a joker, Mum, they're both jokers,' she said.

'Beg your pardon, love?'

'Well, that's what I thought about his son while he was bein' a nuisance,' said Doreen. 'And it's got to be a joke, his dad recommendin' fish and chips for your weak heart. By the way, Mum, was it the doctor who said your heart was weak?'

'It was ages ago, when I was in the worst of me shock,' said Mrs Paterson. 'Yes, I'm sure it was the doctor, but I didn't want to say anything, I don't like burdenin' you with me worries. As for that Mr Edwards, I sent 'im packin'. Him and 'is fish and chips.'

'And a Guinness as well,' said Doreen, keeping a straight face.

'The less we see of 'im and 'is son, the better, love. Did you think the son had sort of shifty eyes?'

'I just noticed he 'ad a lot of sauce,' said Doreen. 'I wonder if a nice retired gent lookin' for lodgings will see our card in the newsagent's window?'

During the morning break at St John's Church School the following day, Mr Hill inspected Boadicea's chariot in company with Freddy and Cassie. A crowd of other pupils looked on agog.

'Seems all right,' said Mr Hill. 'Yes, I daresay that could carry Queen Boadicea without falling apart.'

'Yes, ain't Freddy a clever boy?' said Cassie, which made some kids hoot.

'Oh, yer clever boy, Freddy!'

'Someone askin' for a wallop, are they?' said Freddy.

'Not here, Freddy,' said Mr Hill. 'What's that in your carrier bag, Queen Boadicea?'

'It's me sister Nellie's nightshirt that she don't want any more,' said Cassie. 'It's for Freddy to wear as Caesar's togger.'

'Toga?' said Mr Hill.

'Yes, sir,' said Cassie.

'You Cassie, you ain't brought that with you, 'ave you?' said Freddy.

'Let's have a look at it,' said Mr Hill.

'Excuse me, Mister Hill,' said Freddy, 'but no-one 'ere wants to see her sister's left-off night-gown.'

Kids yelled.

'Yes, we do! Show us it, Cassie!'

'She'd better not if she wants to keep on livin',' said Freddy.

'But you've got to look like Caesar, Freddy,' said Cassie who, being a girl, was a bit vague about what it meant to be a bloke's mate. As far as she was concerned, she was true to her dreams and imaginings, and at present she was imagining Freddy as a noble Caesar in Nellie's cast-off nightie.

'I'm resigning,' said Freddy. 'I'm not wearin' that thing, not when I've got to be run over as well. Would you accept me resignation, Mister Hill?'

'Can't be done, Freddy,' said Mr Hill.

'Come on, Cassie,' sang a girl, 'let's see what Freddy's goin' to look like in yer sister's nightie.'

'It's just right,' said Cassie, and opened up the carrier bag. Freddy swooped, picked her up, slung her over his shoulder and set about carting her back into the school and smacking her bottom. Cassie was enthralled. 'Oh, me 'ero,' she cried, dropping the carrier bag, 'are yer goin' to run off with me in me chariot?'

Into the school Freddy carried her. Kids, rushing, picked up the bag and disgorged its contents, a girl's flannel nightie. They howled with laughter.

'I think a sheet is called for,' said Mr Hill.

'What for, sir?' asked a girl.

'For mighty Caesar's togger,' said Mr Hill.

Inside the school, Cassie was asking an indignant question.

'Freddy, what you doin' of?'

'Smackin' yer bottom,' said Freddy.

Chapter Nine

A French ferry docked at Newhaven at midday. There were enough men at work for the docking to take place, but no porters were available. They were still on strike. All disembarking passengers had to manhandle their own luggage through to passport control and Customs. Mr Ronald Ponsonby, dapper in a light grey suit and straw boater, carried his suitcase into the shed. He showed his passport, that of a British subject by name of Joseph Victor Wright, and went on to Customs, where an officer asked him if he had anything to declare. A bottle of cognac, he said. That's all, sir? That's all, he said, smiling. He had a pleasant smile. The officer asked for no duty to be paid, and Mr Ponsonby passed through the shed and made for the railway terminal. There were no trains running, but he was able after a while to hire a taxi to drive him to London at the stated rate per mile, both ways, plus a tip of two pounds, which the cabby thought handsome. Mr Ronald Ponsonby had an independent income, and if his twin brother Gerald did come to be hanged, that income would be doubled. Not that Mr Ronald Ponsonby wished it that way.

Lodgings. Yes, in Walworth. Well, he would see if anything suitable was on offer. If not, a decent hotel could accommodate him for a couple of days while he searched around. He had the taxi drop him off in the Walworth Road, outside a newsagent. He asked the cabby to wait a moment, then looked at the cards in the window. Well, well.

Room to let for a retired gentleman at five shillings a week. Apply Mrs Paterson, 12 Morecambe Street.

He thanked the cabby for a comfortable journey, paid him and let him go.

Mrs Paterson, answering a knock on her front door, found a middle-aged gent on her step. Yes, a gent all right. What a nice suit.

Mr Ronald Ponsonby, wearing spectacles of plain glass, smiled and lifted his boater.

'Good afternoon, madam.'

'Well, yes, good afternoon,' said Mrs Paterson. 'Might I ask what your pleasure is? I 'ope,' she said, seeing the suitcase, 'you 'aven't come to try and sell me something?'

'Am I addressing Mrs Paterson?'

'That's me.'

'You've a room to let?'

'Oh, that.' Mrs Paterson's fine-looking lashes fluttered. 'I forgot all about it. Well, bless me, me daughter only put the card in the window on Saturday. 'Ave you come to take a look at the room? And are you a retired gent?'

'Indeed I am, Mrs Paterson, indeed I am.' There was a perkiness about the gent. 'I've known better days, but now only have enough to keep body and soul together. Comfortably together, comfortably, you know, as long as I live sensibly. A single room is all I need at my time of life, and five shillings a week will suit me very well. My name is Wright, Joseph Wright. Might I have the pleasure of seeing the room?'

Mrs Paterson looked him over. He didn't have a lot of flesh about him, nor did he seem to have much muscle, just a bit of perkiness. So if he was having her on, if he was hoping to get into the house to pinch something, it wouldn't tax her to give him a couple of backhanders. She was fulsome of body herself and strong-armed, even if people did think she was ailing a bit. It was only natural that a widow didn't want all her children to get married and leave her.

'Well, all right, you can come in and take a look at the room,' she said.

'A pleasure, Mrs Paterson, a pleasure.' Mr Ronald Ponsonby stepped in and followed her through the passage and up the stairs. Mrs Paterson showed him the upstairs back. It was fully furnished, with a single brass-and-iron bed as its main note of comfort, and a fireplace to offer heat and cosiness in the winter. 'Excellent,' said Mr Ronald Ponsonby, 'and as clean as a new pin, if I'm not mistaken. I had just such a room when lodging with my sister, but she, alas, has died. A Peckham lady, you know, poor but genteel, and unmarried, as I am. I'll take the room.'

'You will? Lord, I'm breathless at you bein' so quick at makin' up your mind, Mr— what did you say yer name was?'

'Wright, Mr Wright.'

'You're respectable, of course.'

'Retired, quiet and respectable.'

'Well, I suppose it's all right for you to 'ave the room, and I'll get me daughter to meet you when she comes in from work. I mean, you want to move in straightaway, like?'

'Now, yes. Thank you, Mrs Paterson, a pleasure

to have found you, a pleasure.' He peered amiably at her through his glasses.

'Well, I'll leave you to settle in, then,' said Mrs Paterson, and did so. She might have stayed and had a chat with him, but she couldn't honestly say he interested her all that much. Although he had a perky air, she preferred much more vigorous men, the kind who didn't talk like they worked for solicitors. Still, he'd do as a lodger. She sensed he'd keep himself to himself, but she could always use his presence as something that gave her the kind of responsibilities she couldn't cope with unless she had Doreen's help.

As for that other man, the one lodging with Mrs Martin, he needed seeing to, he did. Eat fish and chips sometimes, with a glass of Guinness, he'd said. What impudence. Mind, at least he didn't talk like he worked for a solicitor, and he had more chat than a flock of magpies. He'd better not call again. She'd show him the sharp end of the parlour poker if he did. A man like that wouldn't have to call more than three times before he'd be telling her she didn't have a weak heart. He'd say he'd healed it. Her condition wasn't his business. It was the condition of a widow who had only one of her children still at home with her.

'You're back from the factory, Sammy?' said Susie, entering his office.

'Yes, this is me in person at me desk,' said Sammy.

'No trouble?'

'It's all gone quiet and peaceful,' said Sammy.

'Good. There's some messages on your desk for

you to attend to as you're there in person. I'm goin' now, it's gone four.'

'Right you are, Mrs Adams, off you go, see you here in the mornin'.'

'Beg your pardon?' said Susie, a picture of a stylish personal assistant in her dark blue costume and white blouse.

'Yes, good night, Mrs Adams, I'm up to me ears myself.'

'What d'you mean, Sammy Adams, you'll see me here in the mornin'?'

Sammy looked up at her. Susie looked down at him. Sammy coughed.

'Jigger me,' he said, 'did I muck that one up, Susie?'

'Sammy Adams, did you forget you were married to me?'

'Temp'rarily, Susie, I wasn't myself, it's—'

'Wait till you get home,' said Susie, 'you'll find yourself locked out. And here's a bit more trouble.' She leaned far over his desk and reached down to his middle. Sammy almost turned a somersault in his chair.

'Perishin' nutcrackers – you Susie—'

'You Sammy,' said Susie, and ran laughing from his office. She met Doreen in the corridor.

'Oh, you goin', Mrs Adams? Good night.'

'Good night, Doreen. How's your mum, by the way?'

'Bearin' up,' said Doreen.

'It's been two years now, hasn't it?' said Susie.

'Yes, but she still feels the loss,' said Doreen.

What a nice girl she was, thought Susie, and the most willing of all of them here. That mum of hers is trying to hang on to her.

'Oh, well, break out now and again, Doreen,' said Susie, and went on her way. Otherwise she might have said more than she should.

The switchboard buzzed and Doreen dashed into the general office.

She answered the call.

'Adams Enterprises. Can I help you?'

'Hello?'

'Adams Enterprises. Can I help you, sir?'

'Is that you?'

'Pardon? Who's callin', please?'

'Me,' said Luke.

'Excuse me, who d'you wish to speak to?'

'Is that Lady Vi?'

The penny dropped for Doreen then.

'D'you mind gettin' off the line?' she whispered.

'I'm in a phone box,' said Luke, 'and it cost me tuppence to get through. Can I give you a lift 'ome at five-thirty? I'll wait outside.'

'Blessed cheek, phonin' me at work.'

'Well, I felt a bit desp'rate,' said Luke.

'Oh, hard luck, then.'

'I'll still try waitin' for you, Lady Vi.'

'That'll be more hard luck,' said Doreen, and rang off.

'Who was that?' asked Lottie.

'Wrong number,' said Doreen.

'Sounded a funny wrong number,' said Lottie.

The switchboard buzzed again.

'Adams Enterprises. Can I help you?'

'Oh, is that Doreen? This is Rosie here, Rosie Adams. Can I speak to Daddy, please?'

'I'll put you through, Rosie.' Doreen connected with Boots. 'It's your daughter, Mister Adams.'

'Right. Thanks, Doreen,' said Boots. 'Hello?'

'Oh, hello, Daddy,' said Rosie. 'I've just got home from school. You know when we were playing garden cricket yesterday and Mummy shut her eyes and lashed out with the bat, and the ball went right over the hedge and broke one of the windows in next door's kitchen? Well, Mr and Mrs Fletcher were away for the weekend, so we couldn't tell them. They've just come back. Mummy's so embarrassed that I said you'd take the blame. Well, you've got ever such broad shoulders and you don't get embarrassed like ladies do, so on your way home could you knock on Mr Fletcher's door and tell him you broke the window and that you'll pay for it?'

'All right, poppet, anything to spare Emily's blushes.'

'You're ever such a sport, Daddy. We don't want Mr and Mrs Fletcher to think the window was broken by burglars, do we?'

'I'll sacrifice my good name, Rosie.'

'I said you would. I'm going next door myself now, just to tell Mr Fletcher you'll be calling to put things right. Anyway, he might not believe that Mummy broke it. I mean, she doesn't look as if she could hit any ball hard enough to break any window, does she? You look as if you could break ten a day.'

'I'm flattered,' said Boots.

'That's all right, Daddy, we all feel for you about having to confess – oh, and don't forget we'd like to have the ball back. Daddy, is that you laughing?'

'Yes,' said Boots, 'I think it's me.'

'Cheeky thing,' said Rosie, and giggled. 'See you when you get home, Daddy.'

Boots smiled as he replaced the phone. Family

life with Emily, Tim and Rosie was never dull. The General Strike was breaking up, summer had brought blue skies even above smoky old London, and once the trial of Gerald Ponsonby was out of the way, the family could look forward to their holiday.

Boots was not to know that a threat to the very existence of some family members had arrived in the shape of a dapper-looking lodger in the upstairs back of the house Doreen Paterson shared with her widowed mother.

Doreen was by herself when she descended the office stairs at the side of the shop and came out through the door. She looked around. He wasn't there. She'd put him off. She began her walk to the tram stop, her heels clicking on the pavement.

Luke, wheeling his bike, crossed the road and caught up with her.

'Evenin', Lady Vi.'

She turned her head and saw him. He gave her a smile.

'Excuse me, do I know you?' she asked.

'Want a lift?' he said.

She looked at the crowds milling around the Junction. She stopped.

'Well, all right,' she said, 'thanks.' She perched herself on the carrier.

'Comfy?' said Luke.,

'Fairly,' said Doreen, 'and you needn't ask about me legs.'

'Off we go, then,' said Luke, and away he went, in and out of the traffic. Young blokes among the crowds whistled at Doreen's flapper look.

'I don't know what some blokes get excited

about,' she said. 'Are you workin' or on strike?'

'On strike,' said Luke, 'but I 'ave to do picket duty. The firm's engineerin' works are in Camberwell New Road.' He cycled steadily towards Walworth.

'You had a cheek, phonin' me at our office,' said Doreen.

'Still, we had a nice chat,' said Luke.

'I think you're a bit forward,' said Doreen.

'I think I'm gettin' fond of you,' said Luke.

'Crikey, you don't give up, do you?' said Doreen.

'Well, 'aving found you,' said Luke, 'I don't want to lose you, Lady Vi.'

'You and your Lady Vi, you're daft,' said Doreen. The warm air lightly brushed her face and flirted with her skirt. Her legs shone and sunlight dappled her knees. A little smile showed. Well, she couldn't help finding him amusing, even if he was persistent when he shouldn't be. If her mum got to hear about that kind of persistence, it would upset her. Poor old Mum, her grievous loss was still giving her a bad time. 'Don't you have a steady girl?' she asked, as they reached the Walworth Road.

'I know a few girls,' said Luke, 'I don't know if they're steady or not.'

'Funny ha-ha,' said Doreen.

'My old man met your Ma yesterday,' said Luke.

'Oh, yes, so he did,' said Doreen, 'I was goin' to mention that. Is he all there? He told Mum fish and chips and a glass of Guinness would be good for her.'

'Well, they're good for most people,' said Luke. Bits of paper skittered about in the road. The street cleaners were still on strike. So were the drivers of the Corporation water-carts. London's gutters hadn't been washed down for a week and more.

'Eye, eye, Gladys,' called a saucy old cove from the pavement as the bike and Doreen's legs passed by.

'Mind yourself, Grandad,' called Doreen, 'or Grandma won't let you out. Listen,' she said to Luke, 'my mum thinks your dad's off 'is rocker. What's he mean, tellin' her that fish and chips would be good for her weak 'eart?'

'Oh, I think he means keepin' her company to the fish and chip shop,' said Luke.

'I'm 'earing things,' said Doreen. 'He'd better not call again, or Mum will go round to the police station.'

'That won't do any good,' said Luke, 'they don't sell fish and chips at the police station.'

Doreen's laugh, choked back, sounded like a gurgle.

'You're both daft,' she said, 'you and your dad.'

Luke turned into East Street and cycled down to Morecambe Street.

'Tell your mum my old man's got a kind heart,' he said.

'I bet. Stop 'ere, please,' she said at the entrance to Morecambe Street. Her mum might just be looking out for her, and she'd get the wind up if she saw her on Luke's bike. Luke stopped and she put her feet to the ground. 'Thanks,' she said, 'and I 'ope you understand Mum has to come first with me.'

'I hope it won't be forever,' said Luke, and let her go on her way without following her. He waited until she'd entered her house before he went on to his lodgings.

* * *

'What?' said Doreen.

'Yes, we got a lodger already,' said Mrs Paterson, sounding as if she'd done well despite not being the woman she'd once been. ''E's a gent all right an' retired, but not all that old. More middle-aged, like. 'E's not been here long, but 'e's settling in. Perhaps you'd best go up and meet 'im. His name's Mr Wright. I'll put the kettle on, lovey, I can do that, and you can make the pot of tea when you come down.'

'Yes, I think I'd better meet 'im,' said Doreen, and up she went. She knocked on the door of the upstairs back. Mr Ronald Ponsonby opened it. The glass of his spectacles twinkled as he peered at her. 'Oh, how'd you do,' said Doreen, 'I'm Mrs Paterson's daughter.'

'Good evening, Miss Paterson, good evening,' smiled Mr Ronald Ponsonby with a perky little nod of his head. 'My name is Wright, Mr Joseph Wright.'

'The room suits you, you're settling in?' said Doreen.

'Everything is excellent.' Mr Ronald Ponsonby looked her over. What a pretty girl, what pretty legs. How nice it would be to stand at the foot of the stairs and to watch her coming down from the landing. 'One room is all I need, yes, all I need.'

'Well, that's good,' said Doreen and on a practical note, 'Has my mother given you a rent book?'

'Alas, I fear not,' he said.

What a funny old geezer, thought Doreen. But he looked all right, very neat and tidy all over, including his moustache and beard.

'Did you pay 'er the first week's rent, Mr Wright?'

'Alas once more, Miss Paterson, I fear not. But I will pay now, yes. Here we are.' He extracted two half-crowns from his pocket and handed them to her.

'Thanks,' said Doreen, frankly happy to have the extra income. 'Oh, you ought to turn the bed-clothes down and air the bed now the weather's warm.'

'Of course, yes, I'll do that. Thank you, Miss Paterson.'

'I'll get a rent book for you,' said Doreen. ''Ope you'll be nice and comfortable here.'

'I'm sure I will.'

'Good evenin', then,' said Doreen, and went to her own room to take her hat off and run a comb through her hair. Coming out, she descended from the landing. Mr Wright appeared in the passage below. He smiled up at her. Delicious, he thought, such very pretty legs, and the suspicion too of the hem of a very pretty slip.

'Ah,' he said, 'I was about to intrude on your mother and ask where the – ah, amenities are.'

'Oh, the little room's on the landing,' said Doreen, 'right next to your room, and there's a handbasin as well.'

'Thank you, Miss Paterson, thank you.'

'Don't mention it, Mr Wright,' said Doreen. 'Oh, and when you want a bath, there's the public baths in Manor Place, which is across the Walworth Road opposite Browning Street. Mum and me go there every week.'

'I shall avail myself of the pleasure, Miss Paterson, yes, thank you.'

'That's all right,' said Doreen, and joined her mum in the kitchen, telling her she thought the lodger was a bit quaint, but that she didn't mind anyone being like that at five bob a week. She'd collected the first week in advance, she said, the usual thing to do, and would buy a rent book for him.

'Yes, I'll let you do that, love,' said Mrs Paterson, 'I'll leave it to you to see to those sort of things. You look after collectin' the rent and put it with the 'ousekeeping. What a blessing I've got you to rely on. The kettle's nearly boilin', so perhaps you could make a nice pot of tea now.'

'Yes, all right, Mum,' said Doreen, but thought of Susie then, and how she'd told her to give herself a break now and again.

Mrs Fletcher, an attractive woman of twenty-five, answered a ring on her doorbell.

'Good evening, Mrs Fletcher,' said Boots with a smile, and little tingles ran down Mrs Fletcher's back. She and her husband were new neighbours of Boots and his family, which included his mother and step-father.

'Oh, hello, Mr Adams.'

'Enjoy your weekend away?' said Boots.

'Yes, we went to my parents.'

'Unfortunately, you've got a broken kitchen window,' said Boots.

'Yes, we thought at first that a burglar might have got in until your daughter explained,' said Mrs Fletcher. She'd been married five years and wished her husband made tingles run down her back.

'I'm the culprit,' said Boots. 'Garden cricket. My apologies. I'll pay the cost of putting a new pane in, just let me know how much when it's done. Apologize to Mr Fletcher for me.'

'He's in the bath just now, but thanks so much for coming to tell me.'

'Could you do me a favour?' asked Boots with another smile.

'Love to,' said Mrs Fletcher, enjoying more tingles.

'Could I have the ball back?'

Mrs Fletcher laughed.

'I'll get it,' she said, and she fetched it, handing it to him with her lashes fluttering.

'Many thanks,' said Boots, and smiled again and left. He found his family in the downstairs kitchen with Chinese Lady, who always prepared a communal supper for all of them. 'I've just seen Mrs Fletcher, Em. Here's our ball back, Tim. Stow it away. I've arranged to pay the repair bill, and there are no hard feelings.'

'What a relief,' said Emily, 'I felt awful about it, me breakin' a neighbour's window when I'm a wife and mother.'

'Oh, I expect Mrs Fletcher didn't mind a husband and father coming to say he broke it,' said Rosie, 'especially when it was Daddy.'

'I don't know why you can't play cricket with a soft ball,' said Chinese Lady.

'Nana, not cricket, not proper cricket,' said Rosie.

'Well, I don't want any more broken windows,' said Chinese Lady, 'or I won't be able to hold me head up. Breakin' windows is like hooliganism.'

'Well, Nana love,' said Rosie, 'Daddy and Uncle Tommy and Annabelle and me won't break any windows now we're playing Saturday afternoon tennis.'

*   *   *

It was Doreen who answered a knock on the front door at half-past seven and found a very manly-looking middle-aged gent in a frock coat on the step.

'Evenin', young lady,' said Old Iron, tipping his bowler hat. 'Might I be havin' the pleasure of lookin' at yer mum's young daughter? If so—'

'Wait a bit,' said Doreen, 'I think I'm on to you. Are you Luke Edwards' dad?'

'I 'ave that honour,' said Old Iron.

'Some honour,' said sprightly Doreen, 'he's a saucebox, and so are you. I like to 'ave respect for people your age, but what d'you mean by tellin' my mum to eat fish and chips more often, with a Guinness?'

'You're Doreen?' said Old Iron, eyeing her with fatherly appreciation for his son's taste. 'Well, Doreen, I 'appen to be a bit of a healer, yer know.'

'No, I don't know, and I'm Miss Paterson, if you don't mind.'

'All the same, I've got to compliment Luke on bein' right,' said Old Iron.

'Right about what?' asked Doreen, liking the cheeky old codger and his weatherbeaten looks.

'Well, 'e said if all the prettiest young female angels was rolled into one, that one would be Miss Doreen Paterson, 'e said.'

'Oh, he did, did he?' Doreen's eyes were bright with laughter.

'Something like that,' said Old Iron, 'and now I'm 'aving the pleasure of seein' you for meself, I concur.'

'You what?'

'I agree.'

'Oh, you do, do you?' said Doreen. 'And I

suppose your son said I 'ad wings as well?'

'No, I can't rightly recall 'e did say that—'

'Well, he's slipped up, then, 'asn't he? Why shouldn't I 'ave wings if I'm all the prettiest angels rolled into one?'

'That's a point,' said Old Iron, nodding sagely. 'I'll talk to 'im about it. Meanwhile, regardin' your dear old Ma and 'er weak ticker, might I 'ave the pleasure of once more givin' 'er the benefit of a consultation?'

'Not likely,' said Doreen. Wait a bit, she thought, why not? Might do her mum good.

Her mum called then.

'Who's that you're talkin' to, Doreen?'

'Just a neighbour, Mum, won't be a tick. All right,' she said to Old Iron, 'go into the parlour and I'll send Mum in. You sure you've got a gift for 'ealing?'

'Sure as chickens lay eggs,' said Old Iron.

'Some chickens lay bad eggs,' said Doreen, but allowed him to step in, at which point the lodger came down the stairs, his boater on and a walking-stick in his hand.

'Just on my way out for a stroll, Miss Paterson,' he smiled, 'I've a liking for being out and about. Good evening,' he said to Old Iron, who gave him a puzzled look. Mr Ronald Ponsonby left the house. Street kids spotted his natty suit and perky boater at once.

'Strike a light, 'oo's 'e?'

'Cat's Sunday dinner, I betcher.'

'Oi, mister, polish yer watch and chain for yer?'

Mr Ronald Ponsonby strolled on.

Old Iron entered the parlour, and Doreen went to talk to her mum.

'Mum, a neighbour wants to see you,' she said.

'What neighbour?' asked Mrs Paterson, looking up from a copy of *Home Chat*.

'A 'elpful one. In the parlour. Go on, Mum.'

Mrs Paterson took herself into the parlour.

'Well, 'ello again, Mrs Paterson,' said Old Iron.

'What d'you want?'

'I'm 'ere in me consultin' capacity,' said Old Iron breezily. 'My, yer lookin' better already. It's that young look of yours, you've got a naturally young look, but I ain't supposin' yer condition still ain't a sufferin' one. Anyway, put yer 'at on and we'll go for a walk, and maybe finish up at the fish and chip shop.'

'I'm not goin' out walkin' with you, I'm not up to any walkin'. What's more, I've 'ad me evenin' meal and don't need any fish and chips, thank you.'

'I've eaten as well,' said Old Iron, 'but by the time we get to the shop, I wouldn't be surprised if we both don't fancy some fried plaice an' chips. Might I ask who the bloke with a beard and specs is?'

''E's our lodger,' said Mrs Paterson. 'Doreen and me decided to let the upstairs back.'

Ruddy tea cosies, I've got competition, thought Old Iron. That's put me on me mettle, that has. He smiled.

'Well, let's go walkin', Mrs Paterson. Good for yer condition, a little walk each evenin'. I knew a poor unfortunate woman once that couldn't 'ardly put one foot in front of the other, but with a little bit of me medicine, I 'ad 'er walkin' a mile every day after a couple of weeks.'

'What medicine?' asked Mrs Paterson, feeling mesmerized again.

'Oh, just the kind that tells a woman 'er feet are made for a jaunt 'ere and a jaunt there, yer know. So put yer titfer on, lady, and out we go.'

'Me 'eart won't stand it, I tell yer,' said Mrs Paterson, but weakly.

'Well, you'll 'ave me right next to yer all the way,' said Old Iron, 'and if yer do come over a bit faint, we won't be far from a pub and a glass of Guinness.'

''Ere, don't you try pourin' drink into me.'

'Rely on me, Mrs Paterson.'

Mrs Paterson could hardly believe herself five minutes later. She was out and walking, her unofficial doctor beside her and giving her the benefit of a fund of cheerful chat. She was out for an hour and a half, and when she got back she collapsed into her kitchen chair.

'Oh, lor',' said Doreen, 'what's he done, worn you out?'

'Where's me smellin'-salts?'

'Here they are.' Doreen brought the bottle to her, from the mantelpiece. Mrs Paterson drew the stopper and took a sniff. 'Mum, you all right?'

'All right?' Mrs Paterson looked dazed. 'Doreen, I don't know if I'm on me 'ead or 'eels. That man, well, 'e's been me death tonight. Don't be surprised if I don't last till mornin'.'

'Mum, where is he, and what 'appened?'

''E saw me to me door, said I was comin' on a treat, and then off 'e went.' Mrs Paterson took another sniff. 'As for what 'appened, I can 'ardly bear to tell yer.'

'You've got to,' said Doreen.

'Oh, lor',' said her dizzy mum. 'Well, I 'ad plaice and chips in the fried fish shop with 'im, then a

Guinness in a pub, and then – oh, me hour of ruination—'

'Mum, 'e didn't!'

'I can't remember what 'e did,' said Mrs Paterson, 'but I did a knees-up. Me, in my condition. Doreen, could yer make me a nice 'ot cup of tea and then 'elp me to me bed?'

Doreen had a coughing fit while she was filling the kettle.

Mr Ronald Ponsonby re-entered the house at ten o'clock and went quietly up to his room. He had done nothing untoward during the evening, he had merely dined in the West End.

Chapter Ten

Mrs Paterson declared herself too ill to get up the next morning. Doreen said never mind, just stay there and I'll bring you a cup of tea and a slice of toast before I go off to work. You're a kind, loving daughter, said Mrs Paterson.

But she was up when the lodger came down at ten o'clock and smilingly informed her he would be out for the day. He was one for getting about, he said, yes indeed, and thought he would let her know. And out he went, in perky style. Mrs Paterson put her best hat on, found some money in a cup on the dresser, and she went out too, to buy herself a new blouse. She ran into Mrs Martin.

'Oh, goin' out, are yer, Mrs Paterson?'

'I thought I would, just to get a bit of air, Mrs Martin.'

'Good for yer, a bit of air is, except there's more of it about in Southend than 'ere. Still, there's enough to go round, I 'ope. I must say yer lookin' a treat this mornin'.'

'Well, I always do me best to try and look better than I feel. Oh, we got our lodger, Mrs Martin, 'e come and knocked yesterday and we've given 'im our upstairs back.'

'Funny you should say that, Mrs Paterson, I thought I saw the gent come out of yer 'ouse a bit ago. Middle-aged, I thought, and dressed quite nice.'

'Yes, 'e's not all that old, but 'e's still a retired gent. Well, I'd best get on.'

'Yes, don't let me keep yer, Mrs Paterson. I must say me own lodgers is provin' friendly and well-be'aved.'

'Pleased to 'ear it, I'm sure,' said Mrs Paterson, and hurried on her way in case the well-behaved Mr Henry Edwards put in an appearance.

Mr Ronald Ponsonby spent the day making enquiries.

Mr Finch, having the day off, met Boots and Sammy for lunch in the pub opposite the shop and offices. He knew a great deal about post-war Germany and its dormant militarism. He considered, however, that the greatest threat to Europe was not the clique of generals still smarting from defeat in 1918, but a political rabble-rouser called Adolf Hitler. Over the beer and sandwiches, Mr Finch seemed to consider it necessary to let Boots and Sammy know just what a menace the man was, having declared himself leader of a National Socialist Party with the intention of militarizing it and using it to overthrow the German government. His further intention was to create a dictatorship and build a greater Germany. That would mean war.

'Not with me,' said Sammy. 'I'm not playing, I've got a business to run. Fortunately for me peace of mind, I'm not able to believe it'll happen.'

'Do you know General Sir Henry Simms?' asked Boots of his step-father, and Mr Finch smiled.

'Slightly,' he said.

'He shares your opinions,' said Boots.

'He's a thinking man,' said Mr Finch.

'Something's takin' the flavour out of my pork sandwich,' said Sammy.

'Hitler will need the support of the German people,' said Boots.

'If he can get the support of armament kings like Krupps and of the German army, he'll convince the German people that he can make their nation the greatest in the world,' said Mr Finch.

'He's a lunatic,' said Sammy. 'Fortunately for Adams Enterprises, I'm sane.'

'Fortunately for this country,' said Mr Finch, 'so are its people. This country, politically, is the most stable in Europe. I only hope that our government will make sure that what might happen won't happen.'

'Let's have another old ale,' said Boots. 'Your round, Sammy.'

'Somehow,' said Sammy, 'there's always someone tryin' to ruin my pocket.'

Luke was again able to be in his waiting position a little before five-thirty. The strike really was tottering. Workers in various parts of the country were going back to their machines, fed-up with a no-hope situation. Picket lines elsewhere were thinner. Luke reckoned the whole thing would be called off in a day or so. He was willing to get back to work himself, his sympathies largely with the coal-miners. Meanwhile, his pursuit of Doreen engaged all his interest.

Out she came, about a minute after other girls had emerged. This time she saw Luke at once, directly opposite. So there you are, she thought. Well, I'm going to tear you into pieces, Luke

Edwards. A break in the traffic enabled her to cross the road and go straight for his jugular.

'How would you like a punch in the eye?' she said.

'What for?' asked Luke, thinking her a gift to his peepers.

'I'll give you what for,' said Doreen, 'sendin' your barmy dad round last night to talk my mum into gallivantin' round the pubs.'

'Me?' said Luke.

'Yes, I bet you encouraged 'im,' said Doreen. 'You ought to be ashamed. He led my mum right up the garden path, tellin' her that a nice walk to the fish and chip shop would start a cure for her weak 'eart, then draggin' her into pubs and pourin' drink into her till she didn't know where she was or who she was.'

'You sure you've got that right?' said Luke. 'What I 'eard from Old Iron—'

'Old Iron?'

'A nickname that got stuck to me dad,' said Luke.

'Serve 'im right,' said Doreen.

'What I 'eard from him,' said Luke, 'was that he and your mum enjoyed a very sociable outin' that put roses in her cheeks.'

'I 'ope I'm not goin' to have to hit you out here in front of people,' said Doreen. 'My mum, let me tell you, came 'ome all worn out last night, and this mornin' she was too faint and feeble to get out of bed.' Doreen wasn't going to let on that she'd nearly died laughing at her mum's confused tale of woe. After all, that didn't alter the fact that it wasn't right for a still grieving widow to be led into doing a knees-up in a pub. 'If I 'ave to get the doctor to her this evenin', I'm goin' to come across to your lodgings and hit your dad with a saucepan. Well, don't just stand there, Luke Edwards, you're goin' to give me a lift 'ome now, aren't you?'

'Be a pleasure, Lady Vi.'

Boots and Sammy, coming out, saw the little cameo across the road of a girl perching herself on the carrier of a young man's bike.

'That's Doreen,' said Sammy, as Luke cycled off.

'The other one's a feller,' said Boots.

'I think I've heard her mum's against fellers,' said Sammy.

'Well, I don't think Doreen is,' said Boots, 'so don't let's tell her mum.'

'Sometimes,' said Sammy, 'I think you're still tryin' to educate me.'

Luke, at Doreen's insistence, set her down before he turned into Morecambe Street. She didn't want kids to start talking, she said, because it might mean her mum would get to know she was friendly with the son of the barmy bloke who took widow women out and poured drink into them.

'I think there's been a misunderstandin',' said Luke, 'but you can believe me, I don't go in for that kind of thing myself.'

'Not much you wouldn't if you had the chance,' said Doreen. 'I bet you and your dad both go in for it. Just tell your dad that if he comes knockin' again, we'll bolt the door on him. Still, I'm grateful again for a lift 'ome. Thanks.'

'Don't mention it,' said Luke.

The moment Doreen got in, she put the kettle on in anticipation of her mum's usual request for a cup of tea. Mrs Paterson said what a nice thoughtful girl she was. Doreen said she'd run into Mr Edwards's son and had taken the opportunity to give him a piece of her mind about his dad.

'Oh, I don't want you to shoulder my burdens, Doreen love,' said Mrs Paterson. 'It's up to me to speak to Mr Edwards when I next see 'im.'

'Are you feelin' better?' asked Doreen.

'I've 'ad one or two 'eart flutters and a bit of a head,' said Mrs Paterson, looking very healthy and handsome for a suffering body, 'but I don't want you to worry, love. It's me good name that's taken the worst knock. I can't 'ardly believe I was led into doin' a knees-up.'

'Crikey, you showin' your legs in a pub, Mum,' said Doreen.

'Oh, don't talk about it,' groaned Mrs Paterson, and Doreen took herself into the scullery to look at the steaming kettle and to smother a giggle. She called, 'Is our lodger in, Mum?'

'Yes, 'e came in about ten minutes ago after bein' out all day, and 'e said 'e'll be goin' out again this evenin'. It's a relief 'e's no trouble.'

'Yes, I shouldn't think he pours drink into women,' said Doreen. 'I told Mr Edwards's son that if 'is dad came knockin' again, we'd bolt the door on him.'

'Pardon, love?'

With the kettle boiling, Doreen made the pot of tea and brought it in.

'Yes, I told Mr Edwards's son that if 'is dad came knockin' again, we'd bolt the door on him,' she said.

'Oh, we needn't do that,' said Mrs Paterson, 'not till I've 'ad the chance of speakin' to 'im to let 'im know exactly what I think of 'im.'

'All right, Mum, I suppose you ought to 'ave the

chance of puttin' him in his place,' said Doreen.

'I owe it to me peace of mind,' said her mum.

'All right, Mum, if he does call, then, I'll show him into the parlour and you can dress 'im down there,' said Doreen. 'There, there's a nice cup of tea for you.'

'Bless yer, love,' said Mrs Paterson.

'Now look here, Old Iron,' said Luke, 'exactly what did 'appen with Mrs Paterson last night?'

'Like I told yer,' said Old Iron, homely in his trousers, shirt and braces. 'A nice walk, a bit of a chat, some fish and chips, and then a Guinness. Mind you, I admit it was a bit lively in the pub, what with the old joanna goin' and Mrs Skinner and Mrs Bigley doin' the knees-up. Well, me new lady friend, your Doreen's mum, suddenly said she 'adn't done the knees-up since she was a girl. I said mind yer ticker, me love—'

'You said what?'

'Mind yer ticker, me love, that's what I said. Well, I ain't ever been a stand-offish bloke, yer know, Luke. She said she'd better 'ave another mouthful of Guinness, and I said that's the stuff for your condition. So she 'ad another mouthful, then up she jumped and there she was, joinin' in the knees-up. Did me mince pies good, me lad, I can tell yer. Well, she's got an 'andsome pair of legs and no wrinkles in 'er stockings. Mind you, she was a bit dizzy when she came back to 'er seat, and I said I'd better take 'er 'ome. She asked me then if I'd made 'er drunk, and I said no, it wasn't me. I said anyway, you can't get drunk on an 'alf of Guinness, just at peace with the world. Then I took 'er 'ome, bless 'er ticker.'

'Well, Doreen thinks you made her drunk,' said Luke, 'and she's goin' to bolt the door on you if you call again.'

'Natural, I suppose, if she thinks I'm goin' to do 'er mum wrong,' said Old Iron. 'I ain't proposin' to do that yet—'

'Nor at all,' said Luke.

'Fetch up, sunshine,' said Old Iron, 'there's always some widows that like a bit of what they fancy, and it's up to understandin' blokes to give it to 'em. Being a widower, I'm more understandin' and more willin'. Now, regardin' widow Paterson and boltin' me out, don't you worry about that, Luke. It's a sort of natural process that tells a bloke 'e's expected to take 'is time. Also, yer see, Mrs Paterson's got to decide if she wants to keep 'er weak 'eart or chuck it overboard in favour of doin' some lively sociable living with me, yer dad.'

'If I read you right, Old Iron,' said Luke, 'you mean the kind of sociable stuff that'll make her expect a proposal from you.'

''Old up there, matey. 'Elping you with Doreen don't mean landin' meself permanent with 'er mum.'

'You said you wouldn't mind marryin' again.'

'So I did, and I ain't denyin' it,' said Old Iron. 'But I don't know I'm keen on becomin' Mrs Paterson's legalized nursemaid. The point is, what we're mainly after is gettin' Doreen untied from 'er apron-strings. Now, pour me out a light ale and 'ave one yourself.'

As for Mr Ronald Ponsonby, he was making neat notes relating to information he had acquired concerning the forthcoming trial of his twin brother. His line of enquiry had taken him to Fleet Street, and to the back numbers departments of various newspapers. He paid for certain back numbers, and brought them back to his lodgings. They contained reports on the discovery of a young girl's body in a Bermondsey scrap metal yard, the verdict of a coroner's court that she had been murdered by a person or persons unknown, and the police investigation. There were further reports on the arrest of a suspect, which coincided with the discovery of the bodies of two more young girls under the floorboards of a deserted fire-damaged factory in Walworth, and then the charging of the suspect, one Gerald Ponsonby, with murder. There were final reports of a magistrates' hearing and the committal of Ponsonby for trial at the Old Bailey. There was no mention, however, of the man, Robert Adams, whom Gerald in his letter had said was responsible for delivering him into the hands of the police. But that, of course, would not have been mentioned. It would only come out at the trial.

Mr Ronald Ponsonby, collating all relevant details in his notebook, regretfully assumed the law had an open and shut case against his twin brother. Gerald had made mistakes. They had always warned each other against making the slightest mistakes. Gerald must have suffered some careless moments.

Mr Ronald Ponsonby put the notebook in his suitcase. He locked the case, then put his boater on and went downstairs. He knocked on the kitchen door.

'Come in,' said Doreen, and Mr Ronald Ponsonby put his head round the door.

'Ah, good evening,' he said, 'good evening. I

thought I would let you ladies know I'm going out again and will be back at about ten.'

'That's all right, Mr Wright,' smiled Doreen, 'you don't 'ave to tell us every time you go out. Mum said you've got our spare key for the front door now.'

'We wouldn't want to interfere with your comings and goings,' said Mrs Paterson. She and Doreen were at supper. 'The only thing we'd mind is if you brought drink into the 'ouse.'

'Drink?' Mr Ronald Ponsonby looked pained. 'Why, of course not, Mrs Paterson, of course not. I don't drink. I'm content with getting out and about. Good evening, ladies.'

Out he went, to the West End again for a restaurant dinner, with which he would drink a bottle of good wine.

'What a funny old bloke,' said Doreen.

'Still, 'e don't pour beer into 'imself,' said Mrs Paterson, 'not like some people I know.'

'Yes, you can point that out to Mr Edwards if he gives you the chance to dress 'im down, Mum,' said Doreen, tongue in cheek.

'That I will,' said her mum.

Mrs Lizzy Somers had a word with her husband Ned when they were in bed that night.

'Ned, what d'you think of Rosie sittin' for an exam that might mean her goin' away to boarding-school?' she asked.

'What brought that up, and at this time of night?' asked Ned.

'Well, would you want Annabelle to go away to boarding-school?' asked Lizzy.

'Not very much,' said Ned, 'but if I know Boots

and Emily, they'll be thinking of Rosie, not of themselves. Boots for one would want Rosie to have all the advantages of a good education.'

'Yes, but if I know Rosie, she'll hate goin',' said Lizzy. 'She won't say so, but I bet you any money you like that she'll hate being away from home. You know how she is about Boots.'

'It's nothing to do with us, Eliza.'

'Yes, it is, it's fam'ly,' said Lizzy, who considered that anything that happened to any of the Adams' concerned all of them. 'It's – Ned Somers, what d'you think you're doing?'

'Well, as a matter of fact, Lizzy Somers, I was just thinking—'

'Leave them alone,' said Lizzy.

'I'm just paying them my respects,' said Ned.

'It doesn't feel respectful,' said Lizzy, and went all weak. 'Oh, you saucy devil.'

'Lucky devil, you mean,' murmured Ned, 'I'm married to them.'

Lizzy sighed and cuddled up.

Chapter Eleven

Sammy, parking his car at the side of the Islington factory, went in to present his personal self to Tommy, Lilian Hyams and the workforce of skilled and loyal seamstresses.

Outside, the large man, name of Ben Skidmore, put in an appearance. He took note of the car. He looked around and cast a glance at the factory office window. He effected a casual advance over the forecourt and tucked himself out of sight in the lee of the wall, from where he eyed the car speculatively. A malicious little grin split his lips.

'Well, how's things today, Madame Fifi?' asked Sammy, entering Lilian's office. She was at her drawing-board, nicely covered bottom perched on a high stool, feet tucked back and resting on a rung. Tommy, at the window, was examining one of her water-colour sketches. Lilian was putting together ideas for Adams Fashions' winter collection. She swivelled on the high stool, a quick smile on her face. She was always pleased to see her electrifying boss.

'Things are coming on, you might say,' she said.

'Mind my eye,' said Sammy. Lilian's short dress was way above her knees.

'Help yourself,' said Lilian, 'I'm not shy.'

'Well, you've got a good-lookin' pair of tent pegs, Lilian, I won't say you haven't, but I'm a married man now, and so's Tommy, and out of respect for our wives we can't take more than a quick butcher's. Have you had yours, Tommy?'

'Not yet,' said Tommy, 'I'm over here, not over there.'

'Just as well,' said Sammy, 'it's a bit blindin' over here.'

Lilian laughed and tucked her legs away.

'What's brought you?' asked Tommy, returning the sketch to Lilian's spacious drawing-board.

'Natural consideration for me workers,' said Sammy, 'and to have a look at Lilian's genius. Her tent pegs were a bonus, I grant you.'

'I'm thrilled, Sammy,' said Lilian. 'Rachel's here, by the way. She's in the workshop, looking at everything that's coming off the machines for Coates. She's agog, my life she is.'

'What's she agog about?' asked Sammy.

'The fac'try,' said Tommy, 'the fact that it's still in one piece and goin' full pelt. I've been treated to a smacker, which I 'ope Vi don't get to hear about.' He winked at Lilian.

'I think I ought to be somewhere else,' said Sammy.

'Sammy, is that you?'

Mrs Rachel Goodman, a lushly beautiful woman of the Jewish faith, entered the drawing office. A cloche hat cuddled her blue-black hair, a jersey wool dress clung to her figure, and her brown eyes swam with light. During her young years she had been Sammy's one and only girlfriend, and she had ways, both frank and subtle, of reminding him of that.

'Mornin', Mrs Goodman,' said Sammy briskly.

'Sammy, come into the office,' said Rachel, 'I

156

wish to speak to you.' Rachel was a director of Adams Fashions. She had bought her way into the business in order to remain part of Sammy's life. She was a faithful wife to her husband Benjamin, a course bookie, and a loving mother to her little girl Rebecca. Sammy, however, she adored, and could not help herself. As a young Jewish cockney girl, she had found delight in having Sammy, a Gentile, for her very own.

'Well, Mrs Goodman,' said Sammy, 'I'm actually here to cast me optics over Lilian's winter progress—'

'In the office, Sammy, if you please,' said Rachel.

Sammy coughed and went, leaving Lilian smiling and Tommy grinning. In the office, Rachel gave Sammy a look.

'What's with this Mrs Goodman stuff?' she asked.

'Business vernacular,' said Sammy, 'and then there's what you might call the politeness of one married person to another. If you get me.'

'I should be rapturous?' said Rachel. 'Sammy Adams, business vernacular is for customers on the phone. How would you like another shiner? Tommy told me you collected one last week, and I can see you did. If you call me Mrs Goodman again, you'll collect a second.'

'Now, now, Rachel, is that nice? Is it ladylike? My eye, Rachel, look at you, no wonder Benjamin wants to have you painted and framed and hung up in the National Gallery. If he does, it's me respectful hope he won't have you painted minus your togs. I'm against the gen'ral public gettin' free eyefuls of you rising rosy from your bath, so to speak. I'm not against it for me personal pleasure, mind.'

Rachel laughed.

'That's my Sammy,' she said. 'Come round at seven tonight.'

'What for?' asked Sammy cautiously.

'That's when I'll be rising rosy from my bath. Sammy, you love, the factory, everything going so well, despite the strike, and Tommy telling me they're well ahead of schedule. Shall I kiss you?'

'Well, Rachel, I appreciate the offer, but it's a principle of mine not to lark about in business hours, and I've got this appointment with Lilian to look over her new designs.'

Rachel consulted her watch. It was noon.

'I'll come and look at them with you,' she said, 'then you can take me to lunch.'

'Rachel, me old love—'

'My life, I'm old at twenty-four?'

'Concerning lunch—'

'Thank you, sweetie.'

'Well, I'll only have time for a fried egg sandwich at Joe's Cafe down the road,' said Sammy.

'Well, bless you, Sammy,' said Rachel, 'haven't I always wanted to share a fried egg sandwich with you at Joe's Cafe down the road?'

'All right, you can have one all to yourself,' said Sammy, 'and then, if you're goin' home, I'll drive you.'

'All is forgiven,' said Rachel.

Sammy, with Rachel in the car beside him, left the factory at fifteen minutes to two. He drove from Islington into Finsbury, and then through Clerkenwell. The open car collected the usual stares, yells and catcalls from kids who should have been at school but had decided either to join the General Strike or attend grandparents' funerals. And although the strike was crumbling fast, restless groups of strikers were fidgeting about on street corners or prowling about and showing the Red Flag. Rachel said that one day perhaps there'd be a decent job for every man in the kingdom.

'One day when?' said Sammy, turning into Gray's Inn Road and joining a jumble of traffic.

'Before they're all dead?' said Rachel.

'What a hope,' said Sammy, motoring cap on his head. 'Parliament's stuffed with top hats and fancy waistcoats, and short on business brains. Not one of 'em could even run a shop.'

'How about Sammy Adams for Prime Minister?'

'I might manage it in me spare time,' said Sammy, 'except I don't have any.'

Rachel smiled. She was enjoying the ride. She always found Sammy's company uplifting. Sammy drove towards Aldwych and Waterloo Bridge. Rachel lived with her husband, daughter and father in a large and well-appointed apartment above two shops in Lower Marsh. It was from there that her father, a widower, directed his business as a merchant. She was very fond of her father, Isaac Moses, known to the cockneys who used his pawnshops as Ikey Mo.

Sammy motored over Waterloo Bridge and into Waterloo Road. It was as he was passing under the railway bridge that his brakes began to fail. He was not moving fast, the traffic wouldn't allow him to, but brake failure at fifteen miles an hour was still dead serious. He pumped on the brake pedal and pulled on the handbrake, but there was no response, and the car was running straight at the back of a slow-moving cart.

'Sammy!'

'The bloody brakes have gone,' hissed Sammy, and took his foot off the clutch. The engine stalled, but the car still ran on. The back of the cart loomed up terrifyingly close, and Rachel had her hand over her mouth and her eyes wide open. Her whole body tensed. Sammy flashed a look at the pavement. It was clear. He spun the wheel, the car took a crazy left turn, bumped and jolted up over the kerb, trundled over the pavement and came to a slow stop against railings. The bump was gentle. People rushed up. A woman shouted.

''Ere, what yer doin', yer lunatic? Tryin' to kill yerselves and us as well?'

Sammy sat back and drew a breath.

'Well, no, missus, I'm not,' he said, 'I ain't in favour of that kind of thing.'

'Well, what did yer come ridin' up on the pavement for? Ain't the road wide enough? It ain't 'ealthy, drivin' on pavements, and it's against the law as well.'

'Bloody right it's against the law,' said a stern-looking elderly gent.

'Force of circumstances,' said Sammy, with Rachel sighing in relief beside him.

'What's force of circumstances?' asked a young bloke.

'Bleedin' dangerous,' said another bloke.

'I bet they're against the law as well,' said the woman.

The law arrived then in the shape of a dignified bobby.

'Stand back, ladies an' gents,' he said, and the

crowd parted for him. He advanced and regarded the car and its occupants with suspicion. 'Now then,' he said to Sammy, 'might I ask what you're doing on the pavement with this here car, sir?'

'I thought you'd ask that,' said Sammy, and got out. 'It's a short story. The brakes failed, constable.'

'Is this your motorcar, sir?'

'It is,' said Sammy.

'Then I have to advise you, sir, that it's against the law to be in charge of a vehicle that's dangerous to the public.'

'Told yer,' said the woman. Rachel got out and smiled at the bobby.

'But, constable,' she said, 'it wasn't dangerous until the brakes failed.'

The bobby blinked into lustrous brown eyes.

'Ah,' he said. 'Well,' he said, 'it's still got no right to be on the pavement.'

'Tell you what,' said Sammy, 'if you could give me a hand we could get it into the kerbside.'

'Ah,' said the bobby again. 'Well, it can't stay where it is, sir, it's an illegal obstruction.'

'I'll lend yer a hand, mate,' said the young bloke, who had the right amount of muscle.

'I'll keep an eye on the traffic,' said the bobby, 'as I'll have to run you in, sir, if you back your motorcar into an oncoming vehicle when acting without authority.'

'We'll be so grateful to have your authority,' said Rachel.

'Ain't she a corker?' said a feller to a young woman. 'I fancy 'er.'

'I fancy the bloke meself,' said the young woman.

The crowd watched as the bobby stepped into the

road, using one hand to divert oncoming traffic and the other to beckon Sammy on. With the help of several volunteers, the car was backed off the pavement, Sammy with a hand on the wheel, and it finished tucked up against the kerb. The crowd cheered. Sammy took a bow.

'Mind you, sir,' said the bobby, 'that there vehicle can't be left here all day. It's unauthorized parking.'

'What's that?' asked the woman who had been taking a keen interest from the beginning.

'Against the law,' said the stern-faced cove.

'Thought so,' said the woman.

Rachel, her smile a vivid lushness, said to the bobby, 'Well, you can authorize it, can't you, constable, while Mr Adams gets help from a garage?'

'Let's see now,' said the bobby and took out his notebook. 'I'll inscribe your name and address, sir, and particulars of the incident, and charge you to have your motorcar taken away as soon as possible.'

'That's fair,' said Sammy, and all was accordingly settled. The crowd drifted away, Sammy extracted his business case from the car, and walked Rachel to Lower Marsh. 'Narrow squeak,' he said.

'You kept your head, Sammy, bless you,' said Rachel. They stopped on the corner of Lower Marsh. The market stalls there were busy.

'Point is,' said Sammy, frowning, 'what made the brakes pack up?'

'They could have been faulty,' said Rachel. 'Won't a garage tell you?'

'I'll go there now,' said Sammy. He knew the area like the back of his hand, and where the nearest garage was. He said goodbye to Rachel.

'Kiss?' murmured Rachel.

'What, on top of a fried egg sandwich?' said Sammy, and made tracks. For all that some of his principles were elastic, Sammy was his mother's son, as much as Boots was, and Tommy as well. If Chinese Lady demanded one thing more than any other of her sons, it was strict observance of their marriage vows. Marriage vows, according to Chinese Lady, were the basis of law and order, and had been bestowed by God. That was why vicars told couples not to take them lightly. For better or worse, that was what marriage meant, she said once, and don't you boys forget it. They were all over twenty at the time. Marriage troubles are no excuse for anyone breaking their vows, she said. Thou shalt not commit adultery, that's what God commands, she said, and don't any of you forget it. Couples do have troubles, she said, I'm not saying they don't. There's drunken husbands that hit their wives, but there's a way of stopping that, which is for a wife to take up a saucepan or frying-pan and hit her husband back.

Chinese Lady's sons assured her they wouldn't turn into drunken husbands or commit adultery, and she said she was pleased to hear it, because if they did they'd wish they'd never been born.

Sammy didn't think Rachel would ever seriously consider breaking her Yiddish vows, but all the same he and she did have a long-standing special relationship, and Rachel once said that he ought to have done it to her when they were young free beings. Done what, Rachel? Loved me, said Rachel. Me do that to you at our age, Rachel? Mmm, gorgeous, said Rachel. Sammy, where you going? I'm running a quick mile, said Sammy, in case I get ideas.

He couldn't now ever see himself being unfaithful to Susie. Then there was Boots, whom that young woman, Polly Simms, looked at as if she was dying to eat him. And Emily, looking in turn as if she was thinking about scratching Polly's eyes out. Well, Polly had given up, she'd gone off to Kenya, probably to look for a big game hunter who could help her to forget Boots. All for the good, that was.

Sammy walked into the garage and made contact with the foreman mechanic. He explained his troubles. Don't like the sound of that, Mister Adams, don't like it at all. Could be a major job. Don't tell me funny stories, said Sammy, I've already had enough laughs today and it's not teatime yet. Just do me the favour of towing the car here and finding out what caused the trouble, there's a good bloke. Phone me at my office. There's my number. And here's a couple of bob in case you're going to tell me you're too busy to get on with it until next week. Obliging of yer, Mister Adams. It's obliging of you not to be on strike, said Sammy. We've had some men out, said the foreman, but they're back now. The union sent them back? No, their wives. I like wives, said Sammy, and he left to find a taxi to take him to Camberwell.

Susie had gone home by the time he reached the offices. He reported his mishap to Boots.

'Hard luck, sonny,' said Boots, 'but I'll do you the favour of keeping it dark from Chinese Lady, or she'll take herself down to that garage and order them to chop the car up for scrap.'

164

'I ain't amused,' said Sammy.

'Further,' said Boots, 'Chinese Lady will also want to know what you were doing with Rachel in the car.'

'I still ain't amused,' said Sammy.

'What made the braking system fall apart?' asked Boots.

'You don't know, I don't know, so I'm waitin' for a report from the garage,' said Sammy. 'On the credit side, I'm personally undamaged and still alive.'

'Glad to hear it, Sammy, you're one of the family.'

'In me business capacity,' said Sammy, 'I *am* the fam'ly.'

Boots smiled. Sammy put his head into the general office and asked where Junior was. He meant Ronnie, the office boy.

'Oh, he's out doing errands, Mister Sammy,' said Doreen.

'In that case,' said Sammy, 'who'll make me a cup of tea, pipin' hot?'

'I will,' said Doreen. She made it and took it into his office with two biscuits.

'Compliments to you, Doreen,' he said. He eyed her. Come to think of it, his switchboard operator and girl-of-all-work was turning into a very nice-looking young lady. 'How's your mum?' he asked.

'Oh, she looks fine, Mister Sammy,' said Doreen, 'it's 'er inner self that's unwell.'

'Her what?' said Sammy, drinking tea, breaking a biscuit and taking note of messages left by Susie. He didn't believe in doing one thing at a time if it was possible to do more. 'Her what, Doreen?'

'Her inner self,' said Doreen.

'Well, Doreen,' said Sammy in his frank way,

'tell her I recommend that after two years her inner self ought to be up and friskin' about.'

'Pardon, Mister Sammy?'

'Did I hear you've got a young man?' asked Sammy.

'Mister Sammy—'

'Tell him from me he's lucky. Is that the switchboard buzzin'?'

'Mister Sammy, I don't have a young man – oh, 'elp, yes, it's the switchboard.' Doreen rushed to answer it. Sammy grinned, thinking of her perched on the carrier of a stalwart young man's bike, and thinking too of all the time she spent looking after her widowed mother. Not good for either her or her mum.

At five-thirty, he got up from his desk and moved to his window, which overlooked the road. A full-up tram was climbing the hill. On the other side of the road, directly opposite the shop and offices, was a young man and a bike, a workman's peaked blue cap on his head. Same bloke, thought Sammy. Same girl, he thought a few moments later, as he saw Doreen cross the road. She spoke to the upright-looking young gent.

'You're here again,' said Doreen accusingly.

What a sweetheart, thought Luke. She was wearing a beret today and a bright summer dress with a flower-patterned hem. Her legs and figure were adorable. Yes, I'll stick with that, adorable, thought Luke.

'I was passin' by,' he said.

'No, you weren't,' said Doreen, 'you're here deliberate. Listen, 'ave you been tellin' people you're my young man?'

'Funny you should ask,' said Luke, 'I'd like to be

166

able to tell ev'rybody that. I'd be proud to.'

'You've got a hope,' said Doreen, 'd'you think I'd go out with any bloke whose dad takes my mum to pubs and gets 'er drunk?'

'Actually, me dad said—'

'Never mind what he said, he's barmy,' said Doreen. 'Still, now you're here, I suppose you want to give me a lift home, do you?'

'Might I 'ave that honour again, Lady Vi?'

'Well, all right,' said Doreen, 'but don't go tellin' anyone you're my young man.'

Sammy was smiling as he watched the bike move away, with Doreen perched on the carrier, her legs shining in the sunlight.

Mr Ronald Ponsonby had conducted himself cautiously that day. He did not wish to become known in the neighbourhood as a man enquiring into the present whereabouts of a family called Adams, a family that had once lived in Caulfield Place, off Browning Street. However, by dint of putting a casual question to a shopkeeper, he had discovered that one of the brothers, Sammy Adams, used to run a china and glassware stall in the East Street market. He sauntered into the market and found the stall and its present owner, a Mrs Walker. He inspected her wares, mused over cheap tumblers, murmured over willow pattern china, and alighted on quite a pretty glazed teapot.

'Charming,' he said, 'charming.'

'Lovely, I'd say,' enthused Mrs Walker.

'I've heard your stall has a reputation for selling quality china at the most affordable prices.'

'Well, Mister Sammy Adams built up that reputation,' said Mrs Walker. 'Of course, bein' his assistant and 'is brother Tommy's too, when Tommy ran the stall, I 'elped build it up, I'm pleasured to say.'

'I don't think I've heard of the Adams', no, I don't think I have,' said Mr Ronald Ponsonby.

'Oh, the fam'ly's got a business in Camberwell now,' said Mrs Walker, always ready for a chat. 'Mister Sammy sold me the rights to this stall a bit ago. It's like a fairy story, the way the whole fam'ly's come up in the world. It just shows 'umble beginnings don't 'ave to hold you back. Of course, if you lived round 'ere, you'd know about the fam'ly, like everyone does.'

'I'm just visiting,' said Mr Ronald Ponsonby, 'just visiting. Yes, what a very pretty teapot. I shall buy it. How much?'

'Well, it's one of me specials,' said Mrs Walker, 'it's a Sunday teapot when there's visitors. It's two shillings, a price you couldn't better, not even in Petticoat Lane, not with glazin' like that.'

'I'll have it,' said the man who was just visiting. 'Does – what was his name? Sammy Adams? Yes, does he run a stall in Camberwell now, a larger one?' The question was put as a polite response to the lady's friendly chatter. Well, that was how it seemed.

'A stall? I should say not.' Mrs Walker, wrapping up the teapot, was emphatic. 'He's got shops and offices and scrap metal yards and Lord knows what else, and he calls the firm Adams Enterprises. Him and 'is two brothers run it. From their Camberwell offices.'

'Most interesting,' said Mr Ronald Ponsonby, but in such a limp kind of way that Mrs Walker begged his pardon for boring him with her chatter.

'Not at all, not at all,' he said. He paid for the teapot and left. He was very satisfied. The information had been volunteered in the main. It would not have done to have stayed and asked questions. He could visualize a possible outcome.

'Hello, Mister Sammy, fancy seein' you. There was a bloke here the other day askin' questions about you and your brothers.'

Very unwise, too many questions when one did not want to be remembered.

He returned to his lodgings during the afternoon, took off his shoes, jacket and boater, placed himself on the bed and went peacefully to sleep.

His method was already taking shape.

Camberwell. The business. Run by all three brothers. Just as Gerald had said. It was necessary now to find out the exact location of their offices.

Chapter Twelve

Two kids watched as Luke cycled into Morecambe Street, Doreen forgetful enough to let him do that.

'Cor, don't yer look pretty, Doreen?' said one of the boys. Well, all the older street kids of the male gender had a soft spot for her and a saucy eye for her legs.

'Got a bloke, 'ave yer, Doreen?' said the other boy as the bike passed him and his mate.

'Oh, now look what you've done,' said Doreen accusingly to Luke as he stopped outside her house. 'You know you're not supposed to ride me up to me door.' She slipped from her perch. 'If my mum's in the parlour, watchin' you, she'll think we're goin' out together.'

'Do me the world of good, that would, goin' out with you, Lady Vi,' said Luke.

'It wouldn't do my mum any good, not in 'er state of health,' said Doreen. 'It's only natural that she wants me to look after 'er till she's better, she's been a good mum to me.'

'Well, I did offer to come and sit with you in the evenings so that we could look after her together,' said Luke.

'Yes, and I bet you'd bring that talkative dad of yours to drive my mum barmy,' said Doreen.

'I suppose you wouldn't like a kiss, would you?' said Luke.

'D'you mind pushin' off?' said Doreen haughtily, and made for her front door. She turned her head. A little smile peeped. 'Thanks for the lift.'

'Pleasure,' said Luke, and went to his lodgings.

Doreen made the usual pot of tea for her mum and herself, and while they were drinking it, their lodger knocked on the kitchen door.

'Come in,' said Doreen.

Mr Ronald Ponsonby presented his dapper person, together with the teapot.

'I'm not interrupting?' he said.

'No, course you're not, Mr Wright,' said Mrs Paterson. Her lodger had been out for hours again, and had returned in the afternoon.

'Good,' he said, giving one of his perky nods. He placed the very pretty teapot on the table and begged Mrs Paterson to accept it with his compliments and as a token of his appreciation for giving him lodgings. Mrs Paterson said bless me, what a lovely teapot, it's ever so kind of you, Mr Wright. Doreen said yes, it was very kind of him. 'Not at all, not at all,' said the lodger, 'I felt myself fortunate to come across it on a stall in the market. In expressing my admiration for it, the lady in charge assured me her stall had acquired a reputation for selling quality china and glassware. She mentioned a well-known Walworth family called Adams.'

'Oh, that would be Mrs Walker,' said Doreen, 'she took the stall over from Sammy Adams.'

'Doreen works for 'im now at 'is other business, don't you, love?' said Mrs Paterson.

'Excuse me?' said Mr Ronald Ponsonby in some disbelief.

'Yes, Doreen works for Sammy Adams now,' said Mrs Patterson, 'at 'is Camberwell offices.'

'My, what a coincidence, what a small world,' said the lodger, nodding very perkily indeed. Extraordinary, he thought. Luck had guided him to a mine of information. But it must be carefully tapped. 'I was told the family had made quite a name for itself.'

'Yes, they came up from nothing, you might say,' said Mrs Paterson.

'How interesting,' said the lodger politely.

'Yes, three brothers and a sister, all such nice people,' said Doreen.

'Ah,' smiled Mr Ronald Ponsonby, 'nice people are much to be admired. Well, I must go out later, to meet a friend. Good evening, Mrs Paterson, good evening, Miss Paterson.'

Out he went later in search of his evening meal, his mind on the family called Adams.

Mr and Mrs Sammy Adams had a small altercation when Sammy, on arriving home, recounted the tale of the failed brakes.

'Say that again,' demanded Susie, looking fetchingly domestic in a pretty apron with frilly edges.

'All of it?' said Sammy.

'No, just the bit about a certain married woman,' said Susie, blue eyes showing warning lights.

'What, Mrs Rachel Goodman, you mean?'

'That's the one, your old sweetheart,' said Susie. If she was jealous of anyone, it was Rachel. 'How did she happen to be in the car with you? Accident'lly, I presume?'

'I wouldn't say that, Susie.'

'Yes, you would if you'd thought of it in time,' said Susie. It was something in his favour that he'd mentioned Rachel, but all the same it wasn't what she wanted to hear.

'She happened to be at the fac'try when I got there,' said Sammy. 'Being a director of Adams Fashions, she likes to take an interest in what's goin' on.'

'Don't I know it,' said Susie, looking for the nearest saucepan. Sammy saw it first and moved it out of her reach.

'Well,' he said, 'I couldn't not offer to drop Mrs Goodman off at Lower Marsh on my way back to Camberwell—'

'Yes, you could,' said Susie, and looked around for something else to hit him with.

'Now, Susie—'

'Don't you now Susie me. Rachel Goodman's a married woman, and so are you.'

'You sure you said that right, Susie?'

'What? Oh, I mean a married man.'

'That's special to me, Susie, being a married man and you being my married wife,' said Sammy. 'I remember sayin' to myself once, Sammy Adams, I said, if Susie Brown gets to be the married wife of anyone but me, it's goin' to pain me considerable, and hurt as well. Bless my heart, Susie, ain't you sweet in that pretty apron and short skirt? Would you like to go out after supper?'

'You're not gettin' any supper,' said Susie.

'Like to go out after I've had some dry bread?'

'Yes, for a walk,' said Susie.

'Where to?' asked Sammy.

'Oh, somewhere where I can push you under a bus.'

Sammy roared with laughter. Susie picked up the wet dishcloth and socked him with it.

Sammy, wet-faced, said, 'Was that you did that, Susie?'

'No, the cat's mother,' said Susie, so Sammy took hold of her and kissed her. 'Ugh, you're all wet,' said Susie, after a gurgling but exciting engagement.

'All part of married life,' said Sammy.

Susie laughed and gave him a forgiving hug. She forgot to ask him why the brake system of his car had failed. Sammy couldn't have told her, anyway. The garage hadn't yet come through with the information.

Tommy and Vi, who liked to enjoy the social activities available in Camberwell, went to the pictures after their supper, leaving little Alice in the care of her grandparents.

Mr Finch did some gardening. Boots did some as well, in addition to kicking a ball about with young Tim. Rosie did some homework, Emily did some reading, and Chinese Lady did some knitting.

Lizzy spent a good part of the evening grooming the hair of Annabelle, Emma and Bobby, applying brush and comb with motherly relentlessness. She'd suffered headlice as a growing girl, and it had given her the horrors. She was accordingly addicted to the care of her children's hair. Headlice weren't exclusive to poverty-stricken people. They were travellers. They travelled on dogs, trams, buses and trains. They travelled from schoolkid to schoolkid. Lizzy was determined they weren't going to find a stopping-place in her children's hair. Annabelle and Emma didn't mind a prolonged combing and brushing of their girlishly abundant locks. Bobby, in his sixth year, regarded a tugging comb as purgatory. Little Edward, in his second year, still had what looked like an innocent head of hair, and so far had only ever received brief groomings. Ned hid himself behind his wine trade magazine and affected to hear nothing of Bobby's protests.

No-one had any idea that the identical twin of a man awaiting trial for murder was thinking of Lizzy and her three brothers as he sat eating dinner in a West End restaurant.

Just after eight o'clock, Doreen answered a knock on the front door.

'Evenin' to yer, Doreen,' said Old Iron with an appreciative smile. A knockout the girl was. Healthy figure as well. Any prospective wife ought to have a healthy figure. After all, there was more to married life than keeping up with the outgoings. 'My, yer lookin' better than Pearl White in 'er Sunday best.' Pearl White was the famous star of serial films.

Doreen, affecting a haughty ignorance of the barmy old coot, said, 'Who are you, might I ask?'

'I'm—'

'Never mind that. Are you a rag-and-bone man? Yes, and how d'you know my name? Blessed cheek, knockin' at our door and addressin' me as if I was someone who pushed your barrow. Go away.'

Old Iron grinned.

'I like yer spirit, Doreen. Mind you, I could get regretful bein' called a rag-and-bone man, seein' I'm a skilled bloke, like me son Luke that's very admirin' of yer. No wonder. Young peach, you are, Doreen. Now, is yer dear Ma in?'

'She's not in to you,' said Doreen. 'Crikey, I know you now, you're the bloke who brought her 'ome drunk the other night. What d'you mean by doin' a thing like that to my respectable mum? And her with a weak heart.'

'I grant yer, it's a problem,' said Old Iron, 'but nothing that kindness and a bit of me healin' gifts can't cure. Kindness to widow ladies comes naturally to me, so do me healin' gifts.'

'If you don't go away,' said Doreen, wanting to split her sides, 'I'll push this door into your face.'

'I don't know 'ow much good that'll do me or yer 'andsome Ma,' said Old Iron, who had something wrapped in brown paper under his arm. 'Be a lot better if you invite me in so's she can 'elp me with the 'Ouses of Parliament.'

'Excuse me, Mister Whatsisname,' said Doreen, 'but I'm not invitin' you in so's you can get my mum in a tizzy – here, what d'you mean, 'elp you with the Houses of Parliament?'

'Put them together,' said Old Iron breezily. 'I'm partial to jigsaws, yer know, which is a recreational way of exercisin' yer brain and yer mental ability, and I know yer Ma's partial 'erself.'

'Well, you know more than I do,' said Doreen.

'It's me intuition,' said Old Iron. 'Also, on top of the 'Ouses of Parliament, I've got a bottle of Guinness in my frock coat pocket, which I'll be 'appy to share with Muriel.'

'Who said you could call my mum Muriel?' demanded Doreen, hardly knowing how to keep her laughter under lock and key.

'Bless yer, Doreen love, that's 'er name,' said Old Iron.

'Doreen love? I'll have a fit in a minute.'

'Doreen? Doreen?' Mrs Paterson made herself heard. 'Who's that?'

'It's Mrs Martin's lodger, Mum, the one who nearly ruined your good name.'

'Oh, me failin' 'eart,' gasped Mrs Paterson, and tottered from the kitchen into the passage. She stared at Old Iron.

'Evenin' to yer, Muriel,' he said happily, 'pleased to see yer 'andsome self. If my peepers don't deceive me, you've got a rosy flush of 'ealth tonight. Might I compliment you, Doreen, on 'aving a fine 'andsome mum? Shall I come in and spread me healin' gifts?'

'Heaven 'elp me,' said Mrs Paterson faintly, and leaned against the wall.

'Now see what you've done,' said Doreen to Old Iron. 'You'd better come in before my mum collapses with the door still open.'

Old Iron stepped in and closed the door.

'Might I suggest we loosen yer Ma's stays?' he said.

'Oh, me gawd,' gasped Mrs Paterson.

'It's all right, Mum,' said Doreen, 'I won't let him get anywhere near your stays. He'll have to go. There you are,' she said to Old Iron, 'you'll 'ave to go.'

'Well, no, perhaps not,' said Mrs Paterson, making a brave effort to overcome whatever was ailing her. 'Now 'e's here, it's a chance for me to give 'im a piece of me mind.'

'I'll be 'appy to oblige yer, that I will,' said Old Iron, 'then maybe we can get down to me 'Ouses of Parliament jigsaw, eh?'

'Jigsaw?' said Mrs Paterson.

'Excites yer, does it?' said Old Iron. 'I thought it would. It's me intuition. We'll use yer parlour table, shall we? Jigsaws could be said to 'ave healin' properties, yer know. Well, they liven up yer brain, and a lively brain leads to a lively 'eart. It's what healers call mental contagion. All right, Doreen, leave yer Ma to me.'

'I hope you're not goin' to send her cock-eyed,' said Doreen, 'or I'll empty hot tea-leaves over you and hit you with our best poker.'

'Now don't you worry, Doreen,' said Old Iron, 'I'll look after her as soon as she's given me a piece of 'er mind. You can go and keep me son Luke company, if yer like.'

'Not likely,' said Doreen. 'I don't 'ardly know him, and in any case I'm not leavin' you alone in the house with my mum.'

'That's discreditin' me integrity,' said Old Iron. 'Still, I understand yer. All right, Muriel, shall we proceed into yer parlour so's you can speak yer piece before we start buildin' the 'Ouses of Parliament?'

Mrs Paterson tottered into the parlour. Old Iron followed her. Doreen, smiling, pulled the door to and left them. From the kitchen, she listened. She couldn't hear anything that related to her mum giving the visitor what for. The door didn't tremble or shake, and there were no sounds like ornaments being chucked about. Still, she did hear the door being opened after fifteen minutes and the voice of Mr Edwards.

'Are yer there, Doreen love? Could yer bring a couple of glasses for the Guinness?'

Doreen took a deep breath to help her keep her face straight, took two glass tumblers from a shelf on the dresser and carried them to the parlour. As she approached, she heard her mum's voice.

'Now didn't I say so, didn't I say that piece went there?'

'So yer did, Muriel, so yer did.'

Doreen went in. There they were, seated side by side at the parlour table, a large number of jigsaw pieces spread before them, and forty or so already fitted. The bottle of Guinness was in evidence.

'Glasses,' said Doreen.

'Yes, put them on the table, love,' said Mrs Paterson.

'You're not 'aving any trouble with him, Mum?'

'No, I gave 'im a piece of me mind,' said Mrs Paterson.

'Well, a man's got to take the rough with the smooth,' said Old Iron, 'partic'larly from a patient whose sufferin' don't make 'er feel too good.'

Doreen made a rapid exit. It got her back to the kitchen in time to bury her laughter in the larder.

Old Iron handed Mrs Paterson back to her daughter at ten. Mrs Paterson was slightly flushed and slightly mellow.

'Any complaints, Mum?' asked Doreen.

'What's that, love?'

'Any complaints?'

'Only me misfortunate widow'ood,' said Mrs Paterson.

'Otherwise, she's comin' on fine,' said Old Iron. 'Temp'rature normal, limbs sound and steady, 'eartbeats 'ealthy.'

'What d'you mean, heartbeats healthy?' asked Doreen.

'That's me medical opinion,' said Old Iron.

'Well, I do feel sort of less sorrowful,' said Mrs Paterson.

'That's the ticket,' said Old Iron. 'We'll 'ave

another go at the 'Ouses of Parliament tomorrer, if I can find time. I commend yer on yer jigsaw abilities. My word, Muriel, you've got a real rosy flush of 'ealth now. I'm proud of yer. Good night now. So long, Doreen.'

Doreen saw him to the door.

'Wait a bit,' she said, 'never mind your medical opinion, how d'you know about Mum's heartbeat?'

'It's confidential,' said Old Iron.

'Oh, you crafty old devil, have you been fondling my mum's bosom?'

'Only professionally, Doreen love,' said Old Iron, and stepped into the night.

'Oh, you wait, I'll 'ave the law on you!' Doreen closed the door, coughed her throat clear and returned to her mum. 'Mum, did he touch you?'

'Touch me?' Mrs Paterson looked and sounded mellow. 'We 'ad a nice drop of Guinness together. I must say it does seem to do a sufferin' woman a bit of good. What was that about touchin' me?'

'Your bosom.'

Mrs Paterson drew herself up.

''Ow dare you?' she said. 'You, me own daughter, askin' a question like that of your own mother? Mr Edwards is very doctorin', I'll 'ave you know. I think I'll go to bed now, me legs feel a bit funny.'

Well, thought Doreen, if I don't fall about in a minute, it'll be a miracle. What's 'very doctoring' mean? I bet it's something Luke would like to try on me. Well, he's not getting his hand anywhere near my bosom.

'Had a nice sociable evenin', Dad?' said Luke.

'Not bad at all,' said Old Iron. 'She enjoyed 'er Guinness and me encouragin' conversation. There wasn't any knees-up. Well, 'er parlour wasn't the place for it, and we 'ad the 'Ouses of Parliament takin' up our time. She looked a bit mesmerized 'ere and there—'

'I bet she did,' said Luke.

'But she sorted out some tricky bits of the jigsaw. We did over 'alf of it, and I'll continue me healin' treatment maybe tomorrow evenin' or the evenin' after. When we get to the point where she fancies a Sunday walk up the park, that'll be the time when you can start courtin' Doreen serious. On the sofa in their parlour, I'd say, while me and 'er Ma are up the park.'

'And earn meself a thick ear?' said Luke.

'Listen, me lad, that's what they call negative talk. Courtin' a girl 'as got to be positive.'

'I'm not twelve years old,' said Luke, 'I can manage to be positive. But I don't see it as positive to grab a girl like Doreen on a sofa. I see it as askin' for a smack in me chops. Doreen's a lady.'

'Well, course she is,' said Old Iron, 'a nice young lady that dresses very tasteful. And did I say you 'ad to grab 'er? No, I didn't, I said start courtin' 'er serious.'

'Stop tryin' to teach me how to suck lemons,' said Luke. 'I am courtin' her, sort of little by little.'

'Well, when I'm up the park with 'er Ma, and you're courtin' Doreen on the sofa, Luke, get a lovin' arm around 'er little by little. Like I did with 'er Ma an hour ago.'

'You old goat,' said Luke, 'you do things your way, I'll do things my way.'

'And may the best man win,' said Old Iron. 'That's both of us. The strike'll be over tomorrow, by the way.'

'Well, it's a fact that our union's said we can go back tomorrow. And if the bus and tram drivers go back, Doreen won't need any lift 'ome on me bike.'

'What's wrong with knockin' on 'er door in the evenin' and takin' the Tower of London with yer? She can 'elp you put it together in 'er parlour. Sit 'er on yer lap—'

'Leave off,' said Luke, but with a grin.

'I'd best get my beauty sleep now,' said Rosie, 'I don't want to grow up all drawn and haggard. 'Night, Mum.' She kissed Emily. ''Night, Daddy.' She kissed Boots.

'I think we'll buy a car,' said Boots, having looked at the family's bank balance.

'What?' said Emily.

'Oh, bliss,' breathed Rosie.

'What do we want a car for?' asked Emily.

'For fun,' said Boots, 'and to help us out whenever there's another strike that affects public transport.'

'Lord above,' said Emily, 'we're goin' to have a fam'ly car?'

'We could have another wheelbarrow, of course,' said Boots, 'but let's opt for a car.'

'Bliss,' said Rosie again, 'but now I won't get any beauty sleep, I'll be too excited. Still, I won't mind being all drawn and haggard for once. Crikey, a family car, Mummy, don't you have a spiffing better half?'

'I think my spiffin' better half is goin' to give your grandma a fit,' said Emily.

Chinese Lady didn't exactly have a fit when she was told of the proposed acquisition at breakfast the next morning, but she did lay down the law about new-fangled contraptions being dangerous to life and limb. She asked why Boots couldn't buy a family horse and cart, which wouldn't do any harm to anyone. Boots said there wasn't anywhere to keep the horse. Chinese Lady said what about the back garden?

Everyone except Chinese Lady then had a fit.

Chapter Thirteen

Sammy, leaning back in his office chair, said, 'Now you've got me thinkin', Boots.'

'Yes, I can hear your clock ticking, Sammy,' said Boots.

'I'm pleased, naturally, that you're goin' to catch up with progress,' said Sammy.

'Don't mention it,' said Boots. 'Point is, what about Tommy?'

'Exactly what I'm thinkin' about,' said Sammy. 'You've got a general manager's salary, Tommy's only got a fact'ry manager's income. You and me with cars and Tommy without, that don't accord with fam'ly rights. So I'll make a proposal.'

'I'll second it,' said Boots.

'You don't know what it is,' said Sammy.

'Try me,' said Boots.

'I propose the firm supplies Tommy with a car. Well, he's got that journey to Islington every day, and he's had a hard time gettin' there during the strike.'

'Proposal seconded and passed,' said Boots.

'Wait a bit, who by?' said Sammy.

'Me,' said Boots. 'Good on yer, sonny, I'll leave you to tell Tommy. I'm busy myself.'

'That's it, break my heart,' said Sammy, 'I'm only up to my eyes meself.'

'I think you'll come out of it alive,' said Boots, and went back to his office.

Sammy received a phone call from the garage a little later. He was informed that the brake system had been crudely sabotaged.

'Come again?' said Sammy.

'It's a fact, Mr Adams,' said the garage manager.

'Well, I didn't do it,' said Sammy, 'I'm against tryin' to commit suicide.'

'Someone chewed away at it, Mr Adams.'

'You sure it didn't just wear out?'

'Not in our opinion. In our opinion, someone played a nasty joke on you. It smells a bit of the jokes played by these people called the Bright Young Things. They're too empty-headed to realize some of their jokes are bloody dangerous. Has your car been parked around the West End lately?'

'No,' said Sammy.

'Well, our opinion is still that you were sabotaged, Mr Adams. Shall we carry out the necessary work? Or do you want the police to look at your car first?'

'Not if it means I won't get the car back for another month,' said Sammy. 'No, do the work.'

'Right, Mr Adams. I'll let you know when you can collect.'

'Thanks,' said Sammy, and hung up.

Doreen came in with his mid-morning tea. He looked her over. Snowy white blouse and a neat office skirt today. Nice-looking girl all over.

'Mister Sammy?'

'I'm here, Doreen.'

'What're you lookin' at me for?' asked Doreen.

'Search me,' said Sammy, wondering about the braking system. 'Must be something to do with my mince pies. Life treatin' you sociably just now?'

'Mister Sammy, you're not on again about some young man, are you?' said Doreen.

'Well, I haven't met him yet,' said Sammy.

'I don't know what's come over you lately, Mister Sammy,' said Doreen, 'you'll drive me potty in a minute.'

'The strike's over,' said Sammy, 'you're all right for trams and buses now.'

'Yes, how thrilling, Mister Sammy,' said Doreen, and went back to the general office.

Mr Ronald Ponsonby, in the Walworth Road post office, consulted the London telephone directory. He found the address of Adams Enterprises Ltd. A tram took him there. He entered the shop. It was large and well-stocked. It was a venture Sammy had started several years ago, and was specifically aimed at the thin pockets of the poor people of Camberwell and Walworth. It offered them Army surplus at knockdown prices. Blankets, overcoats, boots, flannel underwear and so on. In addition, the shop sold cheap men's and women's wear. It still did very good business. As far as Mr Ronald Ponsonby was concerned, what was on offer was all junk. However.

'Can I help you, sir?' asked the young man who ran the shop with the assistance of a war widow.

'An interesting stock, very interesting,' said Mr Ronald Ponsonby.

'Well, yes, you could say that, sir, and it all suits people's pockets.'

'It's your shop?' said Mr Ronald Ponsonby, who knew it wasn't.

'No, I'm just in charge,' said Sidney Pearson. 'It

belongs to Adams Enterprises. They've got their offices upstairs.'

'Interesting, yes.' Mr Ronald Ponsonby's gaze wandered around, and he looked very much as if everything was very interesting indeed. 'I thought I'd have you show me some ties.'

'Plain or striped, sir?' said Sidney.

'Silk?' suggested Mr Ronald Ponsonby.

'Well, no, we don't stock silk ones, they're outside the pockets of most of our customers.'

'Your best, then, and plain.'

Sidney drew out two trays, one containing plain ties, the other striped. Mr Ronald Ponsonby thought them all quite unworthy of adorning his discriminating person. However.

'An excellent selection,' he said, 'excellent.' He fingered a plain one. 'Well, I must say Adams Enterprises is a very go-ahead firm.'

'Two of the Adams brothers run the business from the offices upstairs, and the third brother manages a factory of ours at Islington. They're all go-ahead.'

'Interesting,' said Mr Ronald Ponsonby, and it was, for it was all he wanted to know at the moment. 'I'll take these two, if you'll wrap them up.'

'Pleasure, sir.'

Mr Ronald Ponsonby departed in an equable mood.

He took a tram that carried him to the Embankment, and from there made his way by tube to Stepney Green. There he established contact with an old acquaintance of fairly dubious business references, a man who was always willing to do a favour for people he knew, providing they made the risk worthwhile, which meant skinning their wallets.

In the playground of St John's Church School, a rehearsal of the Empire Day pageant was going on. Among other tableaux, Wellington stood victorious at the battle of Waterloo, his officers and his steed beside him. His steed was a passive Great Dane that belonged to one of the teachers. Sir Walter Raleigh was placing his cloak at the feet of Good Queen Bess, whose crown looked a bit lopsided. Queen Boadicea stood in her chariot, its shaft manned by two boys acting as her fiery steeds. She held her wooden spear aloft.

''Ere, where's Caesar?' she demanded.

'Puttin' 'is togger on,' said a girl, one of a crowd of Ancient Britons.

'He's been an half-hour puttin' it on,' complained Boadicea.

'I think he's having trouble with the safety-pins,' said Mr Hill.

'Well, if I 'ave to wait 'ere like this for another half-hour,' said Boadicea, 'I'll likely fall out of me chariot.'

'He's comin'!' cried the girl.

Caesar appeared in a pinned-up bedsheet, with what looked like a miniature privet hedge on his head.

'Hail, Caesar!' yelled the Ancient Britons on cue.

'Hail, *Mighty* Caesar,' said Mr Hill.

'I'll give 'im mighty,' said Boadicea, 'I'll cut 'is togger off with me spear. Come on, you Caesar, where d'you think you've been?'

'Who, me?' said Mighty Caesar.

'Just as well you've managed to arrive,' said Mr

Hill, 'Boadicea's a little ferocious. Now, you both know your lines? Good. Proceed.'

'Advance, you dog!' cried Boadicea.

'Who, me?' said Caesar. ''Ere, that's not in your lines.'

'Yes, it is.' Boadicea shook her spear.

'Not quite,' said Mr Hill.

'Still, it sounds all right,' said an Ancient Briton.

'It's "Advance, dog of Rome,"' said Mr Hill correctively.

'Advance, dog of Rome!' yelled Boadicea triumphantly.

Caesar, dog of Rome, advanced and tripped over his togger.

'Oh, bleedin' blimey,' he said in disgust. His privet hedge fell off.

Female Ancient Britons giggled, male Ancient Britons hooted.

'Oh, yer clumsy doughnut,' cried Boadicea.

'Rise, Mighty Caesar,' said Mr Hill, hardly batting an eyelid. He was used to chaos. Other teachers were battling against it. On top of that, the Great Dane had weed over Wellington's boots.

Mighty Caesar rose. An Ancient Briton handed him his privet hedge. Caesar put it on. Boadicea could hardly wait to begin her lines again.

'Advance, clumsy dog of Rome!' she cried.

'You wait,' muttered Caesar, 'you just wait till after school.' He cleared his throat. He shouted his first line. 'Rome defies you!'

'Well, take that, then,' said Boadicea, and knocked his privet hedge, masquerading as a laurel wreath, off his head with her spear. Ancient Britons howled in delight.

'Was that supposed to happen?' asked Mr Hill

mildly. 'I think not. Black mark, Boadicea. Restore your laurel wreath, Caesar. Speak your proper line, Boadicea.'

'Well, all right,' said Boadicea. 'Submit!' she yelled.

'Not likely,' said Caesar, 'not while you're wavin' that spear about.'

'Incorrect,' said Mr Hill.

'I say again, Rome defies you!' bawled Caesar.

'Down with 'im!' yelled the Ancient Britons as one.

'Form the tableau,' said Mr Hill.

The Ancient Britons seized Caesar and forced him to prostrate himself before the chariot. His privet hedge fell off again. Boadicea lifted her spear in triumph to the sky.

'Rome 'as fell!' she cried.

'Rome has fallen,' chided Mr Hill.

'Oh, all right,' said Boadicea. 'Rome 'as fallen!' she cried.

'Enough for today,' said Mr Hill. 'You can all go home now, five minutes early. Try to get there without slaughtering each other, or your mothers will want to talk to the headmistress.'

Caesar delivered himself bitterly on the way home.

'That's it, then,' he said, 'that's the end. I'm findin' a new mate.'

'I'll tell me dad if you do,' said Boadicea. 'When 'e was champion boxer of the world, he used to have 'is own chariot, did yer know that?'

Caesar groaned. Boadicea thought she'd like a longer spear.

Mr Ronald Ponsonby passed them at that point, in Browning Street, on his way back to his lodgings in Morecambe Street. He little knew that the girl was to be the chief witness at his twin brother's trial in three weeks.

He entered the house quietly, and Mrs Paterson jumped at a knock on her kitchen door.

'Who's that?' she asked. Her lodger showed himself. 'Oh, it's you, Mr Wright.'

He smiled.

'I thought I'd let you know I'm back,' he said. 'I've had the pleasure of seeing some old friends of mine.'

'Oh, Doreen and me don't worry about yer comings and goings, Mr Wright,' said Mrs Paterson, who might have offered him a cup of tea if she hadn't found him an uninteresting man. He was a bit bird-like with his little nods, and he sort of twittered compared to fruity-voiced Walworth men. That Mr Edwards now, he had a very fruity voice with a manly bit of gravel to it. 'I 'ope you're findin' yer room nice and comfy.'

'Very comfy, yes, very comfy,' said the lodger. 'And Walworth is a surprisingly peaceful place.'

'It wasn't at Easter,' said Mrs Paterson. 'The police arrested a man after finding the bodies of two murdered young girls not far from 'ere.'

'How unfortunate,' said Mr Ronald Ponsonby. He meant unfortunate for Gerald.

'Yes, and I 'eard another young girl only just escaped 'is 'orrible clutches.'

'Dear me, dear me,' said Mr Ronald Ponsonby. The fuss people made. Young girls were ten a penny, there were millions of them all over the world. 'Was the man local? Did you know him?'

''E lived local, but I didn't know 'im, which I'm

grateful I didn't. Name of Pottersly or something. Well, 'e'll be 'anged all right.'

'Most unfortunate,' said Mr Ronald Ponsonby. 'Well, I shall take a little rest now, Mrs Paterson, and go out again tonight, to have supper with friends.'

'Yes, all right,' said Mrs Paterson.

With public transport running again, and the trade unions licking their wounds, Doreen had no trouble getting a tram home. On her arrival, her mum, who was wearing a new blouse, actually made the usual pot of tea herself. She said her weakness was a bit stronger today.

Crikey, thought Doreen, what's all that mean?

Sammy was advised he could collect his car in the morning. Boots, learning that the garage was of the opinion that the brakes had been tampered with, advised Sammy to cast an eye around Islington.

'I prefer,' said Sammy, 'to think it happened accidental.'

'Ask Bert Roper to put out feelers,' said Boots.

'In order to find an excuse for a punch-up?' said Sammy.

'You might, Sammy, have been permanently damaged,' said Boots, and the steel that sometimes broke through his air of good humour, showed in the glint in his sound eye. 'So might Rachel.'

'Well, Boots, much as I value your advice and respect your old age,' said Sammy, 'I ain't in favour of persuading Bert and a couple of his friends to do grievous bodily harm to someone. It wouldn't do, old cock. All me East End friends would say Sammy Adams is gettin' heavy-handed, meanin' too big for his boots. They'd see me as one of themselves if I had a personal stand-up ten rounds with the sabotager—'

'Saboteur,' said Boots.

'Same thing,' said Sammy. 'But if I hired Bert and some of his mates to break the bloke's arms and legs, me East End friends would reckon I'd turned into a gang boss. I'll get Bert to put out some feelers, I'll do that, and if he finds out who chewed up me brake system, I'll ask him to give the bloke an East End talkin'-to, which is a bit different from handin' out a bunch of hospital grapes, but more friendly than breakin' him in half.'

'I think you'll find the bloke's a trade unionist,' said Boots. 'Have you told Tommy he's going to get a car on the firm?'

'Yes, I spoke to him on the phone,' said Sammy. 'He fainted.'

'All of him?' said Boots with a smile.

'Well, there was a dead silence for half an hour before he came back on the line,' said Sammy, 'and when he did he was croakin' a bit. He said he was highly appreciative and would I tell Vi the good news as he hadn't got the strength himself. So I popped over to see Vi at lunchtime and told her she and Tommy were goin' to get a fam'ly car on the firm.'

'That tickled her, did it?' said Boots.

'She fainted,' said Sammy. 'Faintin' must be in the fam'ly.'

'Well, I'm off now,' said Boots. 'By the way, there's been no fainting in my family about our car, just a few words from Chinese Lady.'

'A choice few?' said Sammy.

'I suppose you could call them the equivalent of an East End talking-to,' said Boots.

Tommy and Vi had recovered by the time they sat down to supper with little Alice, and they spent the evening talking excitedly about the pleasures of family outings in the car. They could go to Southend for the day on Sundays, or Brighton. Or Clapham Common, said Tommy. Don't be daft, said Vi, we can always go to Clapham Common on a tram. Well, good on yer, Vi, so we can, said Tommy. His equable, soft-eyed wife six months pregnant with their second child was worth her weight in gold to Tommy.

Aunt Victoria, Vi's mum, spent most of the evening planning calls on her neighbours to acquaint them with the news that her manager son-in-law was going to have a car. Well, a woman had to let her neighbours know she'd chosen the right kind of husband for her daughter.

A knock on the front door made Doreen say, 'If it's that barmy jigsaw lunatic again, Mum, shall I tell 'im to push off?'

'Oh, 'elp,' said Mrs Paterson, and her handsome body quivered. 'No, well, I ought to say good evenin' to 'im out of politeness before tellin' 'im not to come botherin' us.'

But Doreen found it was Luke on the doorstep, with a flat cardboard box under his arm.

'Hello, Lady Vi, how'dyer do?' he said.

'We're not in,' said Doreen. 'Well, we're not to old tramps and loonies. Did your barmy dad send you?'

'No, I came of me own accord,' said Luke.

'Would you like you and me to finish the Houses of Parliament jigsaw?'

'Would I what?' asked Doreen. The jigsaw in question, only partly completed, was still on the parlour table, awaiting the next get-together of her mum and Luke's talkative dad.

'Like you and me to finish—'

'I 'eard you first time,' said Doreen. 'Listen, are you tryin' to make out you're a close friend of mine?'

'Well, I do 'ave a secret ambition to be your closest friend,' said Luke.

'My mum's me closest friend,' said Doreen.

'Who's that, Doreen?' The inevitable enquiry, made in a raised voice, came from the kitchen.

'Oh, just someone from across the road, Mum. You'd best go,' Doreen said to Luke, 'or she might get 'er rollin'-pin out.'

'Not in her state of 'ealth, I hope,' said Luke. 'Shall I come in and say hello to her?'

'If you try to force your way in our house,' said Doreen, 'I'll call Mr Dawkins, our neighbour. He's a six-foot navvy and big as well.'

'Well, listen, if—'

''Ello, Doreen, 'ow is yer, me bonny?' said a tich of a bloke as he passed the gate.

'I'm fine, thanks, Mr Dawkins.'

'Yer look it too. Good on yer, girlie.' The tich of a bloke disappeared down the road.

'That's him?' said Luke. 'That's the six-foot navvy who's big as well?'

'He's shrunk again,' said Doreen. 'Mrs Dawkins keeps puttin' him in her Monday wash. It's 'is own fault, he shouldn't hang about on Monday mornings, he should get off to his work before she starts 'er wash. But I'll still scream for 'im if you put your feet over our doorstep.'

'Well, listen,' said Luke, 'if—'

'You'd better come in for a minute,' said Doreen, 'I don't want everyone to see you standin' on our doorstep lookin' as if you're tryin' to sell me stolen goods. Well, come on, come in, then, but only for a minute.'

Luke entered. Doreen half-closed the door. In the passage, Luke let his peepers dwell on her very nice face. Doreen faintly coloured.

'I was thinkin',' he said, 'that if—'

'Are you lookin' at me?' asked Doreen.

'Yes, I'm treatin' meself,' said Luke.

'Doreen, what's goin' on?' called Mrs Paterson.

'It's young Mister Whatsisname, Mum,' said Doreen, 'he's talkin' to me about that dad of his.'

'Oh, isn't 'is dad there?' Mrs Paterson ventured into the passage, looking fetching in her new blouse. She regarded Luke in suspicion. 'It's you, I see,' she said.

'Yes,' said Luke. 'Dad's nailing new leather soles on 'is Sunday shoes, so he thought you might like to finish that jigsaw with me. He feels a widow like you ought to have some sociable company in the evenings. Good for your condition, he said.'

'You told me you'd come of your own accord,' accused Doreen.

'I did,' said Luke. 'That was Dad's message to me as I left. Would you like a bit of a go at the jigsaw, Mrs Paterson? And I'll take you for a little walk after, if you fancy it.'

'I can't believe me ears,' said Doreen.

'Nor me,' said her mum. 'Of all the sauce. As for that dad of yours—'

'Yes, he said he'll probably pop in to see you tomorrow evenin',' said Luke, 'and bring his 'ealing gifts with him.'

'Oh, lor',' breathed Mrs Paterson. Her new blouse trembled. 'Me legs feel all funny again. I'd best go and sit down. You better finish the jigsaw with 'im, Doreen.' She tottered back to the kitchen, much as if the probable arrival of Old Iron tomorrow was giving her palpitations.

'Now see what you've done,' said Doreen.

'What about the jigsaw?' asked Luke. 'We could leave the Houses of Parliament to your mum and my dad tomorrow, and start on the Tower of London. I've brought it with me.'

'I'm goin' to hit you in a minute,' said Doreen. Still, she thought, imagine her mum saying she could jigsaw with Luke. She must be in a tizzy. 'Oh, well, I suppose now you're here you could stay a bit. But don't try takin' my temperature like your dad did with my mum last night.'

'I wouldn't know how to,' said Luke.

'Not much you wouldn't,' said Doreen. 'Well, let's go in the parlour, then.'

They began the construction of the Tower of London. Luke didn't exactly excel himself. Well, he was far more interested in sitting close to Doreen than in the jigsaw. He felt she was warm, breathing and alive. Should he slip an arm around her? Little by little? He tried it. Doreen asked him what he was up to. Trying to sort himself out on the Tower of London, he said. Doreen smiled.

At just after nine, Mrs Paterson called that she'd like a cup of tea as soon as that young man had gone. Luke took the hint and departed. That left two unfinished jigsaws on the parlour table.

Luke reported to Old Iron that Doreen had been nice and sociable.

'That's the ticket,' said Old Iron. 'Get a cuddle in, did yer, son?'

'No, just a few pieces of the Tower of London.'

'Oh, well, I think you've got more definite 'opes now. See anything of their lodger?'

'Not a whisker.'

'I 'ope he ain't a sly bleeder,' said Old Iron, 'the kind that might be underminin' me when I ain't lookin'.'

Chapter Fourteen

From the offices of the Registrar of Companies, Mr Ronald Ponsonby obtained details of the names and addresses of the directors of Adams Enterprises Ltd. There were four, Robert Adams, Tommy Adams, Sammy Adams and Eliza Somers. He needed the addresses in order to give himself the pleasure of seeing what the quarry looked like. Yes, it would be a pleasure to see the faces of the people on whom his twin brother had laid a curse. But Eliza Somers, who was she? He could ask someone in Walworth, perhaps, if Walworth was her birthplace. She was living now in Sunrise Avenue, Denmark Hill. They were all living in that area, SE5. Family closeness? Could Eliza Somers be the sister? If so, she made up the family of three brothers and a sister. They and their spouses were all to go.

Well, he still had plenty of time to identify all of them, while bearing in mind he did not want anyone to remember him as a man who was always enquiring into the affairs of the Adams family.

He took himself into the City for a pleasant lunch at an old-fashioned but discriminating restaurant. He returned afterwards to his lodgings, and met his landlady just as she was going out. A handsome woman, he conceded, and healthily full-bodied, but of no appeal to him. He and his brother had only ever been interested in young girls, young girls pretty enough to be photographed, and to stay young and pretty forever in the photographs.

'Ah, hello, Mrs Paterson, you are on your way out, I see, and I am on my way in,' he said with a couple of little nods.

'Yes, I'm just goin' to the shops, I'm feelin' I've got the strength,' said Mrs Paterson.

'Good, very good,' he said, peering through the plain glass of his unnecessary spectacles. Unnecessary to his eyesight, that is. 'It's a lovely afternoon.'

'Yes, what a blessin',' said Mrs Paterson, and went on her way.

Ten minutes later, Mr Ronald Ponsonby, as quietly as a mouse, entered Doreen's bedroom. A pretty young lady, very, and would have been delightful had she been a few years younger. However, she was still young enough, perhaps, for what she wore to be sweetly interesting. He pulled open a drawer in her mock Georgian mahogany dressing-table. Its oval mirror stared at him. He closed the drawer. He pulled open another. He smiled. Neatly folded underwear gazed shyly up at him. A dainty man, he took out each garment in turn and unfolded it with the lightest of touches. Eventually, all the garments lay in attractive array on the bed. Lace and little patterns of embroidery decorated some of the delicately feminine lingerie. He moved slowly around the bed, looking.

'Charming,' he murmured, 'charming.'

He refolded and replaced all the items, taking care to ensure they went back in the right order. He returned to his own room, having indulged himself very pleasurably in a visual way.

Mr Ronald Ponsonby, like his twin brother, had very peculiar tastes.

The country and its workforce were sorting themselves out. The Government was making appropriate noises without offering any practical help, but as Boots said to Chinese Lady that evening, governments produce gas and the workers produce wealth, and once that was understood, nobody needed to ask questions about where all the hot air balloons over Westminster were coming from. Chinese Lady asked her husband what her only oldest son was talking about. Gasbags and workers, said Mr Finch, who always enjoyed the evening meal with his wife and ready-made family.

No meals ever proceeded in silence, not in this household. They all made use of their tongues, and Rosie made particular use of hers. She was saying now that what Daddy and Grandpa meant was that Members of Parliament were gasbags and workers industrious. My, said Chinese Lady admiringly, what an educated girl you are, Rosie, and only eleven and all. I don't know why you have to go away to get more education at some school in the country next year. Oh, that's so she can have an advanced education, Mum, said Emily; like Boots did. I don't know it did him much good, said Chinese Lady, it only taught him to say one thing when he means another. But it did teach him to speak nice, said Emily. Well, I did hope none of my children would grow up speaking common, said Chinese Lady. Anyway, our Rosie always speaks very nice, so she doesn't need to be taught that.

Boots glanced at Rosie. She was quiet for once, getting on with her meal. Mr Finch commented that education was important, just as much for girls as for boys. I'm not getting any yet, said four-year-old Tim. You will, said Emily. Tim asked if he could eat his chop with his fingers. I use my teeth myself, Tim, said Mr Finch. Now, Edwin, that's not a proper answer, said Chinese Lady, that's the sort of thing Boots would say. I hope you're not going to catch his complaint. Emily, you answer Tim. Tim, said Emily, you can pick your bone up with your fingers and nibble it, there's still some meat left on it. But don't wipe your fingers on your shirt, my lad, use your napkin. Yes, Emily went on, girls ought to have advanced education as much as boys, shouldn't they, Rosie? Yes, Mummy, said Rosie.

Rosie, at her homework later in her grandpa's study, looked up as Boots came in.

'Hello, Daddy, come to help me with my geometry?'

'Listen, poppet, if you pass this exam next January, how will you feel about going to boarding-school?'

'Well,' said Rosie a little guardedly, 'Miss Simms did say it was a very good school, didn't she?'

'And what do you say?' asked Boots.

'Oh, I'll do whatever you think's best, Daddy. Of course, if Miss Simms hadn't gone to darkest Africa, we could have asked her opinion.'

'Well, I don't think we need her opinion,' smiled Boots, 'it's yours I'm after. Tell me how you really feel about the prospect of boarding.'

'Oh, help,' said Rosie, swallowing a little. The prospect hadn't seriously exercised her mind at first, but she'd been thinking lately that she wasn't going to enjoy being away from home, where she always felt so happy. Imagine being with girls all the time, some of them probably the soppy kind, and not seeing her family for weeks and weeks, especcially the one she loved so much.

'Take your time, poppet,' said Boots gently, and that made her swallow again.

'Well, Daddy, I have been thinking a bit. Isn't there a school I could go to without having to board?' She put the question hesitantly, even shyly. Boots saw the hesitancy, that of a girl who didn't want to go against his wishes. *His* wishes? That was so like Rosie. She was entitled to wishes of her own. He knew the school in question was excellent. Polly had said so, and he believed her. But there was an alternative, a fairly adequate one.

'I think we could consider the possibility, Rosie.'

'Could we? Could we really?'

'I don't see why not,' said Boots. He was thinking about the school he'd attended himself before the war, the only one in Southwark offering the equivalent of a grammar school education. West Square in St George's Road. The girls' establishment was immediately adjacent the boys'. 'What would you think about going to my old school, if your mother agrees?'

'Yours? Yours?' Rosie's eyes shone bluely bright. 'Daddy, d'you seriously mean that?'

'I seriously mean the girls' side. It's right next to the boys. You'll get a grammar school education.'

'Oh, crikey,' breathed Rosie, 'I'd go on a bus or tram every day to the school you went to? Lovaduck, Daddy, wouldn't I be proud, walking in your footsteps every day? Oh, not that I'd get stuck-up about it, I'd be ever so modest about your footsteps.'

'Just as well,' said Boots, 'I'm not famous yet.'

'D'you think Mummy will agree to this, Daddy?'

'I think so. I think your mother will want what you want, Rosie.'

'Well, God bless my mum,' said Rosie.

'I'll talk to her now,' said Boots. 'On Saturday afternoon, by the way, we'll all go to the motorcar emporium in Camberwell New Road and look at what they've got on offer.'

'Bliss,' said Rosie. 'Daddy, I'm not a bother about the school, am I?'

'I don't think so, poppet, I don't think girls like you can be a bother to anyone. I'll see about an interview with the headmistress of West Square.'

'Bless you, Daddy, you're really nice,' said Rosie, eyes over-bright.

'What?' said Emily.

'I'm gratified whenever I hear you talkin' sense, Boots,' said Chinese Lady. 'Edwin, you look pleased too.'

'It's not difficult for me to say I'd miss having Rosie around,' said Mr Finch. He had felt all along that Boots wasn't the man to send his daughter to boarding-school if it meant heartbreak for her. He knew just how attached Rosie was to her home and her family, and to her cousin Annabelle.

'Boots, you sure we'd be doin' the right thing?' said Emily.

'Rosie probably won't get such a polished education at West Square as at that boarding-school,' said Boots, 'but she'll still get a good one. So I think it would be the right thing for Rosie. I also think Annabelle will want to follow her there, and that Lizzy and Ned would be in favour of that.'

'Lord above,' said Chinese Lady, 'I don't know

I've ever heard you talkin' more sense, Boots. I used to sometimes think I'd brought up a music 'all comedian, and that Sammy wasn't much better, but you've both turned out to have a bit of sense. Edwin, do you have to put yourself behind that newspaper when your fam'ly's present?'

'Grandpa's coughin',' said young Tim, about to be put to bed.

'We can all hear him,' said Chinese Lady, 'but it's not a cough, it's some joke he's sharin' with your father.'

'I swear I'm innocent, Maisie,' said Mr Finch from behind his paper.

'I'm goin' to talk to Rosie as soon as I've taken Tim up,' said Emily. She did just that, and when she returned to the living-room that her family often shared with Chinese Lady and Mr Finch, she was smiling. 'That girl,' she said.

'Why d'you say that?' asked Chinese Lady.

'She's happy,' said Emily.

'We all are,' said Chinese Lady. 'Well, I know I am on account of my only oldest son talkin' all that sense at last. Edwin, I think I'd like a little port and lemon.'

''Ello, 'ello, is yer Ma in, Doreen?' said Old Iron.

'I'll have to ask,' said Doreen.

'Good, you do that, Doreen love—'

'Miss Paterson, if you don't mind.'

'No, I don't mind, Doreen,' said Old Iron heartily. 'If you find yer Ma is at 'ome, tell 'er to put 'er hat and coat on and I'll take 'er for a little walk.'

'You won't,' said Doreen.

'Do 'er good, yer know.'

'No, it won't, she'll come home drunk.'

'I trust you ain't implyin' dubious be'aviour on my part.'

'Yes, I am. You brought her 'ome drunk before.'

'Don't you believe it, Doreen. Just lively, she was, from 'aving a bit of what she fancied, yer know.'

'What d'you mean, a bit of what she fancied?' Doreen did her best to look shocked. 'My mum's a respectable widow. I hope you're not talkin' about a bit of what you fancied yourself.'

'What, with a respectable widow?' said Old Iron, weathered face expressing pain. 'Not me, love. What I meant was that yer Ma got lively from 'aving a very healin' time in the fish and chip shop and poppin' into the pub for just a small 'alf of Guinness.'

'Doreen, is that that young man?' called Mrs Paterson.

'No, Mum, it's that barmy dad of his.'

'Oh, lor'.'

'Do I hear that yer Ma's at 'ome?' asked Old Iron.

'Doreen, what's 'e want?' called Mrs Paterson.

'To take you out for a little walk, Mum.'

'Oh, me weak 'eart,' gasped Mrs Paterson.

'What did you say, Mum?'

'Doreen, me legs 'ave gone all funny again.'

'There you are,' said Doreen to Old Iron, 'her legs have gone all funny.'

'Tell 'er not to worry,' said Old Iron, 'I'll 'old her up, I've still got all me muscles. Come on, Muriel,' he called, 'get yer titfer.'

Mrs Paterson appeared. She sailed handsomely from the kitchen into the passage.

'Oh, lor',' she said.

'My, yer lookin' a real treat, Muriel,' said Old Iron, 'I can't recall ever seein' a better healin' job. Look at that, Doreen, ain't yer Ma a picture of 'ealth and beauty? I'll be proud to take 'er walkin'. Would yer maybe feel like a Guinness while we're out, Muriel?'

'Mum, don't you let 'im pour any drink into you,' said Doreen.

'Me a grievin' widow takin' to drink?' said her mum. 'I'll lose all me respectability. Still, perhaps a little walk will do me good.'

'Do us both good,' said Old Iron, wearing his bowler at a saucy tilt. 'And don't worry about yer legs, I'll look after them.'

'I don't like your language,' said Doreen. 'Where's that fast son of yours?'

'Mendin' a chair that fell apart when he sat on it,' said Old Iron. 'Right, yer ready now, Muriel? That's the ticket. Off we go, then, and we'll soon get yer temp'rature up to scratch.'

Doreen watched them go. She giggled.

They returned just after ten. Old Iron brought Mrs Paterson straight through to the kitchen. Her hat was a bit crooked, her face a little flushed, eyes slightly dizzy.

'Bless us, where's me chair?' she asked. She found it, she sat down and she blinked.

'Well, I can't believe it,' said Doreen, 'she's drunk again.'

'No, just lively,' said Old Iron.

'Doreen, I'll 'ave you know I've never been drunk in me life,' said Mrs Paterson.

'Just 'alf of Guinness and a bit of a sing-song, eh?' said Old Iron amiably. 'Done 'er the world of good, Doreen. Heartbeats sound as a bell, you can take me word. Well, see you again sometime, Muriel me love.'

'Oh, good night, Mr Edwards,' said Mrs Paterson dreamily.

Doreen buttonholed Old Iron at the front door.

'I hope I didn't hear you right,' she said, 'I hope I didn't hear something about Mum's 'eartbeats again.'

'Sound as a bell,' repeated Old Iron.

'Mr Edwards, have you had your hands on my mum again?'

'No, just on her titfer, Doreen. It fell off a couple of times.'

'What, when she was only havin' a sing-song?'

'Now you come to mention it,' said Old Iron thoughtfully, 'there was a bit of a knees-up as well. Mind you, it would've gladdened your heart to 'ave seen 'er performin' like a two-year-old.'

'Mum's not a two-year-old.'

'Bless yer, Doreen, course she ain't, she's a handsome woman with a fine pair of legs for a knees-up. Believe me, I was very admirin' of them. I forgot to compliment 'er on 'er tent pegs when I was bringing her 'ome, so maybe you'll compliment 'er for me. Well, I'll toddle across to me lodgings now. I expect Luke'll be knockin' at yer door tomorrer. Good night, love.'

'Oh, you old devil,' said Doreen, 'and as for that son of yours, it's my belief he's no better than you are. No wonder I don't feel safe with him.'

'No worries, Luke reckons you're a lady,' said Old Iron and went on his way. Doreen rejoined her mum, who looked as if she didn't quite know what time of the day it was.

'Mum, did you do the knees-up again?'

'Beg yer pardon, love?'

'Did you do a pub knees-up again?'

'Oh, there was a bit of jollity, I remember, but Mr Edwards was very carin' of me, and I do feel he's got a nice healin' touch.'

'Yes, he said you've got a sound 'eartbeat again, and he also asked me to compliment you on havin' just the legs for a knees-up.'

''Ow kind,' said Mrs Paterson, 'I think I'll go to me bed now.'

Doreen was still silently laughing when she slipped into her own bed. She heard the lodger come up just before she fell asleep.

Chapter Fifteen

Mr Ronald Ponsonby was up early, well before Doreen, who usually rose at seven-thirty, gave herself a little breakfast and took a cup of tea to her mum prior to leaving for her work. This morning, with the house quiet and Walworth just beginning to stir, the lodger went silently down to the kitchen, made himself a pot of tea and drank two cups. He emptied the teapot, washed up the cup and saucer, and was back in his room at seven-fifteen. At twenty to eight he left the house, aiming to get a sight of the man his brother had named in the letter. Robert Adams. He had his address, and surmised he would arrive at his Camberwell office for a nine o'clock start. Therefore, he would leave his house in Red Post Hill sometime before nine.

The hunter took a bus ride to Denmark Hill and alighted at Red Post Hill. He walked from there, checking house numbers. The one he was looking for proved to be some way down, not far from North Dulwich railway station. Reaching it, an old but handsome-looking house with an in and out drive, he crossed to the other side of the road, walked on a little way, then stopped and waited. It was a pleasant residential thoroughfare, tree-lined and quiet, although some people would have said it had an air of boring middle-class respectability.

Boots came out of the family house at twenty to nine, Rosie with him. They usually travelled together in the mornings, Rosie to her school, Boots to his office.

The hunter saw them, and his eyes stirred into quick life. Yes, that must be Robert Adams, and the girl, surely, was his daughter, the daughter pretty enough to be photographed, according to Gerald. Pretty enough? She was delicious in her school dress, boater and white socks. Adams looked tall, long-limbed and self-assured. The girl laughed at something he said. Enchanting, thought Mr Ronald Ponsonby. He watched them walk to a bus stop and wait there. Two young women were also waiting. Within a minute a bus appeared, a monster of grinding power operated by the London General Omnibus Company, its top deck open. Mr Ronald Ponsonby crossed the road behind the bus as it approached the stop. It pulled up. The two young women boarded, and Boots and Rosie followed. The hunter arrived in time to step on to the platform before the bus moved off again. His quarry climbed to the top deck. He took a seat inside and bought a ticket to Camberwell Green.

Another schoolgirl came aboard some way down Denmark Hill, a small boy with her. The girl was Annabelle Somers, daughter of Lizzy and Ned, the boy her six-year-old brother Bobby. Annabelle had a little chat with the cheerful conductor as he clipped tickets for them, then she and Bobby went up to the top deck to join Boots and Rosie, as they usually did.

At the King's College Hospital stop, Rosie, Annabelle and Bobby came down the stairs and alighted. Their school was only a two-minute walk from there. The hunter followed them off the bus, and sauntered in the wake of the two chattering girls and the small boy, his eyes on Rosie. His brother had been quite right. She was charming, utterly charming. He departed from the scene when the two girls and the boy turned in through the gates of St Luke's Church School along with other pupils. He knew now where the pretty daughter of Robert Adams would be each day, and he knew too how he would contrive to complete his mission.

'Susie?'

Susie looked up from her desk to find Sammy beside her.

'Yes, Your Lordship?'

'No sauce,' said Sammy. 'I'm off to collect the car now, and am accordingly leavin' these letters on your desk for your invaluable attention. I'll be goin' on to Islington.'

'Not to bump into a certain married woman, I hope,' said Susie.

'Funny you should mention that, Susie, I was only thinkin' that you bein' a married woman yourself, I wouldn't mind bumpin' into your jumper.'

'I'm honoured,' said Susie. 'Well, my jumper is.'

'Only I don't have time right now,' said Sammy.

'Just as well,' said Susie, 'I don't allow my jumper to be bumped into during office hours.'

Sammy departed laughing.

He arrived at the Islington factory in possession of his car again. Lilian Hyams was out. She was in Kensington, showing her portfolio of winter designs to Harriet de Vere, chief buyer for Coates, a woman under the spell of Sammy's electric vitality and fascinated by Boots.

Tommy was in his office, a sewing-machine on his desk. It had developed a fault and Tommy was applying his mechanical skill to its repair. Tommy kept all the sewing-machines in working order. He was a natural in his understanding of all kinds of machines.

'Hello,' said Sammy, 'how's things?'

'Well, the strike's over,' said Tommy, 'thunder and lightning's gone off for a rest, and the girls are 'aving frequent sing-songs.'

'Tell me about production,' said Sammy.

'Leave off,' said Tommy.

'Me question's superfluous?' said Sammy.

'It's got the makings of bein' upsettin' to me girls,' said Tommy. 'Still, I won't hold it against you considerin' the offer of a car. Vi's over the moon, and I'm fallin' about. Good on yer, Sammy.'

'It's fam'ly,' said Sammy. 'Now, how about all the extra stocks we hold, how are they goin'?'

'The Gen'ral Strike lasted ten days,' said Tommy. 'In that time our competitors nearly cleared us out. You're talkin' about all that stuff you cornered, I suppose?'

'Bought up, Tommy, bought up as a precaution,' said Sammy. 'Where's Bert?'

'In the stock room, puttin' in a new pane of glass that some'ow took an accidental brick on the last day of the strike. Sort of partin' gift from one of the unionists, I'd say. We got off light, Sammy, just this office window and the stock room window.'

'And me shiner,' said Sammy.

'Looks all right now,' said Tommy. 'How's your brakin' system today?'

'The garage fitted a new one,' said Sammy.

'Any thoughts?' asked Tommy.

'Only ones that hurt,' said Sammy, and went to have a word with Bert. Bert wasn't too pleased by what had happened to the brakes. Sammy said he echoed his sentiments. 'Can you ask around, Bert?'

'You want me to, guv?'

'It might be an idea,' said Sammy.

'So it might,' said Bert, 'considerin' it could've been fatal for yer. Now supposin' some 'elpful geezer comes up with a name, what's to 'appen to said name? A brick dropped six times on 'is loaf of bread?'

'No, just give him a bit of a talk,' said Sammy.

'A forgivin' talk?' said Bert, applying putty.

'Not too forgivin'.'

'A brick would 'urt more,' said Bert.

'Still,' said Sammy, 'we've got to consider the strikers all had hurt feelings about the miners. Can't blame 'em. A bit naughty, someone damagin' me brakes, I grant you—'

'Bloody dangerous, guv.'

'All the same, don't let's be heavy-handed,' said Sammy. 'Just a bit of a talk, eh? The right kind of talk. Can I leave it to you, Bert?'

'I'll ask a few questions,' said Bert.

'We had some trouble once with a bloke called Fatty Ford, who sent his heavies in,' said Sammy. 'Remember?'

'I remember,' said Bert. 'We didn't give them a talk.'

'No, brother Boots sent his old soldiers to sort things out,' said Sammy. 'That was different, Bert. Fatty Ford was a boss, and the people round here knew it.'

'See yer point, guv.'

'Thought you would,' said Sammy, and went into

the workshop to give his girls the benefit of a few kind words. Whoops greeted him.

''Ello, Mister Sammy, 'ow's yer manly self?'

''Ow's yer shiner, Mister Sammy?'

'Considerably improved,' said Sammy.

''Strewth, Mister Sammy, it's nearly all gorn.'

'My, don't yer look 'andsome again?'

'Give 'im a treat, Ruby, give 'im an eyeful of yer new garters.'

'Oh, would yer like to see 'em, Mister Sammy?'

'Yes, go on, Ruby, stand up. They're real fetchin', Mister Sammy, and frilly as well.'

'I'll take yer word for it,' said Sammy. 'Wait a bit, have I got something in me eye?'

'Only me new garters,' said the girl Ruby, standing up and flashing the circles of frilly pink around the tops of her stockings. The seamstresses shrieked.

'Oh, that Ruby, ain't she fast?'

'Talk to them, Gertie,' said Sammy, but he gave them five minutes more of his time. He was quite aware that it perked them up to know he had a soft spot for them. He liked being in business, he liked making money, and his seamstresses liked making it for him. Accordingly, he did have a soft spot for them. Before he left he told them they'd get extra bonuses for all the hard work they'd put in during the strike.

'Mister Sammy, yer bleedin' good to us, if yer'll excuse me French,' said Gertie.

'It's fair, Gertie,' he said.

'Ain't you a love, Mister Sammy?' said Gladys. 'Ruby, show 'im yer frilly garters again.'

''Ere we are, Mister Sammy,' said Ruby.

'I ain't lookin', I'm a married man,' said Sammy, and took himself away.

It was lunchtime. In the playground of St Luke's Church School, the pupils were eating their sandwiches or whatever else their mums had supplied them with. Rosie and Annabelle, having finished their sandwiches, were sharing a large apple. Annabelle took it from Rosie and blinked.

'Crikey, Rosie, you didn't half have a big bite, nearly down to the core,' she said.

'Well, you had an enormous bite before,' said Rosie.

'I don't remember,' said Annabelle, and took a modest bite.

'Oh, help,' said Rosie, 'here comes potty Potts.'

Up came ten-year-old Alfie Potts, known for bringing dead mice to school and making girls faint. The pupil count was four hundred, a mixture of riotously energetic young cockneys and equally energetic, if less riotous, boys and girls of the lower middle class.

'Give us a bite, eh?' said Potts, eyeing what was left of the apple, now back with Rosie.

'All right,' said Rosie, a girl so happy with life that she dispensed sweet charity to all, even to boys like Potts. She handed him the apple. He took three snapping bites and returned what was no more than a spindly core to her.

'Well, look at that,' said Annabelle.

'You Alfie, you weren't supposed to eat all of it,' said Rosie.

'I didn't,' said Potts, 'I give yer back what was left of it, didn't I?'

'Yes, just the core,' said Rosie.

'Oh, don't yer like cores?' said Potts. 'I like 'em

meself, I always eat me mum's cookin' apple cores. I'll show yer.' He took the core from Rosie and it disappeared into his mouth, short stalk and all. Crunch. 'There y'ar, all gorn. 'Ere, did yer dads go on strike? My dad did.'

'Mine didn't,' said Annabelle, 'he has to keep my mum and us with our bodies and souls together.'

'What about the workers?' asked Potts, who'd heard his dad say that kind of thing.

'Well, fancy you asking,' said Rosie, 'our dads are both workers. My dad keeps his family's body and soul together by the sweat of his honest brow.'

'I dunno why you talk me ears orf,' said Potts.

Up came a bruiser of a girl, thirteen-year-old Beryl Nicholls.

'Now then, Potts,' she said, 'what yer doin' of with these Lady Mucks?'

'I just ate their apple core for 'em,' said Potts, 'and they ain't Lady Mucks.'

'Yer saucy winkle, what d'yer say that for?'

''Cos I like 'em,' said Potts.

'Oh, yer do, do yer? 'Ow would yer like me knee in yer belly-button?'

''Ow would yer like this down yer drawers?' said Potts, and produced a dead mouse from his pocket. The bruiser of a girl screamed and ran. Potts, grinning, went after her, waving the dead mouse by its tail.

'Ugh,' said Annabelle.

'Still, he did stand up for us,' said Rosie.

'Rosie, d'you think you'll get to West Square School?' asked Annabelle.

'Well, Daddy's taking me for an interview with the headmistress on Friday afternoon, so he said I've got to look brainy and intelligent.'

'Crumbs,' said Annabelle, 'what sort of a look is that?'

'Like this,' said Rosie, and put on an earnest expression.

'That only looks as if you've got toothache,' said Annabelle.

Beryl Nicholls, the bruiser of a girl, came round again, running and yelling, Potts still after her with the dead mouse.

'Potts! Potts!' A teacher was shouting. Potts was deaf. Rosie laughed.

'Oh, help, isn't life a giggle, Annabelle?' she said. 'I wish I could live for ever, and you as well and all the family.'

'What, just getting older and older?' said Annabelle.

'Oh, no, just as we are now,' said Rosie. Potts and the limp mouse caught up with Beryl Nicholls. She shrieked. 'Crikey,' said Rosie, 'she won't live for ever, she's just died the death.'

In another playground, that of St John's in Walworth, Cassie was having a bit of trouble with Freddy.

'What d'you keep on talkin' to Cecily Smivvers for?' she demanded.

'Well, she wants to be me new mate,' said Freddy.

'Well, she can't, or I'll tell me dad,' said Cassie.

'It's like this,' pontificated Freddy, 'I'm lookin' for a new mate, as yer know, on account of 'aving had a lot of sauce from me present one, who's you know who.'

'Yes, it's me,' said Cassie. ''Ere, Freddy, did yer know the King's got a royal plumber that's got a mate that carries 'is bag of tools for 'im? When the King 'as a leak—'

'Cassie, mind what yer sayin'.'

'Well, 'e does 'ave leaks sometimes, in 'is palace,' said Cassie. 'The Queen don't 'ave leaks, 'cos it's not 'er palace, and it's the King that calls the royal plumber in, and 'is mate comes as well, with the bag of tools. Freddy, you best not talk to Cecily Smivvers any more or me dad'll wallop yer.'

'Well, look 'ere,' said Freddy, 'can I trust yer not to give me any sauce in future?'

'Course you can,' said Cassie. 'Freddy, we've got to practise for the Empire Day pageant again tomorrow afternoon.'

'I won't be there,' said Freddy, 'I'll be ill all day tomorrow.'

Mr Ronald Ponsonby stood at a distance from the school gates when the boys and girls were leaving St Luke's at four o'clock. He was reading a newspaper. That did not prevent him sighting Rosie as she came through the gates in company with Annabelle and Bobby. His peering eyes brightened. He was there simply to indulge the pleasure of letting his eyes dwell on the enchantment of the daughter of Robert Adams. It was the enchantment that only young girls possessed, the enchantment of sweet unspoiled innocence. Alas that it was so fleeting. He picked her out easily amid the swarm of girls and boys, and thought her every movement was that of a girl of natural grace. How sad, yes, how very sad that she would be as she was now for only a relatively brief time. He saw the girl beside her, and the young boy. The three of them detached themselves from the swarm, the two girls talking animatedly. The second girl was younger, by a year, perhaps, and she too had enchantment. But the daughter of Robert Adams, ah, she was perfection. Such a pity that she would grow old. He had saved one girl from taking on the ugliness of growing up and growing old, a girl in Nottingham, and another during a visit to Lyons a year ago. The discovery of the body of the latter girl had caused hysterical reaction, and since his hurried return to Dieppe he had contented himself with taking covert snapshots of sweet young angels engaged in active play or frolics in the open spaces of the town.

Rosie, Annabelle and Bobby walked to their bus stop. Mr Ronald Ponsonby did not follow. He took himself off in the opposite direction. There was time to go to the shops, to buy himself a new hat and to discard his straw boater.

Boots stepped off the bus and crossed the road. He was on his way home after his day at the office. Unlike Sammy, he was always able to put the affairs of business behind him once he left his office. His time then, for the rest of the day, belonged to his family. He enjoyed that time, he enjoyed the evening reunion with all of them, with his mother, his step-father, his wife and his son and daughter. He was more the son of his mother than, in his whimsical nature, he might have admitted. To Chinese Lady, the principal reason for living was the family. To Boots, the family meant something that was indefinably precious, never mind faults, irritations or wrangles. All his instincts were of a protective kind. There had been temptation in the shape of Polly Simms, an infectious extrovert. He had not given in, and temptation had taken itself away the day she departed for Kenya. But he missed her occasional appearances in his life.

'Mr Adams – Mr Adams?'

He stopped. He was outside the house of his neighbours, the Fletchers, and Mrs Fletcher was at her open door.

'Hello, yes?' he smiled, and she came to her gate, attractive in a blue dress.

'Mr Adams, I thought I must tell you, I'm sure a man was watching you when you left your house with Rosie this morning.'

'Watching me?'

'I'm sure he was,' said Mrs Fletcher. 'I was upstairs, at my dressing-table, and noticed him across the road and a little way off, by that beech tree. You had your back to him. He crossed the road when the bus came, and boarded it after you and Rosie got on. Oh, you don't think I'm just a silly woman, do you?'

'Far from it,' said Boots. 'What was he like?'

'Quite smart-looking in a boater and suit and spectacles, and middle-aged.'

'Well, I can't say I noticed him, but if he's interested in me for some reason or other, I'll look out for him. You're sure he was a middle-aged bloke with spectacles and not someone like Vilma Banky, the Hollywood heart-throb?'

Laughing, Mrs Fletcher said, 'Oh, you'd like to be followed by her?'

'Not every day,' smiled Boots, 'but once in a while. Anyway, thanks for letting me know. Perhaps a creditor's on my tail.'

'Don't let him catch you, then,' said Mrs Fletcher, and Boots smiled again and went into his house, thinking her suspicions imaginative. Rosie appeared in the hall and kissed him hello. He was home.

Doreen put a question to her mum that evening.

'Would you mind if I went and saw a Douglas Fairbanks film tomorrow night?'

'No, I won't mind, love,' said Mrs Paterson, and Doreen thought well, I'm blessed, nothing about being left alone or that she'd like to come with me? 'I might fancy a small Guinness meself,' added Mrs Paterson.

'Beg pardon, Mum?'

'What did I say?' Mrs Paterson looked flustered.

'I think you said Mr Edwards might come round and take you out for a small Guinness while I'm at the pictures.'

Mrs Paterson blinked.

'I'm not meself,' she sighed. 'Doreen, you sure I said that?'

'Well, something like it.'

The front door knocker sounded. Mrs Paterson jumped.

'Oh, me nerves,' she said, 'can that be 'im?'

'I'll see,' said Doreen. It turned out to be Luke.

'Evenin', Lady Vi, hope you don't mind me knockin'.'

'Well, I do mind,' said Doreen, 'you and that dad of yours are both barmy. You don't think my mum and me like you and him to keep knockin', do you?'

'I can see you're not keen yourself,' said Luke, 'but I'm gettin' fond of it.'

'How can anyone get fond of knockin' on a door?' asked Doreen, who felt she'd lately had a trying time in fighting hysteria.

'Only on your door,' said Luke. 'Look, what

about you and me finishin' the Tower of London jigsaw puzzle?'

'I hope you're not expectin' me to invite you in,' said Doreen, thinking she liked him for the way he always made her want to laugh.

'I can't tell a lie, I'm livin' in hope,' said Luke, thinking she looked nicer and more attractive every time he saw her.

Mrs Paterson appeared.

'Oh, it's you,' she said, 'I 'ope you're not molestin' my daughter.'

'I wouldn't do that, missus, specially not on 'er doorstep,' said Luke.

'I'm glad to 'ear it,' said Mrs Paterson, 'Doreen's only a young girl, and it's me duty as 'er mother to see no-one molests 'er. And I might tell you the police station's not very far from 'ere.'

'Well, Mrs Paterson,' said Luke, 'you don't need any coppers to stand guard for her, I'll be pleased to guard 'er meself. I'll come round and stand guard every evenin' with pleasure.'

It was too much for Doreen. She dashed into the nearest room, the parlour, and smothered her shrieks in a sofa cushion.

'There, see what you've done, young man,' said Mrs Paterson, 'she's gone and probably fainted away at the thought of you comin' 'ere to molest 'er ev'ry evenin'.'

'No, guard her,' said Luke.

'I 'eard what you said, but it wasn't what you meant.'

'I'd better come in and 'ave a look at her,' said Luke. 'If she has fainted on account of misunderstandin' me, I'd better give her some first aid and let her know me intentions are honourable.'

''Ere, who said you could come in?' asked Mrs Paterson as Luke adroitly whipped past her and entered the parlour. He found Doreen lying on her tummy on the sofa, her face buried in a cushion. Strange noises reached his ears.

'Lady Vi, you all right?' he asked.

Doreen turned over. Luke blinked and went dizzy in a happy way. Her knee-length dress was rucked, her imitation silk stockings showing all the way up to glinting metal suspender clips. Well, I've never had a luckier day than this, he thought. What a darling, she ought to be decorated for having legs like that.

'Excuse me,' said Doreen, her face flushed from the effort of smothering hysterics, 'who said you could come in?'

'Your mum thought you'd fainted,' said Luke.

'Me?'

'I feel a bit that way meself.'

'What?'

'Dizzy,' said Luke, 'but I ain't complainin'.'

Doreen sat up. A little shriek erupted as she saw where her dress was. In came her mum.

'Doreen!'

'Oh, me legs,' gasped Doreen. Not that they weren't admirable, or that she was prudish, but really, did her mum have to be there at that particular moment? She pushed her dress down.

'Doreen, don't tell me 'e's been molestin' you,' said Mrs Paterson.

'No, my dress ran up when I fell on the sofa,' said Doreen, pink.

'There, I knew it, young man,' said Mrs Paterson, 'I told yer me daughter came and fainted. You'd better go and get me smelling-salts, they're on a shelf of our dresser in the kitchen.'

'Mum, I don't want any smelling-salts,' said Doreen.

'I'll take her for a walk, if you like, Mrs Paterson,' said Luke, 'and give 'er some fresh air.'

'I'll scream,' said Doreen.

A voice sounded from the open front door.

'Anyone 'ome?' It was Old Iron.

'Oh, me temp'rature,' gasped Mrs Paterson as Old Iron appeared.

''Ello, what's all this, a sociable gatherin'?' he said. 'And did I 'ear you remark on yer temp'rature, Muriel?'

'Me daughter's 'aving trouble from your son,' said Mrs Paterson weakly.

'Not likely I'm not,' said Doreen, up on her feet, 'I don't let any bloke give me trouble.'

'Well, I tell yer what, Doreen love,' said Old Iron in fatherly fashion, 'let's all 'ave a cup of tea, eh? You go an' put the kettle on, Luke, seein' Doreen's a bit flushed and 'er mum's got an agitated pulse, and I'll do a bit of healin' on both of 'em.'

'You'll be lucky,' said Doreen. 'And I'm quite capable of puttin' the kettle on meself.'

Ten minutes later they were all sitting down at the kitchen table, the teapot with its cosy on and Doreen waiting for the contents to brew. When she did pour, the tea was a hot deep gold.

'Very sociable,' said Old Iron, 'and neighbourly as well.'

'I don't know how you two got into our kitchen,' said Doreen.

'Nice of you to invite us,' said Luke. 'Would you like a walk in a few minutes?'

'I'm not leavin' my mum alone with your dad,' said Doreen.

'Still, if you'd like a walk, Doreen, I won't stand in yer way, love,' said Mrs Paterson.

'That's the ticket,' said Old Iron. 'I noticed with pleasure, Muriel, that our jigsaw's still in place on yer parlour table. Kind of yer to wait for me to come and finish it with yer.'

'Oh, I – oh, I don't know about that,' said Mrs Paterson, looking handsome but flushed. 'Well, all right, Mr Edwards, I don't want to be unsociable.'

'Course yer don't, Muriel,' said Old Iron, 'you ain't that kind of lady. Gracious, that's what you are. Luke, you could treat Doreen to some fish and chips while yer on yer walk with 'er.'

'He's not goin' on any walk with me,' said Doreen, 'and I don't need any fish and chips, anyway.'

But she had some all the same. She couldn't resist the aroma when she and Luke reached the shop. And she wouldn't have been a true cockney girl if she'd said no.

When they got back, Old Iron and Mrs Paterson were sitting together over the jigsaw at the parlour table. Doreen examined the progress they'd made on the Houses of Parliament.

'It's comin' on,' said Old Iron.

'Like a house on fire, I don't think,' said Doreen.

'Still, they're 'alfway up Big Ben,' said Luke.

'Truth to tell,' said Old Iron, 'I've been doin' a spot of more healin' work on yer Ma, Doreen.'

'Yes, Mr Edwards 'as been very carin',' said Mrs Paterson.

''Er temp'rature's back to normal,' said Old Iron, 'and me professional pride is proud of 'er heartbeat. Sounder ev'ry day, and I compliment yer, Muriel, on yer recoverin' condition. I'll maybe finish the 'Ouses of Parliament with yer tomorrow.'

'Well, me daughter's goin' to the pictures in the evenin' to see a Douglas Fairbanks film,' said Mrs Paterson, 'so I'll be by meself.'

'Yer won't be lonely,' said Old Iron, 'I'll come round and bring a bottle of Guinness with me.'

'Oh, no you won't,' said Doreen, 'I'm not leavin' my mum so that you can come round, pour more drink into her and feel her 'eartbeats.'

'I think I'll wear me new blouse again,' said Mrs Paterson faintly and absently.

'I'll take Doreen to the pictures, Mrs Paterson,' said Luke.

''Ow kind,' said Mrs Paterson.

'I'm not goin' to the pictures,' said Doreen. Crikey, I'm lying, she thought. I am going. I think something's happening. I think I've got a mellowing mum who likes having her heartbeats examined. What's Luke grinning about? If he's thinking of examining mine, he's due for a black eye. Still, ain't he sweet in a way? He doesn't half know how to come after a girl.

Mr Ronald Ponsonby entered the house and quietly climbed the stairs to his room. He had enjoyed an excellent day.

Chapter Sixteen

Uncle Tom, a distant relative of Chinese Lady and father-in-law of her son Tommy, left his house in Foreign Street, Camberwell, at twenty to eight in order to reach his place of employment, the local gasworks, by eight o'clock. Tommy was with him. He liked to be at the Islington factory by eight-thirty, the time when Gertie and her girls began.

Mr Ronald Ponsonby appeared in the street at fifteen minutes to eight, having correctly assumed that Tommy Adams was the brother who managed the firm's factory. He expected him to leave the house not earlier than eight, for he supposed a manager's starting time was nine o'clock.

Accordingly, he waited in vain. By nine o'clock, he had seen no-one leave the house. Nor by quarter-past. He left then. His presence in a street devoid of trees and traffic had become too notice-able. He decided to return at five and wait at the top of the street, on the corner. From there he could take note of men coming home from their work and which houses they entered. He could not forgo this psychological need to lay his eyes on the people he intended to destroy.

Well, now he had time for a leisurely journey to Stepney Green to collect what had been promised to him by an old acquaintance whose contacts were dubious but very accommodating. At a price.

*   *   *

Mrs Paterson spent part of the morning ironing her freshly washed new blouse. She ironed it in a slightly nervous state. That manly Mr Edwards was visiting again this evening. Oh, lor', with his soothing talk and his healing gifts, he did make a respectable widow really nervous. Still, that didn't mean she shouldn't wear her new blouse, which was a nice decorative covering for a handsome bosom, and no-one could rightly say her bosom wasn't still very handsome.

It quivered a bit then, and her legs went all funny.

At his work, Old Iron thought about her handsomeness and her heartbeats.

'Something ticklin' yer, Old Iron?' said a workmate.

'Yes, me flannel vest,' said Old Iron.

'Tea, Mister Adams,' said Doreen, placing the mid-morning cup on Boots's desk.

'Thanks,' said Boots. 'Who made it?'

'I did. Ronnie's out with Mitch in the van.'

'Good,' said Boots. 'Keep him running about and away from the kettle and teapot. He's a willing lad, but hasn't yet discovered there's a difference between tea and the baby's bath water. By the way, you're looking very eligible.'

'Oh, d'you think so, Mister Adams?' said Doreen. 'I suppose I must be,' she said as she left his office. She put her head back in. 'Well, I think I've got a feller after me,' she said, and disappeared again.

Susie, a self-taught touch typist, placed some letters on Sammy's desk at five minutes to four.

'That's all of them,' she said.

'Your efficiency is remarkable, Mrs Adams.'

'Oh, don't mention it, I'm sure, Mister Sammy.'

'You short at all, Susie?'

'Short of what?' asked Susie.

'Finances?' said Sammy.

'No, of course not, you let me keep all my salary to myself.'

'Still, when winter comes, will you have enough for a fur coat?' asked Sammy.

'A what, Sammy?'

'It's my considered opinion, Susie, that you'd look like Bond Street in a fur coat,' said Sammy. 'It might cost me holes in both me pockets and ruin me wallet as well, but the fact is, Susie, I like bein' married to you.'

Susie's blue eyes turned quite misty.

'Sammy, ain't you lovely?' she said. 'I like it too, I hope we'll both like it for always, even if we do have some ups and downs. I don't really want a fur coat any more than Em'ly does. She's got Boots and I've got you.'

'And Tommy's got Vi, and Ned's got Lizzy.'

'Is that happy fam'lies, Sammy?'

'It's what Chinese Lady ordered for all of us, Susie, as Boots will tell yer.'

'Oh, I adore Boots,' said Susie.

'Eh?' said Sammy.

'Only as head of the fam'ly after Chinese Lady,' said Susie, 'not as my one and only better half. Life's grand, Sammy. I'm off now, see you at home later.' She turned at the door. 'Sammy love?'

'Ask and ye shall receive,' said Sammy.

'Oh, good,' said Susie, 'because I was just goin' to ask if we could start a family.'

'Mother O'Reilly, what a happy thought,' said Sammy. 'I'd better have a second helpin' of afters at supper.'

The hunter was out and about again. He had been to his lodgings, taking with him the items he had purchased during his visit to Stepney Green. They constituted a weighty whole in the innocuous attaché case he was carrying. It was locked. He placed it in his suitcase and locked that too. Then he pushed the suitcase out of sight under the bed.

Now he was on the corner of Foreign Street, the time a little after five. He strolled about. Street kids, home from school, chased after each other. Behind his glasses, his eyes flickered as a man turned into Foreign Street, a middle-aged man in working clothes and carrying a bag of tools. He aroused no interest in the hunter the moment the latter noted his age. But if Mr Ronald Ponsonby had watched his progress down the street, he would have seen him enter the house he'd had under surveillance this morning. The man was Tommy's father-in-law.

Other men appeared from time to time. Some the hunter watched to their doors. At ten to six, Tommy turned into the street, having left Islington just after five. The flickering eyes came to life. Tommy was a tall stalwart, and visibly not yet thirty. The hunter heard him softly whistling. He watched and saw him turn into the house that was marked X on the mental map.

So you're Tommy Adams. And you're whistling, are you? You wouldn't be, oh dear no, if you were locked up in prison and waiting to go on trial for your life, all as a result of the cursed interference of your brother Robert. Well, your whistling days are numbered, Mr Tommy Adams.

Tommy climbed the stairs of the house.

'I'm home, Vi.'

'What a coincidence,' called Vi, 'so am I.'

'Where's me pickle?'

His pickle, little Alice, toddled out on to the landing. Tommy picked her up, tickled her and kissed her nose. He carried her into the room he and Vi had turned into a kitchen-cum-living-room.

'Had a nice day, love?' asked Vi, busy getting supper.

'Busy one,' said Tommy.

'Well, a busy one's better than a troublesome one,' said Vi, fair-haired and lovably equable. She and Tommy were saving to buy their own house, and on Saturday they were going to buy a motorcar at the expense of the family firm. 'No more troubles, Tommy, nothing nasty to report?'

'Nothing,' said Tommy.

How was he to know that only a few minutes ago he had passed a very nasty blot on the landscape?

Mighty Caesar had had another trying rehearsal. He informed Mr Hill, in so many words, that in his opinion Queen Boadicea and her Ancient Britons all ought to be put to the Roman sword. Too messy, said Mr Hill. Drowning, then, said Caesar. Can't be done, said Mr Hill, so try to rise above your misfortunes. Some hopes I got, said Caesar. Boadicea said that Caesar was messing about and his togger wasn't on proper. Caesar said well, it wouldn't be, would it, when he'd been under her chariot wheels three times. Still, said Boadicea, you haven't actually been run over yet.

Caesar gave her another wigging on their way home, and said he'd see to it that she got to play Joan of Arc in next year's pageant. Boadicea asked what for? Well, said Caesar, Joan of Arc got burnt at the stake. That reminds me, said Boadicea, did you know me dad once saved Lady Alfrida from a burning castle? Who's Lady Alfrida? I don't know, said Boadicea, me dad didn't say.

Caesar gave up.

In the evening, Old Iron popped across the street to do more jigsaw with Doreen's quivering mum and to apply some further healing if the lady had any ailing moments. Doreen departed to see the Douglas Fairbanks film, but not before telling Luke's dad that if he did anything to give her mum a heart attack, she'd hurt his bread-basket with her late dad's hammer. Old Iron assured her nothing too excitable would take place. Well, not excitable enough to give her mum a heart attack.

On her way to the cinema, Doreen was smiling. Her mum had encountered a real old cockney character in Luke's dad.

It wasn't until she arrived at the cinema, the Golden Domes, that Doreen felt it just wasn't natural, going to see a film by herself. She could have asked Betty Hooper, a friend of hers. But she'd so liked the idea of an evening out that she hadn't thought of how daft it would feel, arriving at the cinema by herself. Oh, well, she was here now. Several people were at the box office. She advanced, opening her handbag. Someone touched her elbow.

'I've got the tickets,' said Luke.

'Well, if it isn't you,' said Doreen, liking the

moment and what it meant. 'Your dad said you were in your lodgings playin' with your train set.'

'No, he didn't,' said Luke, gone on her. 'Let's go in, shall we? The last programme starts in five minutes.'

'It's blackmail,' said Doreen. 'You know I can't make a scene 'ere. I'd better not tell my mum you as good as dragged me in, she'll 'ave a fit. Oh, all right, let's go in, then.'

They went in. The cinema was nearly full, Douglas Fairbanks being top of the popularity stakes with filmgoers. They found two seats near the back row. They settled down. Doreen's very nice legs glimmered in the darkness. Luke felt he'd won a round in getting her into the cinema, even if she thought she really ought to have stayed home with her mum. Doreen wasn't thinking anything of the sort. She was thinking that what was going on between her mum and Luke's dad was probably a giggle.

The programme began with an animated cartoon about Felix the Cat. Nearby, some old lady made herself heard.

'That ain't a cat, Ellen.'

'It's a cartoon cat, Granny.'

'It don't look any kind of a cat to me.'

'It's a drawin', Granny.'

'What's it runnin' about for, then?'

The cinema pianist ran tinkling fingers along the ivories. Granny sucked an acid drop. The cartoon ran to its end with the pianist playing the song, 'Felix Kept On Walking'. A two-reel Ben Turpin comedy followed, the packed cinema in the mood for a laugh.

'Who's that bloke?' asked Granny.

'Granny, that's Ben Turpin.'

''E's boss-eyed.'

'It's to make 'im look comical, Granny.'

''E don't look comical to me. What's them words up on the screen?'

'It's Ben Turpin sayin' "Get orf me foot, Fatty."'

'Ellen, I just swallered me acid drop.'

''Ave another one, Granny.'

Doreen giggled. The audience laughed its way through the comedy. It was easier to laugh in a cinema than in a dole queue. And aside from the strike, 1926 was fun, with giddy flappers to the fore and the Bright Young Things sending up law and order.

The big film, an American version of *Robin Hood*, featured Douglas Fairbanks at his most swashbuckling. His agile adventurousness aroused cheers. The Sheriff of Nottingham induced hisses.

Behind Luke a girl whispered, 'Geddorf, yer lump.'

'I ain't on yer, Sadie, not yet I ain't,' whispered her bloke.

'You got a hope.'

Friar Tuck bounced about.

'Who's 'e?' asked Granny.

'Granny, it's Friar Tuck.'

'Looks like a dressed-up balloon to me.'

'It's 'is 'abit, Granny.'

'Shouldn't 'ave 'abits like that. 'Abits is common. 'Ave yer got any more acid drops, Ellen?'

Robin Hood swung on a rope with the pianist playing 'The Man On The Flying Trapeze'.

'Crikey, look at that, Granny.'

''E'll fall orf in a minute. There y'ar, told yer so.'

'No, 'e jumped, Granny.'

The Sheriff of Nottingham and his men stole up on Robin Hood a little later. The audience yelled.

'Robin 'Ood, look behind yer!'

Robin Hood turned. Out came his sword.

'Lovaduck, Ellen,' said Granny, ''e 'eard us.'

Doreen enjoyed every moment of the film. Luke liked it a lot. But he liked Doreen more. He liked being with her. She was as lively as any cockney girl, and even when she was giving him what for there was a lot of laughter about. It was a pity she'd persuaded herself that her mum couldn't do without her. Never mind, Old Iron was working on the possessive widow and with any luck might make a new woman of her.

Doreen came to at the end of the film.

'All over, Lady Vi,' said Luke.

Doreen, the lights up, blinked at him.

'Well, I'm blessed,' she said, 'where did you spring from?'

'A doctor's black bag, so my late mum said.'

'Not that, you daft thing,' said Doreen, and the audience stood for the National Anthem, played with rousing patriotism by the pianist. Emerging into Camberwell Road, Doreen said, 'Listen, how did you get in the cinema with me?'

'With a ticket,' said Luke.

'You're barmy,' she said. Barmy nice, though, she thought. 'I've never met a more barmy pair than you and your dad,' she said, as they crossed the road to a tram stop. 'Oh, me gawd, what's he been gettin' up to with my mum this time, I wonder?'

'It's all right, Lady Vi, he won't say anything, 'e'll keep it dark.'

Doreen said that if he was implying her mum had

spent the evening having to fight for her honour as a respectable widow, there'd be ructions all over Morecambe Street. When they reached her house, she told him he'd better not come in, it might upset her mum to know they'd been at the pictures together. Luke said that if her mum had had to fight for her honour all this time, she'd probably have other things on her mind. But he did what Doreen wanted, he said good night to her at the gate. Doreen thanked him for treating her and Luke went home to his lodgings.

As Doreen opened the door, the lodger appeared out of the darkness, smiled at her through his neat beard, peered at her through his spectacles, said what a nice day he had had and went up to his room, wearing a new trilby hat.

Doreen entered the kitchen. Her mum was still up and looking quite happy, and not at all as if she'd had a dreadful evening, even if she was slightly flushed.

'Oh, 'ello, Doreen love, 'ad a nice time at the pictures?'

'Lovely, thanks,' said Doreen. 'Have you 'ad any trouble, Mum?'

'What trouble?'

'Did that man behave 'imself?'

'I don't know why you're so suspicious,' said Mrs Paterson, her new blouse very decorative. 'Mr Edwards 'as been very carin' again. We 'ad some very sociable talk and did a bit more of the jigsaw. He did the honours like a gent.'

'What honours?' asked Doreen.

'Well, 'e made us both a nice pot of tea and complimented me on recoverin' a lot of me 'ealth. I don't know when I ever 'ad a more sociable time.'

Mrs Paterson looked a bit bemused then, but not in a self-doubting way. 'Then 'e went off a bit 'urried, like. 'E 'ad things to do. Doreen, would yer like a nice cup of tea?'

'Yes, I would, Mum.' Crikey, thought Doreen, something's really come over her. 'The lodger's just come in, by the way.'

'Yes, 'e's out such a lot,' said Mrs Paterson. 'I must say we couldn't 'ave a more undisturbin' lodger or a more respectable one. I'll put the kettle on, you 'ave a sit-down, love.'

'I hope you'll be havin' more sociable evenings, Mum,' said Doreen.

'Yer a thoughtful girl,' said Mrs Paterson, putting the kettle on the gas stove in the scullery. 'Of course, I still couldn't do without you, love.'

Oh, blow that, thought Doreen.

'Well, Old Iron,' said Luke, 'how'd you get on this evenin'?'

Old Iron was sitting in a fireside armchair and looking a bit off colour.

'I did a runner,' he said, 'but I ain't sure I escaped.'

'What d'you mean?' asked Luke.

'I've been done for, good as,' gloomed Old Iron. He explained. He and Doreen's handsome Ma, he said, enjoyed a nice friendly time doing the jigsaw over a drop of Guinness. He asked how her health was and she said she'd felt good all day but was a bit faint now. So he put an arm around her to stop her falling off her chair, and she said she was very appreciative of his healing gifts. A bit later, when they were working on Big Ben's clock, she said her legs felt all funny. He told her not to worry, she was sitting down, he said, and wasn't in any danger of falling down. He said he'd make a pot of tea in a minute, a reviving pot. She said she'd be grateful, so he helped her into the kitchen and sat her down and put the kettle on. They drank the reviving tea and she said she felt a lot better but a bit fluttery. So he felt her heartbeats.

'Mind tellin' me how you felt 'em?' said Luke.

'That's confidential,' said Old Iron. 'Private between me and Muriel, and me sense of what's private don't allow me to go into detail, except it related to 'er 'ealth.' He went on to say Doreen's Ma quivered like she was ailing, but he assured her her heartbeats had to be felt to be believed. He complimented her on recovering her health, saying he hadn't had any patient who'd recovered better. She said she appreciated his doctoring, but was still a lonely widow. He said don't you worry, Muriel, you're still a handsome woman just right for a caring widower. Oh, me palpitating heart, she said, fancy you proposing in that nice way. But I'll have to think about it, she said, I'll have to think about Doreen and see if she won't mind living with us so she can still look after me a bit. I'll give you me answer in a week, she said, I won't tell Doreen till I've made up me mind. 'I near fell down dead,' said Old Iron hoarsely, 'I told 'er I'd got emergency things to do and then I did a runner. And 'ere I am, as good as fatally collapsed in mind and body.'

'Wait a minute,' said Luke, 'you've told me more than once that you wouldn't mind gettin' married again.'

'Now did I say I was thinkin' of Doreen's Ma?'

'You as good as said you considered 'er a prospect.'

'I don't remember what I said,' complained Old Iron, 'except I'd do me best to get your Doreen untied from 'er Ma's apron-strings. That didn't mean I was offerin' to get tied to 'em meself. Luke me lad, I'll be ill by this time tomorrow. Don't yer realize that in a week I might get a fatal answer from Doreen's Ma?'

'Old Iron, you shouldn't 'ave told her she was just right for a carin' widower at the same time as you were feelin' her 'eartbeats,' said Luke, grinning all over. 'You tripped up there, sayin' a thing like that while relatin' to her health.'

''Old up,' said Old Iron, 'I was relatin' in a healin' way. Professional, like.'

'You're done for, Dad.'

'Ruddy gorblimey,' groaned Old Iron, 'I ain't waitin' till tomorrow to be ill, I'm ill now.'

Luke roared with laughter. Old Iron couldn't see the funny side of it at all.

Chapter Seventeen

It was Sammy who was the marked man the following morning. The door of his house on Denmark Hill opened at twenty to nine, and Mr Ronald Ponsonby, loitering with intent to discover and identify, observed a young man of about five-feet-ten with a visible air of energy. At the door with him was a young woman, fair-haired and highly attractive.

Susie, because these were still the early days of marriage, saw Sammy off to work at the front door every morning, even though she would be in her office herself by ten o'clock.

'Be good, Sammy,' she said, 'don't flirt on the phone with any widows like Harriet de Vere. Nor with certain married women.'

'Susie, you're hurtin' me sense of integrity,' said Sammy. 'So long, see you later.' He kissed her.

'I liked it,' said Susie, as he departed from the doorstep.

'Liked what?' asked Sammy, making for his car.

'Last night,' said Susie, and laughed.

'Lucky I've got me car,' said Sammy, 'I'm still too short of breath for walkin'.' He got into his car and pulled on the self-starter. The engine fired and chortled into life. Away went Sammy. Susie, smiling, closed the door.

The hunter was also smiling. He had not only

seen Sammy Adams, but a young woman who was obviously his wife. Two at one go. Excellent, yes, excellent. Both of them, no doubt, would be happy to see his brother hang. So, no doubt, would all the other Adams'.

He strolled away. He was wearing a cap and a tweed suit.

Doreen placed post on Boots's desk at five past nine. Exclusive to the switchboard, she could have sat at it all day, knitting in between calls, but she'd always been the Jill-of-all-work. She liked it that way, she liked being busy. There was an office boy now, Ronnie, who stuck the stamps on letters and did errands, but Doreen kept all kinds of little jobs to herself. They took her in and out of the offices of Boots, Sammy, Emily and Susie, which she liked very much, even if she did have to hare back to the switchboard on occasions. She was the favourite general office girl with those four people, and wouldn't have given up her informal and friendly relationship with them for anything, not even if the Maypole Dairy in the Walworth Road offered her their whole shopful of groceries.

'How's this feller who's after you?' asked Boots, running through his post.

'He's fast,' said Doreen.

'How fast?'

'He's nearly catchin' me up,' said Doreen, and departed giggling. She felt life was getting livelier for her. Except that her mum had said she still couldn't do without her. Poor old Mum.

During the afternoon break at St John's, Boadicea reminded Caesar there was another rehearsal tomorrow morning at the school. Caesar said this time he definitely wouldn't be there, he was going on a bike ride to Ancient Greece. Boadicea said there was once a queen of Ancient Greece that was nearly ate up by a fiery dragon, only Hercules came up and bit the dragon's head off with his mighty teeth. Did Caesar know that? Caesar said he didn't know anything except he was going potty.

In her study at West Square Girls School, the intellectual-looking headmistress was interviewing Boots, Emily and Rosie. Rosie sat on the edge of a chair trying to look like a girl no good school should be without. Emily was at her best in a very attractive spring coat and hat, green eyes swimming with faith in Rosie's scholastic eligibility. Boots was himself. Very little disturbed him. His time in the trenches had matured his outlook. Compared to the carnage of that kind of war, the perversities of peacetime life and the quirks of people were almost amusing.

The headmistress, making notes, asked questions of the mother and father. Emily was earnest in all her replies, Boots as natural as the air he breathed, his expression disarming. The headmistress, Miss Warren, began to regard him with interest, and Emily began to smile. Boots had style and a way with women. It made some of them go weak at the knees.

'Rosie is just eleven, you say?' enquired the headmistress, a slim woman in her mid-thirties. 'When was her birthday?'

'The fifth of this month,' said Emily.

'When she began to feel her age,' said Boots.

A little smile appeared on the headmistress's face.

'At eleven, Mr Adams?' she said.

'It happens to all of us,' said Boots, 'some sooner than others.'

Rosie did a very successful job in keeping her face straight.

'Birthday, the fifth of May,' murmured the headmistress, noting it down. 'Mr Adams, why would you like Rosie to attend this school?'

'I attended it myself,' said Boots. 'Among the boys, of course, not the girls.'

'You're an old West Square pupil, Mr Adams?'

'Very old,' said Boots. He would be thirty in July.

'Daddy, you're not even nearly old,' said Rosie.

Miss Warren addressed herself to Rosie, putting her through an oral examination in English grammar, geography, history and the Scriptures. Rosie excelled herself in her answers. She did not suffer nervousness, and she was certainly not inarticulate. She had been brought up in a family where everyone had something to say about everything. She enquired if the headmistress wanted to ask her about her French.

'But you don't take French at St Luke's, do you?' said Miss Warren. 'It's an elementary school.'

Rosie said her father had started her on French, and in that language she informed the headmistress that the pen of her aunt had been left in the garden and the dog from next door had run off with it.

'Of course, ma'am, Daddy was in France during the war, which did his French no end of good, and that was how he got ahead of me. But I'm catching up.'

'I think I'm falling behind,' said Miss Warren drily.

'Rosie, I think you're showin' off a bit,' smiled Emily.

'Oh, help,' said Rosie, 'could you please overlook that, ma'am?'

'I think so,' said Miss Warren, and pondered on her notes. West Square was not an independent grammar school, it was a State-run establishment, providing an advanced education to a mixture of bright cockney girls and aspiring lower middle class girls. 'Mr Adams, Mrs Adams, I'm quite sure St Luke's would have put your daughter's name forward for a place here. As it is, there's no need. When she leaves at Easter next year, we'll accept her.'

'Rosie?' said Boots.

'You say, Daddy.'

'I'll say,' said Emily. 'We'd like that, Miss Warren, we'd all like Rosie to attend this school.'

'We should like it too,' said Miss Warren.

A woman passing the school gate several minutes later noted the emergence of three people, including a very happy-looking girl. Mr Ronald Ponsonby might have noted the same thing had he followed the trio to the school from Camberwell. Loitering in a mood of malicious curiosity that took in the side entrance to the offices of Adams Enterprises, he had first seen a girl go in, a schoolgirl whom he recognized. Not long after, she reappeared, coming out of the door beside the shop in company with a man and woman. The man he also recognized. Robert Adams. Was the woman his wife? She was thin, nicely dressed and, seen from behind, perky in her movements. Mr Ronald Ponsonby followed at a distance as they walked towards the Junction. His adrenalin flowed. He was sure they were mother, father, daughter. He was seeing all three at once. All of them had a place in his plan. He watched as they boarded a tram, and was close enough at that point to hear the woman say, 'Not upstairs, Rosie, inside.'

Rosie. Good. He needed to know her name.

He did not board the tram himself. He watched it go on its way, and then went into Lyons teashop and enjoyed a cup of excellent tea and a fruit bun.

Out of school, Cassie asked Freddy if they could go riding on his bike until suppertime.

'Well, Cassie, I was thinkin'—'

'Oh, good,' said Cassie, 'I'll go 'ome and tell Nellie or Annie I'll be out till suppertime.'

'I didn't say—'

'Freddy, don't forget I want a cushion on the carrier.' Cassie, who always rode astride his bicycle carrier, insisted on having her bottom cushioned.

'You'll want a bloomin' armchair on it next,' said Freddy.

'Oh, did I ever tell yer me Uncle Fred used to ride in an armchair on an elephant in China?'

'Who said they 'ad elephants in China?' asked Freddy.

'Me Uncle Fred.'

'Well, yer Uncle Fred's up the pole, then,' said Freddy, but he couldn't help grinning. That Cassie, she was a trial to a bloke but still a bit of a laugh, in her barmy way. Well, all girls were barmy. His dad agreed, but said blokes had got to accept it as you couldn't cure them.

Coming down Browning Street a little after five-thirty, Mr Ronald Ponsonby saw a boy and girl

246

standing beside a bike on the corner of Caulfield Place. The Adams family, he knew, had once lived in that street. He stopped. Most boys and girls didn't remember a stranger and his questions as much as adults did.

'Hello,' he said pleasantly.

Cassie and Freddy looked up into the face of a middle-aged man with a neat beard and moustache. His eyes were bright behind his spectacles.

''Ello,' said Freddy.

'I'm looking for a family called Robertson. Would you know if they live around here?'

'Never 'eard of them,' said Freddy, ''ave you, Cassie?'

'I've 'eard of the Johnsons,' said Cassie, little knowing that the bright eyes belonged to the twin brother of the man who had abducted her at Easter.

'No, not Johnson,' said Mr Ronald Ponsonby, 'no, not at all. What about the Greenfields?'

'Oh, green fields is in Ruskin Park,' said Cassie. She thought. 'And Peckham Rye,' she said.

'No, 'e means a fam'ly called Greenfield, don't yer, mister?' said Freddy. 'But we don't know 'em.'

'Never mind, never mind,' smiled the enquirer. 'Oh, there was one other family, the Adams. You don't know them, either?'

'Not 'alf we do,' said Freddy, 'me sister Susie's married to Sammy Adams. But the fam'ly don't live 'ere now. They used to, in me fam'ly's 'ouse. Down there.' Freddy pointed to his house.

'Well, I'm unlucky if they've all moved away,' said Mr Ronald Ponsonby. 'There were three sons, weren't there?'

'Yes, and they 'ad a sister name of Lizzy,' said Freddy. 'What d'yer want to see them for, mister?'

'A friend of mine lived here for many years, my boy, and I promised to look up certain people he knew. But it's not important, no, not at all. Thank you, yes, thank you. Some pocket money for being so helpful?'

Cassie and Freddy received a penny each and two little nods from the stranger. Then he went on his way to his lodgings. Freddy had a funny little feeling of being reminded of someone else, but since he couldn't think who it was, away he went again, with Cassie astride the cushioned carrier.

Lizzy, thought Mr Ronald Ponsonby. Lizzy, yes, the cockney equivalent of Eliza. Eliza Adams, now Eliza Somers. He must see what she looked like, and her husband.

Things were going splendidly, splendidly. One could almost believe that the arbiter of life was sympathetically supportive of what he had elected to do to console his brother at his moment of execution. Only if a not guilty verdict came about would there be a reason for reflection.

Ben Skidmore, the large man, brooded bitterly on events. The General Strike a gawdblimey washout for the workers and a bloody tea party for the bosses. And that Sammy Adams had his bleedin' car back good as new, not a scratch on its paintwork nor a fatal dent in his lousy loaf of bread. Sod him.

Downstairs, the front door of the house in Hawes Street, Islington, opened from a pull on the latchcord. Booted feet trod the passage floor and climbed the stairs. The door of his rented room was pushed open. Two dockers showed themselves, one as large as he was, the other taller.

'Watcher, Ben old cock.'

'Whadder you want?'

'Come to talk to yer, Ben.'

'What about?'

'Yer be'aviour, Ben, yer be'aviour.'

'Don't make me laugh.'

'We ain't 'ere to make you laugh, Ben. Just to talk to you.'

''Old it, what's yer game? You're workers of the world, ain't yer? Well, so am I. I ain't a blackleg nor a bosses' man, and I ain't lettin' anyone give me a bleedin' talkin'-to. Shove off.'

'Yer picked on friends of ours, Ben, so we got to talk to yer. Pin yer lug'oles back, mate.'

They gave him a talking-to. Nothing was said about breaking his leg, but the threat was there if he didn't sort himself out and reserve his chopper for sweatshop bosses.

Sod them too, thought Skidmore when they'd gone. And up you, Sammy Adams, I'll still get yer.

'I've been thinkin', Doreen love,' said Mrs Paterson after supper.

'What about?' asked Doreen, who'd bought herself some hanks of lovely blue wool at lunchtime. She was going to knit herself a jumper for the winter.

'Well, feelin' a bit better, as I am,' said her mum from her fireside chair, 'I was thinkin' I'm not too old to get married again. That's if I meet someone that ain't too common and can pay the rent comfortable. If I did meet someone, would yer mind, love?'

'Course I wouldn't,' said Doreen, 'everyone says you're still a handsome woman.'

''Ow kind,' said Mrs Paterson, 'but I want yer to

know I wouldn't not think about you. I wouldn't push you out of me life. You're me carin' daughter that I couldn't do without.'

'But if you got married again, Mum,' said Doreen, 'I suppose I could think of gettin' married meself.'

'Well, yes, but when you're older, you're a bit young now.'

'Not all that young,' said Doreen. 'Is Mr Edwards poppin' across to see you this evenin'?'

'Oh, lor', I'm sure I don't know.' Mrs Paterson quivered. She didn't think she'd better tell her daughter yet that Mr Edwards had offered. Well, she hadn't known him for more than two weeks, and Doreen might think something funny had been going on, something that meant Mr Edwards had to make an honest woman of her. 'No, 'e didn't say 'e'd be callin' – who's that?' She quivered again at the sound of the door knocker going.

'It's 'im, I expect,' said Doreen, hiding a smile.

But it was Luke.

'Evenin', Lady Vi. And compliments on your blue peepers.'

'They're not blue. 'Ave you come knockin' at our door just to let me know you can't see for lookin'?'

'No, just to ask if you'd like a bit of company.'

'Where's your dad?'

'Takin' it easy,' said Luke, 'he's a bit off colour.'

'He's drunk, you mean.'

'No, Old Iron doesn't drink all that much.'

'Where did he get that name?'

'It's a nickname he picked up years ago. He used to bend iron bars at fairgrounds.'

'I don't know you should call your own dad by a nickname like that,' said Doreen.

'He's proud of it,' said Luke. 'You goin' to invite me in?'

Doreen thought of something.

'Yes, come in and be a help to me,' she said, 'but don't upset my mum by gettin' familiar with me, or she'll show you the door.'

'I wouldn't want that,' said Luke.

Doreen took him through to the kitchen, where her mum gave him several kinds of looks.

'Oh, it's you again,' she said.

'Doreen wants a hand with something,' said Luke.

'Just remember she's only a young girl,' said Mrs Paterson, making pertinent use of her new-found formula.

'Sit down and put your hands out,' said Doreen to Luke. Luke took a seat. She pulled up a chair and sat opposite him. He was in favour of that. Well, he wouldn't have felt normal if he hadn't liked her legs. She reached, picked up a hank of wool from the table and slipped it over his hands. 'Stretch it a bit,' she said.

'What's this?' he asked, and a ghastly picture entered his mind, a picture of cousin Alf helping Aunt Rosa to wind wool. 'Wait a tick—'

'Spread your hands a bit,' said Doreen.

'I didn't know you wanted me to 'elp with your knittin',' said Luke.

'I don't,' said Doreen. 'I want you to help me wind all this wool. That's it, keep your 'ands movin'.' She began winding.

'I'm better at fixin' broken doorknobs,' said Luke.

'We don't 'ave any broken doorknobs,' said Doreen. Her mum looked on suspiciously, and Doreen felt it was still going to be some time before she'd be able to have a life of her own.

'Where's your father?' Mrs Paterson put the question to Luke.

'Oh, he's not very well, Mum,' said Doreen.

'He 'asn't got flu, has 'e?'

'No, he's just a bit out of sorts,' said Luke. Old Iron, in fact, had a certain kind of headache, brought on by his feeling that he'd let his tongue over-reach itself. He needed, he said, to talk his way out of it when he felt a bit better.

'I suppose I ought to pop across and see how 'e is,' said Mrs Paterson, then quivered at the thought of being taken advantage of, even if he was out of sorts. After all, a man who'd offered might fancy helping himself in advance. With his son over here, they'd be alone over there. Yes, and that was another thing, if she left Doreen and the son alone over here, there was no telling what might happen. Leaving them might make Doreen think she could have a young man and walk out with him at weekends. 'No, I won't go across,' she said, 'it wouldn't look respectable.'

So she stayed where she was to make sure nothing happened and Doreen didn't get ideas.

Luke helped Doreen to wind all her wool, then had a cup of tea with her and her mum. He left at quarter to ten. Doreen saw him out.

'Any chance of takin' you out tomorrow or Sunday?' he asked.

'No, you can see it's worryin' my mum, you tryin' to take up with me,' said Doreen.

'Is it goin' to last long?' asked Luke.

'I can't say, can I? But I've got to put her first.'

'All right,' said Luke, 'it's your life. Look after her, then. So long, Lady Vi.'

When he got back, Old Iron asked him how he'd got on. He said the damage was done, that Doreen couldn't break the chains and didn't really want to.

'A mother's girl, eh?' said Old Iron.

'It 'appens,' said Luke.

'Still, you've only known 'er a couple of weeks, me lad, you can't expect to take 'er Ma's place in 'er affections in that time.'

'No, it's what's 'appened in two years that's done the damage,' said Luke, 'it's tied her good and tight to her mum's apron-strings.'

'I ain't sure yer right,' said Old Iron, 'she strikes me as too lively a girl to want to be a permanent nursemaid. When I'm meself again, I'll do some more work on 'er Ma.'

'As her prospective better half?' said Luke.

'Steady, me lad, mind me 'eadache,' said Old Iron. 'I've got to talk 'er out of that. There's me other lady friends to consider. I've been neglectin' them lately.'

'I see it all now,' said Luke, 'you're playin' the field, you old Romeo.'

'I'm just a sociable bloke,' said Old Iron. 'Anyway, it won't 'urt to give yer nice young lady and 'er Ma a rest for a while. Maybe we've been pushin' 'em a bit.'

'That's a fact we have,' said Luke.

Chapter Eighteen

Ned Somers, about to leave for work on Saturday morning, said, 'Put your hat on this afternoon, Eliza, and see that the kids wash their faces. I'm taking you all out.'

'What for, a bus ride to Clapham Common?' asked Lizzy, richly brunette and proud of her Edwardian figure.

'No, to look at a bargain of a second-hand car I've seen at Marston's Garage in Herne Hill,' said Ned. 'It's got a gear-lever and pedals that will give my leg no problem. With the kids going on about all the cars your brothers are having, they'll roll about in gloom if we don't have one too.'

'Ned, oh, you sweetie,' said Lizzy, and kissed him smackingly at the open front door.

The hunter, loitering with intent on the other side of Sunrise Avenue, noted the kiss. Husband and wife. Partly effaced by a beech tree, he watched as Ned emerged from the double-fronted house and began his walk to a bus stop in Denmark Hill. It was a slightly limping walk. Ned had lost a leg in a Flanders battle and been fitted with an artificial replacement.

The hunter did not follow him. He had seen him and his wife too, Eliza Somers, the kind of woman who must have been enchanting as a young girl. They were all personable, the three brothers and the sister. But they all had to go, with their spouses, to fully console Gerald.

Now a visit to Brixton, perhaps, purely for light relief, to enjoy looking at young girls in that busy shopping centre. While he was in England he would indulge only in looking.

All the boys and girls participating in St John's Empire Day pageant had gathered for a rehearsal in the playground. The tableaux were being formed fairly well out of initial chaos. The passive Great Dane stood beside Wellington, with Wellington cocking a suspicious eye at the hound. Queen Elizabeth, after a bit of a set-to with Sir Walter Raleigh, had begun her dialogue with him.

'What, what, am I to tread this muddy ground?' she demanded.

'A little louder,' said the teacher in charge of this tableau.

'I ain't goin' to shout,' said Queen Elizabeth, 'me mum don't like me shoutin'.'

Elsewhere, Stanley advanced to meet Livingstone, and King Henry the Fifth led his army on to the field at Agincourt. And Queen Boadicea stepped into her chariot. Her cardboard crown wobbled.

'Blessed thing,' she said.

Henry the Fifth bawled, 'Once more into the breach, mates.'

'Can't someone shut 'im up?' complained Boadicea.

'Not 'im,' said an Ancient Briton, 'no-one can shut Charlie 'Iggins up.'

'Where's me reins?' asked Boadicea. Mr Hill put them into her left hand. She raised the spear in her right hand. 'Charge!' she cried.

'You have charged, you've won the battle,' said Mr Hill.

'Please, teacher,' said a female Ancient Briton, 'don't yer fink there ought to be some blood?'

'Yes, Caesar ought to be wounded and all bloody,' said Boadicea, 'me dad told me.'

'Now look 'ere,' said Caesar, 'I ain't going to be run over an' wounded as well. Blow that for a lark. I've got to tell yer, Mr Hill, that I don't 'alf feel sorely tried.'

'So do I,' said Mr Hill. 'We'll have to put up with it together, Mighty Caesar.'

Caesar sighed. Life was hardly worthwhile these days.

In the afternoon at the motor dealers and garage in Camberwell New Road, Boots, Emily, Rosie and Tim all came to an agreement concerning a Riley car roomy enough to take Chinese Lady and Mr Finch as well as themselves on Sunday outings. Emily was almost dizzy. A family motorcar. Never in her wildest dreams as a girl had she ever thought she would marry into a family able to buy any kind of car. Rosie was in bliss, hardly ever leaving her father's side in her wish to have him share her feelings.

'Blessed heaven, Daddy, it's better than Christmas,' she said.

Tommy and Vi chose a Morris.

'Oh, good on us, Tommy,' she said, 'a new motorcar and a new baby all in the same year. But I've just thought, where're we goin' to keep the car?'

'Outside the house,' said Tommy.

'Oh, yes? What about the street kids?'

'I'll talk to 'em,' said Tommy, 'and hand out pennies for keepin' an eye on it. You can't beat street kids, so you have to join 'em.'

'Clever you,' said Vi.

'Granted,' said Tommy.

Looking, discussing, arguing, agreeing and choosing all took time. Well, as Emily said, you don't buy a new dress in five minutes, so you're entitled to a whole afternoon buying a new car. So even after they'd made their minds up they all spent more time getting in and out of both cars. Sammy and Susie turned up, Sammy to vet Tommy and Vi's choice since the firm was going to pay for it.

A little way down from the dealers' forecourt, Mr Ronald Ponsonby, his back against a lamp-post, appeared to be reading a newspaper. After his trip to Brixton, including lunch in a store's restaurant, he had returned to Camberwell, the urge to prowl again irresistible. Like his twin brother, he disliked people, for people, with few exceptions, were petty and irritating in their lack of understanding and in their intolerance. Instead of delighting in having their young daughters photographed, they were intolerance personified. It was, therefore, quite irresistible, this pleasure of shadowing the particular people whose senior figure was responsible for the incarceration of Gerald, and for his probable death. It was the pleasure of anticipation, the anticipation that they would precede Gerald to the grave.

The brother Tommy was the one who lived in Camberwell, and much to the satisfaction of the hunter he appeared from out of Foreign Street a little after two in company with a young woman and a little girl, a toddler. The woman was obviously pregnant. His wife, of course, and his daughter. He followed them, at a distance, along Camberwell Station Road to Camberwell New Road, on the corner of which was a motorcar dealers. There, to his further satisfaction, they met the senior figure, Robert Adams, together with his wife, the girl Rosie and a young boy. Boots took no notice of a trilby-hatted, blue-suited man who passed by.

From the position he took up at the lamp-post, Mr Ronald Ponsonby heard a general clatter of voices, a clatter that faded when everyone entered the showroom, but came into being again when they left it. Now and then, he glimpsed movements. That was all he could glimpse. It did not affect his satisfaction. They were there, outside the showroom but hidden from him.

Sammy, having fully inspected the Morris standing on the forecourt, said, 'It'll do, Tommy, I like it.'

'I love it, Vi,' said Susie.

'D'you mind if I kiss Sammy?' asked Vi.

'He's charging fourpence a time now,' said Susie.

'It used to be a penny,' said Vi, 'and tuppence when he was twenty-one.'

'He put it up to fourpence on our weddin' day,' said Susie. 'He says I owe him three pounds, one-and-eightpence at the moment.'

'Oh, well, I'll still have fourpennyworth,' said Vi, 'he's been lovely, votin' for Tommy to have a car on the firm. Sammy?'

'I'm here, Vi,' said Sammy, turning.

'Thanks ever so much,' said Vi, and gave him a smacker in front of everyone.

'I'm afraid that'll cost yer, Vi,' said Sammy.

'Yes, I know,' said Vi, and gave him four pennies.

'Uncle Sammy, you're wicked, charging Auntie Vi for a kiss,' said Rosie.

'Well, Rosie, I thought you knew it was a principle of mine,' said Sammy.

'But a whole fourpence,' said Rosie.

'All right,' said Sammy, 'here's a penny back, Vi.'

'Oh, you're so kind, Sammy,' said Vi.

'Crikey,' said young Tim from the back seat of the Riley, 'I think I'm goin' to charge my mum, she's always kissin' me.'

The sales manager joined in the laughter. Mr Ronald Ponsonby heard it.

Boots signed a cheque for the Riley, and he and Sammy signed a firm's cheque for the Morris. There was certain paperwork to be completed, including provisional insurance, and then the cars could be collected and driven away on Tuesday.

Sammy and Susie left, followed by Boots, Emily, Rosie and Tim, leaving Tommy and Vi to linger a little over the Morris. Rosie turned and called.

'Uncle Tommy, don't forget the tennis! Ruskin Park at four o'clock today, not three!'

'I'll be there,' called Tommy.

Mr Ronald Ponsonby clearly heard the exchange.

Four o'clock. It was just gone three now. Excitement animated him. He went into delighted action. He bought a camera and a roll of film. He bought a light mackintosh and a cap. He put them on, placing his hat in a carrier bag. He arrived at the tennis courts in Ruskin Park at ten minutes past four, his spectacles off. Except for his beard, he bore little resemblance to the man who had been at the lamp-post with a newspaper, a man visible to Boots and his family when they left the dealers.

He sighed with pleasure. There they were, Robert Adams and his daughter, his brother Tommy and the other young girl. How deliciously active both girls were in short white tennis frocks. He stood close to the wire surround, eyes bright with perverted pleasure, the carrier bag on the ground beside his feet. The camera, loaded, was in his hands. He was not alone as a spectator. Other people were watching. Good. One did not want to be obtrusive.

Annabelle and Rosie dashed and scampered, Annabelle playing with Boots, Rosie with Tommy. That way the game was more even. The girls shrieked, the men laughed. Short white dresses whisked and flew. The camera, lens aimed between strands of stout wire, clicked from time to time, but was heard by nobody except the owner. He understood cameras, particularly this make. He did not bring it up to his eye. That would have made him noticeable as a man taking photographs. As it was, Boots and Annabelle, and Tommy and Rosie, were far too enjoyably involved in the game to notice anything but the fact that, as usual, there were people watching the play on all four public courts.

Rosie, pedalling backwards because Annabelle had plopped up a soft but high lob, tumbled and fell on her bottom, legs in the air. She shrieked with laughter, and Annabelle giggled herself silly. The camera clicked, and Mr Ronald Ponsonby experienced a darting shaft of exquisite excitement, for he was sure the lens was aimed straight and true at the girl. She was between the net and the wire.

Ah, yes, the arbiter of events surely was in sympathy with him, not only in respect of his designs, but also his very personal predilections. The last frame of the roll of film had captured a picture of a delightful young girl at her most enchanting. He was certain of that.

He left abruptly then, for he was almost shivering with those sensations of exquisite excitement.

Ecstasy kept him company.

Of all girls, the daughter of Robert Adams.

Ah, Gerald, if only you could share this moment with me.

'Oi, mister!'

He checked.

Had someone been aware he had used the camera?

He froze a little, thinking of that which constantly governed so many of his actions, the necessity of avoiding mistakes.

'Oi, mister!'

Avoiding the mistake of running, he turned. A boy came running up, a carrier bag in his hand.

'Yes, yes?' said Mr Ronald Ponsonby.

'Yer left this bag be'ind, guv,' said the boy, 'it's got a titfer in it. Don't yer want it?'

'Goodness me, did I forget it? Thank you, young man, thank you. I'll be forgetting my head next. Here.' He gave the lad a silver sixpence, and the lad gaped happily at the coin.

'Well, ta, guv, yer a sport. 'Ere y'ar.'

Mr Ronald Ponsonby took the carrier bag, murmured additional thanks and went on his way. His hot shivering cooled down. He reflected with calculated pleasure on what his camera held. A roll of undeveloped film of eight frames. Five of one girl, three of the younger. They had changed ends on the court every so often. He would develop the film when he was back in Dieppe.

Empire Day arrived and was celebrated in schools throughout the United Kingdom. The pageant at St John's in Walworth took place in the playground, the hall piano carried out by six men strong and true. A lot of mothers were present, and so were a few fathers, those who were unemployed and actually had very little to celebrate. It was a case of being proud of their dressed-up kids.

One after another, each tableau came into being to a stirring accompaniment on the piano. Wellington was given a rousing cheer when he surveyed the victorious field of Waterloo, his faithful charger, alias the Great Dane, beside him, and his army simulating pursuit of poor old Napoleon with his hand on his bread-basket.

'Dr Livingstone, I persume?' said the explorer, Stanley.

'Yus, that's me,' said Dr Livingstone, forgetting his proper response.

'Once more into the breach, me friends!' bawled Henry the Fifth.

'Charge!' roared the English army of Agincourt.

'Not yet,' bawled Henry the Fifth, 'I ain't ready!'

Queen Elizabeth, resplendent in some mother's spare velvet curtain, spoke her piece next in a shrill voice.

'What, what, am I to tread on muddy ground?'

'Allow me, Yer Majesty,' said Sir Walter Raleigh, and placed his cloak at her feet. She tripped over it, but was equal to the moment.

'Cut 'is 'ead orf!' she cried.

That was cheered to the echo.

It was Boadicea's turn then to excel herself. Her chariot advanced, pulled by her steeds, she sitting in it. It stopped as it reached conquered Caesar. She stood up, reins in one hand, spear in the other.

'Oh, 'elp,' she breathed, 'I've forgot what to say.'

'Advance, dog of Rome,' said an Ancient Briton.

'Oh, yes,' said Boadicea. She yelled at Caesar. 'Advance, dog of Rome.'

'Yer spear's upside-down,' said Caesar, then yelled back, 'Rome defies you!'

'Down, Caesar!' yelled Boadicea, with a teacher playing 'Soldiers of the Queen'. Caesar glowered. 'Go on, down, d'you 'ear me?'

Caesar, wishing he hadn't come, prostrated himself at the feet of her steeds. The steeds trod on him.

'That's it,' growled Caesar, 'that's really the end, that is.'

The heroic death of Nelson at Trafalgar followed, and he made known his wish to be kissed by Captain Hardy. Captain Hardy was played by a fourteen-year-old girl, since Nelson said he'd hang himself in the playground if he was kissed by a boy. The girl put her heart and soul into the kiss, and Nelson, kicking, died a very heroic death indeed.

Eventually, Queen Victoria appeared with Prince Albert. This was the signal for 'Land Of Hope And Glory' to be played and sung with gusto, the audience of parents joining in. Then came the headmistress to extol the marvels of Britain's mighty Empire.

'I don't know what's mighty about it, when it can't find me old man a job,' complained a mother.

'I'd go an' tell the King if I was you,' suggested a neighbour.

'What, go to Buckingham Palace? They wouldn't let me in.'

'Oh, you 'ave to go round and knock on the side door to be let in.'

''Oo do I 'ave to see?'

'Oh, you just knock twice and ask for Archibald, so me 'usband told me once.'

'I'll do that, you see if I don't.'

'It's "God Save The King" now.'

The National Anthem had begun, with all the tableaux in as good a shape as could be expected. True, the Great Dane was licking Wellington's chops, and Henry the Fifth's shield, a dustbin lid, had dropped on his foot, but all in all it was a stirring spectacle of Empire Day.

On the way home, Caesar complained to Boadicea that her steeds had trodden on him.

'Well, they was supposed to,' said Boadicea.

'Who said so? Mr Hill didn't.'

'No, I did,' said Boadicea, 'it was instead of runnin' you over.'

'I'm goin' to 'ave to talk serious to you,' said Caesar darkly.

'Yes, all right,' said Boadicea, 'but yer like me really, don't yer?'

'It beats me, 'aving a dotty mate,' said Caesar. 'Still, come on, I'll buy yer a toffee-apple as it's a nice day.'

'Oh, ta,' said Boadicea happily. 'I think I'll be Florence Nightingale next year, and you can be a wounded solider.'

Caesar grinned. Boadicea smiled.

* * *

The following day there were reports in some papers concerning a near riot in Munich, Germany. The political agitator, Adolf Hitler had rented a beer hall for a rally of his followers, most of whom were dressed in brown shirts, brown breeches and jackboots. Communists, breaking into the hall, had attempted to assault Hitler while he was addressing the rally. A brawl ensued and spilled into the street. The police were called and they dispersed the mob. No arrests were made, however.

The report in Boots's daily paper made him think about all that Mr Finch and General Sir Henry Simms had said to him regarding the menace of Hitler, a fanatic and a warmonger. Knowing exactly what modern war was like, Boots found it difficult to believe even a madman would contrive to start another.

'Dad's frowning,' said young Tim.

'Something's up, then,' said Emily, doing needlework. She always had to be doing something apart from eating little and often.

'It's that new-fangled contraption that's standin' in the drive,' said Chinese Lady. 'He's thinkin' about it blowin' up, I shouldn't wonder.'

'Nana, Daddy wouldn't let it do that, he knows about contraptions,' said Rosie.

'A nice little 'orse and cart wouldn't blow up,' said Chinese Lady. 'Well, I never heard of any that did.'

'It's a nice evening,' said Boots, putting the paper aside. 'Who's for some cricket?'

'Me,' said Tim.

'Me,' said Rosie.

'Me,' smiled Mr Finch. He was into cricket.

'Come on, Mum, you as well,' said Tim.

'I'm doin' needlework,' said Emily.

'Honestly, Mummy, you know needlework's not as important as cricket,' said Rosie. 'Not on a nice evening like this.'

'Give it a go, Em,' said Boots.

Into the garden they went. Rosie whispered to Boots.

'Daddy, when you were frowning, was something worrying you?'

'Only my corn,' said Boots.

'You don't have a corn.'

'I was worrying in case I developed one.'

'Fibber,' said Rosie.

Boots laughed.

Chinese Lady, left to her knitting, picked up the paper her eldest son had put aside. She checked the page he'd been reading. She found the report of the brawl in Munich.

She frowned herself then.

Mrs Paterson suddenly said, 'What's 'appened to 'im?'

'Who?' asked Doreen

'What?' asked her mum.

'Who's him?'

'I was thinkin', that's all.'

'About Mr Edwards?'

'It's funny 'e's not come knockin' lately, nor 'is son.' Mrs Paterson looked quite cross, and to tell the truth, Doreen was a bit miffed herself. 'After the way 'e laid 'is healin' touch on me, you'd 'ave thought he'd come across to see me improvement.'

'His healin' touch, Mum?' said Doreen.

Her mum blushed a little and her handsome person quivered in a familiar way.

'Of course,' she said hastily, 'I'm not sayin' I'm fully improved, I'm still grateful I've got you, Doreen.'

'Perhaps he did have flu, Mum, perhaps he's ill in bed and 'aving the doctor call.'

'Well, you'd 'ave thought 'is son would've come and told us,' said Mrs Paterson, 'specially after 'e said I was recovered enough to make 'im a handsome wife.'

'He said what?' gasped Doreen. 'That son of his said what?'

'No, not that son of 'is,' said Mrs Paterson. 'His dad, Mr Edwards. I don't know what got into your 'ead to say a thing like that. I 'ope I'm not the kind of woman that would encourage some man's son to converse intimately with me. No, it was 'is dad that conversed like that. I didn't want to say anything to you, not till I'd give it a lot of thought and made sure it wouldn't upset you or make you think I wasn't goin' to need you any more.'

'Mum, are you sayin' Mr Edwards proposed to you?' said Doreen faintly.

'In a 'ighly compliment'ry way,' said Mrs Paterson, 'so I don't know why 'e 'asn't come to see me all this time.'

'I'll find out,' said Doreen, who couldn't think why neither father nor son had come knocking lately. 'We don't get messed about by our lodger, so I'm not goin' to let you be messed about by a neighbour who's asked you to marry him. I'll go across straightaway, Mum. You stay there.'

Luke heard the front door knocker rap twice. Twice meant upstairs. He went down to answer the summons and found Doreen on the doorstep. She gave him a look.

'Good evenin',' she said.

'Hello,' said Luke.

'Where's my mum's fiance?' demanded Doreen. 'Eh?'

'You heard,' said Doreen. 'Where's the old Romeo? Not round at his pub, I hope. What's he mean by proposin' to my mum and then doin' a disappearin' act? I notice you've done one too.'

'I think you'd better come up,' said Luke. 'Me dad's just about to go out for a glass.'

'He's got a hope,' said Doreen. 'I'm here to give him two black eyes.'

Luke, not unappreciative of her spirit and her sparks, took her upstairs. Old Iron, on his feet and with his bowler hat on, looked at her and coughed to clear his throat.

'This is Doreen from across the street, Dad,' said Luke.

'So I see,' said Old Iron.

'Don't be funny,' said Doreen. What a girl, thought Luke, she's even better-looking when her blood's up. And what a crying shame, spending her life looking after her mum. 'Mr Edwards, I suppose you've 'eard of breach of promise?'

'Eh?' said Old Iron.

'Breach of promise.'

'Oh, gawd,' said Old Iron. Luke put his hand over his mouth. Doreen looked at him.

'Are you grinning?' she asked.

'What's there to grin about?' said Luke. 'Everything sounds serious to me.'

'It's serious to my mum,' said Doreen, 'she's not used to bein' proposed to and then 'aving her fiance disappear.' She eyed Old Iron. Old Iron coughed again. Crikey, it's true, she thought, he did ask

268

Mum to marry him. That could mean I'd be free of responsibilities. I could have a young man. 'Mr Edwards, what d'you mean by proposin' to my mum and then tryin' to run a mile?'

'Well, Doreen love, I can't tell a lie,' said Old Iron, 'I ain't been tryin' to run a mile. I ain't a welsher, yer know, I got a sense of honour. All me life I've been known as upright and 'ighly honourable—'

'Good,' said Doreen. 'All I need to know now then is when the wedding's takin' place. My mum would like it at St John's, where she's fond of the vicar.'

'Beg yer pardon?' said Old Iron hoarsely.

'St John's,' said Doreen, 'you know, the church in Larcom Street. I'm sorry if I imputed you didn't 'ave a sense of honour, I expect you've been ill in bed. If you'd popped over and told us,' she said accusingly to Luke, 'my mum would've been pleased to come across and minister to your dad while you were at work. It's what any woman would be pleased to do for 'er fiance.'

'I'm sure,' said Luke. 'I've got to admit, me dad 'asn't been feelin' too good. No, I tell a lie, he's been feelin' chronic.'

'There's been a misunderstandin',' said Old Iron, hoarser.

'It's all right, I'll tell my mum you've been very low,' said Doreen, 'that you've been too chronic to come and see her, though I don't know why your son couldn't 'ave let us know. I suppose he doesn't give much consideration to his neighbours, not even your future wife, Mr Edwards. When did you say you'd like the weddin'? July would suit my mum, it would give 'er a bit of time to collect something for her bottom drawer.'

'What d'you think, Dad?' asked Luke, face straight.

'Is there some brandy in the 'ouse?' asked Old Iron, done for.

'I'm glad it's all cleared up,' said Doreen. 'I'll tell my mum the third Saturday in July, shall I? And that you'll come and see 'er tomorrow evenin'. That'll give her a chance to look nice for you. Oh, and perhaps you'd pop over sometime and collect the jigsaws you've left lyin' about on our parlour table,' she said to Luke.

'Dad can collect them tomorrow,' said Luke. 'D'you fancy bein' his step-daughter?'

'I'm sure your dad and my mum and me will get on well together,' said Doreen haughtily.

'Good luck, then,' said Luke. What a waste, a girl like this still wanting to be tied to her mum.

'Well, good night, Mr Edwards,' said Doreen, 'you've been very honourable, I must say. Mum won't wear white for the weddin', of course, probably a nice costume, and I'll look forward to bein' her bridesmaid. The third Saturday in July, then. We'll see you tomorrow evenin'.'

'If I can walk,' said Old Iron brokenly.

'Oh, you're good at walkin',' said Doreen, 'you can take my mum for a nice one round the houses tomorrow. I'll see meself out.' Out she went.

'Where's a chair?' groaned Old Iron. 'I need a long sit-down.'

'You're done for, Dad,' said Luke.

'Don't I know it?' Old Iron sat heavily down. ''Ow did it 'appen, that's what I'd like to know. It was you that was supposed to get churched, not me.'

'It's to me regret, Old Iron, that Doreen doesn't want to get churched,' said Luke.

'Is there a bottle of beer, Luke? I ain't got the strength to get to the pub.'

'What?' gasped Mrs Paterson, fluttering hand to her palpitating bosom.

'Yes, it's all cleared up, Mum,' said Doreen. 'Actu'lly, I think he was a bit overcome at what he'd done, proposin' to you. I think he's been a bit shy about it. Well, you are still a handsome woman, and any widower would be overcome at 'aving you for his wife. Anyway, the third Saturday in July, he said, at St John's.'

'I'm goin' to faint,' said Mrs Paterson, but she didn't. 'Lor', me gettin' married again?'

'He's very manly-lookin', Mum, you'll make a handsome pair. We'd better start thinkin' about who to invite and what sort of weddin' breakfast we can afford. And then there's askin' the vicar to put the banns up.'

'Oh, me poundin' heart,' gasped Mrs Paterson. 'July, you said?' She blinked. 'Just a few weeks away?' She recovered. 'Well, love, I suppose it's compliment'ry, a man bein' a bit impatient. What did that son of 'is say?'

'Nothing very much,' said Doreen.

'You'll be 'is cousin now, sort of,' said Mrs Paterson.

Blow that, thought Doreen, who wants him for a sort of cousin?

Chapter Nineteen

Further, your step-mother, undaunted by all her other commitments, is sponsoring the opening of another orphanage. Her capacity for commitments is inexhaustible, particularly as you're no longer at home. By the way, I saw Boots a little while ago—

Polly threw down the letter that had taken a long time to reach her in Kenya. She had told her father never to mention Boots in his letters, never. Reminders of his existence were no help at all to her. The only cure was to fall in love with one of the bronzed husky white farmers of Kenya, men owning thousands of acres. There was no lack of them in this part of Kenya, the White Highlands. Damn it, why couldn't she fall in love with one of them? They were all masculine, and half of them were unmarried.

She picked up the letter from the floor of the verandah of the huge rambling bungalow owned by family friends with whom she was staying. In an almost fierce way she began reading again.

By the way, I saw Boots a while ago, we had a couple of old ales together, and I spoke to him about a German radical, a man called Adolf Hitler, of whom you've heard. Hitler is dangerous, a menace to the peace of Europe, who has stated the claims of Germany in his autobiography. If he should come to power, war is very possible. I asked Boots if he

would allow me to get him on Officers' Reserve. The
Army would need men like him to command the
training camps for recruits in the event of another
war. In the present climate, however, hardly a
person in this country believes there could ever be
another one. Boots was sceptical and also non-
committal. Having written this, I've just remembered
your command never to mention him. Well, it's done
now and I shall leave it.

Polly threw the letter down again. It went limp in
the heat.

Oh, bloody hell, she hissed to herself. Every
wound was open.

The sun blazed redly.

Oh, for an April shower.

Mrs Paterson herself opened the door.

'Evenin', Muriel,' said Old Iron.

'Oh, good evenin' – er—'

'Henry.'

'Good evenin', 'Enry, would yer like to come in?'

'Might as well, Muriel, seein' we're engaged,'
said Old Iron, and stepped in. 'Mind you, you did
say you'd think it over.'

'Oh, only on account of me troublesome 'eart,
which made me not able to think straight.'

'And how's yer 'eartbeats now, Muriel?'

'Oh, lor', they're all whichways.'

'Well, I've brought me healin' hand with me,'
said Old Iron, and closed the door with his foot.
Unprofessionally, he tested her heartbeats.

''Enry!'

'Well, we are engaged, Muriel,' said Old Iron.
He had taken a philosophical turn. And after all, he
didn't know a more handsome woman.

Or a more handsome bosom, either.

'Oh, 'Enry . . .'

The day before the trial of Gerald Ponsonby began at the Old Bailey, Boots, Cassie and Freddy kept an appointment in the offices of the solicitor acting for the prosecuting counsel. The solicitor, Mr Highway, went through their evidence very carefully with them. It was a repeat of what had taken place not long after Ponsonby's arrest on a murder charge.

'You're quite happy, Cassie, about appearing?' said Mr Highway. 'You know what to say, that's very evident, and I assure you you'll be treated very kindly by judge and counsel.'

'Just watch out for defence counsel,' said Boots.

'I'm not afraid, Uncle Boots,' said Cassie, who had a shy affection for the man who had saved her and had come to see her more than once after her ordeal. She didn't really know what to call him except Uncle Boots. That was what Freddy called him, although he wasn't really his uncle. Boots was the eldest brother of the man who was married to Freddy's sister, Susie. 'I don't like Mr Po'sby, I'm goin' to tell on 'im. Is the Old Bailey like the Tower of London?'

'Not quite,' smiled Boots.

'No, not quite,' said Mr Highway, middle-aged and agreeably professional. 'If the judge speaks to you, call him Your Honour. That goes for you too, Freddy. But he won't mind too much if you forget.'

'Cassie'll probably tell 'im her dad was a judge once in darkest Africa or somewhere,' said Freddy.

'Course I won't,' said Cassie, blushing.

'Make a nice change that will, then,' said Freddy.

'Me and Cassie'll be all right, Mr 'Ighway, and we'll 'ave Uncle Boots with us.'

'A stalwart, mmm?' smiled Mr Highway.

'He's not a wart, he's nice,' said Cassie. 'Ain't you, Uncle Boots?'

'You'll do, Cassie,' said Boots. 'I'll be picking you and Freddy up at nine tomorrow.'

'He's got a car now, Cassie,' said Freddy.

'Crikey, 'ave yer really, Uncle Boots?' said Cassie. 'I 'ad a chariot when I was Queen Board-seer in our school pageant on Empire Day. Freddy was Caesar. One of our teachers called him "O Mighty Caesar", except he didn't 'ave enough safety-pins in 'is Roman togger, and you could see his knees a bit. I had a spear. I hit 'im with it once,' she said thoughtfully. 'Well, he was messin' about. But he didn't mind, I'm 'is best mate and he likes me.'

Boots smiled. There was something very endearing about Cassie, as there was about Rosie and Annabelle and a thousand other young girls.

He hoped Gerald Ponsonby would hang for cruelly ending the lives of three of them.

Mr Ronald Ponsonby, existing quietly and inoffensively as far as Doreen and her mother were concerned, spent part of that day in Stepney Green again, where his old acquaintance, finger on the side of his nose, assured him he could arrange for the hire of a saloon car for a couple of days and no questions asked about the gent. What couple of days did he have in mind?

'I'll let you know by telephone.'

'Could yer oblige me with a couple of days notice, and a small deposit?'

'Of course, yes, of course. The deposit? Here we are.'

'If yer'll pardon me, guv, I didn't 'ave in mind a deposit that small.'

'An extra two pounds, then?'

'I'm obliged. It's a struggle to live, yer know.'

The Old Bailey courtroom was packed. One who might have been there but had decided it was wiser to stay away was Mr Ronald Ponsonby. It would also save the excessive pain of seeing Gerald in the dock.

Emily, Chinese Lady and Mr Finch were present. Emily had felt she must be there, even though she was sure she would dislike every moment. But Boots was one of the principal witnesses for the prosecution, and that had compelled her presence. Chinese Lady had insisted on accompanying her, and Mr Finch had absented himself from his department to be there with them, his mood sombre. Also present were Freddy's parents and Cassie's father, a widower.

In the dock, Mr Ponsonby looked neat and tidy of dress and features, but his attitude seemed to be one of irritation, as if the whole occasion amounted to an objectionable nuisance. Prosecuting counsel outlined the case for the Crown, centred on three young girls who had gone missing. He recounted the discovery of one body in a Bermondsey scrapyard and the other two under the floorboards of a fire-damaged and deserted factory in Walworth. He followed with an account of the police investigation, the abduction by the accused of a young girl in Walworth, one Cassie Ford, the search for her, the discovery of her unconscious person in that same factory, and the apprehension of the accused at the door of the factory by a Mr Robert Adams. He referred to the subsequent confession made by the accused to the arresting officer, Inspector Grant of Scotland Yard. He would read this to the jury. It was exhibit number one, and a confession of murder. In view of that, it was a mystery why the accused had pleaded not guilty. The Crown would show his plea was entirely unacceptable, and leave the jury in no doubt of his guilt.

Prosecuting counsel then read the confession aloud.

'My name is Gerald Ponsonby. I am forty-seven and of independent means. My hobby is photographing young girls while they are still at an age of sweet innocence. Unfortunately, it's rarely possible to do this without them becoming foolishly hysterical. I solved this problem by stealing a bottle of chloroform from the North Middlesex Hospital, where five years earlier I had my appendix removed. I used some of this to help me rob a jeweller and to deceive the police into thinking this was my reason for stealing the bottle. Before this I had secured quietness in one or two girls by giving them money, but I could not be sure they would remain quiet indefinitely, and nor would they pose as exactly as I wished. Further, their acceptance of money tarnished their sweetness and innocence. The chloroform proved ideal. It enabled me to pose three delightful young angels without them making any fuss at all, but regrettably there was no alternative subsequently but to secure their eternal silence. One cannot put up with having hysterical parents shouting and knocking at one's door.

However, people should acknowledge the fact that I saved these girls from ever growing fat or ugly or old. Yes, one of them was the girl whose body was found beneath the shed in a Bermondsey scrapyard, and the other two were those found under the factory floorboards. My method of silencing them was to wind a bootlace around their necks and quickly tighten it. It's very irritating that people cannot understand necessity, nor my need to pursue my hobby. That is all I wish to say.'

Amid an acute silence, broken suddenly and briefly by a woman's exclamation of disgust, prosecuting counsel returned the confession to the clerk of the court. He then advised the judge he would like Inspector Grant to be called.

Inspector Grant, the Crown's first witness, described his involvement in the case and the eventual arrest of the accused at a time when he was being detained at the factory by Mr Robert Adams following the successful search for the abducted girl, Cassie Ford. The Inspector confirmed that the confession was exhibit number one, and that it had been volunteered by the accused after the bodies of two missing girls had been found under the factory floorboards. In the accused's lodgings, a large amount of money had come to light, the proceeds of a robbery admitted to in the confession. In addition, photographic developing equipment had been found, and also a number of photographs of young girls.

In the dock, Ponsonby looked pettishly irritable.

Mr Templeton, prosecuting counsel, then gave way to the defence counsel, Mr Barrington.

'No questions,' said Mr Barrington.

Inspector Grant stepped down, and there

followed evidence from two workmen who had discovered the body of the first young girl in the Bermondsey scrapyard. Freddy's dad might have been called to bear witness to this gruesome event, for he had been in the yard at the time as its new manager, but Mr Highway, the solicitor, had said he wouldn't be needed, which was a relief to him and to Freddy's mum as well.

Defence counsel forwent the privilege of questioning either of the workmen.

Cassie, chief witness for the prosecution, heard her name called then, and the court usher appeared at the door of the witnesses' waiting-room.

'There you are, Cassie,' said Boots, 'your turn.' He gave her an encouraging little squeeze.

'Oh, 'elp,' she gulped.

'You'll be all right,' said Freddy, all togged up in the suit he had worn for Susie's wedding to Sammy.

Cassie went bravely into the courtroom with the usher. She had imagined it would look a bit like a throne room, but it didn't. There was no gilt, no glitter, no chandelier, and not a single Beefeater. She saw panelled walls of brown and rows of seated people. She saw the judge in his robe and wig, and men in black gowns and wigs. The usher guided her into the witness box. It hid all of her except her boater, face and neck. A man near the back of the public benches lifted his hand in a little gesture, and Cassie saw her dad, who had taken the day off from his job as a railway ganger to be present. The clerk of the court helped her to take the oath. She was ready for that, the solicitor and Boots had prepared her. She took it a little shyly. She knew that Mr Ponsonby was in the dock, but avoided looking at him. Her imagination began to work. This could easily be a room in a castle. Well, the judge looked like the king of a castle, even if he did wear a wig and not a crown.

Mr Templeton rose on behalf of the Crown and spoke gently.

'You are Miss Cassie Ford of Blackwood Street, Walworth?'

'Yes, that's where I live,' said Cassie, 'and that's me dad over there that can prove it. And me Uncle Boots is outside, and 'e can prove it too.' The sound of her own voice reassured her, although it seemed to tickle some members of the public. Reassurance took a slight knock. ''Ave I said wrong?' she asked.

'Not at all, not in the least, Miss Ford,' said the judge. 'Would you perhaps like a high stool to sit on?'

'Oh, it's all right, Your Majesty,' said Cassie, 'I don't mind standin' up. Well, that's if it's not goin' to be very long. 'E said it wouldn't be too long.' She nodded at Mr Templeton, whom she'd previously met and talked with. 'I don't mind half an hour, Your Majesty.'

'Very well, young lady.' The judge permitted himself the ghost of a smile. 'Ah – I'm not the King, by the way.'

'Oh, I don't mind, Your Majesty.'

Smiles appeared around the court.

'Sir will do,' said the judge gently. 'Proceed, Mr Templeton.'

Cassie's eyes were drawn to the man in the dock then. He was watching her like a ferret that had sniffed the scent of a baby rabbit. She grimaced.

'Miss Ford,' said Mr Templeton, 'may I call you Cassie?'

'Yes, that's me name,' said Cassie.

'How old are you, Cassie?'

'Ten,' she said, 'and eleven in October.'

'Would you like to tell the court what happened to you last Good Friday?'

'Yes, that's what I've come for,' said Cassie, and in her own articulate fashion she began to recount events. On the afternoon of Good Friday she left her home in Blackwood Street to meet Freddy Brown in Caulfield Place, where he lived. They were going up the park together on Freddy's bike. She had Tabby, her cat, with her. Tabby liked parks, she said. On the way she met a man who lived in Freddy's street. 'Mr Po'sby,' she said, 'that's who it was.'

'Do you see that man here in this court, Cassie?'

'Yes, 'e's over there,' said Cassie, pointing at the prisoner in the dock.

'Carry on,' said Mr Templeton.

Well, said Cassie, with the whole court engrossed, she knew Mr Po'sby, he gave her a peppermint sometimes and had offered to take her photograph. When she met him on Good Friday afternoon, he said he'd photograph her right then. She said she had to meet Freddy. Mr Po'sby said it wouldn't take long, his camera wasn't far away, it was in a studio. He gave her a peppermint and she went with him, carrying her cat, but when they got to the broken gate of a factory that had once caught fire, she told him she wasn't going in there, it was haunted. Her cat jumped down then, and Mr Po'sby put something over her face that sent her to sleep. She didn't wake up for ages, except that sometimes she felt there was something over her face again. When she did wake up she was at home with her family, who told her that Freddy and Mr

Adams, the one she called Uncle Boots, had found her and rescued her.

'Oh,' she said to Mr Templeton, 'did you know there was a princess once that got carried off by a wicked witch that—' Cassie stopped. Somehow, it didn't sound quite right in this place.

Mr Templeton smiled. The judge's ascetic countenance took on an almost benign look. The shorthand writer waited. Chinese Lady and Emily were emotionally touched by Cassie's engaging adolescence.

'I think I know the story, Cassie,' said Mr Templeton. 'The hero was a handsome prince.'

'Yes, I like 'eroes,' said Cassie, feeling she was on the right path, after all. 'Uncle Boots is me own 'ero. Oh, and Freddy, of course, only I don't expect—' She stopped again, conscious of everyone looking.

'Yes, Cassie?' said Mr Templeton, wanting the jury to take note of the unspoiled nature of this young witness.

'Well,' said Cassie bravely, 'I don't expect Freddy could ride a white 'orse as good as Uncle Boots.'

The fascinated court indulged in smiles. Mr Ponsonby alone was unappreciative. Mr Finch reflected on the nature of Boots and the attraction he had for members of the opposite sex of all ages. It was all done without effort, and simply by being himself.

'Perhaps you're right, Cassie,' said Mr Templeton. 'Now, are you positive that the man who took you to the factory gates and put something over your face to send you to sleep is the man you see in the dock?'

'Yes, and I'm sure as well,' said Cassie, looking at Ponsonby again. 'That's 'im, that's Mr Po'sby.'

'Thank you, Cassie.' Mr Templeton resumed his seat. The judge glanced enquiringly at the defence counsel.

'No questions, my lord,' said Mr Barrington. That evoked murmurs of surprise.

'Then you may step down, Miss Ford,' said the judge, 'and thank you.'

Cassie blinked. She'd been told she'd be asked questions by the barrister defending the prisoner, and that he'd try to get her in a fix. Relieved and happy that he wasn't going to, and not wanting to be in the same place as Mr Ponsonby any more, she said, 'Oh, can I go back to Freddy and me Uncle Boots, Your Majesty?'

'You can, indeed you can, Miss Ford, and I hope it won't be necessary to recall you. Usher?'

Cassie stepped down and the usher took her back to the witnesses' waiting-room. Her departure induced a little sigh in Ponsonby, for however much her story may have damaged him, he could not deny she was the epitome of young girlish innocence.

Cassie ran straight into Boots's arms. He hugged her for her courage. And her innocence.

'Oh, I didn't get asked no questions by the other man, Uncle Boots.'

'None?'

'Not one.'

'Good for you, Cassie,' said Freddy.

'Call Master Frederick Brown,' intoned the court clerk.

'Master Frederick Brown!'

'Good luck, Freddy me lad,' said Boots.

Freddy entered the court and took his place in the witness box. He looked around. He saw Ponsonby, and he saw his parents. His mum gave him a little wave. Good old Mum. But what a place, all wigs and solemn faces. And everyone seemed to have staring mince pies. He took the oath gravely. Well, he thought he'd better.

Mr Templeton rose and addressed him.

'You are Frederick Brown of Caulfield Place, Walworth?'

'Yes, me mum and dad are Mr and Mrs Brown,' said Freddy.

'What age are you, Master Brown?'

'Twelve,' said Freddy with some measure of self-importance. 'Well, I will be in November. Your Honour,' he added, looking at the judge.

'Would you please tell the court of your experiences during the afternoon of Good Friday last?' said Mr Templeton.

'Yes, I remember that afternoon all right,' said Freddy, who didn't suffer shyness. He began his account of events. He'd arranged to take Cassie Ford to Ruskin Park, and she was to meet him at his home. Well, he waited and waited, but she didn't turn up, so he went round to her house to see what had happened to her, only there was no-one there. All her family were out. So he went looking for her. There weren't a lot of people about. There never were on Good Fridays, which were like Sundays. He looked all over. Well, Cassie could be a bit dreamy sometimes and just wander about. He couldn't find her anywhere. Everytime he saw someone, he asked if they'd seen her, but no-one had. He started to worry. He went back to her house, but there was still no-one there, and when he went back to his own house there was still no sign of her, and all his own family were out. The afternoon was getting on, so he went to the police station in Rodney Road and told them about her, and they said they'd see what they could do. Again he went back to his own house, hoping she'd turned up, but she hadn't. Then a taxi arrived, and in it were Mr Adams and his daughter Rosie.

'Mr Robert Adams?' enquired Mr Templeton.

'Yes, he's me brother-in-law now,' said Freddy, 'but more like an uncle. He came in the taxi with weddin' presents from 'is fam'ly for Susie, me sister. She was goin' to marry 'is brother Sammy. On the morrow,' he added, and at once thought that that was what Cassie would have said. On the morrow.

'Carry on, Freddy,' said Mr Templeton, the court engrossed again.

Well, Freddy went on, he told Mr Adams all about Cassie, and Mr Adams said he and Rosie would help him look for her, using the taxi. They drove all round Walworth for ages, and it was when they were just about to pass a ruined factory that they saw a cat come out through a gap in the gates. He knew it was Cassie's cat, so Mr Adams told the driver to stop. They all went in through the gates to a door that was barred and padlocked. It was the door to the only part of the factory still standing. There were offices and storerooms inside. He knew that because he'd explored it once when he was with Cassie and the padlock hadn't been closed. The taxi driver got a large spanner and Mr Adams broke the door open. Freddy and Mr Adams went upstairs and they found Cassie in one of the rooms, lying on blankets on some kind of bed, like a camp-bed. She was unconscious. Mr Adams carried her down, and the taxi driver carried her to his taxi to take her straight home. He, Freddy, went with him and so did Rosie, but Mr Adams stayed. He said he was going to wait for the man who had taken Cassie, and he didn't half look grim. Anyway, they took Cassie home, her family were there by then, and the taxi driver then went off to the police station.

'Thank you, Freddy,' said Mr Templeton.

'Is that all, Your Worship?' asked Freddy.

'My learned friend may wish to ask some questions of you.'

'No questions,' said Mr Barrington, which aroused more murmurs of surprise.

'Thank you, Master Brown, you may leave the stand and return to the witnesses' room,' said the judge.

'Oh, thanks,' said Freddy, 'I'd best get back and sit with Cassie.'

He gave his parents a little wave and then returned to Boots and Cassie.

'Well, Freddy?' said Boots.

'I didn't get asked any questions, either,' said Freddy.

'That's a fact?' said Boots.

'The bloke said no questions.'

'That's odd,' said Boots.

'Did yer speak up, Freddy?' asked Cassie.

'Well, I didn't get me north-and-south in a tangle,' said Freddy.

'Did yer see that man, Mr Po'sby?' asked Cassie.

'Yes,' said Freddy, 'but don't let's talk about 'im.'

There was time to call the taxi driver, Gus

Allbury, before the court adjourned for lunch. He described his part in the search for Cassie Ford, and confirmed he was on the spot outside the factory door when Mr Adams brought the girl out alive but unconscious. She was placed in the taxi, with Mr Adams's daughter and young Freddy Brown looking after her. Mr Allbury said he then drove her home to her family, and then went on to the Rodney Road police station with Rosie Adams. Inspector Grant was there, having been called in on account of the girl Cassie being missing. He informed him of what had happened, and that Mr Adams was still at the factory, lying in wait for whoever had brought the girl there. Inspector Grant arranged for a doctor to call at once on Cassie, and then went to the factory with his sergeant and some uniformed constables, some in a police car and some in the taxi. When they arrived, there was a man on the ground outside the door of the factory, and Mr Adams was standing over him.

'Do you see that man in court, Mr Allbury?'

'Yes.' Gus Allbury nodded at the prisoner. 'That's him, guv.'

'Thank you, Mr Allbury.'

'No questions,' said Mr Barrington, defence counsel.

The judge raised his eyebrows. At this rate the trial would not last long. However, he ordered the adjournment for lunch and a resumption at two o'clock.

Mr and Mrs Brown and Mr Ford took Freddy and Cassie for sandwiches and a welcome cup of tea at a little café near the Old Bailey. Chinese Lady, Emily and Mr Finch joined them a minute later.

Meanwhile, the solicitor, Mr Highway, had a word with Boots.

'Cassie and Freddy were both splendid, Mr Adams. Cassie was extraordinarily quaint.'

'Sounds as if she was herself, in fact,' said Boots. 'How's it all going?'

'Strangely,' said Mr Highway.

'How strangely?'

'Defence counsel hasn't asked one question of any of our witnesses so far, Mr Adams.'

'Not one?'

'Not one, which is very strange in view of the fact that Ponsonby put in a not guilty plea.'

'Well, he's not very much like the rest of us,' said Boots.

'Shall we go for a drink and a sandwich?'

'Good idea.' They left the Old Bailey. 'Have the photographs been produced?'

'No, not yet. Inspector Grant will be recalled to identify them as having been found in Ponsonby's lodgings.'

Mr Ronald Ponsonby, now sporting a brown bowler and a brown suit, watched them enter a pub. His eyes glittered for a moment. He was tempted to follow them in and to eavesdrop, if possible. He refrained. He found another pub, where he had a sandwich with a Pernod.

Chapter Twenty

The resumption heralded the arrival of Dr Ernest Sadler in the witness box. Asked by Mr Templeton to describe his part in the events of Good Friday, he said he was requested by the police to attend on a young girl, Cassie Ford, who had apparently been abducted and chloroformed, but was now safe at her home. He found she was indeed suffering from the effects of chloroform, and judged it had been administered more than once. However, apart from that, she was unharmed. When she was sufficiently recovered to speak, she had no recollection of what had taken place from the time when a man she knew, a Mr Ponsonby, had put something over her face. Dr Sadler said he later gave her a sedative to sleep off the sickness she was suffering. He saw her again the next day and found her fully recovered.

'Thank you, Dr Sadler,' said Mr Templeton.

'Mr Barrington?' enquired the judge.

'No questions, my lord,' said Mr Barrington. The general reaction this time was one of curiosity.

Dr Sadler stepped down.

'Call Mr Robert Adams.'

Boots came in to take the stand.

Chinese Lady from her place on the public benches eyed her eldest son with just a hint of pride for the way he carried himself, even if she did have qualms about what he might say in the witness box.

At times, you never knew what he was going to come out with, or what he was thinking behind that sly disarming smile of his. All the same, Chinese Lady sat with a straight back, her tidy and well-defined bosom firm and still. Emily, however, quivered a little, her mind going back to the trial of a neighbour, Miss Elsie Chivers, in 1914. Miss Chivers had been charged with the murder of her own mother. Boots was the final witness for the defence. Emily hadn't been in court, but she'd bought an evening paper on her way home from work and found it full of the remarkable evidence given by a young soldier, Private Robert Adams. It helped to secure a not guilty verdict.

The oath was taken, the preliminaries negotiated. Boots glanced briefly at Ponsonby before he began his recounting of events. Ponsonby's stare was as viciously glittering as that of a basilisk. If he disliked people because they were prejudiced against his kind, he hated the man who had delivered him to the police.

Boots explained the reason for his arrival at the house of the Brown family. He and his daughter Rosie had travelled there in a taxi to deliver a number of wedding presents to Miss Susie Brown, his brother Sammy's fiancée. The family were out, apart from Freddy, who was in the street and in an agitated state. A young friend of his, Cassie Ford, had gone missing. Boots said he used the taxi to conduct as thorough a search of the area as possible, taking Freddy with him. By a stroke of good fortune, Freddy noticed the girl's cat emerging through a gap in a factory's sagging gates. Most of the factory had been destroyed by fire, but part of it was still standing, according to Freddy. They all squeezed in through the gates and approached the door of the standing section. It was barred and padlocked. With the aid of the taxi driver's spanner, Boots broke it open. He went in with Freddy, who had once explored it. The taxi driver and Rosie stayed outside. They found Cassie on a truckle bed in an upstairs room. She was unconscious, and there was a faint smell of chloroform. He carried her down and the taxi driver took her to her home, along with Freddy and Rosie. He stayed behind himself, on the assumption that whoever had abducted Cassie would return. He did. Boots confronted him, and it was necessary then to knock him out and await the arrival of the police, whom the cabbie had promised to alert. When they did arrive they took the man into custody.

'Do you see that man in court, Mr Adams?'

'Yes, I see him,' said Boots. 'In the dock.'

A little hiss, imperceptible to most of the people, escaped Ponsonby.

'Is there more you would like to tell the court, Mr Adams?' asked Mr Templeton.

'A little,' said Boots, and Emily wondered how he could be so calm and matter-of-fact when, in a manner of speaking, the eyes of the whole country were on this trial. But that was his way, of course.

He pointed out that Ponsonby had escaped from police custody the following day, but was recaptured late in the evening. He was discovered hiding in the ladies' cloakroom in St John's Institute, Larcom Street, Walworth.

'Is it true, Mr Adams, that you were again responsible for delivering him to the police?'

'I was in the Institute, yes. The wedding reception

of my brother Sammy and his wife was taking place there, and I discovered the accused man had locked himself in a cubicle after marking it out of order.'

'Thank you, Mr Adams. No further questions, m'lud.'

'Mr Barrington, do you wish to cross-examine this witness?' asked the judge.

'Indeed I do,' said Mr Barrington, and came to his feet at last. The court stirred. Ponsonby betrayed nervous excitement by fussing about with his bow tie.

'Mr Adams,' said defence counsel, 'you seem a very worthy citizen in your readiness to hand over to the police persons you consider suspect.'

'I think you're exaggerating,' said Boots, 'I'm really a very ordinary bloke.'

Chinese Lady's straight back stiffened. Ordinary? Ordinary? She hadn't brought up any of her offspring to be ordinary. Ordinary was almost like being common.

'I doubt, Mr Adams, if ordinary blokes take the law into their own hands,' said Mr Barrington. 'Tell me, in what condition was Miss Cassie Ford when you found her?'

'Unconscious,' said Boots.

'Just unconscious.' Mr Barrington nodded in agreement. 'She bore no signs of harm? There were no bruises or injuries of any kind?'

'I didn't examine her for bruises or injuries,' said Boots. 'My only immediate concern was to get her returned to her family.'

'But did you expect to find her harmed?'

Boots might have said he expected to find her dead, but refrained.

'I had no expectations, I was simply living in the hope of finding her.'

'But weren't you relieved and grateful, when you did find her, that although she was unconscious, she had been treated gently and with care?'

'What kind of a question is that?' asked Boots.

Mr Templeton intervened.

'Yes, m'lud, exactly what kind of a question is it, and what's its purpose?' he asked.

'Mr Barrington?' said the judge.

'I intend, my lord, to prove that the defendant's protective instincts are so strong as to render him incapable of harming anyone, least of all a young girl.'

'Notwithstanding his signed confession?' queried the judge.

'I shall come to that in time,' said Mr Barrington.

'Please continue,' said the judge.

'Bleedin' eyewash,' breathed a woman behind Emily.

'Mr Adams, Dr Sadler advised this court that Miss Ford was quite unharmed,' said Mr Barrington. 'You had seen this for yourself.'

'I'd seen nothing of the sort,' said Boots. 'I repeat, I didn't examine her. That was something for a doctor to do.'

'Come, Mr Adams, there were obviously no injuries. Therefore, why did you assume the defendant was guilty of harmful intent before he had a chance to prove himself innocent?'

'Objection,' said Mr Templeton. 'My learned friend can't know what the witness assumed. He can assume he assumed, but that's only a fly in the wind, m'lud.'

'I think I'll overrule that, Mr Templeton,' said

the judge, 'and let Mr Barrington attempt to make his point.'

'The fact is, Mr Adams, you attacked and assaulted the defendant when he arrived at the factory,' said Mr Barrington. 'That is proof, isn't it, that you did assume him to be guilty of harmful intent?'

'I assumed he was guilty of abducting the girl and chloroforming her,' said Boots. 'I assume you assume that that was harmless.'

'Mr Adams, you did not know who abducted the girl or who chloroformed her.'

'Oh, under some circumstances,' said Boots drily, 'one strikes first and asks questions afterwards.'

'Didn't it occur to you that the man who appeared at the factory door might not have been the man you had in mind?'

'No,' said Boots.

'In this country, Mr Adams, a man is innocent until proved guilty.'

'For which the innocent are grateful,' said Boots. 'Unfortunately, I wasn't in a position to conduct a trial by jury. I was busy trying to ward off an umbrella with a sprung blade, an umbrella like a sword-stick.'

'Is that an exhibit?' asked the judge.

'Number four, m'lud,' said Mr Templeton, and the clerk held up a labelled umbrella. He pressed a concealed spring, and a six-inch blade, deadly in its sharpness, protruded from the end of the brolly. He offered the exhibit to the judge.

'I can see it, thank you,' said the judge. 'Who is or was the owner?'

'The defendant, m'lord.'

'For use only to defend himself when in the more dubious quarters of London,' said Mr Barrington. 'True, he attempted to use it to defend himself against assault and battery by Mr Adams, but it was wrenched from him and he was battered to the ground. After this trial, the defendant will bring a charge of grievous bodily harm against the witness.'

'For the purpose of the present charges, I should like to hear the witness's version of the confrontation,' said the judge. 'Do you propose to ask him for it, Mr Barrington?'

'M'lud, if my learned friend doesn't, I will,' said Mr Templeton.

'The court has heard from the taxi driver that when the police arrived on the scene, the defendant lay on the ground with the witness standing over him,' said Mr Barrington.

'Nevertheless,' said the judge, 'will you give your version, Mr Adams?'

'I'd like to,' said Boots. The glittering eyes of the basilisk bore into him again. 'I heard the defendant approaching the factory door. I was behind it, waiting, certain that he'd show up. I opened the door, and as soon as he saw me he raised his umbrella and jabbed. The blade was out. I knocked the umbrella aside and hit him on the jaw with my left fist. It knocked him out. I took the umbrella from him and kept him grounded until the police arrived. If he was suffering from grievous bodily harm, it wasn't apparent, but then I didn't examine him, either.'

Chinese Lady looked approving. Emily wondered how it was that Boots, born into a desperately hard-up family, could not only stand up to an awesome barrister in an awesome court of criminal law, but also not turn a hair while doing so. She also wondered what Ponsonby thought of her husband. She could not see his face, only the back of his head.

Mr Barrington said, 'Your version, Mr Adams, is not necessarily the correct one.'

'On the other hand,' said Boots, 'it's not necessarily the wrong one, either.'

'The fact remains you chose to make a brutal citizen's arrest of a man without any thought of the possibility that he was the wrong man.'

'I knocked him out to save myself being sliced in half,' said Boots.

'Very amusing, Mr Adams, but it won't do.'

'It'll do for me,' said Boots, 'I'm still alive.'

Someone laughed. The judge lifted his head.

'No further questions,' said Mr Barrington brusquely, and Mr Finch wondered why Boots alone had been singled out for cross-examination.

'M'lud,' said Mr Templeton, 'what exactly has my learned friend established?'

The judge said, 'I think the jury will understand that Mr Barrington has done his best to convince them that Miss Ford, apart from being chloroformed, was treated in – ah – exemplary fashion, while implying the witness may have made a citizen's arrest of the wrong man.'

'Forgive my incredulity, my lord,' said Mr Templeton.

'There is some inconsistency present in view of the fact that it was the defendant who volunteered the confession and signed it,' said the judge.

'I shall refer to that later, my lord,' said Mr Barrington.

'Very well. Mr Adams, you may stand down.'

Boots left the box. He glanced at the public

benches, noting the presence of Emily, Chinese Lady and Mr Finch. He gave them a nod, then returned to Cassie and Freddy. They were happy to have him back with them.

In court, Mr Templeton asked if he might recall Inspector Grant. Permission was given, and the Inspector took the stand again. Mr Templeton asked him what he had found in the room where young Miss Ford had been discovered. The Inspector, without referring to any notes, said a cupboard had contained a camera, a tripod, photographic plates and flashlight equipment. These were all listed exhibits. On the table in the room was an empty paper sweet bag that had a faint peppermint smell to it. Exhibit number six.

Ponsonby looked distinctly irritated at this disclosure.

'Inspector, did you find anything in the defendant's lodgings that the jury should know about?' asked Mr Templeton.

'A large amount of money that the accused admitted came from a robbery he committed, a bottle containing chloroform, a small cardboard box containing chloroform pads, fifty-two photographs and developing equipment.'

'What kind of photographs?' asked Mr Templeton.

'They were all of young girls, including Cassie Ford and the three girls whose bodies had come to light,' said the Inspector.

'Portraits, Inspector?'

'No. All the girls had been photographed while obviously unconscious and with their clothes disarranged.'

'A collective exhibit, m'lud,' said Mr Templeton.

'Number ten,' said the clerk.

'I will see them,' said the judge, 'and then they may be passed to the jury.'

The clerk handed up a packet of photographs. The judge examined several, and glanced briefly at the rest, then allowed the clerk to take them to the jury foreman. The court was silent. Ponsonby looked as if his irritation would snap. His counsel gazed at the ceiling. After quite some time, the photographs were returned to the clerk, and Mr Templeton addressed Inspector Grant again.

'The accused was present when you searched his lodgings?'

'He was.'

'What did he say when you showed him the photographs?'

'He said such interference was intolerable, that he wished to put an end to it and would do so by making a confession. Which he did, at the Rodney Road police station, and to the effect that his hobby was to photograph young girls while they were still at the age of sweet innocence, that it was rarely possible to do so without them becoming foolishly hysterical, and that the chloroform, stolen from a London hospital, solved this problem.'

'And regrettably, as we heard when the confession was read, he then had no alternative but to silence them,' said Mr Templeton. A woman expelled angry breath. 'With a rider, I recall, to the effect that they would never grow old and ugly.' Mr Templeton glanced at the man in the dock.

Ponsonby was muttering, 'So much prejudice, so much intolerance, what a day, what a day.'

'Is the prisoner attempting to say something?' asked the judge.

The constable in the dock with Ponsonby, tapped him on the shoulder and requested his silence.

'That is all, Inspector Grant, thank you,' said Mr Templeton.

'No questions,' said Mr Barrington, at which the judge adjourned proceedings until ten o'clock tomorrow morning.

'All rise,' said the clerk. Everyone stood up and the judge departed.

'Well,' said Chinese Lady, 'after all that, perhaps we can go home now and have some tea.'

'Happily, Maisie,' said Mr Finch, 'there's no better alternative.'

'I'll just see if Boots is takin' Freddy and Cassie back to their homes,' said Emily.

'You go with him, if you want, Em'ly,' said Chinese Lady. 'That's if you don't mind ridin' all the way home in that contraption of his. Your dad and me will go on a bus. It's safer.'

Mr Finch winked at Emily. Emily, coming out of her slightly traumatized mood, smiled at him. They both liked Chinese Lady's use of the word 'dad'.

'We'll have a talk at home,' said Emily, and went to find Boots. She ended up riding home in the Riley with him and Cassie and Freddy. The girl and boy knew they had to attend again tomorrow, in case it was necessary to recall them to the witness box, but the prospect gave them no nervous worries. The excitement of the car ride was uppermost at the moment, anyway. Boots had brought them in the Riley and was taking them home in it.

'Crikey,' said Cassie in delight, as the car headed through City streets towards London Bridge, 'I feel like a lord, Uncle Boots.' As a treat, she was sitting next to him. Emily was in the back with Freddy.

'You mean a lady,' said Freddy.

'No, a lord,' said Cassie. She felt as if she ought to be waving a lordly hand at people on pavements. 'You could be me butler, Freddy.'

'Can't wait, can I?' grinned Freddy.

'Uncle Boots,' said Cassie, 'I didn't mind about today. 'Is Majesty was ever so kind to me.'

'His Majesty the judge?' smiled Boots, handling the Riley in the fashion of a man who meant to be its master.

'Yes, 'im,' said Cassie.

'You're supposed to call 'im Your Honour,' said Freddy.

'I forgot,' said Cassie. Boots overtook a trundling horse and cart on London Bridge.

'Don't land us in the river, Boots,' said Emily.

'Oh, 'e wouldn't do that, would you, Uncle Boots?' said Cassie.

Emily smiled. Boots had won himself another admirer.

Everyone came round after supper that evening, Tommy and Vi, Sammy and Susie, and Lizzy and Ned with their children. They all wanted to know about the trial. They'd read some reports in evening papers. Chinese Lady said it was all shocking, that it was criminal young Cassie and Freddy having to stand up in court with that heathen man there. They should have given their evidence in private, she said. She didn't know if they ought to be talking about it now, not in front of Rosie and Annabelle.

The younger children were playing elsewhere.

Lizzy said, 'Well, I don't suppose anyone wants to talk about the weather, Mum.'

'I don't see why not when it's been such a nice day outside,' said Chinese Lady. 'I could of done a bit of special washin' and had it dry in no time.'

'How did Boots perform?' asked Ned.

'Like he always does,' smiled Emily.

'Auntie Emily, how's always?' asked Annabelle.

'Like he was lord of the manor,' said Emily.

'Still, I must say he didn't disgrace us,' said Chinese Lady. 'I suffered disturbances that he might, knowin' how he can talk like a music hall turn even when the house is on fire.'

'Nana, we haven't had the house on fire,' said Rosie.

'True,' said Mr Finch gravely.

'Never mind that,' said Chinese Lady, 'we all know he'd say something comic if the roof fell in. All the same, I must say he stood up very commendable in court, which was a great relief to Em'ly and me. Mind, it was a bit queer, Boots bein' the only witness that was – what was it, Edwin?'

'Cross-examined,' said Mr Finch.

'Yes, that was it,' said Chinese Lady, conducting the discussion in brisk matriarchal fashion. 'But Boots still stood up very commendable, which made me think he might turn out a credit to the fam'ly, after all.'

'We all hope and pray he will, Nana,' said Rosie, and that drew a smile from Boots.

'As for Cassie and Freddy,' said Chinese Lady, 'well, I never saw a braver girl and boy, they both spoke up very admirable. Yes, and there was Cassie callin' the judge Your Majesty, would you believe.'

'We can all believe, Ma,' said Sammy.

'Don't call me Ma,' said Chinese Lady, and

added, not for the first time as a mother, 'we might all 'ave been poor in our time, but never common.'

'Freddy did really well, Mum?' asked Susie.

'You can be proud of 'im, Susie.'

'Well, bless him,' said Susie, but looked as if nothing and no-one could make the nature of the trial any less horrid than it was. Boots was saying very little, he was leaving descriptions of the courtroom scenes to Chinese Lady and Emily. Sammy was serious, Tommy fairly quiet, and Ned saying not much more than Boots. Susie felt all four men, and Mr Finch as well, were thinking that hanging was too good for the man Ponsonby, whose counsel, it appeared, had only asked questions of Boots.

However, Emily lightened the atmosphere by mentioning that Cassie was such a funny girl.

'Freddy calls her his mate,' said Susie.

'That really is funny,' said Vi.

'She's Boots's new little sweet'eart,' smiled Emily.

'Well, I'm blessed,' said Rosie, 'I just don't know when you're goin' to stop, Daddy. You've got me and Annabelle and Emma and goodness knows who else, and now there's Cassie as well. I call that – well, I don't know what to call it.'

'Acquisitive?' suggested Mr Finch.

'Over-ambitious?' said Ned.

'Over the top?' said Tommy.

'Greedy?' said Sammy.

'Exaggerated,' said Boots.

Rosie laughed. She didn't mind how many girls wanted to be his little sweethearts. She knew she was special to him, she knew it and felt it. They'd always be together, she'd made up her mind about that, and when he was older and Emily liked to rest a bit, she'd do everything for him.

Outside the house, a man who had been strolling began to make his way to Denmark Hill. Mr Ronald Ponsonby had thought the whole family might gather, and they had. From a distance, he had watched them all arrive. Robert Adams had been a star witness along with young Cassie Ford, the *Evening News* late edition had said so. Inevitably, the rest of the Adams brood had come to this house to gorge themselves on firsthand details of the day's proceedings, details that had dominated the news. The hunter felt he might, in his consideration of events, have guessed in advance that such a gathering would take place. He could then have made plans to destroy them all now. But no, young girls were also there, and he could not destroy young girls who had served him no purpose.

The brothers, the sister, and their spouses would gather together on another occasion, and by themselves. He would see to it that they did.

He talked pleasantly to himself as he strolled with his head perkily nodding. Mrs Fletcher, going up to the marital bedroom to draw the curtains, just missed seeing him. In the saga of events, she was the only person who had taken specific note of the hunter.

'Not all of it's in my evenin' paper, Mum,' said Doreen, 'not in the one I bought, anyway.'

'I suppose the paper 'ad to start bein' printed before the judge rose,' said Mrs Paterson. 'Fancy one of the witnesses bein' one of the Adams' that you work for.'

'I told you that ages ago, Mum,' said Doreen.

'The paper doesn't give all of 'is evidence.'

'You'll be able to ask 'im all about it when the trial's over, lovey.' Mrs Paterson spoke with the affection of a widow happily engaged to a widower who was very appreciative of her handsomeness. Mind, his healing hand had got very saucy lately. Still, that showed natural appreciation. 'I'm sure Mr Adams'll do 'is best to 'elp get that man hung. It's funny 'Enry's son still 'asn't come knockin', not even to compliment me on bein' 'is future new mother. I will say 'e looks upstandin' and not as shifty as I first thought.'

'Oh, him,' said Doreen. Blow him, she thought, I suppose he's one of those blokes that blow hot and cold. All over a girl at first, then acting as if he's forgotten he ever met her.

The hot and cold bloke knocked on the front door then. Doreen eyed him coolly, noting he had a wrapped bunch of flowers in one hand.

'Hello,' he said, 'is your mum in?'

'Yes,' said Doreen haughtily, 'and so am I.'

'I can see you are.'

'Well, fancy that, I thought you might not 'ave noticed.'

'Some hopes,' said Luke, 'you're always noticeable. Anyway, would you like to give these flowers to your mum, and pass 'er me compliments on her engagement to me dad?'

'Why can't you come in and give them to her yourself?' asked Doreen, feeling cross. 'You won't get eaten, I'm sure.'

'All right,' said Luke, and went through to the kitchen, where he presented his future step-mother with the bouquet. 'Compliments on gettin' engaged to me dad,' he said.

304

'Well, I never,' said Mrs Paterson, ''ow kind of yer, Luke.'

'Don't mention it,' said Luke, and gave her a smile. She'd outflanked Old Iron. However, Old Iron was accepting defeat like a man. 'Hope you'll both be good and happy. I'll be best man. So long now.'

'Here, where you goin'?' demanded Doreen, following him from the kitchen.

'Back to me lodgings,' said Luke, turning at the front door.

'Oh, that's polite, that is, I don't think. I suppose you think we've got fleas or something.'

'You don't look as if you 'ave,' said Luke.

'I'm thrilled,' said Doreen, 'but I don't think my mum is, 'aving you run off like a rabbit that's seen a new lettuce.'

'I'm playin' in a darts match with me dad,' said Luke. 'Down at the pub.'

'Oh, beg your pardon, I'm sure,' said Doreen, 'don't let me keep you.'

'Let's see, I suppose when the wedding's over, you'll be my sister,' said Luke.

'Don't you have any good news?' said Doreen, and shut the door on him. She almost gave it a kick.

Much later that evening, with everyone else in bed, Mr Finch spoke to Boots.

'Boots old chap, I find it quite peculiar that the defence counsel ignored all prosecution witnesses except you. He asked questions only of you. Have you any idea why? It doesn't make sense of the fact that his client pleaded not guilty.'

'Ponsonby's a queer fish and a nasty one,' said

Boots. 'I think all his bile is directed at me, and he instructed his counsel accordingly.'

'It still doesn't make sense,' said Mr Finch.

'I've a feeling Ponsonby's got something up his sleeve,' said Boots.

Chapter Twenty-One

'Prosecution has no more witnesses, m'lud,' said Mr Templeton on resumption the following morning.

'I note that, Mr Templeton,' said the judge. 'Mr Barrington?'

'Defence offers one witness only, my lord.'

'One?'

'The defendant.'

'Mr Barrington, you are sure?' said the judge. It was unheard-of, defendant in a murder trial to take the stand and leave himself wide open to the prosecuting counsel.

'Quite sure, my lord.'

'Very well, the prisoner may take the stand.'

Members of the public opened their eyes wide as Ponsonby was escorted from the dock into the witness box. He moved almost daintily, a neat and pigeon-toed man of middle age, hair parted down the middle, eyes peculiarly bright. He would, with a beard and moustache and spectacles, have looked exactly like his twin brother Ronald.

While Boots, Cassie and Freddy were in the waiting-room again, Chinese Lady and Emily were in court once more. Chinese Lady's firm mouth tightened as she watched Ponsonby take his place in the witness box. Like Boots, she thought he had something up his sleeve.

The man took the oath in a piping voice. Then Mr Barrington addressed him.

'You are Gerald Francis Ponsonby, formerly of Caulfield Place, Walworth?'

'Yes, yes.'

'Do you now propose to offer the court a true explanation of the events that have brought you here?'

'I do, most certainly, yes.'

'Please proceed, Mr Ponsonby.'

'First,' said Ponsonby, 'it's not I who should be here, but my twin brother, wanted in connection with the disappearance of a young girl in Nottingham.'

The judge looked up. The court gasped. The jury sat up and quivered. Chinese Lady blinked, Emily's huge green eyes swam with astonishment.

'Please enlarge on that, Mr Ponsonby,' said defence counsel.

Mr Ponsonby did. He declared his twin brother Ronald to be extremely fond of photographing young girls, but most regrettably was given to ending their lives once the photographs had been taken. He, Gerald, was given to protecting his twin while doing what he could to make him change his ways. Unfortunately, Ronald seemed incurable. It was not possible to detail his victims, but the girl in Nottingham was certainly one, as were the girls whose bodies had been found in Bermondsey and Walworth. Ronald had said so and he, Gerald, had confiscated all the photographs his twin had shown to him on one occasion.

'Did you live with your brother, Mr Ponsonby?'

'No, no, never. We were twins, yes, twins, but with very different interests. Mine mainly concerned visiting museums, art galleries and places with historical backgrounds. Attendants will confirm I visited the Tower of London many times. We had independent incomes, Ronald and I, but no, we never lived together, and he was no sooner in one place than he was moving to another.'

'Do you know if he did so in order to keep himself out of the arms of the law?'

'I do know, yes. He made that quite clear to me. The only time I was sure of where he was living was when he was making use of the deserted factory in Walworth. A bed has been mentioned, and there were blankets, yes, blankets. Also a table and a cupboard. It is not assumed, is it, that I lived there myself? No, no, I could not be in two places at once, there and in my lodgings in Caulfield Place. I was aware Ronald had not changed, and it was while he was virtually secreting himself in that factory that I learned of the unfortunate young girls who'd become his victims. Dear me, yes. It was then that he showed me a number of photographs, those that I confiscated, pointing out that his ownership of them put him at great risk.'

Mr Templeton intervened.

'M'lud, we're listening to a great deal of hearsay.'

'Necessarily so,' said the judge, 'and the jury will take note of that, no doubt.'

'May I continue?' asked Ponsonby fretfully.

'You may,' said Mr Barrington.

While his twin was existing in the factory, he, Gerald, saw more of him than on previous occasions. Each time he warned him to put a stop to the activities that would surely bring him to a sad end sooner or later. On the afternoon of Good

Friday, he went to see him, to point out not for the first time that the police were investigating the demise of a young girl whose body had been found buried in a scrap metal yard.

'You have admitted you are responsible, I told him. Yes, fatally responsible. It was my intention to persuade him either to give himself up or to vanish. But, oh dear me, he had a girl there, a girl I knew and saw in this witness box yesterday. She was unconscious and Ronald had photographed her. I knew, to my shame and distress, that she was now in danger of losing her life. For once, however, he listened to my persuasions, and agreed to leave the district immediately. Go abroad, I urged him, go abroad. He said he would, asking only that he should keep the photographs he had taken of the girl, who was still unconscious. I refused to concede, and I insisted on confiscating them. He packed, and I was sure, oh, yes, I was sure I had saved the girl. But then his obsession took hold of him again, and he began to argue for the return of the photographs. I added force to my persuasion, I have very strong wrists and I also had my umbrella with me. A defensive weapon, I assure you, defensive. But I threatened Ronald with it, and told him that despite my love for him I would have to kill him unless he left. I don't claim that my defence of the girl made an heroic figure of me, but I was determined to save her, determined. Ronald left. I forced him to, going with him. We reached the New Kent Road, which was not far, and there I waited until he had boarded a tram and gone on his way. I then hastened back to the factory, to the girl, and there I was confronted and attacked by a man whose name I discovered to be Robert Adams. I identify him as the man who was in this witness box yesterday afternoon.'

'Mr Ponsonby, why did you volunteer a confession that made no mention of your twin brother and led you to being charged with crimes committed by him?'

'Why, why?' Ponsonby looked as if the question had been asked by an idiot. 'For the same reason that I never betrayed him to the law, sir, the law. We are identical twins and our love for each other has never wavered.'

'But the jury, Mr Ponsonby, may well think you are betraying him now.'

'Upon my soul,' said Ponsonby impatiently, 'can no-one see that by my false confession I have given Ronald time to be out of the country and beyond its malignant law?'

'My learned friend might ask you to prove you have a twin brother called Ronald.'

'Come, come,' said Ponsonby, 'your clerk secured copies of our birth certificates from Somerset House yesterday, did he not?'

'He did,' said Mr Barrington. 'Exhibits sixteen and seventeen, my lord.'

The judge and the jury examined the certificates. So did Mr Templeton.

'Most entertaining,' he said.

'Mr Ponsonby,' said Mr Barrington, 'the witness Miss Cassie Ford identified you as the man who took her to be photographed, the man who put what was obviously a chloroform pad over her face.'

'Oh, dear me, haven't I made it clear that that was Ronald?' said Mr Ponsonby, now looking exasperated. 'She thought I was the one, oh, yes, but it was Ronald. A natural mistake, sir, and I can't hold it against her.'

'Will you tell us, Mr Ponsonby, why your brother was existing in such primitive circumstances in the factory when he had independent means?'

'As a recluse, a hermit, with no known address, he was more secure from police investigation than if he had been living in a hotel or in lodgings. As you know, the Nottingham police were investigating him—'

'The court does not know,' said the judge.

'My lord,' said Mr Barrington, 'I have written confirmation from Nottingham CID that they are indeed looking for a Mr Ronald James Ponsonby in connection with a missing girl of twelve. Exhibit eighteen.'

This too was examined.

'Continue, Mr Barrington,' said the judge.

'Continue, Mr Ponsonby,' said Mr Barrington.

'So many interruptions, what a day, what a day,' said Mr Ponsonby. 'Where was I?' Emily, looking at him, thought him as cunning as a fox with a smile on its face. 'Ah, yes. Not only were the Nottingham police interested in Ronald, but there was an investigation going on in Walworth and Bermondsey concerning an unfortunately dead girl and two missing ones. My brother, therefore, existed as he did as a matter of discretion, sir, a matter of discretion.'

'No further questions,' said Mr Barrington.

'Mr Templeton, do you wish to examine the witness?' asked the judge.

'Thank you, m'lud.' Mr Templeton rose, advanced to the witness box and gazed with interest at the accused. 'Oh, dear me, Mr Ponsonby.'

'What? What?'

'A likely story, don't you think?'

'It's my unfortunate brother's story,' said Ponsonby.

'So you say. Would you like a peppermint, Mr Ponsonby?' Mr Templeton produced a paper bag of peppermints.

'Not now, not now.' Ponsonby waved a hand in fussy dismissal.

'You like them, don't you? And you've been known, haven't you, to offer them frequently to the girls and boys you came across while lodging in Walworth?'

'I may have, I may have.'

'I can recall Miss Cassie Ford and Master Freddy Brown to the stand and have them confirm your frequent generosity.'

'Very well, yes, I believe I did make a habit of it. Everyone likes peppermints.'

'Miss Cassie Ford testified that the man who took her to the factory gave her a peppermint on the way. Would that have been you, Mr Ponsonby, or your twin brother, the hermit?'

'My brother, of course.'

'Your identical twin, so identical that he too made a habit of handing out peppermints. The paper bag that was found in the room in which Miss Cassie Ford was discovered, had a peppermint smell. Would you have left the bag there or your brother?'

'My brother, of course,' snapped Mr Ponsonby.

'Really? But the fingerprints found on it were yours, Mr Ponsonby.'

'Then I left it there, not my brother. What does it matter? I was there, and have said so, and I won't be browbeaten, sir.'

'Let me refer you, Mr Ponsonby, to the photographs taken of Miss Cassie Ford, unconscious from chloroform. You say your brother took them?'

'I did say so. His camera was found there.'

'How strange, then, that the fingerprints on the camera were all yours.'

'What, what?'

'The fingerprints found on the camera were all yours.'

'Nonsense, sir, nonsense.' Ponsonby's eyes glittered. 'But wait, it was I who put the camera away in the cupboard while I was arguing with Ronald.'

'Yet there were no other fingerprints on it except yours,' said Mr Templeton evenly. 'Tell me, Mr Ponsonby, where did your brother develop the plates if he indeed did take the photographs?'

'In the same way he always did, by using the developing amenities of a professional photographer for a suitable fee.'

'I see. He left the unconscious girl after he had photographed her to go to the studio of a professional photographer. There's only one in Walworth, Mr Ponsonby. Jerome's. They have no record of your brother's visit. How could they? They were closed on Good Friday.'

'Then he processed the plates in the factory, sir, in the factory.'

'There are no developing facilities in that place, Mr Ponsonby, no running water, no dark room.'

'Then you must find my brother and ask him your questions, oh, yes, you must ask him.'

'I suggest, Mr Ponsonby, that it was you who processed the plates. Developing equipment was found in your lodgings.'

'And why not?' said Ponsonby irritably. 'I dabble

in a little photography myself, my subjects places of interest, such as Tower Bridge or the Tower of London.'

'Oh, dear me, Mr Ponsonby, you've made no mention of that before, nor of where you keep your camera. No camera was found in your room, nor any photographs of places of interest. Only of young girls apparently asleep.'

'I mislaid the camera on one of my many outings.'

'How careless of you, Mr Ponsonby. Can you tell the court, by the way, how you came to be in possession of a bottle of chloroform, some chloroform pads and money from a robbery?'

'Really, how childish,' said Ponsonby. 'I find it difficult, sir, difficult, to contain myself.'

'Nevertheless, you must answer the question,' said the judge.

'I will,' said Ponsonby. 'In my protective attitude towards my brother, I took the bottle of chloroform and the pads and the money with me when I forced him to walk to the New Kent Road and board a tram.'

What an implorable liar, thought Chinese Lady. He's horrible, thought Emily.

'You are asking the jury to believe you were able to forcefully persuade your brother to leave while carrying your umbrella, together with the bottle of chloroform and the box of pads?' said Mr Templeton.

'I am asking them to believe I was taking desperate measures, desperate, to protect my twin from the consequences of his regrettable actions.'

'You intended to return to the girl and to see her to her home after your brother had gone on his way?'

315

'I have said so.'

'Taking the chloroform bottle and pads back there? If so, why was it necessary to remove them in the first place?'

'So that I could take them to my lodgings before I went back to the girl.'

'I suggest you did nothing of the sort, Mr Ponsonby. I suggest the chloroform and the pads could be found in your room at any time except on the occasions when you were possessed by one of your devilish inclinations. I suggest that in a mood of hope you had the bottle of chloroform and a pad in the pocket of your frock coat when you met Miss Ford on Good Friday afternoon.'

'You may suggest what you like, sir, what you like. I am concerned only to protect my brother.'

'Mr Ponsonby, you have called no witnesses who might vouch for your integrity or your singular devotion to your erring brother. Not even your parents.'

'This is intolerable!' Ponsonby slapped the edge of the witness box. 'My parents are dead, sir, dead, and my independent income derives from that unfortunate fact.'

'Then do you have sisters or other brothers or friends who might vouch for your character and your credibility, Mr Ponsonby?'

'My brother is my only relative of note,' said Ponsonby crossly, 'and I have never found it necessary to have close friends. Close friends become possessive, and I have a fondness, a fondness, sir, for being a free spirit.'

'I see,' said Mr Templeton. 'A free spirit. Mr Ponsonby, why didn't you destroy the photographs you confiscated from your brother, including those of Miss Ford? They were objectionable photographs, don't you agree?'

'Ah, there you have made your first acceptable point,' said Ponsonby. 'I confess I should have burned them, and in omitting to do so I was guilty of stupidity. I am guilty of nothing else, nothing, sir, oh dear me, no.'

'So, Mr Ponsonby, having taken the chloroform, the box of pads, the money, and the photographs of Miss Ford to your lodgings, you then returned to the factory to release her?'

'I did.'

'I suggest, Mr Ponsonby, that the confession is as it stands, your own, and that you left the factory not to escort your brother to a tram but to process the plates in your room.'

'Must I say it again?' Ponsonby glared at Mr Templeton. 'All I said in the confession was, in its essence, the confession of my brother Ronald.'

'The jury will decide that, Mr Ponsonby. No further questions, m'lud.'

'Does the defence rest, Mr Barrington?' asked the judge.

'If I may put just one more question, my lord?' said Mr Barrington, rising.

'You may.'

'Mr Ponsonby,' said the defence counsel, 'do you swear that all you have said while under oath is true?'

'I swear,' said Ponsonby.

'Thank you.'

Ponsonby was escorted back to the dock. The court adjourned for lunch. Cassie and Freddy were still in the waiting-room with Boots. He had provided them with a girls' annual and a boys' annual to help them while away the time. Cassie had absorbed herself. Stories fascinated her. Boots went out to make enquiries about what had happened during the morning.

'Oh, are we wanted now, Uncle Boots?' she asked when he returned.

'No, everyone's gone to lunch, Cassie. Would you and Freddy like to come and have some sandwiches?'

'Not 'alf,' said Freddy, 'I'm starvin'.'

'Is there fish an' chips, Uncle Boots?' asked Cassie.

'Afraid not, Cassie, not round here,' said Boots.

'Oh, all right, I don't mind sandwiches,' said Cassie blithely. 'Uncle Boots, 'as the judge done anything?'

'Not yet,' smiled Boots, 'he'll do it this afternoon, he'll do his talking to the jury, if the counsel don't take the rest of the day to do their own talking.'

'Will we be wanted?' asked Freddy.

'Hope not,' said Boots, 'you and Cassie have done your stuff like heroes.'

'Uncle Boots, you're ever so nice to us,' said Cassie. ''Ave you ever been to tea with the King and Queen?'

'Not yet,' said Boots, bringing them out of the room.

'Oh, I expect you'll get invited soon,' said Cassie.

They joined Emily and Chinese Lady outside. Sammy appeared.

'Thought I might just catch you and see how things are goin',' he said. 'I'm on me way to Islington. Hello, Cassie me angel, hello, Freddy me lad. Both dressed up, I see, and lookin' like Harry

318

Champion in his best togs. Where you all off to, Boots?'

'Sandwiches and tea in the cafe,' said Boots.

'I'll join you,' said Sammy.

'Well, I never,' said Chinese Lady, who had her best hat on, 'my youngest son offerin' to stand treat.'

'Did I offer?' said Sammy. 'Ain't it Boots's turn? I concur, him bein' older.'

'Come on,' said Boots.

They lunched in the café on sandwiches and tea, and while Chinese Lady engaged Cassie and Freddy in conversation, Emily let Sammy know that Ponsonby had taken his stand in the witness box.

'Ruddy 'ell,' said Sammy in an undertone, 'that was askin' for it, wasn't it?' Emily acquainted him with Ponsonby's story and finished by saying, 'He made himself out to be his brother's lovin' keeper.'

'Well, if I had the geezer in my keepin',' said Sammy, 'I'd drop him down a hole and pour boiling oil on the bleeder.'

'Language, Sammy,' murmured Emily.

Prosecuting counsel and defence counsel addressed the jury in turn. The former took time to lay out all the facts that justified a verdict of guilty. The latter pointed out that the accused man had never been in trouble with the law until now, that there was no record and no evidence that he had lived a perverted life, and that he did indeed have a twin brother whom the Nottingham police wished to question concerning a missing girl. It was not at all unlikely, in the case of identical twins, for the devotion of one to induce desperate protection of the other. And so on.

The judge's summing-up was fairly brief. He too pointed out that a twin brother did exist, and asked them to dwell on how credible they considered the accused man to be in his own defence. Was it true or otherwise that the photographs found in his lodgings had been confiscated from his brother? You must decide, he said. Was it true that the brother developed the photographs of young Miss Ford? If so, was there any member of the jury who could put up a theory on how the brother might have accomplished this? Further, could identical twins be identical in their habits and inclinations to the extent that they were both perverts? It was possible, of course, although not according to the accused man's evidence on oath. If you disbelieve his testimony, you must consider a verdict of guilty. If not, this is a factor that you must weigh against whether or not you find his stated reasons for making the confession quite believable. A not guilty verdict must then be considered.

The jury retired. They were out until ten minutes to six, by which time Emily and Chinese Lady were in the waiting-room with Cassie and Freddy, helping the girl and boy to get over their fidgets. And Mr Finch had arrived.

The foreman of the jury delivered the verdict.

Guilty.

Ponsonby slowly turned his head until he sighted the foreman, and the foreman saw a strange glittering smile on his face.

The judge donned the black cap and sentenced the prisoner to death by hanging.

Out rushed the gentlemen of the Press, and so did the representative of the new BBC wireless service. Anyone owning a cat's-whisker set with earphones would be among the first members of the public to receive news of the verdict.

Mr Ronald Ponsonby, watching people coming out of the Old Bailey, stopped a woman.

'Pardon me, madam, has the verdict been made known?'

'You bet it has. Guilty.'

'Thank you.'

'Yes, I'm pleased meself.'

Mr Ronald Ponsonby strolled thoughtfully to a bus stop.

Well, the public hangman was not the only person who had execution in mind.

Chapter Twenty-Two

'There,' said Mrs Paterson, serving a supper of liver and bacon to Doreen and herself. The plates of food arrived hot on the kitchen table, covered by a white ironed cloth.

'Well, you did it, Mum, it's the first meal you've cooked for ages,' said Doreen.

'I suppose I've got Mr 'Enry Edwards to thank for that, love. 'E's got the gift for healin' women sufferin' the grief and ailments of widow'ood. I didn't believe 'im at first – my, what nice tasty liver. But 'e proved 'e's got natural gifts, I feel more recovered ev'ry day.'

'You'll be bloomin' with health on your weddin' day, Mum.'

'I 'ope so, I wouldn't want to be an ailin' bride for 'Enry. I must say 'e's 'appy that 'e'll have a new fam'ly in you and me. We're goin' to live 'ere, with 'Enry takin' over payin' the rent. I don't think we'll need any lodger then, I'll 'ave to think about givin' Mr Wright a week's notice sometime in July. What a quiet lodger 'e's been and no bother at all, specially seeing 'e's out most of the time. Mind, I can't say I take to 'im very much, not the way 'is eyes peer at a woman through them spectacles of 'is. Still, we can't complain about 'im, 'is rent's still useful and 'e pays up prompt in advance. Did I tell yer that 'Enry says you're a very nice young lady, and complimented me for the way I've brought you up? 'E says 'is son Luke also thinks you're a credit to yerself.'

'I didn't know he could think,' said Doreen, 'I thought his 'ead was as empty as a basin with nothing in it.'

'I wouldn't say that, love, not when he's 'olding down a skilled engineerin' job. He'll be a nice upstandin' new brother for you.'

'Ugh,' choked Doreen.

'Beg yer pardon, love?'

'Some new brothers can make a girl feel sick,' said Doreen. 'Here, he's not goin' to live in this house too, is he?'

'Well, 'Enry and me were talkin' on our little walk last night, and when the lodger goes and the upstairs back is free again—'

'I'll leave 'ome,' said Doreen.

'What?' said her mum.

'If that young man moves in 'ere, I'll leave 'ome,' said Doreen.

'Oh, lor',' said Mrs Paterson, and thought it best to change the subject. 'Did you bring an evenin' paper 'ome? Was there anything about the murder trial in it?'

'Yes, but not about any verdict,' said Doreen, 'just about the man defendin' himself in the witness box. He said it was his twin brother that committed the murders. It sounded potty to me. I don't know if Mister Adams will be out of the office again tomorrow, but there's a lot of work on 'is desk. I think I'll go and see Freddy Brown after supper. I mean, he's been at the Old Bailey again with his young friend Cassie Ford, and he'll know if the jury went out or not.'

'All right, Doreen, you 'ave a walk down to Freddy's, I'll be able to entertain me new future 'usband when he comes across.'

'Don't get up to any larks,' said Doreen.

'I don't know 'ow you can say a thing like that to your own mother.'

'I'll give a loud knock on the door when I come back,' said Doreen.

The first person she saw when she left the house was the object of her derision. He was walking up the street towards his lodgings.

'Evenin', Lady Vi,' he called from the other side of the street.

'Good evenin',' said Doreen haughtily and without stopping.

'Lookin' forward to bein' my sister?'

'No, just to bein' sick,' said Doreen, and on she went, stepping out.

'Yes, 'e got found guilty,' said Freddy. He was outside his house with Cassie.

'They're goin' to hang 'im,' said Cassie, 'but I ain't goin' to watch.'

'Did you or Mister Adams have to go into the witness box again?' asked Doreen.

'No, the judge didn't want us to,' said Cassie. 'Freddy and me read annuals all day. Well, I read Freddy's as well as mine. Uncle Boots nearly bought us fish an' chips for our lunch, only there wasn't a fried fish shop 'e could take us to, so we 'ad sandwiches instead. I saw yer young man a bit ago, in Brownin' Street. Is 'e goin' to be yer sweet'eart?'

'No, he's goin' to fall under a Corporation water-cart,' said Doreen.

'Crikey, how d'yer know that?' asked Freddy.

'I'm goin' to push him,' said Doreen. Freddy grinned. Cassie giggled.

'Oh, did yer know me Uncle Elijah once pushed a train all by 'imself when—'

'Now, you Cassie,' said Freddy, with Cassie swinging on the gate, 'you don't 'ave an Uncle Elijah.'

'Yes, I do,' said Cassie. 'Well, I did 'ave before 'e fell in a castle moat and didn't come up. Anyway, 'e pushed this train all by 'imself when it broke down. The Queen was in it and thanked 'im when he got it to Windsor Castle, she said goodness, my man, I dunno what I'd 'ave done without all your 'elp. I've got the Princess Daffodil comin' to tea, she said.'

'And they all lived happy ever after?' smiled Doreen.

'All except her uncle,' said Freddy, ''e fell in the moat.'

Doreen laughed. She looked at Cassie. Everyone who knew Cassie was aware of her narrow escape from the man who had just been found guilty of murder. However, Cassie, whose imagination conjured up fascinating stories, not nightmares, had never seemed fearfully affected by what had happened to her. Her funny little friendship with Freddy occupied her mind to the probable exclusion of anything unpleasant.

'Are you two sweethearts?'

''Ere, give over, Doreen,' said Freddy, 'you shouldn't ask questions like that out loud, not round 'ere.' He glanced at the ever-present street kids running about. They'd be out all hours now that the long evenings of June were here.

'Me dad says I've got to be a bit older before I can be Freddy's sweet'eart,' said Cassie.

'I'll be off to Australia by then,' said Freddy.

'I'll foller yer,' said Cassie.

''Bye,' smiled Doreen, and began a slow walk back to Morecambe Street. She saw the lodger approaching.

'I'm out again, Miss Paterson, out again,' he said, giving her a smile and one of his bird-like nods as he went by.

'Enjoy yourself, Mr Wright,' said Doreen, thinking him a bit of a character.

When she reached Morecambe Street, she saw Luke again. He was standing on the corner talking to Pam Billings, who lived at the other end of the street, and always had a ravishing smile fixed to her face whenever she was in company with a personable bloke. Doreen always hoped it would fall off one day and break into little pieces.

'Oh, 'ello, D'reen,' said Pam.

'Can't stop,' said Doreen, ignoring Luke as she swept straight past them. Now I know for certain he's a bloke who blows hot and cold. Well, he's welcome to blow hot for Pam Billings. She'll eat him and put his bones in the family dustbin.

Indoors, Doreen found her mum was out. Gone walking with her Henry, of course. Fed-up, Doreen tried to settle down with a library book. But a knock on the front door ten minutes later brought her face to face with Luke again.

'Well, fancy that, you've escaped,' she said.

'Have I? What from?' asked Luke.

'Bein' eaten,' said Doreen. 'D'you want my mum?'

'I thought you'd mention your mum,' said Luke.

'I 'appen to be her best friend,' said Doreen. 'Anyway, she's out.'

'Probably playin' darts with Old Iron down at the pub,' said Luke.

'I hope he's not tryin' to turn her into a common pub woman,' said Doreen. 'Might I ask what you're here for?'

'Well, it seems we're all goin' to be one happy fam'ly,' said Luke, 'so I thought you might let me take a look at your upstairs back.'

'Let you what?'

'See what your upstairs back is like.'

'What for?' asked Doreen.

'Well, if it's goin' to be my bedroom—'

'You've got a hope if you think you're goin' to live 'ere,' said Doreen.

'Seems a sensible arrangement to me, sis,' said Luke.

'What did you call me?'

'I was thinkin' about you bein' my sister,' said Luke.

'I'll be sick in a minute,' said Doreen, then suddenly thought about what it would be like, having him in the house. 'Of course, if that's what my mum's arrangin', for you to have the upstairs back, I can't stop her. But we've got a lodger rentin' the upstairs back.'

'Is he in?' asked Luke.

'No, he's out.'

'All right, I don't suppose he'll mind if I take just a look at the room. I won't pinch anything.'

'Well, I suppose you'd better go up, then,' said Doreen. He came in and she closed the door.

'I seen yer, Doreen,' called a saucy kid, 'I'll tell yer mum you got a feller!'

Luke climbed the stairs, Doreen following. He turned the handle of the lodger's door. It was locked. He looked at Doreen.

'You sure he's out?' he whispered. 'He's not in there with his fancy bit of stuff, is he?'

'Oh, d'you mean someone like Pam Billings?' said Doreen.

Luke grinned.

'Now now, Lady Vi,' he said, and Doreen couldn't repress a smile. For some reason, she liked his pet name for her.

'Well, it's not my fault you're fond of tarty girls,' she said.

'I'm not,' said Luke. 'But why's this door locked?'

'I don't know,' she said, 'but I do know he's out, he passed me in Browning Street.'

'Hasn't got a body in there, I suppose?'

'That's not very funny,' said Doreen.

'No, it's not,' agreed Luke, 'not under present circs.' The partly ruined factory in which the bodies of the two murdered young girls had been found was not far from Morecambe Street.

'The man was found guilty, did you know?'

'No, I didn't,' said Luke, 'the evenin' paper I bought on me way 'ome from work just had the sensational news that the filthy sod had put 'imself in the witness box, and that he was sayin' it was all his twin brother's doing.'

'Well, the jury didn't believe him,' said Doreen, 'they found him guilty. Excuse me, but did you use a swear word just then?'

'Did I? Sorry, Lady Vi.'

'You're not goin' to stand up here all evenin', are you?' said Doreen. 'Don't you want to do more standin' on the street corner with Pam Billings?'

'Not much,' said Luke. 'Well, I'll push off and take a look at me future bedroom another time.'

'I suppose you couldn't stay and 'ave a cup of tea with me,' said Doreen. 'No, I suppose you couldn't.'

What a girl, thought Luke, and not for the first time. Health and good looks all over her. Ruddy criminal, tying herself to her mum, especially now there was going to be a wedding.

'A cup of tea would go down well, Lady Vi, thanks,' he said.

'Come on, then,' said Doreen.

When Mrs Paterson arrived back in company with Old Iron, she said, 'Well, I never, you two sharin' a pot of tea?'

'Yes, it's keepin' him off the street corner,' said Doreen. 'Mum, have you been in the pub again?'

'No, 'Enry and me 'ave been for a nice walk, it bein' a lovely evenin',' said Mrs Paterson.

'It's me pleasure to inform you, Doreen, that yer mum's walkin' legs 'ave improved considerable,' said Old Iron. 'Still, you'd better 'ave a sit-down now, Muriel, and I'll put the kettle on and make a fresh pot. I see you're sittin' comfortable yerself, Luke. It strikes me there's the makings of an 'appy fam'ly in the four of us, eh?'

'Well, I'll say this much,' said Luke, 'I've been gettin' to know me future sister over our pot of tea.'

'That's nice,' said Mrs Paterson, and Luke smiled.

'Me your sister?' said Doreen. 'Some hopes.'

'Luke'll be a fond brother to yer, Doreen,' said Old Iron, putting the kettle on.

'Pardon me if I fall over,' said Doreen.

Tommy and Vi were having a chat with Aunt Victoria and Uncle Tom about the trial. Aunt Victoria, being a woman who considered respectability would secure people pride of place in heaven, hadn't been too happy about having a relative attending a murder trial. Well, Boots was very much a relative, since he was her son-in-law's brother, and although she had a soft spot for him, she would have preferred him not to be – well, not to be tainted by being called as a witness. His name had been in the newspapers this morning. Her own daily paper had had a headline. *Star witness, Robert Adams, says 'It'll do for me, I'm still alive.'* Her neighbours were bound to have seen it. They would have thought Adams, that's Tommy's name. They would stop her and ask her about it. They'd think it wasn't very respectable.

'Anyway, it's all over now,' Tommy was saying. He'd phoned Boots from a public call-box, having said the family couldn't all descend on Boots and Emily again, like they had yesterday evening. 'Guilty as hell. All that eyewash about a twin brother didn't work.'

'He'll dangle all right,' said Uncle Tom, lighting his pipe.

'What d'you mean, dangle?' asked Aunt Victoria.

'From the rope,' said Uncle Tom.

'Don't be common,' said Aunt Victoria.

'Well, Mum,' said gentle Vi, 'a rope is what the beast deserves.'

'I don't like your father talkin' about dangling,' said Aunt Victoria. 'Still, Tommy's right, it's all over now, thank goodness, and Boots won't be mentioned in the newspapers no more. Any more,' she added hastily. She liked to be respectable in her talk as well as in her behaviour.

Vi refrained from saying he'd be in tomorrow's dailies. They'd be bound to mention all the witnesses, especially as Boots in his exchanges with the defence counsel had taken the fancy of the reporters yesterday. He and Cassie had both had prominent mentions.

'The fam'ly can sit back now,' said Uncle Tom, as easy-going as Vi.

'I think the fam'ly ought to have a nice get-together,' said Vi, 'a sort of celebration in honour of Boots—'

'I'll divorce yer,' said Tommy.

'But Boots is the 'ero of the fam'ly,' protested Vi, 'he was the one who knocked that 'orrible man out and captured him.'

'Can't say fairer than that,' observed Uncle Tom. 'There y'ar, love,' he said to Aunt Victoria, 'we've got an 'ero in the fam'ly.'

Aunt Victoria visibly swelled with pleasure. Well, her bosom did.

'I hadn't thought of that,' she said. 'I must say it's a real pleasure, knowin' I can be proud when I'm talkin' to the neighbours.'

'There you are, then,' said Vi, 'a fam'ly get-together to honour Boots.'

'Your dad and me would be happy to have it here,' said Aunt Victoria, thinking of neighbours watching from their windows to catch the arrival of the family hero.

'What about honouring me?' asked Tommy.

'What for?' asked Vi.

'Well, I'm married to yer,' said Tommy.

'But you should honour Vi, Tommy, as your wife,' said Aunt Victoria.

'I have honoured her,' said Tommy, 'and she's goin' to have another little Adams.'

The old Vi would have blushed. The new Vi, the happy and knowing wife, shrieked with laughter.

'Well, I just don't know you should've said a thing like that,' said Aunt Victoria.

'Takes some doin',' said Uncle Tom, 'but it came out soundin' funny, don't yer think, old girl?' And he laughed. So did Aunt Victoria.

'What a fam'ly, the Adams',' said Vi.

'Just right for a get-together,' said Uncle Tom.

There was one in the offing. Mr Ronald Ponsonby was planning it.

'Thank goodness,' said Lizzy.

'Thank goodness,' said Annabelle.

'I'd like to say something myself,' said Ned.

'What?' asked Lizzy.

'Thank goodness,' said Ned.

'What a coincidence,' remarked Lizzy, 'that's what Em'ly said on the phone.'

'Just that in all of half an hour?' enquired Ned.

'Daddy, of course not,' said Annabelle. 'Crumbs, you talked to Uncle Boots for ages first. What did he say?'

'Thank goodness,' said Ned.

Annabelle, with a shriek and a bursting giggle, jumped on him. He had his feet up on the sofa, the evening paper on his lap.

'Got you!' she exclaimed.

'Mind my arm,' said Ned.

'What's wrong with your arm?' asked Lizzy.

'My mistake,' said Ned, 'I meant mind my leg.'

In came Bobby, Emma and little Edward to see what all the noise was about. They joined in.

'What a fam'ly,' said Lizzy. 'Bed, you lot.'

'Thank goodness,' said Ned.

Lizzy smiled. The trial was over, a cloud lifted, and the family could forget a horrendous character called Ponsonby.

'So Boots'll be back at work tomorrow?' said Susie.

'And Freddy and Cassie back at school,' said Sammy.

'Bless them,' said Susie. 'It shouldn't have been allowed, a young girl and boy at a murder trial.'

'Due process of the law, Susie.'

'Blow the due process of the law,' said Susie, 'there wouldn't have been any need if the police had let Boots finish Ponsonby off in the fact'ry yard.'

'I've got a feelin' Boots would have enjoyed breakin' his neck,' said Sammy.

'Well, I'm relieved it's over,' said Susie, 'except they'll be talkin' about it all day in the office tomorrow.'

'In which case, they won't get paid,' said Sammy, 'I ain't running a home for gossipin' female girls and chatty book-keepers.'

'Doreen's a bit funny lately,' said Susie, seated on the sofa with him. She was doing some needlework, and Sammy was simply enjoying the fact that he had a legal right to her permanent company in the kitchen, at the table, on the sofa and in bed. 'She's not her usual bright self. I think she's got some problems at home.'

'What, when her dear old widowed mum is about to get churched with a widower?' said Sammy.

'Perhaps she doesn't want her mum to get married again,' said Susie.

'She's got a feller,' said Sammy.

'Well, he doesn't seem to be makin' her very happy,' said Susie.

'Mother O'Reilly,' said Sammy, 'I trust he ain't done her wrong, not our Doreen.'

'If he has,' said Susie, 'find out where he lives, then go round and knock his head off.'

'Me?' said Sammy.

'Yes, you, Mister Adams. It's – oh, no you don't!'

'Well, Susie—'

'Never mind well, Susie, get off!'

'Immediately and right now, Susie?'

'All right,' murmured Susie, 'not immediately, then. I think we'll invite Cassie and Freddy to tea on Sunday.'

'What a relief,' said Chinese Lady for the umpteenth time.

'Oh, yes, I do agree, Nana, a blessed relief,' said Rosie.

'We're all in favour, Maisie,' said Mr Finch.

'I must say my only oldest son has come out of it like a credit to you, Em'ly,' said Chinese Lady.

'Oh, and me, Nana,' said Rosie, proudly wearing stockings for the first time. 'And Tim, and you, and Grandpa. Everyone, really.'

'And the neighbours?' said Boots.

'And Jack 'Obbs,' said Tim.

'Who's he?' asked Chinese Lady.

'Hobbs,' said Boots, 'Hobbs, Tim.'

'Yes, I said 'im,' declared Tim.

'Tim, you're losing your aitches,' said Rosie.

'Where've they gone, then?' asked Tim.

'Into the unknown,' smiled Mr Finch.

'I expect the man in the moon will pick them up,' said Boots, ruffling his son's hair.

'Who's Jack Hobbs?' asked Chinese Lady.

'Oh, lor', Mum, what a question in a fam'ly like this,' said Emily.

'Nana, I don't want to despair of you,' said Rosie, 'but Jack Hobbs is the best batsman in the world – well, next to your only oldest son.'

'I'm grateful to be informed, Rosie,' said Chinese Lady, mouth twitching.

'It's a pleasure, Nana,' said Rosie. 'Nana, could we have a tea party on Sunday, inviting everyone, as we're all enjoying great relief?'

'I don't see why not,' said Chinese Lady. Nothing gave her greater pleasure than organizing a Sunday tea party for the whole family.

'And can we have cricket, Dad?' asked Tim.

'Yes, your Grandpa can oil the bats and you can polish the stumps,' said Boots.

'Bliss,' said Rosie.

'The garden's goin' to be like a fairground,' said Emily.

'Never mind, Mummy,' said Rosie, 'what with great relief, Daddy a credit to everyone, a tea party on Sunday, me in stockings and treading to school next year in Daddy's famous footsteps, it's like happy ever after for always. Oh, and perhaps we could invite Cassie as well on Sunday. You know, Daddy's new sweetheart. And Freddy could come too, he's good at cricket.'

'Well, I just hope it will be like happy ever after, Rosie, and not like a bunch of 'ooligans,' said Chinese Lady.

'I'm a hooligan,' said Tim, 'a lady down the road said so when I fell over her dog.'

'Join the club, Tim,' said Boots.

'What a fam'ly,' said Emily, and laughed. She was still putting on regular ounces. Boots was roasting monkey nuts for her and shelling them. They were easy to eat between meals.

Chapter Twenty-Three

The following morning, Mr Ronald Ponsonby was having a nine o'clock breakfast at Toni's Refreshment Rooms close to East Street market in the Walworth Road. He had discovered the place early on. It was run by an Italian couple, Toni and Maria, Toni being voluble and temperamental, Maria placid and smiling.

He tucked into the breakfast of bacon and eggs, with tea. He had asked for coffee on his first visit.

'Coffee?' Toni had said. 'Where-a you come from, eh? You a bloody foreigner? We don't-a drink coffee here.' He and Maria drank it themselves, of course, in their private rooms above the café, but they had long learned the cockneys of Walworth only ever drank tea. The market costermongers regarded coffee as being on a par with old men's water laced with a dash of Southend mud.

There were several costermongers in the place now, but Mr Ronald Ponsonby was living in his own world. He was not only devouring his breakfast, but also two daily papers he'd bought on the way from his lodgings. Details of the trial were fully reported, the verdict splashed in bold letters. He ate his way into his food and the reports. The verdict of guilty, well, he had expected that. There was too much that had damned Gerald. Even so, it consumed him with the need to revenge and console. But he set

those feelings aside as he read the accounts of
Gerald in the witness box, defending himself with a
recitation of double identity. It was brilliant in its
concept, but quite unavailing, of course. However,
he lapped up the details with such appreciation that
a little smile appeared on his bearded face. But the
smile went when one report made special mention
of two star witnesses for the Crown, Robert Adams
and the young girl, Cassie Ford. There was a
photograph of them coming out of the Old Bailey
together. He took off his spectacles and peered. He
had seen that girl somewhere. Where? And when?
Wait, there was also a boy in the photograph. He
too was faintly familiar.

Mr Ronald Ponsonby remembered then. A boy
and a girl and a bike. He had spoken to them, and
the boy had said his sister was married to Sammy
Adams. Forgetting for a moment the lethal enmity
he felt towards the Adams family, Gerald Ponsonby's twin brother smiled again. Walworth was a
very small place. One never knew whom one might
run into.

Finishing his breakfast and his reading, he left.
Maria smiled at him. He gave her an amiable nod.
He returned to his room and spent most of the day
busying himself. He did not lock his door, but he
did have a chair jammed under the handle to check
the entrance of the uninvited. His landlady had
never bothered him, but it would be foolish to take
chances, or to be as reckless as Gerald had been.

His time bomb came into being. He had followed
the instructions with great care, checking each step
over and over again. Now it only needed to be set.

'The lodger's been in all day, would yer believe,'

338

said Mrs Paterson to Doreen when her daughter arrived home. 'Well, except for goin' out to get a bite to eat at midday. I called up to 'im this afternoon to see if 'e'd like a cup of tea. I'm better lately at doin' things like that, but 'e called down and said no, thanks. Very politely, mind.'

'I hope he's not plannin' to rob a bank,' said Doreen, 'only when he went out last night as usual, he left his door locked. It stopped your future husband's son from takin' a look at the room. He wanted to see if it would suit 'im.'

'Oh, yes,' said Mrs Paterson, blooming with the good health of a widow whose prospects were rosy, 'I thought 'e could 'ave that room for 'imself when we're all livin' together. He'll pay 'is way, so what with 'Enry lookin' after the rent and givin' me 'ousekeeping, we'll be much better off, love, and it'll be nice you 'aving a new brother.'

'If anyone mentions brother again, I'll put me head in the gas oven,' said Doreen.

'All right, I won't say no more,' said Mrs Paterson, 'and I can't see Mr Wright robbin' any bank. I expect 'e just likes to keep his room and his belongings private, and 'imself too, which suits me. Well, I don't want 'im comin' down and makin' up to me. I'm sure 'Enry wouldn't like it. A strong man like 'im could be very bruisin' to anyone who 'ad designs on me. Oh, I've got the supper goin', love, I'm up to that now, thanks to 'Enry bein' a very healin' fiance. Doreen, I 'ope you don't actu'lly dislike Luke.'

'I'm not goin' to be a sister to him, I can tell you that,' said Doreen, putting the kettle on. 'I can't make him out most of the time, anyway.'

'Well, you're still young, love, you'll understand

men better when you're of an age, like.'

'I'm of an age now, I'm nineteen,' said Doreen, 'and I'd like to 'ave someone who'd take me out on Saturday nights.'

'Oh, you can always come out with me and yer future step-dad, Doreen.'

'I can 'ardly wait,' said Doreen. The lively willing girl of Adams Enterprises general office was fed-up.

Their lodger went out later, locking his room.

His time in the upstairs back was nearly at an end.

The large man, Ben Skidmore, sat at a corner table in a gaslit Islington pub. Two men were with him, one thin and foxy, the other thickset and moon-faced.

'Right, then,' said Skidmore, 'yer know what to do, and do it next time 'e's at 'is bleedin' sweat-shop, grindin' 'is workers into the mud. You'll 'ave to do a bit of 'anging about, seein' 'e ain't there ev'ry day, but you ain't got much else to do except draw yer dole. There's a quid in it for both of yer, and me boot up yer backsides if yer let me down. You're doin' the performance, Tiddler, and you're the witness, Bonzer.'

'Right on,' said the moon-faced man, 'Tiddler's the indiarubber act, I'll get injured if I try it. Spring-'eeled Jack, that's our Tiddler.'

'And remember,' said Skidmore, 'I don't want any mention of my monicker, you got it?'

'Course we got it, Ben,' said Tiddler, 'we owe yer a favour and we ain't keen on 'aving our backsides killed stone dead. Where's our quids?'

*　　*　　*

340

'Mrs Paterson?'

'Oh, is that you, Mr Wright?' said Mrs Paterson from her kitchen. It was a few minutes to ten the following morning, Friday. She opened the door. The lodger smiled at her. He was carrying his suitcase in one hand, an attaché case in the other. 'Oh, yer not leavin', are yer?' she asked.

'No, no, certainly not,' he said. 'I'm visiting a friend in the country for three days, and thought I'd let you know. I'll be back on Monday, dear me, yes.'

'Well, I appreciate you lettin' me know,' said Mrs Paterson. 'Which reminds me, I 'ope you won't mind, but I'll be wantin' yer room from the last week in July. I'm gettin' married again, and me future 'usband'll be movin' in here with his son. It means I'll want yer room for 'is son, if you could see yer way to findin' other lodgings, which I'll do me best to 'elp you find. I can recommend yer as a good lodger.'

'My compliments, Mrs Paterson, my compliments, and don't worry, I'm sure with your help I'll be able to find another room in the area. Thank you for telling me well in advance. I must go now.'

'Well, 'ave a nice weekend in the country,' said Mrs Paterson.

'I intend to enjoy myself. Goodbye until Monday.'

He took himself off to Stepney Green once more, where the hired car, a Morris saloon, was waiting for him.

'Suit yer, guv?' said his old acquaintance.

'Perfect. How much for the two days?'

'Special price for you, guv. A small pony. Er – exclusive of deposit.'

'Twenty-five pounds? Slightly extortionate.'

'Yer right, guv, cheap at the price, specially as it's 'ired in the name of Aubrey Carstairs of Beech Lodge, Broxbourne.'

'And who is Aubrey Carstairs?'

'Well, it ain't you and it ain't me, guv. In fact, it ain't anyone I've ever 'eard of. Might I take 'old of the twenty-five smackers?'

Mr Ronald Ponsonby paid up. He placed his suitcase and attaché case in the boot and a few minutes later was heading back south. He stopped in Soho, where the traffic, the inhabitants, the shopkeepers and the scenes were a fascinating mixture. From a theatrical costumiers, he collected an outfit he had ordered over the phone yesterday. He tried it on before he paid for its hire. It fitted perfectly to the measurements he had given.

'I'm off to Islington this afternoon, Mrs Adams,' said Sammy.

'Very good, Mister Sammy,' said Susie, busy at her desk.

'I'm meetin' Lilian and Miss de Vere there.'

'Very good, Mister Sammy, you're meetin' two widows there,' said Susie, studying pencilled notes Sammy had made on the day's mail.

'Would you mind lookin' at me when I'm in business converse with you, Mrs Adams?'

'What for?' asked Susie.

'It's yer blue eyes, Mrs Adams, I like 'em.'

'Well, fancy that,' said Susie, 'when you've been married to them all this time, two months.' She looked up at him and smiled. Sammy winked.

'Harriet—'

'Miss de Vere,' said Susie.

'See your point, Susie.'

'You'd better,' said Susie.

'Miss de Vere is hopin' to approve Lilian's final winter collection, and I'm hopin' I can discuss a contract with her for same. The stuff'll have to be delivered in October, early October.'

'Atta, boy,' said Susie.

'I disapprove of American verbage, Susie. It might be all the rage in Clapham, but not here in me business headquarters.'

'Very good, Mister Sammy.'

'I'll deal with you tonight, Mrs Adams.'

'Yes, please,' said Susie, and Sammy went back grinning to his own office, having lost one more verbal contest with the light of his life.

His old friend and valued business contact, Mr Eli Greenberg, well-known rag and bone merchant, called on him at noon. His black beard flecked with grey, his round black hat rusty with age, he was wearing a long dark serge overcoat with capacious pockets. He wore it summer and winter.

'Hello, Eli, how's yer prosperous self?' said Sammy.

'Sammy my poy, vhen vas I ever prosperous, vhen did I ever know vhere me next crust vas comin' from, ain't it?'

'I know the feelin', Eli, I'm in the same boat meself,' said Sammy. 'Still, as long as we keep hold of the oars we might end up headin' straight for cake with icin' on it.'

'Ah, a pointed vay, Sammy, of referrin' to vhat I'm headin' for, the veddin' cake,' said Mr Greenberg mournfully.

'I'm happy for yer, Eli,' said Sammy. Mr Greenberg, by reason of the unexpected, had been

343

compelled to contract marriage with a Mrs Hannah Borovich, a widow with three curly-haired sons. He was still in mournful shock.

'I should have a friend like you happy for me, Sammy?'

'Do you good, Eli.'

'My life, Sammy, but vhat about my pocket? Ain't it sufferin', as always?'

'So's mine,' said Sammy, 'and I grant it hurts, Eli, but as long as Susie leaves me enough for overheads the pain won't be too considerable. You'll get hot breakfasts in the winter, and drive your horse and cart home to a hot supper and, if I might mention it, a warm bosom. A warm bosom, Eli, is invaluable to a married man and also worth a lot.'

'Vell, Sammy,' sighed Mr Greenberg, 'I'm contracted, ain't I? Mrs Borovich and me vill be highly pleasured to have you and your fam'ly attend the veddin'. I vould myself and personally, consider the occasion in August sad vithout the Adams fam'ly. I have brought the invitations.' He drew a number of envelopes out of a capacious pocket. 'For you and Susie, Sammy, Boots and Em'ly, Tommy and Vi, Lizzy and Ned, and, yes, most of all, ain't it, for your fine mother and her husband. Vhat could give me more pleasure than to see all of you or some of you there? Expenses bein' vhat they are, vould you kindly hand them out, Sammy? Postage is crippling, ain't it?'

'I'll save it ruining you, Eli,' said Sammy, 'and on behalf of all the fam'ly, I'm informin' you we're complimented at bein' invited.'

'Sammy my poy, vhat a consolin' friend you are,' said Mr Greenberg.

'Happy days, Eli.'

'Vell, a hot breakfast in vinter is also consolin', ain't it, Sammy?'

'That and other things,' said Sammy cheerfully.

A little after two o'clock, Mr Ronald Ponsonby entered the shop below the offices of Adams Enterprises. The young man in charge, Sidney Pearson, recognized him as the cluckety-cluck neat gent who'd bought a couple of ties a week or so ago. He had an attaché case with him this time.

'Good afternoon, sir,' said Sidney, 'pleasure to see you again.'

'My word, you know me?'

'Once a customer, always known, sir. Our motto – well, mine, really – is all our customers are our friends, even if they only patronize us once.'

'Commendable, yes, commendable. Now, do you sell blankets? Yes, of course you do, that's why I've returned. I need twelve.'

'Twelve, sir?' Crikey, a nice bit of commission on that, thought Sidney.

'Twelve. Blue. Yes, they must be blue. They're for a Salvation Army hostel for unfortunate down-and-outs. Do you have blue?'

'A dozen? Yes, sir,' said Sidney, 'a few here in the shop and plenty in our storeroom. And I can find a large cardboard box to put them in. That all right, sir? We can deliver them in the firm's van if you live round here.'

'Thank you, but I don't. I'll be taking them myself. If you'll pack them in a box for me, I'll call back for them later.'

'Pleasure, sir.'

'I'll pay for them now, of course, then I'll know

you'll be sure to have them ready for me. I've to go up to Liverpool Street now – ah, perhaps along with the blankets I can leave this attaché case in your care? It's a little heavy.'

'You can leave it with pleasure, sir. I'll look after it.'

'Thank you, yes, thank you. When do you close?' The eyes behind the glasses were brightly enquiring.

'Half-five, sir.'

'Good. I should be back before then. Take care of my attaché case, won't you? The contents aren't worth much, but they've an intrinsic value. Two vases belonging to the family and which I'm delivering to an aunt.'

'I'll put the attaché case behind my counter, sir.'

'Excellent, yes, just the place. Thank you. Now let me settle for the blankets.'

He paid for them and left. Sidney put the attaché case, heavy, behind his counter. The little tick of a clock, thickly muffled, was imperceptible.

Sammy and Lilian together had won the promise of a new contract from Harriet de Vere of Coates. It meant a huge bonus for Lilian, so she gave Sammy a smacker. He departed in a hurry in case she closed the door of her drawing-office and let her gratitude and enthusiasm run away with her. She was a generous and warm-hearted example of how to be a bosom chum without hardly trying. A bit like Rachel, come to think of it, except that Rachel was kind of elegant and purring.

Bert came out just as Sammy was about to drive off.

'Keep yer peepers peeled, guv,' he said.

'Goliath's about?' said Sammy.

'Not 'im personal, guv. Rumours.'

'Rumours are about, are they, Bert?'

'So I 'eard,' said Bert. 'Cheeri-o, guv.'

'So long, Bert.' Sammy drove out of the factory yard and turned right. The street was clear, only a few kids about. It was twenty to four and most were still in school, those who went. He motored into the next street. Two men were talking to a lamp-post, or so it seemed. They stepped off the pavement as he drove up. Sammy, never having been an idiot, and never having failed to listen when he was being spoken to, stood on his foot-brake as the thinner man of the two took a running dive into the path of the car. Unfortunately, the sudden halt of the car made his dive premature. He hit the ground with the car a yard away. A woman, head out of her upstairs window, yelled at him.

'Yer cock-eyed fish-'ead, think yer divin' orf Southend pier, do yer? If you've made another bleedin' 'ole in our street, I'll make yer fill it in!'

Tiddler, who was supposed to have landed on the bonnet of the car and then had Sammy arrested for dangerous driving, with Bonzer swearing witness, turned over. He had a shocking hurtful pain in both kneecaps.

'Yer a bleedin' maniac!' he bawled at Sammy.

''Ere, I 'eard that!' shouted the woman. Sammy lifted his driving cap to her. ''E saved yer silly life by stoppin' in time. 'Ere, ain't you the bloke that diddled yer old dad of 'is watch and chain?'

Bonzer leaned over Tiddler.

'Yer buggered it up, yer dozy lump,' he hissed.

Sammy, standing up in his car, said, 'Do us a favour, cully, move yer friend out of me way, would yer? Only if I run him over, you'll have to scrape him up.'

'Well, sod yer,' growled Bonzer, and heaved Tiddler up.

'Oh, me bleedin' kneecaps,' panted Tiddler.

'Serve yer right,' called the woman.

Kids were gathering. Bonzer got Tiddler back on the pavement, where Tiddler could hardly stand up without falling down again. Sammy sat down and drove away. He knew the score. A fake body collision with a car and then a demand for damages, settled on the spot, or a complaint to the police, with a witness present.

Lucky that Bert had heard a rumour.

At fifteen minutes to four, a teacher ran into a classroom at St Luke's Church School.

'Rosie – Rosie Adams – quickly!'

Rosie stood up and slipped from her desk. She hurried to the classroom door, with everyone looking.

'Miss Purvis—'

'Come with me, Rosie. It's your father – there's been a little accident – a police superintendent is going to take you to him.'

Rosie turned white.

'Miss Purvis—'

'Here we are,' said Miss Purvis. A bearded man in the uniform of a police superintendent approached from the entrance hall.

'This is Rosie Adams?' he said, his cap under his arm.

'Yes,' said Miss Purvis. The headmaster appeared. He looked at the superintendent, who nodded.

'I'll get her there, sir,' said Mr Ronald Ponsonby. 'Rosie, I'm going to drive you to see your father. He's in St Thomas's Hospital.'

'Yes, yes,' said Rosie, stiff-faced and swallowing. 'I'll come – we must hurry? I mean, is he—?'

'I'll tell you about him as we go.'

'Good luck, Rosie,' said the headmaster.

'Her hat—'

'Never mind her hat, Miss Purvis.'

They watched her hurrying across the playground to the gates, in company with her smartly uniformed escort, his cap back on his head.

'Here we are, Rosie.' He opened the passenger door and the girl almost flung herself in. He closed the door, came round the car and slipped into the driving seat. He pulled on the self-starter, the engine fired and away he went. 'Don't worry too much, it's not a fatal accident. Serious, perhaps, but not fatal. He came to as soon as the ambulance reached St Thomas's and asked for you and your mother. She's on her way and is probably there by now.'

'Yes. Thank you.' Rosie sat stiff and taut and praying, her young heart in pain. 'Please, was it an accident in his motorcar?'

'Yes. At the Elephant and Castle, a busy junction, busy. Chin up, Rosie, we shan't be long getting there.' He sounded the horn, giving Rosie the impression of urgency as he overtook a tram on the inside and then a cart on the outside. They were quickly motoring through Camberwell Road. 'He's in good hands at the hospital, Rosie, good hands.' His own hands were gloved and in firm control of the wheel. Rosie wanted to urge him to hurry, hurry, but knew he was driving as fast as he could, using his horn frequently, with all the authority of a senior police officer. Down the Walworth Road he went. 'We'll cut through the back streets, Rosie, and avoid the Elephant and Castle.'

Rosie swallowed again.

'Oh, is the car still there, is it wrecked?' she asked, her whole being concentrated on her adoptive father and all he meant to her.

'It may not have been moved yet, there may still be a hold-up in the traffic there.' He took a right turning that would bring them out to the New Kent Road.

'Please, do you know about his injuries, what they are?' she asked.

'Serious, the ambulance men informed me, but not fatal, no, not fatal, I'm sure.' He entered the New Kent Road traffic and turned left into Harper Road, on the corner of which was a public telephone box. He pulled into the kerb and stopped.

'Why have we stopped?' asked Rosie.

He switched off the engine and turned to her. His eyes were bright. He wore no spectacles.

'Rosie, would you like to speak to your father?'

'Oh, but how can I? We must go on, we're not at the hospital yet.'

'He isn't in any hospital.'

'What d'you mean? Oh, please tell me.'

'Are you fond of your father, Rosie?'

'Yes, yes!'

'You would not like to have him dead?'

'Oh, no! Why are you talking like this when you're a police officer?'

'I'm not a police officer, Rosie. I have an extreme dislike for all of them. But I have the power to put your father to death, and for reasons of my own.'

'No!' Rosie could not believe what she was hearing, but she could see the bright eyes, peering into her very soul, and she suddenly hated those eyes. Ice travelled down her back.

'If you will do exactly as I say, you can save your father. I will only beggar him, not cause his death. If you argue, if you irritate me and refuse to do as I say, you will never see him alive again.'

The ice travelled all over her body.

'I'll do anything you say,' she said in a whisper.

'Good. But understand, if you try to escape and succeed, you will still never see your father alive again. I can promise you that. Do you see that promise in my eyes, Rosie Adams?'

Rosie saw it, the glitter of sheer evil.

'Please don't hurt my father. I'll do what you want, really I will.'

'Good. No harm will come to you. I need money, and will have all I can get from your father and his brothers. You understand?'

'Yes.'

'Very well. Stay there a moment.' He got out of the car and looked around. What he did not want was to come up against any patrolling men on the beat. He came round to the passenger door and opened it. 'Get out, Rosie.'

Rosie slipped out, a figure of young girlish charm in her school dress, her fair hair taking on golden tints in the sunlight. He sighed to himself. Oh, for a camera and for her to pose for him. No, he must put that kind of thing aside. Inclinations must not lead him into a single mistake.

'Where are we going?' Rosie asked, her throat dry, her heart painful.

'Why, to speak to your father.' He locked the car and walked with her to the public call-box. It was empty. The New Kent Road traffic rumbled. At the Elephant and Castle two constables were on point duty. He had avoided coming up against them by cutting the junction out. He opened the door of the call-box and took Rosie in with him. He knew the number he wanted. He put in two pennies. The operator came through. He asked for the required number. Rosie quivered. It was the number of the firm's office at Camberwell Green. The operator made the connection, he pressed button A, the pennies dropped and Doreen spoke at the other end of the line.

'Adams Enterprises. Can I help you?'

'Thank you. Put me through to Mr Robert Adams.'

'Who's callin', please?'

'I'm speaking for his daughter, Rosie Adams.'

'Oh. Oh, hold the line, please, sir.'

Boots came through.

'Who's that?' he asked.

'You don't know me, Mr Adams, no, not at all. But I know you, and must ask you to do as I say.'

'Don't arse about, who is that?' said Boots.

'I have your daughter Rosie with me, Mr Adams, and because of that you'll do exactly as I say, do you hear?'

'For God's sake, man—'

'Here she is. She will speak to you.' He put his hand over the mouthpiece and said, 'You will not tell him where we are, only that he must do as I ask. You understand?'

'Yes,' said Rosie, and he gave her the phone. Her breath caught in her throat. She swallowed painfully. 'Daddy?'

'Rosie, what's happening?'

'Daddy, please do as the man says, then he won't harm you or me. Please, Daddy. I can't say any more except – Daddy, I love you.' The phone was pulled from her hand.

'You heard that, Mr Adams, you recognized your daughter?'

'Yes, I did, you bat out of hell. If you harm one hair of her head, God help you.'

'Come, don't be childish, Mr Adams. What I'm going to ask of you is not very much, and I'm sure you'll agree to it and so spare yourself fatherly suffering. I shall arrive at your Camberwell offices at five minutes to eight this evening. You will be there, you and your wife, your brother Tommy and his wife, your brother Sammy and his wife, and your sister Eliza and her husband. All eight of you, yes, all eight. I have something to say to every one of you. Not six of you, or seven, but all eight. Therefore, no absentees, not one, if you care as much as you should for Rosie. Further, each of you will have one hundred and twenty-five pounds ready to hand to me. When I have spoken to each one of you and have received the money, I shall depart and see to it that Rosie joins you in your offices fifteen minutes later. That is guaranteed, Mr Adams, guaranteed. Should any attempt be made to detain me or to call on the police for help, then, alas, as a father you will suffer lamentably, sir, lamentably. Remember, five minutes to eight, with all of you there.'

'You win, whoever you are,' said Boots, 'I've no alternative, and you know it.'

'Say goodbye for the moment to your father, Rosie.' He put the mouthpiece to her stiff lips.

'Daddy, I love you.'

'Don't worry, Rosie, don't worry – and don't say anything, I think I know who has you. Trust me, poppet—' The phone was slammed back into place.

'What did he say, Rosie?'

'He told me not to worry and not to do anything I shouldn't.'

'Good. Obedience has its saving graces. Come along, back to the car now.' He took her back to the car. He looked like a police superintendent shepherding his daughter, for his hand was around the back of her neck and resting lightly on her shoulder. He unlocked the passenger door. 'Get in, Rosie.' She got in. She did not think about what he might do to her, she thought only about what he might do to Boots if she did not obey him in every way. 'Stay there, stay there and sit quietly. I shall be back in a few minutes. Do you understand?'

'Yes. I won't do anything, I promise.' Rosie forced out every word.

'Good girl.' She was perfect in her reactions. There were no hysterics, no panic, nothing that made things difficult for him. Ah, how he would like to take her back with him to France. 'A few minutes, then, that's all.' He closed the door on her and locked it, and Rosie sat very still. He returned to the call-box. There was still traffic, trams, buses, vans and other vehicles. And people. He lifted the phone and slipped in two pennies.

The shop phone rang. Sidney Pearson answered it.

'Hello?'

'Ah, it's you, young man. I'm calling about the blankets you've boxed up for me.'

'Oh, yes, sir, they're ready.'

'Thank you, but could you please hold them for me until tomorrow morning? I'm stuck in Liverpool Street and shan't be able to get away in time to be at your shop before you close. You did say you closed at five-thirty?'

'Yes, sir.' Sidney hesitated. He didn't want to be too late home, he and his wife of a year were going to see a Clive Brook film. Clive Brook was her favourite film star. 'I could hang on for twenty minutes, say.'

'No, no, I still couldn't be sure of getting there in time, with my vehicle. I have a vehicle for the box of blankets. No, keep them for me – oh, and my attaché case too, I'm sure it can be safely left behind your counter.'

'Yes, sir. Tomorrow morning, then.'

'Yes, tomorrow morning. Thank you, yes, thank you. Your shop has been doing well this afternoon?'

'Usual Friday afternoon business, sir.'

'Goodbye, then, young man, thank you again.'

'Pleasure, sir.'

He replaced the phone and left the call-box. No panic had reached the shop. It was being confined to the offices above, to the Adams brothers. He returned to the car and to his hostage.

Chapter Twenty-Four

The first thing Boots did when his shock and fury were under control was to telephone the headmaster of Rosie's school. The headmaster's initial reaction on being spoken to by a man he knew well and whom he'd thought at death's door, was to momentarily lose contact with his mental processes. Recovering, he answered Boots's first question.

'Yes, Mr Adams, Rosie left the school at about a quarter to four.'

'Why?'

'A Superintendent Craven of the Walworth police arrived to inform us you'd had a motorcar accident, that you were seriously injured and had been taken to St Thomas's Hospital by an ambulance. He further said you were asking for Rosie.'

'So he took her away?'

'Yes, in his car.'

'What was he like?'

'A smart-looking, bearded man of middle age, slim and about five feet ten.'

Yes, a beard makes sense, thought Boots, it's the best of all facial disguises. He thought then of the man Mrs Fletcher had said was watching him.

'He's played a practical joke on you and me in the worst possible taste,' he said, and rang off.

With Sammy not yet back from Islington, he then phoned Tommy at the factory.

'Hello, what can I do for yer, Boots?'

'Has Sammy left?'

'Yes, and he should just about be with you.'

'Right. I want you to get here yourself as soon as you can, Tommy.'

'Why, what's up?'

'I'll tell you when you get here, but get here, Tommy, the family has a crisis on its hands.'

'Right, count me in, Boots, I'm leavin' now.'

Boots next rang Ned, manager of a wine merchants' establishment in Great Tower Street.

'Ned, when you get home this evening, arrange for you and Lizzy to be here in our offices by half-seven.'

'Have to ask why, Boots.'

'A crisis. I'll fill you and Lizzy in when you get here. Take it that it's necessary and make sure you both come.'

'You sound rough, Boots.'

'I feel rough. Can I rely on you?'

'Need you ask?' said Ned, who had always had a very close relationship with Lizzy's eldest brother.

Sammy came in as Boots put the phone down.

'Promisin' news, Boots, Harriet liked—'

'Forget that, Sammy. Close the door and take a seat.'

Sammy looked hard at his brother's face, then closed the door and sat down.

'You've got trouble,' he said.

'I've got very personal trouble,' said Boots through gritted teeth, 'and the family's being dragged in.'

The iron's showing, thought Sammy, and it's showing as if he'd like to murder someone.

'Let's have it, old soldier,' he said.

Boots, tight of jaw, explained rapidly and concisely. At the end, he said, 'We're on the rack, Sammy.'

Sammy knew just how painfully it was stretching Rosie's dad. His kids were the great fun part of his life, Rosie especially.

'Well, yer know, Boots, what's a thousand quid? The bugger's got us handcuffed and trussed. He wants a thousand quid and we want Rosie back.'

'The banks are closed,' said Boots.

'Our shops aren't,' said Sammy. 'Peckham, Brixton, Kennington and New Cross. And here. I'll collect the takings from all of them. That'll add up to more than a thousand quid if I collect the cash takings from our scrap yards as well. Sidney'll hand you his takings, as usual, I'm off to the other shops and the yards. Look, ring Peckham, New Cross and Brixton, and tell the manageresses not to go home until I get there. It might take me a while. Boots, help yourself to a large Scotch. The bottle's in me cabinet. Don't ring Susie. I'll tell her.'

Sammy vanished.

'Christ Almighty,' said Tommy, 'our Rosie. It's bloody unbelievable. I'll 'ave to break the news gently to Vi.'

'Vi's got enough character to take it, Tommy. But tell no-one else. It's to be kept to us and our wives, and Lizzy and Ned. I'll go home at my usual time and talk to Emily—'

'And have supper?' said Tommy. 'Who's goin' to be able to eat anything?'

'I'll tell Chinese Lady that Emily and I, with Rosie, are going to a theatre and eating in town.

I've rung Emily and told her Rosie's here with me—'

'When you get home, Chinese Lady'll be cookin' the supper,' said Tommy.

'Not for us,' said Boots, 'I asked Emily to tell her we're going out.'

'Then Em'ly asked questions, didn't she?'

'I told her I'd answer them when I got home.'

'Well, you're thinkin' straight, Boots, that's something. I'm off now to have a special word with Vi – wait a bit, why's the ugly bugger wantin' to talk to all of us?'

'We'll find that out, Tommy.'

'Oh, dear God,' whispered Emily.

'Say nothing to Chinese Lady or anyone else, Em.'

'I won't, no, Chinese Lady'll want you to tell the police. Boots, hold me, my legs are goin'.'

The shops and the offices were empty now. The offices were in an eerie state of waiting. Camberwell Green was quietening down, the workers either at home or still on their way. The rush hour traffic had melted away.

The time-set clock ticked on imperceptibly.

'No, I can't eat,' breathed Rosie, pale of face and stiff of body. The car was in a quiet cul-de-sac near the Bermondsey docks, and there were warehouses all round the area. Everything seemed deserted.

He had actually bought fish and chips. He was eating his from the newspaper. Rosie was staring unseeingly at hers.

'You should eat something, Rosie.'

'I can't.'

'But everything is going to be all right now.'

'You promise, you promise?'

'I've promised already, yes, dear me I have. Rosie, what a very pretty girl you are. How old are you?'

'Eleven.'

'Delightful, delightful. Such sweet innocence. Come, eat a few chips at least.'

'I can't,' whispered Rosie again. There was something about this man that chilled her blood and put her in anguished fear for Boots. She was sure, terribly sure, that he had the means to kill her adoptive father if she did or said the wrong thing. She licked her dry lips, swallowed a catch in her breath and ate three chips. Each one was difficult to take down.

She sat there in the car with him, waiting for the time when he had said he would release her. A little while after eight o'clock.

Mr Ronald Ponsonby enjoyed his fish and chips. If Rosie was waiting in a state of anguish, he was waiting in pleasurable anticipation.

By seven-thirty, they were all there in the offices above the shop, Boots and Emily, Tommy and Vi, Sammy and Susie, and Lizzy and Ned. Lizzy was shaking with agitation and anger, Vi was appalled. They were all in the picture now. Boots had given his very precise account of events, and was as hard as steel. Susie felt he was ready to lynch the man.

'Boots, we've got to keep our heads,' she said. 'We've got what he wants, the money, and we're all ready to take our turn to hand our shares over to him.'

'What's worrying me,' said Ned, 'is can we trust a

twisted character like that to hand Rosie back?'

'Lord above,' breathed Emily, 'don't say things like that, Ned.'

'My own feelin',' said Sammy, 'is that he will hand her back. I'm against pessimism, and a thousand quid ain't quite like a packet of tea.'

'It's ruddy peculiar, though, wantin' to say his piece to all of us in turn, and wantin' each of us to 'and him a hundred and twenty-five quid,' said Tommy.

'He's 'orrible,' said Lizzy. 'If he touches Rosie, if he does her any kind of harm, I won't rest till I see him dead.'

'Boots,' said Vi quietly, 'who can he be?'

'The identical twin,' said Boots.

'What?' gasped Emily.

'His voice over the phone,' said Boots, 'the way he spoke and put his words together. Identical with Gerald Ponsonby's way of talking. But he's grown a beard, according to Rosie's headmaster. I think that makes sense, since he's a wanted man, wanted in connection with a missing girl in Nottingham. I think we're dealing with Ronald Ponsonby.'

'Christ,' said Ned.

'He'll be dangerous,' said Boots. 'When he arrives, do nothing. He intends to talk to all of us in turn. It'll be a succession of malicious speeches and crazy curses, all on account of his brother being found guilty. We all know, don't we, that while he's here with us, he won't be with Rosie. That might make some of us feel we could take him, but he'll be aware of that and he'll have guarded against it.'

'Boots, we wouldn't know where to look for Rosie,' said Susie. 'She might be tied up somewhere, she might die of starvation if we couldn't

361

find her and if he refused to tell us. He's a horror, Boots.'

'Susie's right,' said Sammy, 'we've got to let him talk to us and we've got to hand over the money. On top of that, we've got to trust him to hand Rosie back. I've met all types all over London, and there's occasions when you've got to let someone kick your ribs in and hope that that satisfies him.'

It was now fifteen minutes to eight.

'Something doesn't make sense,' said Boots, jaw tighter.

'And what's that?' asked Ned.

'According to Gerald Ponsonby's evidence, he and his brother have independent means,' said Boots, 'so what does the bugger want a thousand quid for?'

'Oh, gawd,' breathed Tommy.

'That worry only applies if your assumption's right, Boots,' said Ned, 'if the man is the identical twin.'

'Even if he isn't,' said Emily, 'I'm beginnin' to feel something's not right. Apart from what's happenin' to Rosie and the money.'

'Think,' said Boots, and they all set their minds to work on what they could do to ensure the safe return of Rosie.

They waited and they made assumptions. Down below, the door to the world outside was unlocked to permit the entry of the kidnapper. The tension mounted as the time of his arrival grew closer.

Sidney Pearson, manager of the shop, had no worries. He was at the pictures with his wife. He had a nice bit of commission on the sale of a dozen blankets to look forward to, the customer's purchase was awaiting him and so was the attaché case.

Then there were the savings he had in the Post Office to put down for a deposit on the little house he and his wife were presently renting on the corner of Love Walk not far from his work.

He might not be as prosperous as the Adams', but at this precise moment he had no worries.

He knew nothing of the ticking clock.

The car was now parked on the forecourt of a closed engineering works a little way down Camberwell New Road.

Rosie's heart was in turmoil, beating erratically, her teeth biting on her lower lip. The June evening was clear. The rooftops of Walworth had an old grey look that was mellowing in the gentle sunshine, and here in Camberwell the Green was looking warm and bright. But it could have been bleak winter to Rosie.

'Come, Rosie, you are still worrying. Ah, how I would like to remove you from all worries and take you with me. Would you like that?'

'No, you know I wouldn't.'

'In any case, it's impossible. And any moment now, Rosie, I shall let you run free.'

Rosie trembled.

In the offices, the people who loved her waited with tension at its peak. The arrival time of five minutes to eight went by, and Emily could have screamed that no footsteps marked its passing. They could do nothing but wait further.

At precisely eight o'clock the bomb went off with a great explosive roar, and while all eight people were still waiting in the offices above the shop.

Chapter Twenty-Five

The sound of the explosion reached beyond the limits of Camberwell Green. A man and a woman, walking past a car parked on the other side of Camberwell New Road, stopped as they heard it. They looked at each other, then began to run towards the Green.

In the car, Rosie, startled, breathed, 'What was that?'

'A roll of summer thunder?' said Mr Ronald Ponsonby. A roll of avenging thunder, he thought. Would that it had reached the ears of Gerald in Pentonville Prison.

Rosie, disturbed, though not to the point of thinking a bomb had exploded, whispered, 'Please, you haven't been to the offices to see my father, to get the money.'

He smiled.

'Well, I don't think I'll go, after all, Rosie, no, I don't think I will. I've put a scare into your father and the others, yes, and for my own reasons. Let them stew for a while. We'll drive a little way. Then I shall release you, I promise.'

He started the car, pulled off the forecourt and drove down to Wyndham Road. He turned into it and proceeded towards Camberwell Road, Rosie sitting and praying beside him. As he crossed Camberwell Road, he saw a policeman heading at a run towards the Green. He tensed just a little, but the policeman did not notice the uniformed driver or the girl passenger. He was intent on investigating the explosion. The car entered Church Road, and then began to head towards Peckham and Kent. Rosie clenched her teeth. Just why hadn't he gone to see her daddy and the others, and where was he going now, where was he taking her?

He took her, in fact, as far as a street off Peckham Road. He stopped the car halfway down the street.—

'Please—'

'You may go now, Rosie.' The eyes she hated smiled at her. 'But speak to no-one, do you hear? Down there is Peckham Road. Take a tram back to Camberwell and to your father's offices.' What was left of them, of course. 'Here's money for your fare.' He gave her a shilling, putting it into her quivering hand. 'With the change, buy your-self some chocolate and eat it while thinking of me, a man who was kind to you. Goodbye, Rosie, my pretty one.' His hand lightly touched and caressed the skirt of her school dress as she opened the passenger door. Gladly, wildly, she slid out, her heart pounding. 'Goodbye, Rosie, good-bye.'

She closed the door, her breathing jerky, for she could hardly believe he really meant to let her go. But he did, for away he went, turning into a side street before reaching the main road. She ran then, she ran like the wind, her heart beating fast. A tram was travelling towards her as she sped into Peck-ham Road. She hared across the road. The tram's bell clanged in warning, but she reached the stop in advance of the public vehicle.

It pulled up and it carried her towards Camberwell Green.

The Clive Brook film stopped running, and the audience groaned. Some films were always breaking down. A notice flashed up on the glaring white screen.

Will Mr Sidney Pearson please go to the manager's office

Sidney went, and his wife went with him. There was a policeman with the manager.

'What's all this about?' demanded Sidney.

'Yes, just as we were really enjoyin' the film,' said his wife.

'You're Mr and Mrs Pearson?' said the constable.

'That's us,' said Sidney.

'Well, I'm sorry to spoil your evenin', sir. One of your neighbours informed us you were here. Look now, d'you think either of you could've left a gas tap on when you left your house?'

'We never have done,' said Sidney. 'Why'd you ask?'

'I'm very sorry, sir, but I'm afraid I've got some un'appy news for you,' said the constable. 'Your house blew up a little while ago. At eight o'clock, in fact.'

'What?' gasped Mrs Pearson, a young wife.

'You're joking, constable,' said Sidney.

''Fraid not, sir. It exploded.'

'Gawd help us,' breathed Sidney, 'you sure it was our house?'

'The corner house in Love Walk, sir, next to Grove Lane.'

'Oh, me gawd,' said Mrs Pearson.

366

'Sorry to spoil your evenin', said the constable, 'but I'd be obliged if you'd come with me. My Inspector would like to talk to you, to make sure you didn't leave a gas tap on. What's left of it is on fire, but the fire brigade's there. Other houses were damaged, but at least there's been no loss of life.'

'Gawd save the starving crows,' breathed Sidney.

'It must've been a gas leak we didn't notice,' said Mrs Pearson faintly.

'Let's get there,' said Sidney.

In his conscientious consideration for a customer's property, two vases of intrinsic value, Sidney had taken the heavy attaché case home with him, just to make sure it would be safe. Shops did get burgled sometimes. A locked attaché case would have been a magnet to any acquisitive hands.

The roar of the explosion had galvanized Sammy and Ned into rushing from the offices in an alarming suspicion that it had something to do with Rosie and the man who held her. They were back now, satisfied that leaking gas had caused a house in Love Walk to blow up. In ten minutes it would be nine o'clock, and all eight people were present, still tense and strained.

'He's not comin',' said Sammy.

'He's got to,' said Susie desperately.

'Boots, do something,' breathed Emily.

'Suppose,' said Boots, 'suppose his idea in getting us all here was to make sure that he kept us out of action? He knew we'd wait and wait, that we'd be doing nothing except wait.'

'While he spent the time taking Rosie miles away?' said Ned.

'He didn't need the money,' said Boots.

'If he's the same as his brother,' said Tommy, 'he likes—' He checked himself. He'd been going to say the man liked young girls.

'Boots, we just can't wait any longer,' said Lizzy, 'we've got to do something. He's got a car, we've got to tell the police.'

'Right, Lizzy,' said Boots, 'we've—' He stopped. Someone had opened the door downstairs, and that someone was running up the stairs.

'Daddy, Daddy, are you there?' Rosie ran into the corridor and into the general office, the largest room. 'Daddy!' She flung herself at Boots and wound her arms around him.

'Bless you, poppet,' said Boots, and hugged her.

'Rosie – oh, Rosie,' said Emily, and her tears ran. Rosie transferred her joyful self into Emily's arms.

'It's been a long time waitin', Rosie,' said Sammy, 'can we all have a cuddle?'

'Oh, hundreds,' said Rosie. Her eyes were moistly bright, her joyful smile misty. 'Daddy, I've got the number of his car.'

Mr Ronald Ponsonby had two things to do before he caught the night ferry from Newhaven. Get rid of the police uniform and change the car's number plates. He had already changed direction, he was now heading for Croydon, Lewes and Newhaven. Once well out of Croydon he'd reach open country-side. Rosie, of course, would be with the police now, a tragic young figure stunned by the loss of her parents and her aunts and uncles. The police would want her to talk. Perhaps she'd already talked. Poor sweet young girl, perhaps, after all, he should have ended her life too. But Gerald would not have asked for that. Eight lives would be consolation enough. The news would get to the inmates of Pentonville.

He motored through Croydon, eyes alert, watching for signs that policemen who were on point duty were checking number plates of cars. He drove on to Purley, the car engine humming, the quiet of the countryside beckoning, the June twilight soft. But he could not risk waiting for nightfall before he changed the number plates. A quiet lane was the place. Traffic, already light, became thin. He put his foot down through Coulsdon and raced for the countryside. The sharp bend at Hooley was his undoing. He took it too fast. A lumbering lorry appeared on the other side of the road as the car lost its course. The brakes of the lorry squealed and shrieked, its driver aghast. The car shot across in front of it, hit a pile of boulders in the grass verge and somersaulted. Mr Ronald Ponsonby burst through the windscreen, shattering it. He died instantaneously. The car, yards away, exploded into a ball of fire. A camera containing a roll of undeveloped film melted in the searing heat.

'Now look here, Lady Vi,' said Luke.

'Oh, yes?' said Doreen, who had no idea that the Adams family had been in crisis, only that the brothers had spent unusually long minutes in Boots's office.

'I'm fed-up with all this,' said Luke, standing on her doorstep.

'All what, might I ask?' enquired Doreen, putting on her haughty look.

'It's ruddy ridiculous,' said Luke.

'If you've come knockin' at our door just to swear

at me,' said Doreen, 'you can go away again.'

'Now look,' said Luke, 'your mum's goin' to marry my dad. Old Iron's not goin' to be the kind of 'usband that'll make your mum feel she still needs you.'

'I should 'ope not,' said Doreen, 'I should think he wouldn't be any kind of a husband if he did.'

'There you are, then,' said Luke.

'There I am what?' said Doreen.

'You don't 'ave to tie yourself to your mum once me dad has promised her 'imself and all his worldly goods.'

'I should 'ope I won't,' said Doreen.

'Well, can I come in, then?' asked Luke.

'What for?'

'Because I'm gone on you, and I'm not goin' to stand on your doorstep for ever with the street kids gogglin'.'

Doreen smiled.

'Would you like to come in, Luke?'

'Pleasure,' said Luke, and stepped in.

'And would you like to take me to the pictures tomorrow and up the park on Sunday?'

'Yes, and I'd like to do that permanent,' said Luke.

'Well, then?' said Doreen, lifting her face.

'Well what?'

'Don't I get a kiss?'

'Stone the crows,' said Luke, 'I thought you'd never ask.' He bent his head and kissed her. He liked it very much.

'Oi, I seen that, Doreen,' called a street kid, 'bet yer muvver don't know.'

'Luke, you loony,' said Doreen, 'what d'you mean by kissin' me with the door still open?'

'My mistake, Lady Vi,' said Luke. He closed the door and kissed her again.

''Ello, 'ello,' boomed Old Iron, appearing from the kitchen, 'what's all this, then?'

'Oh, nothing very much,' said Doreen, eyes bright, 'except your son doesn't want me for a sister.'

'Come to 'is senses, has 'e, Doreen love?' grinned Old Iron.

'Yes, and we're goin' to finish the Tower of London tonight,' said Doreen, and laughed.

Later that evening, police investigating the accident at Hooley thought at first that the skull-crushed dead driver was a senior officer of the uniformed branch. Subsequently, they discovered a passport in the name of Joseph Wright. It was stamped and it showed he had come from France. They also discovered a letter written by an inmate of Pentonville Prison who had signed himself Gerald. The envelope bore the name of Joseph Wright and an address in Calais. The letter itself had been written to the inmate's twin brother Ronald. The police began to put two and two together, particularly as the name of Robert Adams was mentioned and the import of the letter disturbing.

'Daddy?' Rosie called softly from her bedroom as she heard Boots on the landing. He went in. She was in bed, her bedside light still on.

'Not asleep yet, Rosie?'

'Oh, I will be in a tick, I can hardly keep my eyes open,' said Rosie, 'but I heard you and I just wanted to ask you something.'

'Ask away, poppet.'

'Daddy, am I really worth a thousand pounds?'

Boots laughed. His relief had been huge, his admiration for her total. She had come out of her ordeal like a trooper.

'Well, a fiver at least,' he said, and bent and kissed her forehead.

'Crikey, as much as that?' murmured Rosie. Her heavy lids fell and she slipped into the blissful sleep of a girl secure again.

Sidney knocked on Sammy's door at nine the next morning and went in.

'Hello, Sidney,' said Sammy. 'Here, don't you live in Love Walk, where that house blew up last night?'

'You bet I do, Mister Sammy,' said Sidney, 'it was our house, and I've come to ask if I can have today off, only Nora and me have lost everything. Her parents are putting us up—'

'Say no more,' said Sammy, 'take the day off. Was it a gas leak?'

'Well, that's it, the police now say no. They couldn't do much last night, not even after the fire brigade put the fire out. But they were there as soon as it was light, and they've just told me they suspect it was a bomb.'

'A what?' said Sammy.

'I'm knocked cold meself,' said Sidney. 'I mean, a ruddy bomb.'

'Someone's off their chump,' said Sammy, 'unless you've got Bolshevik friends.'

'Well, I've been thinking,' said Sidney, and told Sammy then about the bearded bloke who'd bought blankets, had arranged to collect them but had phoned to say he couldn't manage it until Saturday morning, today. He'd left a heavy attaché case, which he said he'd collect with the blankets, so Sidney took it home with him to ensure safe keeping. The man had said it contained family heirlooms.

'Mother O'Reilly,' said Sammy.

'I've just mentioned all that to the police,' said Sidney.

'A perishin' bomb,' said Sammy, 'and a bloke with a beard.'

'He seemed all right,' said Sidney, a young man shouldering a great load of worries. 'A sort of genteel way of talking.'

'Sidney, you go and comfort your wife,' said Sammy. 'Let the police take on the worry of the bomb. Was your furniture insured and so on?'

'Yes, we had insurance.'

'Well, I'll give you a hand sorting it out with the insurance company, and if you need any financial advance, just let me know. And listen, d'you realize that if that case did contain a ruddy bomb, you saved this place bein' blown up by takin' it home? We owe you, Sidney, and I'll talk to you about that when your headache's better. Off you go.'

'Thanks, Mister Sammy.'

Sammy had an immediate word with Boots.

'So that was it,' said Boots. 'Those blankets won't be collected, I'll wager.'

'See it all now, don't we?' said Sammy.

'He got us all here to blow us up,' said Boots. 'The ransom he asked for was a red herring, and his insistence on talking to each one of us guaranteed we'd all be here when the bomb went off. He said we were to be here when he arrived at five to eight. That ensured we'd certainly still be here at eight.'

'You were right, Boots, it's got to be the identical twin.' Sammy grimaced. 'Mother ruddy O'Grady, he was after all of us.'

'And he's still on the loose, Sammy, if the police haven't caught him,' said Boots. He had phoned the police last night after Rosie's return, and told them that the twin brother of Gerald Ponsonby, wanted in connection with a missing girl in Nottingham, had been seen in the uniform of a Superintendent driving a black Morris saloon car in the vicinity of Peckham half an hour ago. He gave the car number and then said put me down as a friend of the law. Whether or not they had acted and had caught Ronald Ponsonby, he did not know. He felt he must assume that the man was still at large.

'You think he'll try again?' said Sammy. 'What the hell for, and why in the first place?'

'Perhaps he didn't like the fact that I helped to catch his brother,' said Boots.

'Well, the sooner the police clap him in irons, the better,' said Sammy, 'I ain't in favour of lookin' over my shoulder every five minutes. It'll put me off me efficiency. Further, we'll have to keep Rosie under lock and key.'

'That's on my mind, Sammy, as well as yours.'

'Boots, old soldier,' said Sammy, 'the fam'ly's closin' ranks.'

The police arrived at the offices at ten past eleven, asking to see Mr Robert Adams. Doreen showed them in. They advised Boots of the death in a car accident at Hooley of a man whom they believed to be Gerald Ponsonby's twin brother Ronald. They gave him details. Boots listened, made comments and asked questions, but said

374

nothing about the events relating to Rosie and the family. He wanted all that kept quiet. He did not want newspaper reporters clamouring to see Rosie. The police, CID officers, then showed him the letter that had been found on the dead man.

'D'you note mention of your name, sir, and the threat the letter posed to you and members of your family?'

'I note it looks as if we could have expected something heavy falling on our heads from a great height,' said Boots.

'On account, sir, of the fact that you were responsible for apprehending Gerald Ponsonby.'

'Some people, Inspector, aren't very good losers,' said Boots.

'Some people, Mr Adams, are a little worse than that. Did you know a house not far from here blew up yesterday evening?'

'I do know, yes. Mr Sidney Pearson, manager of our shop below, was renting that house, with his wife.'

'And did you also know, sir, that Mr Pearson took home an attaché case left in the shop for collection this morning?'

'I do know that as well,' said Boots. 'Mr Pearson came in first thing and reported it. He said you told him it was a bomb that blew his house apart.'

'Your shop and offices would have been blown up, Mr Adams, if that case had been left in the shop overnight.'

'Yes,' said Boots. He smiled. Ronald Ponsonby was dead. His smile was for Rosie and the lifting of any further threat. 'We come back to the same thing, Inspector, some people aren't very good losers.'

It was the turn of the CID men to smile.

'Well, with the bomb-planter managing to kill himself, Mr Adams, the matter's closed now, except for the inquest, but I thought I'd come and talk to you.'

'Thanks,' said Boots. He told Sammy, and he phoned Tommy at the factory and told him. Then he rang Lizzy and told her.

'Well, I'm a Christian, I hope,' said Lizzy, 'but I'm glad he killed himself. I know I'll never suffer a worser hour than I did last night.'

'Worse, Lizzy.'

'You and your education,' said Lizzy, 'you're still the same old Lord Muck.'

'Love you, Lizzy old girl. Regards to Ned and the kids.'

'Good on yer, old boy,' said Lizzy, 'we're all comin' to the Sunday tea party tomorrow.'

'Yes, and you're opening for the Somers' cricket team.'

'Can't wait, can I?' laughed Lizzy, who was actually a walloper with a bat, having played street cricket when a girl.

'Cassie, you can't,' said Freddy.

'Yes, I can,' said Cassie, 'tabby likes Sunday tea parties. Will there be kippers? 'E specially likes kippers.'

'Now look 'ere, gormless,' said Freddy, 'you ain't takin' that barmy cat to any Sunday tea party at Uncle Boots's 'ouse. D'you 'ear me, Cassie?'

'But I'm not askin' you to carry 'im there,' said Cassie, 'he can come on the bus with us. Me dad said so.'

'No, 'e didn't.'

'But you do like me, Freddy, don't you?'

'That don't mean I'm in love with yer daft cat. Cassie, 'e's not comin'. That's me final word.'

'Yes, all right, Freddy.'

The Sunday tea party had a very special atmosphere, not only because Chinese Lady had bought herself a new summer hat that was a bit like a white basket of flowers, but because she insisted on wearing it on the grounds that the tea was going to be served in the garden. And also because Cassie's cat had arrived with her in a cat basket. It must have had some of its young mistress's fancy ideas, for it interfered with the cricket by imagining itself to be a dog. It chased after the ball and evoked hysterics among the younger generation. Freddy apologized, saying he couldn't do anything with Cassie or her cock-eyed cat. However, the cricketers soldiered on, although Lizzy took a very dim view of being run out by Boots.

'Well,' she said in disgust, 'my own brother and all, you just can't believe it, can you, Rosie?'

'Yes, it's very sad, Auntie Lizzy,' said Rosie, 'but Nana always says you can never trust her only oldest son.'

Chinese Lady, coming out into the garden bearing a tray of tea china, looked at the scene in the sunshine of June. They were all there, all of them, her sons and daughters-in-law, her daughter and son-in-law, her husband and her grandchildren. And Freddy and Cassie too. Well, the Lord had been good to her, and she couldn't say otherwise. But she did have a few remarks to make when the cricket was over and tea was being served in the garden.

'Something's been goin' on,' she announced the moment she had a chance to make herself heard.

'Ah,' said Boots.

'Ah what?' said Tommy.

'Ah who?' said Sammy.

'Not me,' said Emily.

'I've got eyes and I've got ears,' said Chinese Lady, 'and I know something's been goin' on. I'm not goin' to ask what it was, I'm just goin' to say I hope and trust it wasn't something uncreditable, which it might of been if Sammy had anything to do with it. Still, I'm sure we all feel that now he's a married man we can look forward to Susie improvin' his disreputable ways. Now, who'd like some more shrimps?'

'Please, Mrs Finch,' said Cassie, 'is there any kippers for me cat?'

'I told yer, ev'ryone,' sighed Freddy, 'I told yer I can't do anything with Cassie.'

July, and the day was warm but cloudy. The vivid-looking woman sat in her little open car, parked a short way up Denmark Hill. She was watching the Adams' shop. She knew Boots had a habit of going regularly to the pub opposite when all he wanted for his lunch was a glass of ale and a beef sandwich. She hoped he would go there today. The time was ten to one, and she was waiting, though not very patiently. Her nerves were jangling.

He emerged from the door at the side of the shop at five minutes past one. Her eyes, quickening, followed him as he crossed the road and the tram-lines. His familiar walk, his easy stride, tugged at her heart-strings. She had been in Kenya several months, solely for the purpose of getting him out of her system, but it hadn't worked. And seeing him now, she knew it never would. She watched him enter the pub. It wasn't long before she entered it herself. The saloon bar was busy, the cold roast joints on their white stands adorning the marble top. Businessmen of Camberwell favoured this pub and its sandwiches made of new crusty bread and generous fillings.

She saw Boots sitting at a table. He had his glass of old ale and was waiting for his sandwich to be made by the white-aproned, white-capped barman-chef. A newspaper was keeping him company. From just inside the door she eyed him, her lashes flickering. God, she wasn't actually nervous, was she?

She had a golden suntan, and a brown velvet beret sat on her dark brown bobbed hair, the curving frontal points lightly touching her cheeks. The months seemed to have made no difference to him. He looked as he always did to her, a man of distinction, a man of France and Flanders, an ex-Tommy. Because of her four years as an ambulance driver during the Great War, Polly Simms had a weakness for all ex-Tommies, more especially this one. He had been blinded on the Somme, and although an operation had restored his sight, she knew his left eye, lazy-looking, could see very little.

She crossed the floor to his table. He looked up from his paper. If he was astonished to see her, he didn't show it. He smiled.

'Hello, Polly.'

'Hello, darling,' she said.

'Are you back?' he asked, coming to his feet.

'Yes. For good. I hate chasing lions. Are you glad?'

'I'm ignorant about what it feels like to chase lions,' said Boots, 'but I'm fairly sure I'd hate them chasing me.'

That remark, so typical of him, felt as refreshing to sun-baked Polly as the April showers she had sometimes longed for.

'Are you going to treat me to a drink and a sandwich?' she asked.

'I'll order when Joe brings me my own sandwich. Sit down, Polly.'

'Dear old thing,' said Polly, and sat down beside him. 'Listen, loved one, is there something really nice you can say to me?'

'Yes, I think so,' said Boots. 'Come to tea on Sunday as an old and special friend, and bring your mum and dad with you. Can Sir Henry play cricket?'

'Ye gods,' murmured Polly, 'is that what I've come home to, cricket and Sunday tea?'

'With shrimps and winkles,' said Boots.

Polly laughed.

THE END

ON MOTHER BROWN'S DOORSTEP
by Mary Jane Staples

The big event of the Walworth year was to be the wedding
of Sammy Adams, King of Camberwell, to Miss Susie
Brown. Everyone was looking forward to it, and Susie was
particularly overjoyed when her soldier brother suddenly
turned up on leave from service in India in time for the
approaching 'knees-up'. The reason for Will's extended
leave wasn't so good, for bad health had struck him and he
didn't know how long the army would keep him, or how
he could find a civvy job in the slump of the 20s. When he
– literally – picked Annie Ford up off the pavement in
King and Queen Street, his worries were compounded, for
Annie was a bright, brave, personable young woman and
Will knew that if he wasn't careful he'd find himself falling
in love.

And over Walworth hung a greater anxiety – the mystery
of three young girls missing from their homes – a mystery
that was to draw closer and closer to the Adams and Brown
families, and finally culminate – along with Will's personal
problems – on the night of the wedding.

0 552 13975 0

SERGEANT JOE
by Mary Jane Staples

Everyone liked Sergeant Joe. From the huge jolly Beavis family with whom he had lodgings in Newington Butts, to Mr George Singleton, Charing Cross Road bookseller, who employed Joe in a little lucrative and harmless forgery, Sergeant Joe was a universal favourite. Quite a few people wondered why he didn't get married.

But it wasn't until he bumped into Dolly Smith – in a London pea-souper, that he met a girl who made an impression on him. Dolly was quick, lively, and full of cockney cheek. She was also a little frightened – running from a vicious-looking thug and a sinister foreigner who seemed to think she had stolen something valuable. When Joe took Dolly under his wing he thought he was just helping her in a momentary predicament. He didn't realize his peaceful existence was going to be wrecked. For Dolly was both bewitching and beguiling – and she was also involved in something quite dangerous that was finally to give Sergeant Joe the surprise of his life.

0 552 13951 3

TWO FOR THREE FARTHINGS
by Mary Jane Staples

Horace was ten, Ethel seven, when Jim Cooper, home from the trenches, minus an arm and just about managing on his own, found them huddled in a doorway on a wet night in Walworth. Slightly against his better judgement he took them in, fed them cocoa, and put them to sleep in his bed. A few days later he found that – somehow – he had become the unofficial guardian of Horace and Ethel. It was him, the orphanage, or separation for the gutsy little pair who would have to be farmed out to anyone who would take them, and Jim felt a sudden affinity for the two cheeky cockney kids. The first thing he had to do was find fresh lodgings for them all.

Miss Rebecca Pilgrim was a woman of strict Victorian principles, eminently respectable, and determined to keep her privacy intact. She had reckoned without her new lodgers – Horace, Ethel and, above all, the irrepressible Jim Cooper. And thus began the humanizing of Miss Pilgrim, who turned out to be younger, prettier, and far gentler than any of them had suspected.

0 552 13635 2